Fathers, Sons, Unholy Ghost

V.J. DASWANI

ROBERT HALE · LONDON

First published in Great Britain 1995

ISBN 0 7090 5765 2

Robert Hale Limited
Clerkenwell House
Clerkenwell Green
London EC1R 0HT

For
Cathy

Photoset in North Wales by
Derek Doyle & Associates, Mold, Clwyd.
Printed in Great Britain by
St Edmundsbury Press Ltd, Bury St Edmunds, Suffolk.
Bound by WBC Book Manufacturers Limited,
Bridgend, Mid-Glamorgan.

Author's Note

If the Chicago Grain and Metal Exchange does one day come into existence, I shall strongly urge it to make $1 an ounce the daily limit for trading in silver futures, such as takes place in this piece of fiction. (The Chicago Board of Trade, too conservative for my liking, allows a mere 20 cents). In London, the silver price is 'fixed' daily by a select band of insiders; should, however, the London Minerals Board ever be created, the commodity must be dealt in it by open outcry as it is here.

No book can be written without other people giving up their valuable time. Heartfelt thanks to: Donald Ackerman, Sir Richard Acland, Carole Blake, Jonathon Brown, Nick Brown, everyone at the Bunch of Grapes in Galway, 'Tim' Burton, the Chicago Board of Trade, the Connemara Heritage Project, the Coolmore Stud, Tim Corballis, Audrey Cotterell, Liam Coyle, Donald Cross, Anne, Bobby, Gina, Joanne and Naresh Daswani, the Drummona House Stud, Joan E. Duck, Daithí Ó Dufaigh, Durga Edson, Huguette Florens, Sandy Friedman, Mike and Gaye Galliver, Michael Gibbons, John Goodall, David Grossman, John Hale, Compton Hellyer, John Illman, Inter Commodities Ltd, the Ireland Office of Public Works, Irish Ferries, Patrick Janson-Smith, Lesley Kermond, Roy and Paddy Kibby, Lind Waldock Commodities Inc., the London Metal Exchange, Terry Melia, John Mottershead, M. and Mme. Moulu, Colin Murray, Edward O'Grady, Dushyant and Lois Patel, Jack Powell, 'Prospero', Santos, the Hon. Christopher Sharples, Freddie Smith, Neeta Thakrar, George Thompson, Laurette and Edouard Vilain, Steve Watkins, my parents and my children.

Prologue

Condrieu Hall finally opened to the public on a Wednesday in September 1995. After buying tickets in the main entrance hall, visitors could view the magnificent state rooms of the south block, the chambers of the first two Dukes of Marylebone, and then tour the outhouses and gardens.

They queued from dawn on that first day. Elizabeth Greville, the dowager duchess, was there in person throughout the morning to sign copies of the guide book.

Simon Winchester arrived at midday. Elizabeth had already by then received several hundred invaders to what had been her private sanctuary since her marriage at the age of nineteen. She was seventy-five now. She recognized Winchester immediately from afar and smiled her acknowledgement.

At first he thought she'd mistaken him for someone else. Then he bought a guide book and came over to have it signed.

'Well, Mr Winchester, you're the last person I expected to see here.' She held out her hand and he shook it.

'Coming up was the last thing I'd planned to do. But I'm a great believer in doing the first thing that pops into your head when you wake up. I remembered Condrieu was going public this morning, felt I shouldn't miss it, and took the 8.45 from St Pancras. So here I am.'

'I *am* pleased you came. It's such a long way from London.' She signed his book with a little flourish and glanced at her watch. 'I was about to take a spot of lunch ... will you join me?'

He was surprised. 'You can't have forgotten?'

She shook her head. 'Forgotten, never. But sixteen years is long enough to forgive.'

They lunched in the west wing apartments which the duchess had retained for herself. Vichyssoise soup, rabbit in cider with rice, green salad, cheese, sherry trifle; a fine 1985 Gevrey Chambertin for Winchester, Muscadet diluted with mineral water for Elizabeth; coffee.

'If only they'd stuck to training horses,' she said.

'I agree.' Winchester had never approved of O'Donnell.

'The Margaret Thatcher era was like that: greedy people sticking their fingers into any pies they could, out to make killings with other people's money. Thank goodness they got rid of Maggie.'

Shifting the blame for her husband's failings on to Mrs Thatcher clearly made Elizabeth feel better, so Winchester prudently didn't mention 'Prospero'. This was an obnoxious financial 'guru' from Utah, a smart-aleck who had hijacked the name of Shakespeare's most godlike character as a desperate marketing ploy, and he had trumpeted to the world that he had made over $20 million from what had gone on in silver in 1979. It had been Prospero's prophesy which had set the whole thing off in the first place that year.

Elizabeth said, 'I know the profit motive was very important for everyone concerned except you.'

He nodded. She had been the biggest loser. When he'd been with the Grevilles, it was unthinkable they would ever have to open Condrieu to the public.

Elizabeth read his thoughts. 'You may find this hard to understand, Mr Winchester, but it all went so horribly wrong because James never believed I could love him. You see, I had to find some way to prove that I did.'

Book One

January 1963

That winter, it got so bad that the waterfall on the border of the O'Donnells' field froze solid. But still Christy never imagined his ma could die. Molly kept working out on the land, not always well covered, and began to feel a little off-colour. She just shrugged it off at first.

Then, on the day they went to the Connemara cattle fair at Maam Cross, a biting gale blew. Every bone in Molly's body ached after that.

The 15-year-old Christy shifted her bed from the back room of their stone cottage to near the turf-burning hearth. But Molly's brow got so inflamed that she told him the same evening: 'You'd better be stopping at the doctor's on your way to Galway tomorrow.'

The boy drove off early next morning, with the milk cans clanking on the back of the cart. At Dr Conroy's surgery in the village of Rosscahill, six miles across the frost-bound bogs, Christy said to him, 'Ma's got a bad fever. Could you please be coming out?'

Conroy put Molly O'Donnell's name in his visiting book and shook some pills into a brown bottle. 'I'll be out the day after tomorrow now. The whole of western Ireland's down with the same epidemic, it seems. She's to take two of these tablets four times a day until I come and stay warm. And she's to eat oranges.'

Christy knew a greengrocer's in Galway City where he'd get oranges; he'd go there straight after delivering the milk.

'You're a fine lad, you know, Christy,' the doctor called after him as he left. 'Not all the boys would keep away from the girls and look after their ma instead.'

The boy gave an embarrassed nod. He was already five foot ten, with keen hazel eyes and an appealing mop of dark curly hair, and he would break girls' hearts when he grew up. He didn't keep away from the fairer sex out of choice; it was just that he and his ma lived alone miles out on the bogs.

An hour and thirteen more miles later Christy was in Galway City, unloading the milk cans in the yard of Sharandon's Creamery. Happily, the precious contents hadn't frozen and he declared, 'My luck's in today!'

Old Sharandon, who was stamping his feet on the cobble-stones to keep warm, chuckled, *'Is fearr a bheith sona ná saoithiúil.'* The ancient Gaelic proverb meant: 'It's better to be lucky than wise.'

Christy nodded. 'That's the truth sir, to be sure.' Bringing milk out all the way here from Connemara on a day like this could hardly be considered wise, especially since very few folk from his part of the county would do it in *any* conditions. Dairy farming was almost unheard of on the bogs; Connemara calves were usually sold off young, to be fattened up for slaughter.

But Christy had always felt it to be terribly wrong that the calves which he and his ma reared should be consigned to such a grim fate for only a few pounds. The idea to milk them – so obvious really – had come to him at one of the cattle fairs eighteen months ago, when a dairy farmer from east County Galway had bought a calf they called Nell to rear as a milch cow.

'Why don't we keep our she-calves for milking ourselves?' Christy had said to his ma. 'We could always be selling the milk.'

Molly had replied: 'The bog land's no good for the grazing.'

Christy, however, made enquiries. One night, he told his ma: 'Farmer Macarthy keeps cows, you know, and he says that, as long as you've got a little area for pasture, the local milk's all right for churning into butter. He sells gallons down at the Galway creameries, and he gets money week in week out. We could do the same ma. We've got that small stretch of grass by the road. Getting money in every week's better than waiting ages between selling calves, isn't it now?' He even took her along to John Macarthy's place near Derryerglinna to see the cows for herself.

Molly eventually agreed to try it out. Within a short time they saw that it could pay, and Christy left school to help his ma full-time. Their cows now yielded three to four gallons a day and Christy took ten gallons to Galway City every Monday and Thursday. At two pence a pint, he got thirteen and four for each trip. Twenty-six and eight a week. It was enough for them to get by on. The little else they made, like any surplus arising after selling a sheep and paying for feed, they put aside. Christy had resolved they'd get a decent farm one day, like his da had always promised his ma.

When today's cans were unloaded, Old Sharandon handed over a ten-shilling note and two florins. The boy proffered eight pence change, but the creamery man waved it aside. 'You deserve it for making it out here in this weather.'

'Thanks, sir!' The tip would come in very handy for his ma's oranges, he thought happily.

Old Sharandon winked. 'You're determined to be rich, Christy, so here's another tip: if you've got any spare turf back home, take it down to Screeb Power Station. They've run right out of fuel because of this murthering cold.'

The cottage reeked of fowl droppings. The O'Donnells kept their hens in the lower part of their large dresser, and Molly had just mucked the straw out of this coop. The stink was sharpened by the sweet pungent scent of the turf burning in the hearth. Molly was sweeping straw and feathers off the floor when Christy burst open the door.

'There's a fortune to be made in Screeb ma!' he cried.

She shivered in the draught. 'Will you shut ...'

Christy slammed the door behind him, his face radiant. 'We've got to be quick! The power station's paying thirty shillings a bag for turf!'

She was well past being surprised at most things, and worn out by her fever. But this did catch her off-guard. Thirty shillings for a bag of turf? She had never known it to go for more than five shillings.

'Get in front of the fire,' she said, seeing his teeth chattering. 'And don't go giving me any more nonsense about thirty-shilling turf.'

He hurried over to rub his hands above the spitting little flames. 'But it's true, ma. Power stations all over Ireland have run right out of fuel.'

This merited deeper contemplation, and Molly went thoughtfully to stir the bacon and cabbages stewing in the big cast-iron pot – the *corcan* – which hung by a chain in the hearthplace. She was aware of the black, brick-shaped turf sods stacked to one side; there were acres and acres of the stuff out on the bogs which could be cut and dried for fuel. It was impossible that a bag could be worth thirty shillings. There must be some catch. There always was. Her hopes were forever being dashed. 'You didn't say when the doctor was coming out,' she muttered.

'He can't make it until the day after tomorrow, ma.' The boy hurriedly fished the bottle of pills out of his pocket. 'He said to take these and eat oranges. I was after getting you some from Teale's....'

Molly clucked her tongue with frustration. 'That's just typical. Here everybody is, all excited about thirty-shilling turf, but can Michael Conroy come when I need him? No. All he can do is send pills and keep me waiting. Everyone keeps me waiting. Take your da now ... he never even sent the American letter this last Christmas.'

Christy, feeling wretched for her, mumbled, 'We might get one next year, ma.' He knew they wouldn't. His father had disappeared eleven years ago, and she'd persuaded herself he'd gone across the Atlantic to make his fortune. Every December, she watched out for the 'American letter' – the money packet which the emigrant men sent to their families. One had never come for them.

Tears brimmed in her eyes. 'When you were born, Christy, my Stephen was so proud that he promised he'd build me a castle. 'It'll have a moat,' he'd say, 'and we'll pour boiling oil on invaders from the battlements.' Such grand words, Christy, and then he'd go off to gamble on the blessed horses in Galway or Dublin. Or across the water in England. And he'd always come back penniless. And one day he never came back. I still remember that day ... And here I am, waiting and waiting, and we don't even have electricity.'

She coughed and coughed for a good minute, then she hacked, and this brought the phlegm up in her throat, which she swallowed back. 'Thirty shillings a bag, is it now?'

Christy's eyes brightened. Unusually, she wasn't going on and on about that castle business. 'That's right. We could get fifteen pounds if we sold ten bags' worth.'

'And that's what you call a fortune? Fifteen pounds? We'd get more than that for a cow.'

He pleaded, 'It's a lot of money, ma. And we'd still have enough turf left to get us through this cold snap.'

She smeared her tears off her cheeks with the back of her hand. 'No, we're not selling ten bags of turf, Christy. We're going to sell every sod that's in the shed, that's for sure.'

'Every sod?' he repeated. She couldn't mean that.

Molly nodded, ladling the dinner on to his plate. All traces of self-pity had vanished from her face. There was now a determined glow. 'It's going to get warmer again any day now, and then a bag of turf won't fetch thirty shillings, will it? So we'd be better off cashing in by selling all we have. There's enough wood outside to keep us going at least a week.'

They did have some wood by the shed, Christy knew. And if they got a bit low, there were plenty of branches on the dead larches out by Ross Lake he could help himself to. 'All right ma,' he said, yielding to her logic. So, after wolfing down his bacon and cabbages, he went to pack all the turf in the shed. There were seventeen and a bit bags' worth in total. Molly told him to top this up to a full eighteen bags by adding the sods stacked next to the hearth. He had to make two journeys to get it all to Screeb Power Station; but by dusk he and his ma were richer by twenty-seven pounds.

When Dr Conroy came out to the O'Donnell farm two days later, the weather had got worse. The temperature recorded at Clifden on the Atlantic coast was 17 degrees Fahrenheit. It was the coldest day for forty-six years.

The stethoscope which the doctor pressed about on Molly's chest was a circle of ice. She sighed with relief when he unhooked it from his ear and turned her over to take her temperature.

'I thought as much,' he said as he withdrew the thermometer from her anatomy. 'Yet another case of Asian flu.' After cleaning the instrument and putting it away in his black bag, he stuck a needle in her rump. Then he wrote a prescription. 'You're to stay in the warm for at least five days now, Molly Joyce, and take a spoonful of this mixture twice a day.'

Molly beamed happily at Michael Conroy from her bed; the familiar way he used her maiden name warmed her more than any medicine he could ever prescribe.

It began to snow the next day.

With the ground frozen solid, the snow settled easily; by late morning, Connemara was several inches under.

Molly stayed indoors while Christy did the milking, went to Galway, brought the firewood in to stop it getting wet, and got two of the cuckoo wrasse rock fish out of the salting barrel for their midday meal.

The snow kept falling as he continued the outdoor chores: fresh straw had to be stuffed in the cracks in the roof; snow cleared off patches of bog for the sheep to graze; the eyes of the old potatoes in the shed whittled out to use as seed at next month's planting; the cow shed mucked out; the mixture of bran and potatoes for the donkey and cows prepared; the animals brought in under shelter and fed.

The snow was still teeming endlessly down when he made his way back at dusk, worn out, wet through and chilled to the bone. He had no inkling of what had gone on in the cottage. As he opened the door, a blast of heat hit him in the face, searing his eyes. The place had become an oven, and his ma, wearing just a thin cotton dress, sat in a chair in front of the hearth. Her pasty face had swollen up in the heat, and her eyes were red.

'I wanted to make a feast for your da, see Christy,' she babbled, 'for when he comes to take me to my castle ...'

She's cracked, Christy thought.

'... but there was only the cuckoo wrasse, so I thought I'd make the place really warm for him instead ... and then I thought it would be nice to toast my toes by the fire....' A guilty expression lurked behind her red eyes. 'I've used up the wood, see now ... could you go get some turf out of the shed?'

The curly-haired lad stared at the hearth. All that remained in it were a few glowing embers. On the mantelpiece above, next to the clock, was the chipped old teapot containing the twenty-seven pounds he had brought back from Screeb only three days earlier.

'We haven't any more turf, remember, ma?' he cried. 'And you can forget all about that precious castle of yours and the American letter! Da's abandoned us for the bloody horses and he's never coming back. All right?'

Now her stare turned haughty, but there was a glimmer of comprehension in it. He led her to her bed by the hearth and tucked her in. 'You're not to move from there, understand now? I'll go and get fuel from somewhere.'

She nodded weakly.

In the eerie white glow of the yard, Christy harnessed old Tony the donkey to the cart, his thoughts crowding upon each other. Farmer Regan, four miles away, was the nearest neighbour and the best hope; the return journey there normally took less than an hour; allowing for the snow on the ground and that still swirling down, he should be back in an hour and a half at most. Yes, that should be all right. The cottage would stay hot for several hours yet ... Now another idea flashed into his head: as a precaution, he should bring one of the cows into the cottage for extra warmth, as folk did in the old days.

When he had done this, he got on the cart and set off over the bog. Almost immediately, he drove into a deep drift. It took more than a minute to get through this, then he drove into another drift moments later. It was obvious now that he'd be away longer than he'd thought. But he had no alternative but to plough on, and more than an hour went by before he reached the first of the ancient standing stones by the road. From this, Christy worked out he hadn't even covered half the distance. Here, he drew up the cart, wondering if he should go back and fetch his ma out to the Regans'. Then he remembered Dr Conroy saying she must stay in the warm and not go outdoors. Even as he pondered this, the cart tracks behind him had already disappeared under fresh snow. The fall was thickening all the time.

Christy decided to press forward, really force old Tony along. The faithful old animal had been doing great so far, and it would take a long time for the cottage to get cold enough to put his ma in danger.

Another two hours went by before he reached the Regan farmstead. Here, billows of smoke rose from the cottage chimney and filled the air with the tang of burning turf. As soon as the farmer opened his door, Christy shouted, 'I need fuel Mr Regan! We've run out, see now?'

Farmer Regan, a ruddy-cheeked man with a vast belly, rocked back on his heels at the sight of the shivering boy with snow-matted hair. 'Of course you could be having fuel now, son. And more's the pity I can't take you back in the Bedford. But the murthering battery's flat, see now?'

'I should be all right if we're quick,' Christy cried, explaining how his ma had made the house oven-hot. It took them only a minute or so to load turf and logs on the cart before the boy set off again into the night.

Storm winds were sweeping across the bog now, and squalls of powdered snow lashed the cart. A mile or so out from Farmer Regan's, the donkey began to falter in its stride. Then, a few hundred yards further, it just stopped in its tracks.

Christy yanked at the reins and yelled at the animal to carry on. Reluctantly, it lumbered forward again. The boy managed to keep goading it on until they came to the mid-Connemara moraine ridge. The narrow passage through this was packed now with snow higher than the donkey's head. Here Tony came to another halt. This time, it sank on to its knees; then it tried to lower itself further but couldn't, frustrated by the shafts to which it was attached. It began to thrash its hind legs about in the snow.

Christy jumped off the bench and tugged at the donkey's cheek piece. 'Come on, Tony!' he shouted, 'Get up! We've got to get home now!'

The donkey shook its head free, snorted steam from its nostrils and tucked its head between its forelegs. The boy unfastened the leather traces by which it was bound to the shafts and tugged the cheek piece again. 'You're free! Get up now, get up! We've got to get back to ma.'

Tony dropped its hind quarters and stretched flat in the snow.

Christy knew it must die within a couple of hours if it didn't get moving. It had already closed its eyes. He realized wretchedly he had no time to lose: the cottage was losing heat every second that he stayed with Tony, when the only thing that mattered was his ma. He made a sign of the cross over the animal's head, took four logs off the cart and scrabbled his way through the snow-blocked passage.

Even after he cleared this, he could only inch forward in that blinding snowstorm. Mountainous drifts reared up all the time, forcing him off course and concealing the familiar standing stones along the route. The blizzard began to weaken with the dawn, but by then Christy was quite ground down with fatigue. As he struggled on homewards, still more hours dragged by.

When at last he made out his cottage in the distance, the snow had long stopped falling and the sun was high and brilliant in the sky. Mustering up one last effort, he made it past the frozen waterfall and up to the stone dwelling. He opened the cottage door and his heart leaped with relief.

His ma was still on her bed in front of the hearth, and her lips had lit up in a welcoming smile. Christy grinned inanely back. 'Ma?' he mumbled.

She didn't reply.

He was suddenly drenched by the knowledge that her eyes were closed. And that her lips weren't moving. The terrible realization dawned on him that there had been no smile; that it had just been a trick of the light sweeping across her face with the opening door. 'Ma?' he muttered again, the terror dragging at his throat. She still didn't respond. 'You all right, ma?'

Only the cow chomping straw by the bed made any sound.

'Ma ...' Christy whimpered once more, creeping towards her, staring at her lips, seeing they were blue-black, willing them to reply, feeling so much colder here than outside....

Before he could reach her bedside, his legs gave way and he fell on his knees. The freezing spasm gripped the rest of his body, and his head pitched to the floor.

Still holding the logs, he had a last glimpse of the dead ashes in the hearth, then his eyes stopped seeing.

His life was saved by Farmer Regan. Not a deep sleeper at the best of times, the good farmer had passed a particularly bad night. His big farmhouse had been cosy enough indoors, but the storm outside had been disturbing and he had worried about the livestock. There had also been that other concern nagging the back of his mind.

He rose well before dawn to go out and see to the animals. The blizzard was abating by now, but this didn't allay his other worry: that the O'Donnell boy might not have made it home last night.

As soon as he had fed the animals, he hurried back into the farmhouse. On the table in the kitchen was the battery of his Bedford van. It was rigged up to a charger, which was making a loud buzzing noise.

The farmer saw on the charger's dial that the battery was up to only one-third of its effective charge. Deciding it would have to do, he took it out to the garage and connected it back to the leads under the bonnet of his snub-nosed blue Bedford van. Then he got in and turned the ignition key. In common with other vehicles of the era, the 1956 model van had a starter knob to make the engine turn over. As Regan pulled this, he muttered a prayer to Mother Mary.

At the first attempt, the engine turned over and over but wouldn't catch. The second time around it was the same, only now the revs were weaker. The farmer heeded the warning and got out to wait. While he did, he cut two lengths from some rope he had in the garage, and tied these around the back tyres, fastening up firmly with truck knots. He also put a spade in the van.

A quarter of an hour having passed by now, Regan decided to have another try at starting the vehicle. He got back in, turned the key in the ignition again and, as he pulled the starter knob, jammed his foot down hard on the accelerator.

The engine spluttered into life. Regan stamped repeatedly on the accelerator pedal and the spluttering got livelier. Then the engine caught and began to run smoothly.

The farmer, sending his heart-felt thanks to Mother Mary, revved it a number of times with a combination of accelerator and choke knob, before carefully engaging gear and driving out across the white yard and through the gate.

It was just getting light and barely snowing now. Regan knew if he didn't go higher than second gear, he should be all right for most of the journey. He did need to get out more often than he'd expected to shovel away drifts on the road, but he was heartened by the way the van furrowed along through the snow for much of the route because of the rope around the tyres.

The biggest hold-up was at the mid-Connemara moraine ridge, where the road was blocked by the boy's cart and dead donkey. It took him half an hour to drag these out of the way and shovel a passage through, during which he dreaded what else he might find further down the road. His fears were realized when he eventually reached the O'Donnells' cottage.

The boy was stretched out, unconscious and cold, on the flagstones in front of the hearth, but thankfully still breathing. Poor Molly O'Donnell, though, lay completely still on her bed. Regan put his ear to her chest. There was no heartbeat. Then he took her hand, which was as cold as ice, and checked for her pulse. There wasn't one. The last test was to gently thumb up one of her eyelids. The eye beneath was without a flicker of life.

His heart heavy, the kind fellow went across to the mantelpiece and stopped the clock. By tradition, everyone had a right to see when a person had died or when a body had been found.

5.1.79

It was at just about the moment the burly man let himself into the Lincolnshire country mansion that, 250 miles away, Charles Greville finally lost his fight for life. The lights had come on in the palatial lobby here at Condrieu Hall, and still more staff were mustered, waiting desperately for news. Those who saw the Hon. Henry Brewer enter passed the word around quickly, and the chattering subsided.

'Any news from Dublin?' Brewer asked an elderly valet.

The man shook his head. 'No, sir.'

Brewer carved his way through. An intimidating figure with wire-brush eyebrows and a grim set to his jaw, he was the Agent of the Condrieu Estate. His position here in relation to the duke was similar to that which the prime minister enjoys with the Queen: the estate was his to govern on his sovereign's behalf, but only as long as he got results. The methods Brewer used sometimes had earned him the nickname 'Trouble Brewing' by the staff. Now, they melted out of his path.

Many had come from far-flung parts of the estate – gamekeepers, gardeners, foresters and home-farm workers – to wait for news with the uniformed maids, valets and cooks who worked within the Hall premises. Sixty to seventy employees here tonight. On the faces of young and old was the same sense of helplessness. Charles Greville, Duke of Marylebone, was much loved, and it was happening so far away.

The agent pressed on and into the Blue Drawing Room. Gathered here, in the company of Lady Elizabeth Greville, the duke's daughter-in-law, were friends and acquaintances of the family. Lady Carole Markeston sat in the main window alcove with Elizabeth, while the others stood around, some chatting, a few smoking. The lack of news for over an hour from across the Irish Sea oppressed everybody. With night closing in, it seemed to Brewer that a black shroud had been drawn behind the room's immense stained-glass window. In it, Philip Boucherett, the Huguenot forefather of the family, sat proudly on horseback.

'I'm afraid your husband wasn't at Moresby Road either,' Brewer said, approaching Elizabeth.

'I can't imagine where else he could be,' she said with frustration. In her late fifties, Elizabeth Greville was a handsome woman with intense blue eyes and ivory-brown hair which she wore swept back up from her forehead. The duke had not remarried since his wife Letitia's death almost half a century earlier, and Elizabeth had been mistress of Condrieu ever since.

'Have you tried his club?' piped up Lady Carole Markeston. She was forty-two and a former star of the TV soap opera

Brazen Hussies. Now the wife of politician Sir John Markeston, she was Elizabeth's closest friend, and this despite James Greville having been besotted with her to the point of almost raping her when she had refused to have sex with him.

Brewer cast a brisk nod at Lady Carole, and surveyed Elizabeth with concern. He wondered how her husband would react when he was located and informed about his father's accident; knowing James Greville, he would probably try to nail her to the cross. 'I'd left messages with Simon Winchester and at the Scimitar club....'

She shook her head. 'Neither of them has called back.'

Brewer racked his brain but couldn't think of anywhere else Greville could be. Simon Winchester, Greville's comptroller down in London, had told him on the phone that Greville had left Marylebone House in a hurry soon after lunch. No-one else at the House knew where he had gone or when he'd be back. The Condrieu agent himself had just returned from Horncastle, a few miles across the Lincoln Wolds. James Greville's mistress – Lady Sarah McGonagle – had a detached property there where the two met. But no-one had been in tonight, and none of the neighbours had seen them for days.

'He rang this morning to ask about Charles,' Elizabeth recalled. 'He wanted to know about Charles's movements across at the Grange. But he didn't say he was going anywhere.'

Carole Markeston offered helpfully, 'What about the silver vaults, Henry?'

'He wasn't at any of them when I tried earlier.' Brewer had called the secure warehouses of London Minerals Board, where Greville sometimes went, half a dozen times that afternoon. Now, with the tension building over both the duke's accident and the search for his heir, he was close to letting rip his feelings about James Greville: that Greville wasn't fit to be duke if Charles died; that he should never have dragged the family into this silver thing. But, of course, this was hardly the time or place for anything like that. 'I'll try Marylebone House again,' he said instead.

The drawing-room phone rang as he approached the satinwood Hepplewhite console on which it stood. It had rung all afternoon. He barked into it with frustration, 'Condrieu Hall.' Staff waiting out in the hall crowded by the open door to listen. Brewer turned and said to Elizabeth: 'It's Early from the hospital in Dublin, ma'am. He wants to talk to you, and only you.'

Silence descended on the room and a young man, Dennis

Whyte, a gardener, let himself in from the hall. Orphaned at an early age, his father had used to be head gardener at the Estate, and Whyte's subsequent upbringing had been paid for entirely by the duke. He worshipped Charles Greville. Brewer frowned at the intrusion, but the gardener didn't notice.

Elizabeth stood very still as she listened to the subdued voice in the telephone, one trembling hand pressed against the console for support. The man speaking was the assistant trainer of the duke's horses at Eden Grange in Ireland. He had been the person driving the Land Rover. 'I'm sorry, ma'am,' he concluded.

Other staff members were slipping into the drawing room in huddles, and Brewer made gestures at them to be silent.

Elizabeth's brain screamed that it couldn't be true. But if it was, then thorough enquiries would have to be made and this man punished. She was unaware she had turned ethereally white.

'What is it, Liz?' said Lady Markeston, trying to sound nonchalant.

Into the telephone, Elizabeth said, 'Your words of sympathy have been noted.' She put the receiver back in its cradle and glanced around vaguely. Servants and friends pressed closely, desperate for news.

'Is he going to be all right, ma'am?' someone said.

Right next to her, a junior laundry maid from Leeds called Karen Dodds burst out sobbing.

Other voices jabbered:

'I'm sure it's bad news....'

'But he can't have been that badly hurt....'

'If he dies, we'll be in the hands of Mr James....'

She refused to listen to any of them. She spotted Brewer in the crush of faces and said, 'He must be found at all costs. Get the police in to track him down if you have to.'

The agent nodded solemnly. It was obvious the duke hadn't pulled through.

Matthew Brown, ex-Mayor of Horncastle, said hopefully, 'He will recover, won't he, Liz?'

'No,' she said quietly, wanting just to go to her room and cry for hours. He had been one of the giants of the twentieth century and she had adored him. No-one else would ever make her laugh in the same way. She smiled kindly at the sobbing laundry maid and put her hand on the girl's shoulder. 'The surgeons did everything they could but they couldn't save him.

He had a massive brain haemorrhage and died.'

The maid lurched away, bawling. Others broke down in tears. Some left the Blue Drawing Room in desolation. The gardener, Whyte, just stood there, staring at Elizabeth.

To anyone still listening, she announced, 'Before he died, he expressed total faith in James.'

It was a bare-faced lie. Everybody knew Charles Greville's true feelings for his son. But she had to have the staff behind the family just now. 'His Grace was sure every one of you would back the new duke to the hilt.'

In the cold drizzle, the pall bearers carried the coffin up the mausoleum steps. The Reverend Arthur Holdsworth climbed after it.

James and Elizabeth Greville were at the front of the column of following mourners. Estate employees held umbrellas up for them. Behind were their daughters Deborah and Jane, then countless black umbrellas stretching a hundred yards back to the family's private chapel.

The Rev. Holdsworth turned at the top of the vault steps to face the gathering.

James Greville's pale grey eyes gazed past him. They were trained on the coffin, which was being manoeuvered into position above an opening in the vault floor. Fifty-nine years old, the new duke had a face mottled with livid red blotches. He suffered from hypertension. His hair retained some blond strands amidst the silvering of age, but his eyebrows and moustache were pure white.

The elderly priest observed him from above, conscious that millions around the world had been appalled by the manner of Charles Greville's death: an unexpected fall out of a Land Rover; a wheel riding over his head. James Greville had been seen by a number of people in Dublin that same day and at Heathrow Airport later that evening, and rumours had spread that he had been somehow involved. The chaplain preferred not to believe these without concrete proof, but he was nevertheless saddened at the complete absence of distress the heir had exhibited throughout the funeral service. With a sigh, he opened his black book and began to read the Committal:

'For as much as it hath pleased Almighty God of His great mercy to take unto Himself the soul of our dearly beloved here departed ...'

'I can't believe you were actually in Dublin,' Elizabeth said in a low tone. 'Actually waiting outside the hospital at the moment Charles died?'

'So what?' Greville didn't look at her.

The coffin was placed on canvas webbing ropes held by the undertaker's men and lowered out of sight.

'Do you know anything about the accident that I don't? You must tell me, James. Did you have anything to do with it?'

'No!' A shade too loud. Yet the reaction was somehow just what she had expected.

'We therefore commit his body to the ground; earth to earth, ashes to ashes, dust to dust …'

The chaplain tossed a handful of earth in after the coffin. A few pebbles rapped against its lid and bounced on to the marble floor below.

'It was Prospero, wasn't it?' Elizabeth sobbed. 'His prophesy.' It was Carole Markeston who had shown her the article in the *Washington Journal*, the day after the accident, and she had understood. Her daughter Deborah held her shoulders now to comfort her, but she was racked with sobs.

Greville turned his blotchy face on her. 'It's not like you to break down in public, Liz. You're just making it obvious that you and he disgraced yourselves together.'

She shook her head with despair. 'He's dead, James. Can't you see he's dead?'

February 1963

'I can't accept that she's gone,' Christy said glumly. He stood by his ma's grave at Killertoon churchyard, his legs still throbbing with pain. A simple headstone of Connemara granite marked Molly O'Donnell's last resting place.

Farmer Regan, who had brought him here from Galway's Merlin Park Hospital, didn't respond. Death can overwhelm the most communicative spirit. They got back in the Bedford van and drove off. Regan eventually remarked, 'It hasn't hit you yet lad … you're a tough young fellow and you're fighting it off.'

A few patches of snow remained in the hollows in the fields

they passed, thin and almost transparent now. The rest had melted right away during the last six days.

Regan steered the van through the gates of his farmstead, carefully avoiding the calves grazing near the cattle grid. He drew the vehicle up to a halt in his yard and racked up the hand-brake. Christy looked blankly on at the calves, not wanting to get out. That glazed look was probably due to anaesthetics they'd used at the hospital, the farmer decided. 'You'll feel it sooner or later that your ma's left this earth,' he breathed. 'The Lord bless her poor soul.'

Mrs Regan opened the farmhouse door and from behind her emerged Nellie Orme. She was Christy's middle-aged spinster cousin, who had come down from Sligo for Molly's funeral four days earlier. Christy, recovering in hospital from frostbite and exhaustion, hadn't been able to see his ma buried. Nellie had visited him every day. She was the O'Donnells' only known relative.

Now, after helping him out of the van, she led him into the cottage and sat him down on a stuffed armchair by the hearth. 'You take the weight off your poor little pins, now.' She raised his legs and placed a stool under them.

'I'll get you a nice cup of tea, now,' Mrs Regan chimed in, 'and some gingerbread I baked this morning.' She bustled off towards the kitchen.

An involuntary grin lit up Christy's face. He wasn't used to all this attention being showered on him.

'And don't you worry yourself about the cows,' Nellie said. 'I went down to your place this morning with Farmer Macarthy – he's ever so kind – and we fed them and milked them and took the milk to Galway, and old Mr Sharandon gave me two pence a pint for it, and I've kept all the money for you....' She broke off. Christy's smile had vanished and his eyes were vacant again. He didn't want to know about the cows and the farm and the milk. Least of all about the money.

People came that afternoon to offer their condolences to the boy: Father Deeny, John and Mrs Macarthy, Dr Conroy, Thomas Symes (the hay and feed supplier), Eammon Halliday (an old friend of his da's), Caitlin Entwhistle (his last teacher at the National School), Old Sharandon from the Creamery and, last but not least, the assistant at Teale's greengrocer's, who went by the name of Santos. A dark-skinned middle-aged man with frizzy greying hair, this fellow swore he was of Brazilian descent, though locals sniggered he was what had resulted when an Irish colleen of dubious morals had checked the size of an African sailor's anchor when he had berthed in Galway.

Molly's praises were sung, while Eammon Halliday kept repeating that it was tragic, really tragic the way she had left the earth and this led to great choking moments of sadness. Thankfully, Santos told a few self-deprecating jokes about his origins, and Mrs Regan kept bringing in gingerbread, small cakes, tea and glasses of stout on trays throughout the afternoon, so the mood never got too oppressive.

It was after dark by the time the mourners had all gone, with Christy's cousin Nellie the last to leave. She was taken off by Thomas Symes to Galway's Ceannt Railway Station where she'd try to catch the 7.35 back to Sligo. Mrs Regan gave the boy supper, then led him upstairs to the room she'd prepared for him.

'We're just next door my dear,' she said. 'And don't worry about disturbing us if you need a shoulder to cry on during the night.'

'Thanks, Mrs Regan.' But he hoped it wouldn't come to that. They had already done so much for him and his ma.

Four nights later, he dreamed for the first time about Molly. She was making boiled bacon and cabbages for him. 'You left school to help me on the farm, Christy. Why didn't your da stay and help me?'

He woke up sobbing, 'Ma. You're gone, aren't you?'

'You're sure you're doing the right thing, now?' Farmer Regan asked.

'Aye, Mr Regan.' The boy had no doubts. They stood in the O'Donnell farmhouse, three weeks after Molly's death, and Christy had been back home eleven days. 'I'll sell off the animals at the market, then see what I can get for this lot.' He threw the last of his ma's clothes on to the heap by the threshold. There were two cardboard boxes there too, in which he had put all the household things and knick-knacks and the couple of bits of jewellery Molly had had. Set apart was a wire cage full of cackling hens. 'The poultry's for you and the missus. To thank you for everything you've done.'

'Oh, you needn't bother,' Regan retorted, but he beamed nonetheless. 'Maureen will be pleased.'

Christy retrieved his cash from the old teapot on the mantelpiece. Four pounds, thirteen shillings and seven pence was all that was left. Out of that, three pounds was thanks to the rag-and-bone man he'd called from Clifden yesterday to take away the scant furniture in the house. The windfall he and his ma had had from the turf and whatever else they'd squirrelled away over the years to buy their new farm had been swallowed up by the funeral expenses, the cost of the headstone, and by back debts they owed to a feed supplier.

'Come on,' said Regan, a lump growing in his throat. 'Let's be away. I wouldn't want to be late getting to Galway.'

They loaded the things – without forgetting the milk cans from the shed – into Regan's van. The farmer was an expert at herding livestock with the vehicle and soon got the O'Donnell cows and sheep trotting down the road in front of them. Christy didn't look back as the party advanced across the bog.

'I can understand your not being able to bear to live here any more,' remarked Regan. 'But where will you be going after you finish down at the market?'

Christy wondered how much of his plans he should reveal. 'County Kildare,' he said. 'There's likely to be work in the big stables out there.'

'Stables?'

He wouldn't say a lot more, he decided. That way he'd keep the idea fresh in his mind until he achieved it. And achieve it he would. Even if it took him fifty years. 'Aye, Mr Regan. Racing stables. The money's grand in the racing game.'

Regan grinned. 'Aiming for the jackpot, eh? Well, don't go forgetting the folk in Connemara when you rake in the millions!'

'Oh I won't forget anyone. I'll be coming back.' His tone was so determined that Regan's grin slipped right off his face. But Christy didn't elaborate. What was the point of telling anyone, even the good farmer, about his da's failed promises? No-one would understand if he tried to explain how his ma had yearned for the castle she always believed her husband would give her....

All the snow was long gone, and the sun was out, and after Rosscahill they came across other folk on the Galway road herding animals down in the same direction. The sun had brought families out on the bog too, to work at replenishing the turf stocks consumed during the cruel winter just gone. The whole of Connemara had heard how Molly O'Donnell had died; nobody else wanted to be caught out the same way. The men were busy cutting the peat turf with their slanes; the women and children arranged the sods in low dolmen-shaped stacks for drying. Some of them waved as the van drove by, but Christy kept his gaze stolidly on the road.

When the party arrived in Galway, Regan parked beside the market stalls and said he was off to the bank, and then after that to see if any of his pals weren't down at the Dog and Duck. The boy herded his livestock into the mêlée of complaining sheep, goats, cattle and pigs in the square. Everywhere, farmers and breeders bawled out the merits of their animals or argued over prices. Christy listened for a moment or two, then started shouting too.

A farmer from the village of Cloonboo came by and took a fancy to Nancy, his best cow. 'How much?'

'Twenty pounds, sir.'

'Never in a million years!' The farmer waved an ash plant in Christy's face in a gesture of dismissal. 'She's worth no more than ten.'

Now a 'tangler' – one of the free-lance negotiators who were always present at markets – materialized. Staring at the cow as if struck by lightning, he remarked, 'You can smell the milk in that animal's udders from here. She's bound to bring money in week in week out.' He'd heard Christy shouting this a few moments earlier.

The farmer waved his weed at the tangler now, to shoo him away too. To Christy he said, 'I'll give you fifteen pounds for that cow.'

The tangler intervened, 'Oh, that'd be robbery! That animal's worth no less than thirty.'

The Cloonboo man protested. The tangler counter-protested. The farmer raised his price. The tangler dropped his. A couple of minutes later, the farmer and Christy spat into their hands and clapped them together. A deal had been sealed at nineteen pounds twelve shillings and sixpence as long as Christy threw in one milk can with Nancy. Then, before the Cloonboo man led the cow away, he tied a knot in her tail to ensure that the 'luck of the beast' would remain.

The rest of Christy's livestock was also disposed of with the tangler's help, and the boy gave the fellow a pound for his trouble. Then he set out his ma's clothes and the other wares in the back of the Bedford van and accepted whatever the market-goers were prepared to pay for anything. There was only one item which he couldn't part with: a little silver locket with photos of his parents on their wedding day. Someone offered him up to fifteen shillings for the locket, but Christy refused. Instead, he stashed it away in the calf-skin pouch which Mrs Regan had given him to keep his cash.

When he had finally disposed of everything else to do with his ma and their cottage and his old life, he went across the square to the Dog and Duck with a dull ache in his heart. Farmer Regan had indeed run into a couple of old cronies in the pub, and the three were taking copious swigs of Conneely's poteen, the local illicit firewater, with each trying to tell the tallest tale. A Garda man had been detailed to put a stop to these goings-on, but he could be seen propping up a corner of the bar with a glass of the same poison in his thick hand.

Christy tapped Regan on the shoulder. 'I'll be off on my way now Mr Regan ... I just wanted to be thanking you again for everything you've done for me.'

Regan, focusing on who it was, rose and clapped the boy heartily on the back. 'Now you take good care of yourself, son. And don't you forget us. We'll be looking out for you when you're back this way.'

At the bus station, while he waited for the bus to the east, Christy counted the cash in his pouch: fifty-seven pounds sixteen and eight. Even in 1963, and in Ireland, that amount of money wasn't going to buy anyone a castle. But he needed every penny of it to fulfil that one aim in life.

17.1.79

Sir William Butts's assistant made a slight adjustment to the lights trained on the subject standing grandly by the tall lattice windows which gave on to Marylebone Park.

'Tilt your head a little to the left,' Sir William said. James Greville obliged. Sir William pressed the trigger and the camera clicked, wound on, clicked, wound on, clicked, wound on....

Tall, distinguished, with a perfect crop of white hair, Sir William had already taken over three hundred photographs of the new duke for his portrait. He never painted with the sitter before him, but observed carefully all aspects of his subject's environment, studied his photographs for weeks, and only went to his easel when his imagination was ready to take over. An idea already burgeoning in his mind was to depict Greville as a posturing emperor with no clothes.

To start with, there was that hand forever creeping on to his chest. Sir William guessed it was a nervous tic of some sort, but Greville nevertheless appeared feebly Napoleonic because of it. Then there was that smug expression on his blotchy face, which the zoom lens magnified and sharpened. Most important of all, though, was the egregious vanity of the man for having turned this 4,000-square-foot ballroom, easily the biggest room in Marylebone House, into his den.

Sir William had danced here on many occasions before 1973. Then, when James Greville had seized control of Greville Holdings, he had hijacked this place and now virtually lived in it. He had made an office area at the orchestra end, where there were Chippendale desks for himself and his comptroller; in the middle stood a vast mahogany dining-cum-conference table ringed by two dozen button-backed chairs; and, at the fireplace end, there were leather sofas, ships' chairs, Chinese lacquered cabinets and a hi-tech hi-fi system with enormous black out-curving speakers. The only thing missing, Sir William had observed wryly as he had taken pictures from different angles, was a bed.

'The panic just goes on,' called out Simon Winchester, the comptroller, from his desk. He had a sheaf of telexes before him. The markets had gone mad with the news of the Shah fleeing from Iran yesterday.

'That's it,' said Sir William. He handed his camera to his assistant, who put it away in its case.

'Thank you.' Greville swivelled his gaze on to Winchester. 'I've told you. Prospero's prophecy is coming true.'

'Nonsense!' Winchester protested. In his late thirties, with a long pinched nose, tiny blue eyes like a pig's and mousy hair, Winchester wondered why he'd agreed to quit his own room two doors along and come and work in here. He'd never get through to Greville, no matter how close he was. He tried, nevertheless. 'The market's full of froth. None of the fundamentals support this rise. Silver just has to fall again. If you've any sense, you'll sell now from the stockpile while the going's good.'

Greville lit a Romeo y Julieta. 'I'm not selling one troy ounce.'

'Then you haven't any sense.'

More messages chattered up on the telex. The machine, on the low orchestra stage, was on line to the London Minerals Board and the Chicago Grain and Metal Exchange, the world's principal silver markets. Near the telex, on music stands once used by the orchestras, graphs displayed the movements in the silver price.

The comptroller tried again. 'If you don't want to reduce your total holding, sell now and buy back at a lower price. It's a golden opportunity to get in some cash.'

Greville drew on the cigar. 'The price isn't going to get lower, Winchester.'

Sir William said, 'Thank you, James, I'll be back if I need to take any more shots.' He headed for the double mahogany doors, followed by his assistant, who wheeled the cameras and lighting rig out on a purpose-designed trolley. The head butler, Milton Diamond, ushered them out into the high-arched vestibule beyond, which was occupied by Greville's secretary, and drew the doors shut behind them.

The comptroller muttered with frustration: 'Over the years, there have been dozens of peaks you could have sold into. But all you've ever done is go on buying. You've got over 67 million ounces now, and here's a heaven-sent opportunity to take profits in millions of dollars. And God knows we need the cash.'

Greville nodded knowingly, loosing cigar smoke through his lips in a way that made Winchester cringe. 'You can't imagine I'll sell silver now, when the Shah has fallen? Don't you remember Prospero's words?'

Winchester did. By heart. *'Watch for the fall of the head of a dynasty, friends. I think you have enough confidence in me by now for me to call you friends. A head must fall and a tail must wag. Then watch silver finally lift off. Watch it go to at least fifteen dollars before the end of this year.'* He protested, 'But this is no long-term lift-off!'

Greville didn't hear. He raised his eyebrows in the direction of the telex. 'What do they say now?'

Winchester stepped up on to the stage, as curious as Greville for an update, though he would never have admitted it. On the telex, the prices of silver bullion and futures continued to tap up in a constant stream. The markets remained in turmoil.

'Spot silver last traded at $6.75.'

'That's now 37 cents higher than last night's close!'

Winchester tore off the message sheet and stomped back to

his desk with it. 'You mustn't be fooled by this. It's not just silver; gold has jumped by seven per cent and platinum by five. There are rumours flying about that Iranian oil production will be cut by half by this Ayatollah fellow; speculators are panic-buying all the precious metals as hedges against inflation. It can't last. In a few days the price will be right back down again.'

'It won't,' Greville said with finality. He rubbed his chest again. Blast that nagging ache.

The blue chauffeur-driven Bentley Continental, Charles Greville's last car, passed Borehamwood on the A1 at nine the next morning, heading south from Lincolnshire. In the back were Elizabeth Greville and the Hon. Henry Brewer. The agent of the Condrieu Estate had his diary open on the little walnut table on the back of the driver's seat. 'At the EGM this morning, I've asked Lindsay Owen, as General Manager, to give a summary of the company's performance over the last eighteen months. This afternoon it'll be the bankers.' He glanced to the top of the next page. 'Tomorrow morning, the three department heads will each make an hour-long presentation....'

Elizabeth listened with only half an ear. Outside, the drab clusters of homes on the outskirts of the capital grew more dense, and she wondered whether this was Blake's Jerusalem. She hated straying from the sanctity of Condrieu Hall. But today's trip to London had to be made; the strings gathered together even though Charles had never wanted her involved closely. Making her the Chairman of Greville International Corporation had been done out of simple necessity ... 'I have to keep at least this company out of James's clutches, and I'm afraid I need to use you.'

He had sometimes teased her: 'Chairman of the GIC isn't the only position I'd like to have you in, you know Liz ... If I'd been twenty-five years younger, and had not met Letitia, it's you I would have wanted for my wife.'

'Stop it,' she would laugh. 'I'm married to your son.'

Once, he had come up to the Hall after a stormy session with James with huge sadness in his grey eyes. 'Nobody can bring out the good in him, not even you. He's rotten through and through, and I had the misfortune to father the swine. He's now come up with the idea that you and I are having an affair.'

Her laughter had disappeared. 'What rubbish. If we're together here for much of the week, it's only because Marylebone House has been made into a no-go area for you.'

He had then chuckled, unexpectedly: 'You do make me perk up as Letitia never did.' Taking a lance from amongst the coats of armour and weapons on the staircase, he had walked around with it projecting from his hip at an angle of sixty degrees. It had looked hilariously rude seen from the side, and she had squealed with laughter.

'You're not trying to make love to me, are you, Charles?'

'I can think of many worse fates.'

Of *course* she had loved him. But never in the way James supposed.

'... After lunch tomorrow it'll be Andrew Levinson: he's the senior partner of Menzies & Fry, Greville International Corporation's chartered accountants. Two hours should be more than enough to put the figures under a microscope. Then at four o'clock it's Sir Roy Marchand.'

The name of her solicitor brought her back to earth. 'I hope you've explained everything thoroughly to Sir Roy?'

Brewer knew that she feared, more than anything else, a legal challenge by her husband for control of Greville International Corporation. 'I have. He was expecting our brief. Remember, it was Sir Roy who set up your majority shareholding in GIC in the first place. He's still consulted the two best QCs who specialize in Chancery matters – Sir Jeremy Downton and Martin Benedict.'

'Thank you for whatever you're doing, Henry, even though GIC's affairs are outside your territory. I do have to have the help of someone I trust completely.'

He gave a brisk nod and she smiled. She had already decided on a suitable reward: she would make him Managing Director of Greville International Corporation.

At Highgate, the Bentley forked right to tackle the morning traffic as far as Marylebone House, which remained at the heart of what was left of the Greville family empire.

In 1714, Sir Richard Boucherett-Greville purchased eight and a half acres of land in Marylebone Park to be able to have a home not far from that of his friend, the Duke of Buckingham. In those days, land in the Park went for £500 an acre and Sir Richard, having been told he should spend more on the building than on the land, threw in a further £5,000 on the construction. The first Marylebone House was nevertheless a plain rectangular affair, though with Italianate door and window carvings to lend it some distinction.

Half a century later, King George III bought the Buckinghams' mansion and turned it into the royal palace. From 1821 to 1835, it was extensively reconstructed by John Nash.

When Frederick Greville became the first Marquess of Marylebone, William IV was King of England. The Greville family's land holdings stretched by then from London through Essex, Suffolk, Norfolk and Lincolnshire. Frederick, both clever and lucky, purchased still more land in Yorkshire, Durham and Northumberland, and watched with delight as the values of all his properties shot up during the boom years of the Industrial Revolution. After being dubbed 'Emperor of Eastern England' and 'Richest Man in London', Frederick became immensely vain. He decided that Marylebone House should be reconstructed, as Buckingham Palace had been. In 1844, he commissioned Decimus Burton, the disciple of John Nash who designed the magnificent neo-classical screen at Hyde Park Corner, to develop the whole of his Marylebone Park estate. The original House was demolished and its place taken a year later by the present colonnaded edifice. The new House dominated a square around which a hundred and eighty townhouses were also built. All the buildings were in the grand Regency style, with sweeping gardens laid in the central quadrangle. The result was a masterpiece; many exterior aspects are unchanged to this day.

At the beginning of the twentieth century, Robert Greville, the fourth Marquess of Marylebone and Charles's father, entirely refurbished the interior of Marylebone House. The family was now the richest in England, and Robert – who had made generous donations to the Liberal Party – was awarded a dukedom by Herbert Asquith.

On 17 June 1909, the first Duke of Marylebone threw the new House open to the world. The *People* newspaper commented:

> £870,000 has been spent on renovating Marylebone House, but no attempt has been made to render it cosy. Size and grandeur are everything. In the ballroom, a hundred couples and more may waltz without fear of colliding; then, the Great Hall and the other state rooms are adorned with gilded ornamental ceilings, crystal chandeliers, Carrara marble mantelpieces, Gobelin tapestries and fine Louis XIV furniture. There are marvellous paintings on every wall. In one dining room, there are twenty-seven masterpieces, six of which are Rubenses. There is

also a purpose-built picture gallery in the west wing, which houses canvases by Gainsborough, Rembrandt, Stubbs, Renoir, Hogarth, Claude Lorraine, Murillo, Velázquez, Titian, Van Dyck and Reynolds; over three hundred in all.

But Marylebone House is a monument, not a home. Lord Harbingdon finds it 'most expensively furnished, but in exceedingly bad taste.' A senior House employee confided that the duke wanted 'King Edward's gorge to be raised' when he saw its treasures. His Majesty, it is to be noted, declined to attend the opening.

Charles Greville crumpled the newspaper after reading the last paragraph. Only ten years old at the time, with his genius already legendary, his indignation blazed in his light grey eyes. 'Take them all to court, father!'

Robert laughed. 'Every person in town who has a home with three rooms to a floor thinks he's fit to criticize our House. It's envy, dear child, that's all.'

'But they're saying you wanted to see the king's gorge being raised. It's a nasty slur. You mustn't let them get away with it.'

'Forget it. It's too petty for words.' Unable to admit he *had* said that to a House steward, also that the man would be dismissed for revealing it to the press, Robert added grandly: 'It isn't with possessions that we show our worth, you know, Charlie. It's name and reputation that count. And we've spent centuries building up ours; we can boast today the highest title in the English peerage.'

'Oh, father, I'm so pleased you say that. Ted Reade and the others claim you're only a duke because you paid the prime minister for it.'

Robert Greville could never warm to the honest audacity which was the hallmark of his son. When Charles grew up, accomplishing breath-taking coups in business and society, Robert's coolness towards him became more marked. The first duke left the management of the firm to Charles when the latter attained the age of thirty, and divided his own time clubbing in London, hunting at Condrieu, or yachting off the Côte d'Azur. He doted on young James, and his devotion for his grandson became total when Charles's wife Letitia died giving a still birth to her second baby.

Just before the 19-year-old Elizabeth Orpen-Birley married the 20-year-old James Greville in 1939, the young woman remarked to her mother: 'Robert's blind worship of James all through his life must be why he's so utterly spoiled.'

A year later, after the birth of their first daughter Jane, Elizabeth further confided to her mother: 'I can't forgive James for his political beliefs. He wants Hitler to be given the concessions he demands, and uses this stance for not fighting for his country. I'm ashamed to admit it, but it does smack of cowardice.'

The first duke, however, turned a blind eye to his grandson's lack of patriotism. He also ignored James's dissolute ways. In 1958, shortly after Charles raised the family to being the richest in Europe, Robert Greville amended his will and the articles of Greville Holdings UK Ltd. He believed that precocious talents decayed prematurely, and he wanted Charles to hand over the reins of the company to James when the former turned 65 in 1963. Robert himself died in 1960, at the grand age of eighty-six. In 1963, James demanded control of Greville Holdings from his father, but Charles refused to relinquish it. He believed Robert's intentions were misguided. 'You haven't yet understood the challenges,' he told his son. 'And you won't while you go on whoring about. Your best bet is to work conscientiously under me for a few years. There are things you've got to learn and you'll only learn them when you're not the boss.'

But James Greville embarked upon litigation, and it went on for ten years. In 1973, he finally gained control of Greville Holdings UK Ltd, and then proceeded to dismantle in the space of five more years the property empire built up over two and half centuries.

'That painting goes back in the Great Hall!' James Greville growled.

'The room was empty without him,' Elizabeth said. She knew he would take this wrongly, as more proof she had slept with Charles. But she wasn't going to be intimidated. 'His picture needs to be here.'

Charles Greville, the second Duke of Marylebone, looked over the two of them from above the fine fireplace in what had been his study. His light grey eyes had seen a thousand arguments between them. This portrait had also been painted by William Butts. In it, Charles stood imposingly in the gardens at Condrieu, the Hall behind him, a shotgun under his arm. Elizabeth had ordered the canvas brought in here from the Great Hall on her arrival this morning with Brewer.

It was after one o'clock now. Greville International Corporation's Extraordinary General Meeting had finished half an hour earlier. The announcement to the board about who would replace Charles Greville as managing director would be made by the chairman, Elizabeth, tomorrow. She was now taking lunch with her husband by the windows in the study which gave on to the Park. Outside, it was blustery.

Greville said: 'William Butts started preliminary work on my portrait yesterday. It's to go next to Charles's in the Great Hall when it's finished.'

'I'll ask Sir William to make a copy of Charles's to hang in the place of the original.'

'A copy can never be the same as the original.'

Elizabeth laid down her knife and fork with a quizzical smile. 'Why do you care so much for his image when you hardly cared for him living?'

'Now that's unfair! I had nothing to do with his death. Nothing. Do you hear me?'

'Aren't you protesting too much?'

Milton Diamond came and served sherry trifle, Elizabeth's favourite dessert.

Greville said, 'I can't understand why he made you the chairman and majority shareholder of GIC. It should have been me.'

'You've done more than enough damage to the family assets.'

'I've done no damage!'

'No doubt you believe that. But he didn't want us to lose the overseas assets the way we lost the UK ones.'

'The UK ones are not lost!'

'Of course they are. The office blocks and so on are one thing; but how could you have sold off all the townhouses in Marylebone Park?'

'They're on leases, not sold.'

'Selling ninety-nine year leases on them is as bad as selling the freeholds.'

'But don't you realize the townhouses will eventually revert to the family?'

She smiled sadly, 'Yes, when you and I and our children are long dead.'

'But we've got the silver in the meantime.'

Her smile disappeared. 'And that was what killed him. Your craving to have the world's biggest stockpile of silver.'

'Winchester recommended I invest in silver when the property market collapsed. And he was absolutely right.'

She countered: 'As I recall it, your comptroller told you to make some short-term investments in it, to tide us over the depression. Not to sell off every property we had, nor to hang on to the silver for grim death.'

Greville's face darkened. 'When you do something, you should do it whole-heartedly, never mind the consequences.'

Elizabeth gave up. She knew he would never budge over the silver, which *was* what had killed Charles. She was sure she'd done the right thing in having his portrait brought in here.

Greville came into the study again the next morning. Henry Brewer was in here with Elizabeth now, and the beefy Condrieu agent sat across the great oak desk from the duchess. The rage rose in Greville's breast when his eyes fell again on the portrait of Charles above the fireplace.

Lining one wall of the study were glass cases containing scale models of GIC's overseas properties: the Boucherett Towers office buildings in Auckland, New York, Johannesburg and Buenos Aires; the shopping mall in Montreal; the industrial estate in Philadelphia; the châteaux and farms in France; the fishing fjord in Norway; the sheep station in Wagga Wagga; the Eden Grange stables in Ireland's County Kildare.

Greville strolled by them, pretending to show interest. Then he turned his blotchy face on his wife. 'Silver keeps going up you know Liz. It's just traded at $7.28 an ounce.'

She and Brewer had suspended their conversation and were watching him. 'I'm so pleased, James,' Elizabeth said. 'It must be the perfect opportunity to sell and get back into property?'

'Madness to sell while the price keeps going up ... I'm buying more ...'

He walked across the study and stared out of the window at the Park. He had no intention of leaving her and Brewer alone.

Elizabeth resumed talking to the Condrieu agent. 'So will you accept the position of Managing Director of GIC, Henry?'

Brewer felt the skin on the back of his neck crawl at the presence of Greville behind. 'I'm not sure I'll be able to do such a job, ma'am.'

'You will. You're the only person I can think of to take over from Charles.'

Greville turned and thundered, 'Now wait a minute, Liz. Charles made you Chairman of GIC out of convenience. He didn't mean you to go around making anyone you fancied managing director.'

She retorted, 'You have no authority in GIC's affairs. It's an offshore trust outside the provisions of your grandfather's will. Charles wanted it out of your clutches, and I intend to keep it that way. Henry here will make the perfect managing director if he accepts my offer.'

'Thank you, ma'am, for your confidence,' the burly man said.

'Thank you, Henry, for your support through this dreadful period. Will you accept?'

Brewer looked at Greville and replied slowly, 'Yes.'

'A bloody farmer!' shouted Greville. 'That's all he is, and you hand over what's precious in our family to him. Don't you have any sense of values?'

'Oh, James,' she said sadly. 'Don't be such a hypocrite. You sleep with a mistress in Horncastle not ten miles from Condrieu and still lecture me on the family and values?'

Brewer blanched and looked into his lap.

Greville breathed: 'Come on, Liz. You know Sarah's just a plaything.'

'Do you really imagine that *I* toy with the idea of the two of you together?'

'You know she's not important....' His eyes hardened now. 'You always bring up Sarah to cover up your own disgrace. Everybody knows what you and Charles got up to.'

She said easily, 'Your father was a wonderful man. He had qualities I've never seen in anybody else. And yes, he did make me happy in a certain way.'

Leering foully at his wife, Greville said, 'He made you "squeal with delight", didn't he, in your own words? You know, Liz, I'm amazed you managed to make him perform at his age. You must have done the Indian rope trick on him to get it up. And God knows what other tricks to keep him shacked up with you at Condrieu....'

'You're being obscene and ridiculous,' she snapped. 'You know he only spent so much time at Condrieu because he was no longer master here. You took away his pride.'

Greville rubbed his chest. 'It wasn't my fault Robert wanted me to have control when Charles turned sixty-five.'

'No,' she said, 'perhaps not. But did you really have to fight him in the courts for ten years? Couldn't he have groomed you properly for the task instead if you'd let him?'

He shook his head with disbelief. 'You don't mention *his*

legal actions against me, do you?'

She said firmly, 'That was only after you'd taken control. He had no choice then. Your behaviour was outrageous. Selling our properties at rock-bottom prices. If only you hadn't snatched control ...'

Greville screamed, *'I had to do that, you stupid bitch! He was taking the family down the road to ruin!'*

Elizabeth gave an ironic laugh. 'That's nonsense and you know it. That's why you have to yell at me. He made the family the richest in Europe and one of the richest in the world.'

Greville stormed out of the study. 'We'll see who makes you squeal with delight when silver goes up to $15 an ounce.'

Sir Roy Marchand confirmed to Elizabeth that her husband's grounds for a challenge on Greville International were very thin.

'Plus, appointing Henry Brewer as managing director is a sound move. He's tough enough to face off your husband if he does try to work the company round to his influence.'

'The Condrieu Estate Management Committee will endorse Henry's capacities if it's ever necessary,' Elizabeth said.

Marchand smiled. 'I doubt it will be. Your husband will have to spend a fortune if he takes you and Brewer on. All the odds must be that he won't get anywhere.'

Elizabeth returned to Lincolnshire that evening, pleased with her work in London over the past two days, and reassured that Greville International Corporation was in good financial order and well-managed. And safe from any designs James might have for selling off its properties to buy still more silver. He was obsessed, possessed by the stuff, with only one craving, and that was to prove to the world that he was a better man than his father. And silver was what he had latched on to as his means for achieving that end.

March 1963 – December 1965

I

The tall wrought-iron gates of Eden Grange opened on to a long tree-lined avenue. At the far end was a grey Georgian mansion with annexes tacked on each side, and numerous chimney turrets. Smoke spewed from several of these. There must be a lot of people living here, thought Christy as he walked up the avenue with a small bag in his hand, past white statues planted in the sweeping lawns to either side.

Yesterday, after going from Galway to Limerick, he had taken another bus to Newbridge in County Kildare. A weary night with little sleep in the local YMCA had followed; then, first thing this morning, he had gone to the Curragh racecourse to ask about work.

A man checking race-cards in the Stewards' room told him: 'You want to try down at Eden Grange. Charles Greville's place – he's the Duke of Marylebone if you didn't know, from England. I've heard they're taking on a lad or two there just now.' The Grange, on the main Dublin Road, had been easy to find.

Forty yards before the house, the avenue widened into a sweeping gravel forecourt, in the centre of which was a bronze statue of a man in a frock coat on a majestic stallion. It was Robert Greville on Bucephalus, Ireland's champion sire in 1902. Large gleaming cars were parked around the statue. The boy's apprehension grew.

He approached a uniformed driver polishing the wing of a maroon Bentley with a chamois-leather, and was directed along a path leading down behind the house. Spread out on a lower terrace to the left of this path was an oval-shaped straw-bedded exercise track for the Grange's thoroughbreds. Beyond that, to the northwest, as far as the eye could see, was rolling land cross-hatched with hedges, ditches and banks, where the steeplechasers were schooled. Horses were working out there now.

A group clip-clopped past Christy as he headed along the path to the stable complex, and a couple of the riders – stable lads and apprentices – exchanged nods of greeting with him. More sleek, clipped horses grazed alongside cattle in the paddocks surrounding the stables buildings. In one paddock, early foals tottered adventurously about their mares. The Grevilles combined breeding and training here at the Grange.

Stretching along three sides of the main yard, which was over an acre in size, were lines of horse boxes. In them, thoroughbreds munched feed from their mangers. Compared to these animals, the racehorses in Christy's old world of County Galway could best be described as sturdy, or sound, or willing.

The boy sheepishly asked an elderly lad in a barn manipulating hay bales with a pitchfork where he should report concerning work. The lad led him to the trainer's lodge, one of the individual houses in the adjacent group of buildings. It had a white picket fence overgrown by rose bushes.

The trainer sat at a table in his kitchen-cum-study, a bald man who had a curious habit of running his fingers through imaginary hair. He was fifty-seven and his name was Ken O'Flaherty. 'You done any work with horses, now?' He looked Christy up and down.

The boy stammered, 'I worked on a farm, see, sir, and we had a donkey ... it used to pull our cart.'

The trainer smoothed back some non-existent strands along each temple. 'A donkey, eh?'

'That's right sir, he was a good and loyal animal, who was always willing....'

O'Flaherty chuckled. 'Willing, eh? A willing donkey, no less. And I thought I'd heard everything. Now here's a boy in front of me who thinks that driving an ass and cart qualifies him for working here, with our thoroughbreds. For winning prize money on the racetracks for the Duke of Marylebone.'

'I couldn't pretend to be an expert with the horses, sir,' Christy said. 'But I know all about being up at four in the morning to muck out cow sheds. Farm work is hard and dirty work, and I've been doing it all my life. Surely that kind of experience could be useful?'

O'Flaherty nodded. The boy was honest, and the trainer appreciated the spirited way he had answered. He was obviously anxious for work. Plus he understood about mucking-out, and that had to be an asset. He could do well here.

'All right then, O'Donnell, we'll try you out for a couple of weeks.' He stood up. 'If you shape up I might let you stay till the end of the flat season. You'll be starting on thirty shillings a week, all found. Gather up your tack: I'll show you where you're to be quartered.'

Only a couple of hours later, Deborah Greville came into Christy's life.

He was raking smooth gravel in the yard, after the last string of horses had returned from the gallops, when the 17-year-old girl came along the path from the great grey house. Walking alongside her, virtually licking her black riding boots, was the head lad Terry Molony. The trainer and another man followed some way behind.

She was dressed in a white polo-neck sweater, khaki jodhpurs and those boots. Her hair was blonde and swept carelessly back, and her legs were very long. Striding by Christy, she glanced into various horse boxes, while he gaped after her, hypnotized by her glorious self-possession, aware that she must be something to do with the owners. But she didn't notice him.

He watched as she chose a black colt from one of the boxes and let Molony saddle it up for her. The head lad helped her mount, then led the horse out through the yard gate and on to the schooling fields. As she rode off, she tossed her head back with a laugh and said something which made Molony go crimson.

Christy stared on after she had cantered out of sight.

A commanding English voice behind him said, 'Keeping an eye on our fillies, eh?'

Christy whirled around. A few feet away stood the man who had been walking up with the trainer. He was in his mid-sixties, and he wore a trilby hat, tweed jacket and cavalry twill trousers. There was such a steady and penetrating gaze in his light grey eyes that the boy felt his knees sag.

'His name's O'Donnell, your Grace,' O'Flaherty said semi-apologetically. 'He only joined us earlier this morning.'

Charles Greville bared his teeth in a grim smile. 'I'd say he needs a good dose of work to keep his mind on the right track.'

Christy had to be on duty extra early the next morning, at four o'clock.

'That's a time you're used to waking up at,' O'Flaherty said, 'so let's see what you're made of.'

The other lads slept on while he took a 'skip' – a manure basket – to the stable boxes and collected the droppings. The horses, used to a different routine, eyed him curiously; some snorted their displeasure. For the rest of that day he dug ditches in the schooling fields where new hedges were to be planted.

For three days, he performed the same tasks. Then O'Flaherty called him in. 'You've done your time for giving the duke's granddaughter the eye,' he said with a laugh. 'From tomorrow you'll be starting at the regular time and doing the normal routine for the new recruits.'

Mucking out the next day was at the mercifully late hour of six-thirty. Then, when the 'strings' – the sets of horses – went out, he had to scrub and disinfect their box floors and their drinking-water buckets, collect droppings from the boxes at various intervals during the day, load the manure on the tractor from time to time, and tidy the yard after the last string was ridden back in from working.

In the afternoon, the tack had to be cleaned. Then, the divots in the gallops and the paddocks repaired, the manure unloaded out in the fields, the feed room tidied after the feed had been mixed.

Pay-day came around at last, and Ken O'Flaherty put two notes in his hand: a pound and a ten shilling one. The boy gazed at the thirty shillings. It was the exact sum the power station at Screeb had paid for a bag of turf, he remembered. He had sold eighteen bags down there.

'It's the Derby, then the Derby, then the fucking bloody Derby,' Terry Molony grumbled.

Sitting on one of the four beds in the dormitory room, the head lad shuffled a deck of playing cards and dealt. He was playing canasta with Johnnie Early, a freckle-faced boy from Wexford, who had flaming hair and green eyes. Early was the other new recruit at the stable beside Christy.

They glanced up from their cards as Christy came in. Both noticed the banknotes in his hand.

Molony tossed down a card. 'It's that bitch Deborah who wants it most of all in the family. Whenever she's here from England she goes on that they've had this place a hundred years and never won the Derby. She says she'll give me whatever I want most if I can get a horse of ours to win it.'

Christy opened his locker and put his wages in the calf-skin pouch. Then he transferred three shilling coins from the pouch to an empty molasses tin on another shelf. This was for his weekly spending: two shillings put by in the kitty towards clothes, shoes, haircuts and so on; a shilling for entertainment. Going to see a film at the Rex Cinema cost one and six, and if he allowed himself sixpence for refreshments, he could go there once a fortnight. It was enough. It meant he didn't have to touch the other twenty-seven shillings.

Christy put the pouch and tin back in the locker, and looked at the silver locket propped open on the middle shelf. In the left-hand side picture was his father, wearing an NCR's uniform, his cap tucked proudly under his arm. On his ma's face was a smile as broad as Ireland.

'What she means is, I can have it off with her if we win the Derby,' Molony went on. 'I mean, she spreads it around up at the house with the blokes she brings across from England. That's what she comes for. It's not the horses she gives a fuck about, just her own satisfaction. She'd strut about like the Queen of England if we won the Derby.'

Christy locked his locker and carefully put the key away in his pocket.

The following morning, Terry Molony strolled up to him in the yard as he was shovelling manure on the tractor.

'All right, Terry?'

Molony nodded. Then: 'Got some cash stashed away, have you now?'

'Maybe I have, maybe I haven't.' Christy wondered what business it was of the head lad's.

'I saw you put it in your locker yesterday.'

'So what of it?'

Molony tapped him on the chest. 'You shouldn't leave it there. Money's gone missing from some of the dormitories before.'

'I'm going to put it in the bank on Monday, see, Terry.'

Molony held his sides and laughed. 'Oh, I see. Going to get as rich as the Duke of Marylebone eh? Now I wonder if he made his money by hefting horse shit about the place.'

Annoyed, Christy turned away to resume his work.

'Listen to me.' Molony pulled Christy back up by the shoulder, looking seriously disapproving. 'If you want to get ahead in life, there's no use putting your money in the bank. You have to make it work for you, see.' Glancing around to make sure no-one was watching, he lit a cigarette. The lads weren't allowed to smoke anywhere in the stable area: it was bad for the horses – adding to the ever-present risk of chronic obstructive pulmonary disease – and also dangerous with all the hay and straw around. In a tall barn only a few yards away, straw bales were stacked to the ceiling. Molony shook the match to kill the flame and tucked it away in his pocket. 'Just put every penny you've got on Garden of Eden in the Leopardstown Handicap Chase on Wednesday.'

The horse was the top jumper at the Grange; everyone was predicting its certain victory in the race.

'Oh no, Terry,' Christy retorted. 'I couldn't do that.'

Molony snarled, 'I fucking thought you wouldn't. You're a stuck-up cunt and you don't trust anyone. You're in the horse-racing game but you won't even back your own stable, not even on a sure winner.'

Christy knew that many of the hands had either put or were going to put money on Garden of Eden. But he could think of nothing else just then except his ma's cold body on that morning two months ago, and the promise he had made to her memory. 'It's just that I'm not really a gambler by nature, see now,' he said meekly, before resuming the loading of manure on to the tractor.

Garden of Eden duly won the Leopardstown Handicap Chase on the Wednesday.

'I told O'Donnell to back it, but of course the cunt didn't trust me,' Molony crowed to everyone in the stable. He added, for good measure, that his judgement wasn't flawless but that it could always be counted on for the big ones.

When someone asked Molony how much he had won himself, he claimed that in the pressure of getting Garden of Eden ready at Leopardstown, he'd forgotten to put down his own stake. The other lads who had gone to the course knew that wasn't true: the head lad had lost all his money on the three preceding races, and hadn't a penny left in his pocket when the stable favourite's turn had come to race.

Johnnie Early, one of the lads who had followed the tip, had a delighted grin on his face for days. He had become richer by twelve pounds, equal to eight weeks' wages for him and Christy.

By the Friday, Molony was spreading another tip far and wide: Willy Nilly in the four o'clock at Punchestown tomorrow.

For a few hours, Christy was tempted to back the horse. It had ante-post odds of 5–2, and looked a sure-fire winner just as Garden of Eden had. He could more than double his money in one swoop and his savings programme would get a tremendous boost. Why not try a punt of ten shillings, or even five, he wondered, just to give himself a chance?

But when the other lads went to the bookies down the town that afternoon, he chickened out and stayed back at the Grange. The idea of losing even sixpence from his savings was too hateful to contemplate. Yet, he recognized, this was not the same sort of thing his da had used to do; he worked in a stable, whereas Stephen had operated by pure guesswork, and he had inside knowledge, so there was no point looking a gift horse in the mouth; sometimes, it paid to take a chance. He decided that if Willy Nilly won, he would definitely put a few bob on Molony's next tip.

The following day, the horse was withdrawn from the race at the last minute because of a strained tendon. Everybody who had placed money on it in ante-post betting lost their stake. It jolted Christy into believing nothing was ever a dead cert, and he never again thought of making a wager on the horses.

Due to Garden of Eden's earlier victory in the more important race, Ken O'Flaherty remained in a good mood. It was pay-day and, as he handed thirty shillings to Christy for the second time, he declared, 'I'm happy with the way you're measuring up, and, if you want to, you can stay until the end of October.'

The boy profusely thanked O'Flaherty, who was growing in his esteem with every passing day. On the Monday, he banked twenty-seven shillings from this lot of wages too. Ninety per cent again. It was a percentage he would never fall short of.

The other lads began to realize that Christy had some mission, but he never told anyone what he was saving for. A few of them, like Molony, were uncomfortable in his company. One colleague with whom he got on well was Johnnie Early, who was simple, earnest and hard-working. The eighth of twelve children, young Johnnie had run away from home with a touring circus, had worked with the circus horses, and had been dumped in Newbridge, where someone advised him to apply for work at Eden Grange.

It was to him that Christy once confided, 'I'm going to make it to the top in the racing world. I'm going to be as good a trainer as Mr O'Flaherty.'

Johnnie Early was the sort of person who was easily drawn into other people's dreams. And these words made the wish to become a top trainer grow in him too. One day, he said to Christy, 'Wouldn't it be wonderful to be a success and live in a place like the Grange, eh?'

The reply Christy gave totally baffled him. 'Oh no, Johnnie, that wouldn't do me and my ma at all. I need a place with a moat, see now?'

The flat season brought a buzz of anticipation and excitement to the Grange which National Hunt racing couldn't equal. Flat racing was the sport of kings, and every person at the Grange felt some of the royalty rub off on to himself whenever a thoroughbred from the stable won a race.

On his mornings off, Christy would ride out on one of the Grange's hacks to watch the various strings doing their fast work on the exercise track. Ken O'Flaherty sat on Pegasus – the stable's retired champion hurdler – on the knoll overlooking the circuit. His judgement in sorting the geese from the swans was legion. Mansion staff and Greville family members who came along to look over the thoroughbreds inevitably ended up at his side, listening to his opinions.

'It's all in the race-planning,' he would say. 'There are horses for courses and what I try to do is enter our hopefuls correctly. Every half-decent horse can do something over a particular distance and in the right class of opposition.' To Christy, whose interest in the racing business pleased him, he once said, 'Watch the horses closely. Feel with them.' He placed a forefinger on an eyelid, then on his heart. 'You have to listen to them with your eyes and your heart. They're talking to you all the time, telling you about themselves, telling you what they want and what they'll give in return. It's a language you have to master if you want to become a horse man.'

Christy followed O'Flaherty to schooling sessions and racecourses, desperate to learn more. He quickly understood that the trainer's eye and heart business was one thing, but what also made him a top horse man was the attention he gave to detail. He was quite meticulous in everything. The only bedding he allowed in the boxes, for instance, was the best quality wheat straw – short, clear, golden-coloured, dry, rustling and crisp; otherwise it went back on the lorry. Similarly with the feeding, which was now a fine art at the

Grange. The horses were fed three times a day, and each animal's feed was mixed separately, according to its age, temperament, likes and dislikes, the work and exercise programmes it was on, its exact state of health and so on, and O'Flaherty or Molony personally checked the mixes for the forty-two horses before they were fed. If the rations weren't correctly balanced, the manger would be emptied, the components of the feed reweighed and the mix made up again.

When he was in the calm of his lodge, O'Flaherty studied closely everything which went on in the bloodstock industry; no-one in the county knew more than he about the breeding, pedigree and form of the hundreds of thoroughbreds running in Ireland, England and France. And so on; the list of the trainer's concerns was endless.

And then, when all was said and done, there was the love of his horses just for themselves. O'Flaherty knew them as well as he knew himself, spoke to them lovingly and encouragingly, and provided – and demanded from the lads and apprentice jockeys – patient, tactful and firm treatment. Sharp rebukes and even sackings resulted if the hands ever mistreated the animals.

Tickled by Christy's thirst for knowledge, he remarked to the boy one warm May afternoon, as they trotted back together from the gallops, 'You know, I've spent my whole life trying to master the racing game, and in all that time I've only learned one hard fact: a good horse is a horse that's first past the post in a good race. What makes it achieve that, nobody knows exactly. That's what makes racing so fascinating.'

Christy said loyally, 'But you've a great record, Mr O'Flaherty.'

The trainer nodded. 'Perhaps. But there's just one thing that would make it better.'

Christy knew what that one thing was. 'It'll come one day, believe me, Mr O'Flaherty, the Derby'll come one of these days. There's no way a man like you can miss out on winning that.'

As a reward for the dedication Christy showed, the trainer gave him grooming tasks and even allowed him occasionally to exercise the horses. These jobs were normally the preserve of more senior hands, and some complained. O'Flaherty told them, 'The boy's been putting in so much extra effort, he deserves to do more than just mucking-out.'

Despite becoming the trainer's pet, Christy didn't travel with

Oberon and the Grange party to England for that year's Derby. The horse finished unplaced in the race, and when they all returned to County Kildare, O'Flaherty muttered despondently, 'Another shot at the Derby gone begging ... Will it ever come in my lifetime?'

The weekend after that 1963 Derby, Christy was at work in the box of Black Bullah, 'wisping' the colt with the wet rope of hay known as a wisp. In a form of massage designed to develop a horse's muscles and produce a shine on its coat, the animal was struck on specific parts of its body with the wisp.

The box door creaked open and Lady Deborah let herself in. Christy had seen her around the place earlier, but was surprised she'd come in here. From her came a lovely fragrance which cut through the piquant odour of straw, horse sweat and droppings in the box. He tore his eyes away and carried on wisping the colt's neck.

In that small box, it took the blonde girl three strides to be up against him. Before Christy knew it, two firm pads of her body pressed against his upper back, and he realized these were her breasts. A thrill shot through him and his penis went erect. In a state of consternation, he moved aside. 'Oh sorry, Miss,' he muttered, and tried to strike the horse again but only managed a lame swipe.

Deborah kicked over the bucket in which he'd been wetting the hay rope. Water flowed out on to the straw. Christy watched the bucket for a moment, then kneeled to set it upright.

'I'm surprised you're paying so little attention to me. I could have you sacked if I felt like it, you know?' she said.

Christy rose. 'The colt's just come in from work, Miss. Wisping is best done when he's still warm. I didn't want to stop and let him cool down, see now?'

Deborah leaned against the box wall and looked him up and down. 'You're Donnell, aren't you?'

'O'Donnell, Miss,' he replied, unable to gaze directly at her face. He had never been so close to such a stunning girl before.

'They say you're a quiet type, that you don't mix much with the other lads here?'

'I just try to do my job as best I can,' he mumbled.

'You spend loads of extra time with the horses when you're off-duty too, I'm told.'

'Oh yes!' he blurted. 'I want to learn as much about them as I can so that ... ' He stared nervously down at his feet. He was saying too much.

'Yes?'

He glanced up again. Her cool grey eyes showed interest. This made him feel bold, decide he could tell her more. 'I want to be a successful trainer one day, see, Miss. A real horse man.'

She tossed her head back and laughed. It was a lovely sound. 'So you want to be a real horse man? A great trainer?' She touched her eyelid and heart, as she must have seen O'Flaherty do. 'Well, that means you'll give your heart and soul to the job, make sacrifices, miss out on all the fun of being young.'

Christy thought about this. Fun hadn't been high on his list of priorities, he realized. 'I suppose you'd be right.'

Deborah took the wisp out of his hand and flung it to the side of the box. Then she took both his hands in hers. 'Let me tell you if you're going to get what you want.' She turned his hands palm up and stared at them.

Christy's heart leaped into his mouth. Her hands were so soft. He didn't know why she was holding his hands like that, but it was a delicious feeling. He gazed down at the crown of her head, taking in the deep sheen of her blond hair. The smell of her perfume was very strong and his penis came close to bursting in his pants.

She ran a finger down his left palm a few times. 'You have a long money line, a longish life line, and a love line which splits in two.'

Without releasing his hands, she looked up into his eyes. 'Who will the two lucky women be, I wonder?'

Christy had the wild urge to kiss every inch of her face, but managed to restrain himself. There was no doubt if he tried anything he'd be out of the Grange before Black Bullah next dropped a turd in the box.

Deborah smiled sweetly, reading his every thought. Slowly, she raised his hands and pressed them against her breasts. Then she dropped his hands and rubbed her own right hand against the throbbing bulge in his trousers. She had a bangle on that wrist. It was all too much for him and he came in his pants. Paralysed with shame, he felt his face redden. But Deborah didn't seem to notice anything.

'Yes, you'll have to forget all ideas of having fun with girls.' She turned and strolled out of the box.

That night, as he lay in his dormitory bed, Deborah Greville filled his every thought. He could tell from the levelling-off of the breathing sounds all around him that the other lads were dropping into sleep. But he couldn't fall asleep.

His mind boiled with the fantasy of what he could have done to her in Black Bullah's box. He turned over and over the image of grasping her firmly around the waist, working her boots and jodhpurs off, then the two of them falling back on the straw – the way James Bond and Pussy Galore had done it in *Goldfinger* at the Rex last week – then him pumping everything into her. He didn't care if he had got the sack. It would have been worth it. Eventually, drained by his fantasies, he drifted off into an uncertain sleep.

The next time he saw Deborah, she totally ignored him, and he was cut deep. She behaved the same way every other time she came down, until Christy became certain it was because he had ejaculated when she had rubbed his crutch and she knew it. So he threw himself into his work with greater fury whenever she was around. Gradually, he got her to figure a bit less prominently in his thoughts. But his desire for her burned unabated in his heart.

'Stephen was always wanting much more than he could have, see, Christy,' Molly had used to say. 'That's why he was never satisfied with the farming. He could never accept it was only by working harder on the farm that he'd make more money. That way we could have moved away from the bogs like everybody else, and got ourselves a decent holding in east County Galway. Who knows? That would have been better than any castle in the air, to be sure! But your da … whenever he went down to the fair at Maam Cross and saw the horses at auction, he would always come home sure he knew which would be the winners and which the crocks. If only he hadn't tried to be so clever … Promise me, Christy, you'll never try to be so clever now. All I ever really wanted was electricity.'

As Christy looked at the statement from the Irish Linen Bank in the middle of September 1963, he saw his savings had topped the hundred-pound mark by a few shillings. Out of this, one pound and some shillings had been earned in interest. He could never imagine Stephen O'Donnell trying to milk the system the way he was doing.

'I'll never follow da, ma,' he muttered to himself, checking the statement to ensure there had been no error in the bank's favour, either in the totalling-up of the weekly deposits or in the calculation of interest.

II

October approaching heralded the end of the flat season.

O'Flaherty explained kindly to Christy and Johnnie Early that the staff at the Grange had to be thinned down between November and February. 'So I'm afraid priority has to go to the longer-serving hands.'

Both had expected the chop. Christy was quick to ask around for work at other stables. But there was none to be had anywhere over the winter. 'Try again next March,' they all said.

Four days before his tenure was due to expire, Christy was out by the garages, hosing out the trailer in which Black Bullah was to be taken off to a race. His thoughts were on the nagging question of the winter ahead: if he didn't get work, how would he make his precious resources last through to next spring? He had been told that labouring work on building sites in Dublin might well be available. But this meant he would lose touch with the horses. He hated that idea. Not to mention that he would have to get digs, pay for food....

His mind thus occupied, he sprayed the inside walls of the trailer until he noticed Black Bullah come across the yard in his direction. On its back was apprentice jockey Harris, a small dark-haired fellow with bright red cheeks and hopeful hazel eyes. Terry Molony walked alongside. They'd taken the colt for a perking-up run on the exercise track before the race. Christy turned off the hose and went into the trailer to sweep the water out briskly with a stiff brush. Harris dismounted and, as Christy emerged from the trailer, Molony tried to lead Black Bullah in. The horse came up to the entrance, refused to go in and pawed the ground in front fretfully instead.

Molony grumbled, 'Of all the fucking times to get trailer fright....'

Harris went to Black Bullah's rear and tried to push it in. The horse shook its head and let out a loud, tortured scream. A couple of lads popped out of a dormitory to see what was going on. Black Bullah was pawing the ground more vigorously now and whinnying horribly. Its coat was staring and sweat beaded out on its mane.

'He must have colic!' Molony cried. 'Here, take over,' he said, handing Christy the reins. 'I'll get O'Flaherty and call the vet.' He went off in a hurry towards the trainer's lodge.

Black Bullah was trying to get down on to its knees now, but Christy, grasping the reins tightly, saw its terrified face and just knew he mustn't let that happen. If the colt went down, it might never want to get up again. Like Tony, the donkey, had never got up again. He should walk the horse, he sensed; so, tugging it firmly but kindly, Christy led it, still fretting and pawing, into the yard.

Harris, following, said, 'Don't tire him out. He might have a twisted gut.'

But Christy carried on walking the horse, remembering it was really fit, in hard condition and properly fed. He took it for a circuit around the yard.

Molony came storming back out of the lodge. 'The vet won't be able to come for at least two hours.' O'Flaherty followed, bearing a rug. A few other lads were with him, including Johnnie Early.

'Stop walking the horse, will you there,' O'Flaherty shouted.

Reluctantly, Christy did so. The apprentice stepped up to take the reins from him. None of the people present could have foreseen what happened next.

It was a fact that a trainer of the quality and experience of Ken O'Flaherty should not have approached Black Bullah from its right-hand side, and certainly not in haste. But everyone is vulnerable to a lapse of concentration. O'Flaherty's whole intention was to get to the horse quickly, to soothe it by talking to it and get the rug on it to prevent it catching cold from its sweating. Nevertheless, horses shouldn't be approached from the wrong side, especially if they're skittish. Black Bullah was already terrified. At the sight of the figure hurrying towards it from the 'dangerous' side, it spun around, yanking the reins out of Harris's hands, and it kicked high and hard with its rear right hoof. There was a sickening crack as this struck the small apprentice on his temple, and he collapsed on the ground in a heap. Christy grabbed the reins and dragged Black Bullah away from the prostrate figure to prevent him being trampled. O'Flaherty shouted at Johnnie Early beside him to call an ambulance, and took up the limp body of Paul Harris up in his arms. He tried mouth-to-mouth resuscitation, and thumped the young fellow on the chest several times to get the heart going again. But the rosy-cheeked lad was dead.

The Grange was laid low for days. The inquest established it was an accident, but Ken O'Flaherty was devastated. He asked for an audience with the duke.

'Here's my resignation, your Grace.' O'Flaherty handed an envelope to Charles Greville.

The duke tore it up. 'The coroner is satisfied it was an accident.'

'I can't carry on, sir.' He had tears in his eyes. 'It was my negligent approach which made the horse kick out at the poor young fellow.'

'His family has agreed to the figure of eight thousand pounds compensation from our insurers,' the duke said. 'We need you more than ever now, Ken.'

O'Flaherty shook his head. He had thought long and hard about this. 'My heart's gone out of the job, your Grace. I'll never be able to give you a hundred per cent again.'

So Charles Greville was forced reluctantly to accept O'Flaherty's resignation and arrange an early pension for him.

The trainer did ask, as a final favour, that Christy and Johnnie Early be allowed to stay on through the winter. A show of solidarity amongst the hands was essential, he believed.

'Plus,' he added, 'both lads acted well in the crisis. O'Donnell walked Black Bullah around and around the yard until the vet came. This helped it get over the worst of its colic symptoms, and it responded well to medication. In the meantime, Johnnie Early drove out to fetch the doctor for me, believing I would be in a state of shock. And he hasn't even got a driving licence.'

The duke agreed automatically to both lads staying. Thus did Christy get a macabre reprieve from losing his job.

To everyone's surprise, Charles Greville appointed Terry Molony as trainer. The old assistant trainer Johnson, in retirement for a year now, had been expected to come in and do the job provisionally until an eligible outsider was brought in.

Christy's own standing at the Grange went up hugely because of his action with Black Bullah, even though he agonized for months over Harris's death. None of it seemed to have an effect on Deborah, who continued to ignore him whenever she came across from England.

During the National Hunt season of 1963–4, Garden of Eden started doing wonders again. He once more proved the stable's top steeplechaser by winning the Naas November Handicap and then coming second in the Irish Cesarewitch at the Curragh. By March, Christy, who had now become six feet tall, found his wages going up to two pounds ten shillings.

'You've done a year here, and you're becoming quite useful,' Molony said. The new trainer didn't add that Christy's knowledge and understanding of the training game had developed into assets he hated losing to a rival stable. He sensed more keenly than anyone that Christy was the only one at the Grange who had O'Flaherty's 'heart and eye' instincts with the animals.

Nonetheless, despite the best efforts of the hands, Molony was hopeless at race planning, and during the whole of the next flat season, no Greville thoroughbred won a Group One race for the first time in the stable's history. The poor results continued into the next National Hunt season, so it came as no surprise to anyone when Charles Greville arrived at the Grange one day in a dissatisfied frame of mind, and the following day Molony and his head lad Les Randall were gone.

The old assistant trainer Johnson did come in at this time, and his first duty was to send for Christy.

'Now, lad, with me not able to handle all the work like I used to because of my illness, and after all I've seen and heard about you, I'd like you to be taking on some of the responsibilities. I'm ready to promote you above more senior lads here, as you're a prospect for the future in my book. You've been here two years, and I'm prepared to stick my neck out and ask you to be the head lad.'

'Oh, that'd be great, Mr Johnson,' Christy replied at once. 'And would that be affecting my pay?'

'Well, naturally I'll see that it goes up in compensation. How much are you on now?'

'Two pounds ten, sir.'

'Then I think five pounds fair, don't you?'

'Yes sir!' he cried, his mind racing at the impact which an increase of a hundred per cent would make on his savings programme. 'Very fair indeed.'

There was a lot of griping by older staff at the appointment of a 17-year-old to such an important post. Johnson effectively told them to like it or lump it. One hand left the Grange in protest. Johnson, to emphasize his point, increased Christy's pay by another ten shillings.

The new head lad's burgeoning nest egg was given a further boost in the summer of 1965. The Newbridge branch of the Irish Linen Bank mistakenly made a credit entry of four hundred pounds nineteen shillings to his account instead of four pounds nine shillings. Christy wondered whether he should bring it to the attention of the bank.

He went into the branch the same day. 'I want to close my account, please,' he informed the cashier. 'Can I take all my money out now? In cash.'

'Oh, that's a shame, Mr O'Donnell,' the cashier said, recognizing the young man who came in every week with his few pounds. 'Hasn't our service been good enough?'

'Oh no, on the contrary, it's been excellent. Much better than I could have been expecting.' He winked, realizing it would be sensible to have a reason. 'I've had a hot tip and want to cash in, see now?'

'A hot tip? What is it?'

He winked again, much more conspiratorially. 'I daren't tell you in so many words in case you lose any money. That would stay on my conscience for ever. But just watch every horse in our first string, and you'll work it out for yourself.'

Accounts were consulted, then something in excess of £762 in cash was passed across the counter. Christy counted it all, stuffed it carefully in his pockets and made his way to Kildare Town. There, he deposited the money into that town's branch of the same bank. The Irish Linen did, after all, pay the highest rate of interest on savings accounts. To soothe his conscience, Christy also reflected that if the Newbridge branch discovered its error, it could easily trace his account seven miles away in Kildare Town.

It never did.

By the end of 1965, with the help of this windfall, Christy's total savings were just over £900. A little fortune already.

During that time he rarely went out to meet the Newbridge girls, despite Johnnie Early and the others proposing it to him every Saturday night. One reason was that none of them looked like Deborah. Another was financial, since Christy found the local lasses expected a lot. First he had to treat them to the pictures, then to drinks and chocolates during the film, then they always asked after that if they could have fish and chips.

But when Christy would think he was entitled to even a half-decent return for his investment, they would pout at him – with the fishy vinegar on their breaths much more sour now than when they had been kissing – and they would say, 'I'm not that kind of girl, you know. I'm the marrying kind.'

Christy had long ago decided he had better uses for his money.

14.2.79

'He killed Charles.'

'He didn't. It was an accident.'

'How could you have promoted him, James? How could you have made him the full trainer after what he did?'

'He's deserved it for his loyalty. He's been with us since 1963. You can't hold Charles's death against him.' But Greville had done it to punish her, of course; she'd had no right to make Henry Brewer the Managing Director of GIC.

Up at Condrieu Hall, Elizabeth hung up without another word.

In Marylebone House, unaware that it was St Valentine's Day, Greville hung up too. A great grin on his face, he rose from his desk and went to put a dated soul record on the Bang and Olufsen hi-fi. He'd got under her skin, he knew. She'd deserved it.

'That's six days in a row now. Nothing will stop the fall,' Simon Winchester said. He stood on the ballroom stage, watching the prices chatter up on the telex.

Greville's grin disappeared. 'You're to keep buying, Winchester.' He raised the volume of the music.

The comptroller spoke louder.

'Spot's currently trading at $6.33.'

Greville glared at him. 'It'll rise again. The price can't keep going up without a slight breather. As a professional commodity dealer, you should know a 'lift-off' can't come to a halt overnight. Keep buying.'

Winchester returned to his desk and picked up the phone. There was no use arguing with the man. A bullion dealer had told him that morning that he had a block of silver he wanted to offload, and it might as well be bought for Greville's account. The comptroller made a token protest nevertheless: 'Your so-called "lift-off" has never even started, except in your mind.'

The duke turned the music up still louder. Nat King Cole sang:

'... Faith can move mountains ...'
'... Darling you will see ...'
'... I can move mountains ...'
'... If you have faith in me ...'

7.50 p.m. Simon Winchester glanced frequently from his watch to the restaurant door. She should be here within the next ten minutes.

He was at a table for two in the Lemonia Greek Restaurant in charming Primrose Hill. Playing softly in the background was the Bee Gees' song: 'More than a Woman', from the hit film *Saturday Night Fever*. The Lemonia was clearly more in touch with current musical tastes than James Greville.

'Expecting a lovely lady, Mr Simon?' Kostas beamed. He set a glass of white retsina on the table.

Winchester grinned sheepishly. 'I certainly hope she *is* lovely. She's had the advantage of seeing what I look like.' He had secured the blind date by replying to a Box No. in *Time Out* magazine, with a photograph of himself.

At 8.01, a squat female wearing a tweed coat with flared lapels over a dowdy mid-length skirt came in and squinted about, looking for someone. Winchester had a sinking feeling when she spotted him and made a beeline for his table.

The Comptroller of Greville Holdings UK Ltd rose and mumbled insincerely, 'Glad you could make it.' On top of that awful squint and the short stubby legs, Daphne had buck teeth, a dull complexion, premature streaks of grey in her hair and no breasts. She draped her coat over the chair, sat down and began to talk.

'I'm quite daft really. I'm only interested in the simple things in life.'

This was the very description she had given in her letter, which Winchester had found rather charming; understatement of that sort often concealed an interesting personality. But it immediately emerged that the one 'simple thing in life' the unlovely Daphne wanted to talk about was her boss, from the 'What-A-Bastard-He-Is!' point of view. It was a theme Winchester might have warmed to if Daphne had had even one more inch on her breasts.

Kostas, to his credit, never smirked throughout the evening.

When he finally brought the bill, Daphne said with buck-teethed brightness, 'I'll pay my share. Then we can go back to your place for coffee and just laze about on the settee. I'm in no hurry to get home.'

Winchester was a gentleman to the last. He ordered coffee from Kostas, declined Daphne's kind offer to laze about on his settee, and put her in a minicab bound for Palmers Green.

When she was gone, Kostas served him a raki on the house. 'Better luck next time, Mr Simon.'

Winchester nodded, wondering whether he shouldn't go to Argyle Square in King's Cross. The area was prowled by prostitutes, some of whom at least resembled human beings instead of flat-chested gophers.

After the third free raki, he went home to his mews house around the corner. Encounters with prostitutes made him even lonelier afterwards, and he might as well conserve his strength to cope with Greville tomorrow. His evening had failed to make him forget how unsatisfactory his time at Marylebone House had become. If only he wasn't bound to the place by silver handcuffs.

The day five years earlier when Greville and Winchester had met for the first time had held so much promise for both of them, despite the previous night's election result.

'Sixty thousand pounds a year,' Greville said. He'd heard a lot about Simon Winchester, and his first encounter with the man already convinced him that here was the person he should appoint as his comptroller.

The figure, Winchester knew, could never be matched by MacIntyres, the commodity brokerage firm for which he worked. At most they might raise his present 22,000 to 30. Business confidence and foreign investment had evaporated over the winter, and darkness lay over the country. The coal miners were on strike, the Arabs had hijacked the price of oil, and Britain's fuel stocks were dwindling to nothing. Electricity was available for only three days a week. The worst-hit business sector was property, where market values were in free-fall. And James Greville had wrested control of Greville Holdings – the country's largest landlord – out of his father's hands only five months earlier.

Winchester had followed the story of the battle for control from afar. He'd gone to Cambridge with Lady Jane Cooper – James and Elizabeth's first daughter – and, with her family's affairs in the news every day that winter, he had hardly been able to avoid it. It had started when a press hound had sniffed out that in the period since James Greville had been at the helm of the UK property company, the family's assets had plummeted in value from £575 million to 370 million, and they were no longer the richest in Europe. Then the whole media circus jumped on the bandwagon. A myriad details emerged, abetted by revelations by some staff members who received sizeable cheques from the papers.

> James Greville ... a notorious womaniser and wastrel ... refused to go to war against Hitler ... was totally distrusted by his father.... *(Daily Mirror)*
>
> ... the legal costs borne by the family during the ten-year court battles have exceeded twelve million pounds.... *(Sunday Times)*
>
> ... Robert Greville was so jealous of Charles's genius that he willed control of the company to his grandson James. This, according to everyone intimate with the Grevilles, is what really undermined the family's fortune.... *(Daily Express)*

Nothing piqued Winchester's interest as much, though, as the telephone call he had received only two days ago from Marc Weintraub, boss of Barbican Commissions, a top City head-hunting firm.

'I'll be brief, Simon,' Weintraub said. 'James Greville has been on to me to find a successor to Julian Lockwood. That, in case you didn't know, was his comptroller, who he's just sacked. I suggested you.'

'That's very kind, Marc,' Winchester had replied. 'But I'm not a property man.'

'I know that. But he wants to break clear of the family's traditional business. According to him, recent events prove the property game belongs to yesterday's men. He wants to move into something less vulnerable to today's investor power. 'Financial instruments' interest him, he says. Shares he finds too complicated, commodities more attractive. He says they're basic, old-fashioned, but as relevant today as they've ever been. I don't know a better commodity man than you.'

'Sixty thousand pounds a year,' James Greville repeated now. He grinned, 'You did go to Selwyn College with Jane, after all.'

It was the first time Winchester had ever been in the

ballroom at Marylebone House. That March 1974 morning, the nation was breakfasting to the news of the Conservative government's defeat in the General Election. A television set had been placed on the conference table in the ballroom, and late results were coming in from the Hebrides and other remote constituencies. James Greville had a bowl of All-Bran before him, Winchester a plate of bacon and eggs.

'My father got us into trouble, which is why I took over. Naturally enough, I had to sack the previous comptroller, who'd given my father all the wrong advice. So now I've got to try to sort out the mess. You've got the knowledge and experience in commodities which I need for that. Are you interested?'

A three-year contract worth £180,000 plus bonuses was on the table together with the cooked breakfast. Money like that couldn't be refused. Simon Winchester took the job. 'Though I'll have to have a detailed look at the whole company before I come up with any concrete recommendations. It might take up to a month.'

On television, Edward Heath's piano was being loaded on to a removal van.

Winchester's assessment landed on Greville's desk only one week later. 'In a nutshell, we have to sell off our lowest yielding properties and invest in silver, for the short to mid-term at least.'

James Greville read Winchester's report quickly and closely. He didn't hesitate to start selling off land assets and invest in stocks of the precious metal. It stood then at $1.47 an ounce.

At first, only the bad properties were disposed of. Then it began to dawn on Winchester that the silver buying was becoming an uncontrollable obsession for James Greville, and that an increasing number of the properties which shouldn't be sold were. By the end of the year, the silver price had risen close to the two dollar mark and Greville Holdings already possessed 20 million ounces. To finance his mounting purchases, Greville was by now auctioning properties off wholesale. He did much of this in a hurry, and increasingly often for lower than the market values. Winchester's doubts about his employer's judgement deepened.

Then Prospero came on the scene.

About eight months after Winchester moved into Marylebone House, a City friend of James Greville showed the future duke a publication entitled *Nothing shines brighter than silver.*

Greville devoured its contents and asked Winchester to dig out for him everything else produced by its author, this 'Prospero', a man whose prophecies Wall Street and the City of London were taking some notice of.

Winchester discovered that because of a few uncannily accurate predictions in the past, Prospero had become popular with that peculiarly insecure type of small investor who lives in perpetual fear of the future. Writing in the *Washington Journal*, he had successfully forecast both devaluations of the dollar in 1971, advising readers of the *Journal* to invest in quality works of art, fine wines and antiques; those who took his advice salvaged something each time the dollars in their pockets were suddenly worth a great deal less. Then, in 1973, Prospero warned that the Arabs would hike up the price of oil to 'between three and five times its current value, and this will happen three to four weeks after the autumn equinox.' On this occasion, he recommended the purchase of shares in Exxon, Texaco and the other oil companies. When he was proved right again by Saudi Arabia, the Kingdom of the Hejaz and the other Arab nations in the OPEC cartel unilaterally quadrupling the price of oil, he took pains to have his name known not only throughout America, but also across the Atlantic. Having noisily bought thousands of oil company shares himself and made half a million dollars' profit, Prospero sent photocopies of his share certificates and account forms to newspapers and magazines like *Time* and *Newsweek*, and also to New York and London investment houses. The subscription list for the pamphlets he published privately grew longer.

When Winchester told Greville about these previous coups by Prospero, his paper *Nothing shines brighter than silver* became a holy tract for the future duke. In it, Prospero expounded why silver was the best investment for the 70s. Thirty pages of relentless logic found their focus in one central paragraph:

> 'Industry uses 351 million ounces of silver annually, and the mines produce only 247 million ounces. This gap is partly plugged by scrap: by the accumulation of silver from melted-down coins or unwanted family silver. There are twenty-two recent developments that will increase the demand for silver in industries ranging from aerospace to pharmaceuticals. But the greatest demand of all doesn't require any new developments; try though they might, Eastman Kodak, the world's largest producer of photographic materials, cannot

discover any substitute for the chemical salts, made from silver, that react with light in such a way as to give the clearest picture. They will therefore have to continue using silver in film manufacture at least until the end of the decade. There seems nothing, then, to prevent this gap between silver demand and supply increasing, and the price rising.'

From then on, James Greville's disposal of Greville Holdings properties became a fire-sale. Even prime sites went willy-nilly.

'You're insane to sell off the family silver like this!' bellowed the old duke.

'It's the family rubbish I'm selling off, to buy silver. Literally. Keep your advice to yourself. You've proved you've passed the limits of your usefulness.'

The following spring, Charles Greville instituted proceedings in the Chancery courts to contest Robert's will and regain control of Greville Holdings UK Ltd. His case was based on the diminished responsibility of his son. But his efforts were to no avail. James Greville retained Sir Timothy Bryant QC to defend his sales of the family's properties. Bryant based his case on the continuing recession in property, while galloping inflation – which reached an unbelievable 26.6 per cent in October 1975 – went on boosting silver's value. Bryant was also too good a lawyer to fail to point out to the court that Charles Greville was now seventy-six, well past the retirement age in any business. The duke finally gave up the fight. He had long since learned that hate within the family was the most potent of all the hates.

Elizabeth kept trying to reason with her husband: 'Why won't you listen to Charles? Why won't you see that you're destroying the foundations of the family?'

He answered: 'If Robert willed the company to me, he must have had a good reason. He made our family the richest in England, and won for us a dukedom. What did my father ever achieve, except spend ridiculous amounts of grandfather's hard-earned money on useless property around the globe? The minute that recession hit, we were in trouble. Thanks to me, we're coming out of it.'

He continued to invest heavily in silver.

When Simon Winchester's three years expired, he signed a further three-year contract, its value £270,000, or £90,000 a year. In 1977, there was nowhere else in Britain he would get this kind of money for his kind of work.

By that time, James Greville's silver holding stood at 43

million ounces. The price, $4.40 a troy ounce. His purchases continued into 1978.

Many of the land assets such as Marylebone House, Condrieu Hall and other country seats were entailed in perpetuity to the family line; thus these could not be sold off. But Greville discovered that money to continue financing the silver buying could be raised by granting leases of up to ninety-nine years on the Marylebone Park townhouses.

Even Winchester was mortified when he began to do this.

Charles restricted his visits to Marylebone House now to once a week. He did still run Greville International Corporation, which he'd had the foresight to keep apart from Greville Holdings since its inception. The rest of the time he spent at Condrieu.

'You're a bloody bastard, dad,' Greville said to him. 'You can't bear me being so successful with the silver, so you've decided to have an affair with Liz up at Condrieu instead.'

It was on 1 January this year, 1979, that Prospero made the following prophecy in the *Washington Journal*:

> 'Watch for the fall of the head of a dynasty, friends. I think you have enough confidence in me by now for me to call you friends. A head must fall and a tail must wag. Then watch silver finally lift off. Watch it go to at least fifteen dollars before the end of this year.'

James Greville, on reading that, was convinced Prospero had addressed him personally.

On 5 January, during Charles Greville's next visit to Eden Grange in Ireland, the old duke fell out of the Land Rover and died. The same day, James Greville started having tremors in his chest.

Prospero.

It was all down to Prospero really, Winchester knew. That devil had aroused the deepest evil in the heart of his boss.

On 15 February 1979, the day after Winchester's romantic soirée with Daphne, spot silver closed on the Chicago Grain and Metal Exchange at $6.29 a troy ounce, another 7 cents down.

In London, at 6.30 p.m., the lights of the Marylebone House ballroom were on. The telex had gone quiet and Simon Winchester stood helplessly by his desk. 'Sell as much as you can before the price fall accelerates,' he said, his voice almost begging.

Greville said, 'Keep buying. The price has dropped so much, this is the perfect time to buy.'

'Our sterling cash reserves are almost exhausted. In dollars, we're down to under three million. The situation has suddenly taken a dangerous turn. If the price dips below $6.20, we'll have to expect margin calls from brokers. The fact is, you bought too much at the top. Every cent the price falls now makes some of our brokers very nervous.'

Greville went to the windows and gazed out at the Park. Head- and tail-lights blazed on the cars crawling around the square in the rush hour. 'Find a way to get cash in without selling.'

Winchester scratched his head. 'The only way I can think of is for you to get in the duchess's good books and persuade her to mortgage or sell some of GIC's properties.'

Greville hadn't much tried in the past to get into Liz's good books. Now, though, it seemed to him that the matter demanded some consideration. His father had been dead over three weeks and couldn't maintain his powerful influence over Elizabeth indefinitely. She was a forgiving sort. She'd soon forget about the horse trainer.

February 1966 – June 1968

I

Vincent Johnson's health continued to deteriorate, so Charles Greville drafted in a new trainer at the stable. He was Brendan Byrne. To everybody's surprise, the duke then promptly handed over ultimate responsibility for Eden Grange to his son James.

'But they're fighting in the courts, aren't they?' Johnnie Early said to Christy. Both lads had turned eighteen by now.

The old trainer Johnson, on quitting the lodge for the last time, gave them the explanation. 'I've heard it's all down to the duke's daughter-in-law, Lady Elizabeth. Seems she told the duke to give her husband more responsibility in the hope that he'd drop his legal battles. But they're still at it, unfortunately.'

Brendan Byrne's record as a trainer wasn't bad, but Christy, who remained as head lad, instinctively distrusted him. He had a face like a weasel's and he disliked not always being right.

'You can help me pick out which of our yearlings we should keep, and which we should sell,' he said to Christy. Byrne explained he wanted to 'rationalize' the Grange stock and that the forthcoming bloodstock sales at Goff's in Ballsbridge gave him a good opportunity to do this. 'I also want to buy a future Derby winner – a colt with a dam which isn't from our own stud.'

Christy disagreed with Byrne about one yearling which the trainer wanted to sell. 'It's got no prospects,' Byrne said, while Christy's opinion was: 'I like his broad noble head. He's a horse which is going to do something, I guarantee you.'

Byrne finally succumbed, grumbling that he wanted the head lad to agree with *his* decisions, not the other way round.

At Goff's, neither of them saw any animal they particularly fancied. A visiting breeder, though, invited them to his stud to see some late foals which he hadn't entered in the sales. The following week, Christy and Brendan Byrne drove down to County Tipperary and bought three foals from that breeder. The animals looked not bad and would probably pay their way overall, though not much more. Christy wouldn't have bothered with them, but Byrne had got to that point where he just had to buy something.

Arrangements were made for the payment and eventual transport of the animals, and the two men left the town in the late afternoon. As they drove back northeast past the Rock of Cashel, Byrne suggested they stop overnight when dark fell. Then, just before the Slieverdagh Hills, as they rounded Leprechaun's Finger, Christy saw it.

It was high up on the cliff. A thirteenth-century Norman castle. Warm and massive in the red rays of the dying sun. It was so familiar and so right. Distant memories strained to penetrate the forefront of Christy's mind as he gazed up at it. Hadn't he come down here once with his father when he was a toddler? He was sure he heard Stephen O'Donnell's voice in his mind's ear ... 'Like that son ... the castle I'll be building for your ma ... like that beauty up there, Kit.' They'd been on a bus, he seemed to remember....

Byrne and Christy stopped in Kilkenny for the night. While the trainer played darts with a couple of the regulars in the pub after supper, Christy fell into conversation with a local shopkeeper.

'That castle up on Leprechaun's Finger, you know that really old castle, just inside the County Tipperary line ... would you be knowing anything about it?'

'The one that looks like the King of the Gaels himself must have lived in it, you'd be meaning?'

'Aye.'

The shopkeeper nodded. 'It's known around here as 'Kirkpatrick's Folly'. I've heard it's always being let out to tourists, mostly Americans. Owned by a man called Seamus Kirkpatrick. I've never met the fellow myself, but he's a nutcase by all accounts.'

All night, Christy dreamed about Kirkpatrick's Folly. The next morning, as Trainer Byrne drove the car back towards Eden Grange, the head lad's mind remained in turmoil. It was impossible to believe, but he'd seen it at last. The castle he'd be buying for his ma.

The chestnut colt they'd kept against Byrne's wishes began to show promise, at least as far as Christy was concerned. There was no denying its blistering brute speed when going at full gallop. Unfortunately, even several months later, it retained its unconditioned, backward air.

'He's growing sideways,' Byrne complained one day at the exercise track. They watched the horse finish a run, sheened with perspiration. It was still only working in the third string. 'He'll become a monster. Then he's bound to lose that pace, you'll see now.'

But the head lad didn't agree. The smouldering power he felt in the animal was a tangible force which no other horse at the stable possessed. 'Give him time Mr Byrne,' he insisted. 'That's all he needs now. More time.'

One weekend that autumn, Deborah Greville came across from England with a group of friends. Christy saw them strolling about the yard as he 'lunged' the reddish-brown colt – made it trot and canter around him at the end of a long rein in the outdoor manège. He did this every day to improve its balance and transitions.

The little English party came over to watch. There were three young men and two other girls, all of Deborah's age. Deborah had a riding whip in her hand and she pointed at the horse with it. 'Now here's a colt we were going to sell, but then it became a great hope for the Derby.'

Christy completed his work and walked the horse by the party.

Deborah said, 'And this is Mr Christy O'Donnell. I should have introduced him first, really.' To Christy: 'You *are* more important than the horse aren't you, Mr O'Donnell?'

Her friends chuckled softly beneath their breaths.

She explained, 'Mr O'Donnell's our head lad, and he's the one with the almighty faith in this colt.'

'He's got the golden touch, all right,' Christy said, wondering what these highbrow folk did for a living and why they weren't away doing it.

Deborah said around to the party, 'The colt's provisionally down in the stud book as Saucy Red, but no-one's really happy with the name. Can anyone suggest anything better?'

'Trigger!' said someone.

'Bo-ring,' was the general verdict.

'I've got it!' shouted one of the girls excitedly. 'The Duke of Marylebone!'

'We've already had three by that name, Paula,' Deborah laughed. 'What about Thick as a Mick, gang?'

Everyone glanced at Christy. One or two looked embarrassed.

Then a young man in tweeds, who had wavy brown hair and eyes of china blue, spoke. 'I know, Deborah darling.' His plummy accent and the spotted yellow silk scarf he wore at his neck made Christy's scalp crawl. 'Mr O'Donnell says the horse has got the golden touch, so why not call him King Midas?'

'Oh yes, Peter,' Deborah said. Her eyes glowed. 'That's perfect. King ... Midas ... Everything he touched turned to gold. Oh yes. I think it's wonderful.'

'It does suit him,' said the girl named Paula. There was a chorus of agreement.

Deborah placed her whip on the colt's head. 'I hereby dub thee King Midas.'

'First horse's christening I've been to!' someone cried out.

Everybody laughed.

Deborah turned and linked arms with the Peter fellow. Christy, realizing grudgingly that the fellow was bloody good-looking, hated having to witness her loving manner towards him. 'Come on, gang,' she said. 'Tea should be up. I could murder a scone.'

Christy watched them go off. Deborah and Peter were nuzzling right up to each other now. She rubbed her face against the fellow's shoulder and he bent down to whisper something in her ear. A lock of his hair fell on her cheek; she blew it away. Then she glanced back at Christy, gloating.

He looked away, rage boiling in him. The bitch was surely fucking with the man! And she wanted him to know it. Is that why she had mocked him? To show off to that la di da plum-voiced bastard? Of all the people to have thought up the name King Midas, why him? If only it wasn't so bloody perfect.

The winter was a mild one and in the spring of 1967 King Midas stopped growing. His power could be channelled more easily now. Christy explained over and over again to the apprentices that they had to handle the colt really well if they wanted to get the best out him. Then he would reward his rider with the scorching bursts of acceleration which only top thoroughbreds could produce. But if the King sensed even slight touches of jockey carelessness, he was a devil to work with.

'He's got a mind of his own Christy,' complained one of the apprentices, a fellow named Pat Jordan. 'He's impossible to control on the gallops when he gets his head up. You made a mistake keeping him, you know.'

'I agree he's got a mind of his own,' Christy replied. 'And that's why he's a class horse. Just see that handsome head he's got. Strong and powerful, and broad between the eyes. Any horse with a look like that has to be handled delicately, and you know it. Get a better grip of him when you go full throttle.'

The head lad, who had himself previously begun to doubt whether King Midas would be ready until the autumn, was proud and delighted by the 2-year-old's progress in the spring. The colt performed particularly well when it was dry, and Christy quickly realized he would always run best when the going was firm. The King won both races he was entered in over May, and Deborah wanted him tried out on the Epsom Downs.

After much insistence on her part, Byrne managed to get King Midas entered in the prestigious Coronation Cup during Derby week, which gave Christy his first chance to visit England. The colt came in fifth behind the great Charlottown, last year's Derby winner, and Deborah was delighted with the result. It was, after all, King Midas's first test amongst the highest class opposition. Christy, though, couldn't avoid a slight feeling of disappointment. He had been hoping for at least third place. But the promise was there for all to see, and it was later fulfilled to a greater extent by King Midas's next runs at the Curragh. At the end of July, the chestnut colt won the important Probationers' Stakes in brilliant style.

It was after this that Byrne called the head lad into his lodge. 'Look, Christy, the both of us know you have much more of a feel with the King than I have. So, between you and me, I want you to have the responsibility of getting him ready for next year's Epsom Derby. You're to spend all your time with him from now on.'

Christy was thrilled. 'But would there be any extra compensation for me in that, Mr Byrne?'

Byrne thought about this. 'Lord James Greville seems like a decent enough gentleman despite all the family feuding. I won't tell him the exact reasons why – I mean, let's keep that between ourselves, eh? – but I'll ask him if I could put your wages up to fourteen pounds a week. How's that now?'

Christy's confidence had grown since his predictions with King Midas had begun to be fulfilled. He responded: 'Sixteen would be better.'

Byrne grinned, 'I see *you've* become a saucy so-and-so now. But all right then, I'll ask Lord James for sixteen.' A serious look came over his face. 'You'd better be sure to do the business in that case.'

'Don't you worry, Mr Byrne, I'll do everything humanly possible. The only thing is, the other lads are going to be pissed off at me sticking to one horse only and them having more work piled on to do.'

The trainer nodded. 'It's true that there is a lot of jealousy in the racing game.' He thought for a moment. 'Tell you what. They won't bother you if I make you official assistant trainer and partition off a private room for you in the dormitory.'

James Greville scribbled a note to Byrne confirming the posting and the higher pay.

Christy was able to put aside fifteen pounds four shillings from his new wages, ninety-five per cent. Sixteen shillings, he decided, was more than adequate for his expenses.

Even though he had a room to himself now, he could hear

the other lads joking and ribbing in the adjacent dormitory.

'I reckon O'Donnell's a bloody homo,' said somebody one evening on the other side of the dividing wall. 'Doesn't like the girls.'

'Don't you believe it, Mick,' said another voice. 'He likes them all right. But he's got his eyes on you know who in the jodhpurs. Aims high, does our Christy O'Donnell. The ones from Newbridge that we go with are too low for him. Either that, or he's too bleeding tight to take them out. Reckons he can be having it free with the goddess sooner or later. Probably thinks he's better looking than King Midas's arse!'

There was raucous laughter. Christy recognized the voices, but didn't go and take issue with their owners. He knew they all fancied Deborah Greville like mad themselves. He was more concerned that his savings were already only just short of two thousand pounds. It was a long way off from possessing 'Kirkpatrick's Folly', that was sure. But he would get there.

That autumn, Deborah came by to chat more often than ever to Christy. The main subject of conversation was, naturally enough, the horse, which was now being tipped for next year's Derby by the smart money all over the British Isles. King Midas had won his last three races in Ireland with ominous ease, and the full-time work Christy invested in him was paying handsome dividends.

'What's your secret with him?' Deborah said to him once. 'How do you get him to perform so well?'

'It's love, see now, Miss. The kind of love no man could give to a woman if he was very involved in his work.'

She giggled, not catching the reference. But Christy had never forgotten their encounter in Black Bullah's box in his first summer here. Hadn't she said the horses would have to matter more to him than the women if he was to succeed?

One Sunday afternoon, Deborah rode up to him on a grey gelding as he was getting King Midas ready for schooling.

'I want to watch you put our golden wonder through the paces,' she said.

'All right miss, I'm just about to take him down to the track.'

She gazed down at him from her saddle. 'Can we do it in private, with just you and me around? I don't want any distractions.'

'I'm afraid there are other lads already down at the gallops.'

'Well, get rid of them,' she commanded.

Christy shook his head. 'I've a better idea.' He mounted King Midas. 'Follow me.'

They rode beyond the fields where the steeplechasers were schooled, then across the ditch on the border of the Grange's grounds. Christy pulled King Midas up in a wide, well-grazed field. 'Is this private enough for you?'

Deborah looked around at the unfamiliar terrain. 'Why have we come off our land? This is Farmer MacBride's property, isn't it?'

'I often bring King Midas here,' he winked.

Deborah didn't seem very amused. 'I didn't realize you did schooling off the Grange premises?'

He explained: 'There's less loam in the soil here, see, so the ground is harder than up at our own gallops. The horse likes a firm going.'

'And doesn't the owner object?'

'Not at all. I give him racing tips in return.'

'Trust you, O'Donnell,' she laughed. 'You're one of the few to come up with something clever like that. Just don't let Grandy hear about it. He'd be livid if he knew our horses were trained in someone else's field.' She suddenly shouted, 'Come on!' and galloped off, waving at him to race against her.

He did. For an hour. He won easily every time. She finally signalled at him to stop. Drawing her gelding up against the colt, she said breathlessly, 'You don't have a girl friend, do you Christy?'

It was the first time she'd ever called him by his first name. He looked away. The feelings he had for her, and which he had suppressed these long years, stirred in him.

Deborah laughed. 'I thought not.' They sat in silence in their saddles for several seconds, until the horses started champing about with impatience. 'Why don't we take a rest by that tree?'

They rode up to an oak and dismounted. Deborah stepped up to him, undid the top three buttons on his shirt and rubbed his chest. 'You're a very sexy man, you know.'

Christy thrust his lips down on to hers. She responded to the kiss, snaking her tongue in and scouring the roof of his mouth with it. He pulled his face back. Raggedly, he asked, 'Is that what you do with your snooty blue-eyed friend Peter from England?'

'Peter?'

'Yeah, that la-di-da git.'

Deborah's grey eyes clouded. 'I never guessed you were so

infantile. You're being offered what you want on a plate and all you can do is sulk. See you in a hundred years' time, or whenever you grow up.' She remounted her gelding and rode back across the ditch into the Grange property.

II

After that episode, she became very frosty again with him, and he responded by going out to the local dances with his colleagues.

These took place in Newbridge Town Hall on Saturday nights. A priest would sit on a raised platform at one end of the dance room and keep a stern eye on the proceedings. Girls clustered sheepishly about on one side, boys on the other; all sipped soft drinks, which was the only strength of beverage allowed. Many of the boys, not boldened by Dutch courage, never asked a girl for a dance. Refusals were common whenever a boy did cross the floor to proposition a female. There would then be lots of giggling on the girls' side and cat-calls from the boys. It always seemed a miracle when a couple actually did start dancing. By the end of the evening, though, things usually livened up. This was when the priest would come down from his pulpit and circulate on the dance floor, pulling couples apart if he saw them make bodily contact.

Christy had already met Mary O'Riordan, a pretty shop assistant, in Newbridge. She had been totally smitten by the Grange's assistant trainer for a long time. As they danced one evening she whispered to him that she'd meet him down the road after the dance. This was a common practice, because the priest ensured that the girls and boys left the Town Hall separately.

Christy escorted Mary back to her parents' house in Leitrim Street, kissing her full on the mouth all the way. They reached the front door, and she tried to say good-bye, but he undid her blouse buttons, dug her breasts out and sucked her rose-pink nipples right there on the doorstep.

'Come on now, Mary,' he said, trying to drag her round to the back garden, the blood pounding in his groin. 'Let's not finish at this.'

'No, Christy,' she whispered, tugging herself free. 'Not here. Not outside my own ma and da's place. But next Sunday we could go down to Bull Island, and we can do it as long as you bring along a packet of Johnny Bags ... What do you say to that, then?'

He nodded curtly. It was about time he lost his virginity.

But when the appointed day came, he never showed up at Mary's place to take her to the island park near Dublin as planned. What had happened was that Deborah had come to the Grange that weekend and Christy, shocked into realizing what a different plane she dwelt on, couldn't bear the thought of touching Mary again.

King Midas started having problems at the worst possible time.

In the spring of 1968, short months before the Derby, the colt unaccountably went off the boil. He lost pace towards the finish of two pre-Irish Derby trials, loping in a miserable last each time. Unimpressive performances in other races followed. At first, this was put down to the poor weather and the soft going on the racetracks that spring. But when the weak finishing also happened in schooling and on the harder surface of Farmer MacBride's field, James Greville called Byrne into the Grange mansion for a conference.

The trainer mouthed lame excuses, then came looking for Christy. 'I told you that when the time came the horse would start losing its speed. Now we've gone and raised everybody's hopes and it'll all backfire on me.'

'It'll sort itself out,' Christy replied. He didn't show the worry he felt himself.

They pulled the King out of the Two Thousand Guineas at Newmarket in May, and were prepared to make other changes to the horse's race plan if the need arose.

Every morning, Christy carefully watched his colt when he went out with the first string for schooling. He also took the King for extra work in the afternoon, either on the track or in MacBride's field. He observed the animal ceaselessly, both as spectator and rider, searching for the key to its finishing problem. As a 3-year-old this year, King Midas couldn't qualify for the Derby ever again if he missed out this time around.

One morning just over a fortnight before that all-important race at Epsom, Christy noticed something strange happen to the colt. He was down on the exercise track, standing near the finish. An apprentice was riding King Midas. They came round, two furlongs out; the apprentice turned on the gas for the final spurt. The horse's tongue lolled out of its mouth. At the next tug of the reins, the tongue disappeared back in. It only lasted a second, but the King never recovered his blistering pace after that.

Christy decided to try a new bit. That afternoon he put in a 'Dr Bristol' double-jointed snaffle, which had a central rectangular plate to hold the horse's tongue in more firmly. Then he took him out for a run himself. He worked him up to an adequate gallop then, as he hit the button for the extra surge, he watched the King's mouth closely. The tongue slipped out again, and now he was conscious of a dying of power in the animal which he couldn't quite re-establish, no matter how hard he thrashed at the reins.

As soon as they came off the track he went to the trainer's lodge and told Byrne about his discovery.

Byrne came out to King Midas's box and looked in the horse's mouth. 'Oh, it's nothing serious,' he said casually. 'There's just a slight jaw conformation defect. Obviously when he's under pressure, the jaw flexes in a particular way and pushes the bit out of line. The tongue will never be properly held in, no matter what bit you use. I've seen it happen before. I can guarantee you it's got nothing to do with him losing speed. That's just a coincidence.'

'Well it's a funny thing Mr Byrne ...' Christy scratched his head, ' ... but as soon as that happened, he went completely cold.'

Byrne said, 'Forget about the tongue, I say. Work more on his morale and confidence. It's obvious that he buckles under pressure when a lot's asked of him at the end. See if there's some way you can get him to take the pressure in his stride.'

The next morning, the King's tongue stayed in its mouth and he finished well. The morning after, the tongue lolled out and the colt slowed down again. Christy realized the problem was an intermittent one. He talked more and more to King Midas, and he performed well on the exercise track more often. But he never quite maintained that top pace for long enough. All that the assistant trainer could do after that was to hope that his talks would have an extra good effect on the day of the Derby. The race was the hardest in the world.

It was scheduled for 6 June. For days before, everyone at the Grange prayed for good weather in England, and the prayers were rewarded when the Home Counties began to bask in a heatwave during the last days of May.

Two days before the Derby, with the weather holding, the

Grange party took the car ferry across the Irish Sea from Dun Laoghaire to Holyhead. Then they drove down to Epsom in Surrey. The King rode in splendour in his horse box, which was freshly painted for the occasion.

The colt was taken for schooling runs on the Epsom Downs the following day by both Christy and the race jockey. As they didn't want to use the King up by riding him at full gallop, there was no way of checking whether the finishing problem had cleared away.

That evening, a buffet party was thrown by James Greville at the Robin Hood Hotel in Ewell for the Grange team. Byrne was staying at the hotel, unlike Christy and the other hands, who were billeted in bed and breakfast establishments. Deborah, who was also staying at the Robin Hood, hosted the party. She was dressed in a black top and white miniskirt, and her face and limbs glowed under the tan she'd acquired while on holiday in Mustique. She spent the evening chatting with Brendan Byrne, her father, the race jockey, the lads and everyone else there. Except Christy.

Just before the end of the do, Christy overheard a fairly drunken Byrne say to James Greville, 'I have the solution, sir … I know exactly what's wrong and I'll be putting it right. I can guarantee you that King Midas will win the Derby tomorrow.'

Christy was intrigued and wanted to know what the trainer meant. Before he could ask, Deborah came across and raised an eyebrow at him. 'Going back to your B and B?'

'No, I'll be checking on the King down in his box first.'

'I'll give you a lift there if you like.' She inclined her head in the direction of the hotel exit.

'Glad to see you're so concerned about the colt,' Christy said, climbing into her roadster. He sensed, though, that her interest just then went beyond King Midas.

In the enclosure at the Epsom racecourse, Deborah watched as he tucked King Midas in for the night. Then she said, 'It's time you were taken to your bed too, don't you think?'

'Aye. I'm all in now.'

They drove off again in the roadster. But she didn't take the turning for the bed and breakfast place where Christy was staying. After a few minutes driving in silence, during which the suspense grew in Christy's mind, Deborah pulled up beside a farm gate. 'We've arrived.'

Her look left him in little doubt about what she wanted. They got out of the car, and she slipped her hand in his. She led him through the field, towards a tall barn which loomed up in the night. 'I saw this place this morning, and knew it would be perfect.' Her teeth gleamed in the dark as she smiled.

Christy's head was pounding. He couldn't take in that this was actually happening at last. He had always suspected she fancied him quite a lot, from the way she was always either very nice or very rotten to him. But he had never dared hope that this day would come.

His throat dry, he asked, 'So you don't think I'm infantile any more then?'

Deborah laughed and picked her way into the barn. 'Come on horse man,' she whispered.

He followed her up on to a bed of hay.

In Surrey that night, the temperature stayed at a gloriously balmy 67 degrees Fahrenheit.

He jiggled the tight miniskirt down Deborah's legs, the hunger-ache in his groin monstrous. When the skirt was off, he dragged her panties down hastily, hurting her with the elastic fastenings. She squealed with pain and laughed in one breath, then lay back to watch him clumsily unbutton his trousers and shirt.

He didn't try any preliminaries, just fell on her, kissed her hard on the lips, cheeks, neck, thrust up her blouse to chew her breasts, and rammed his prick into her slippery warm vagina. She carried on laughing as her body sucked on his sex, clamping it with little membranous muscles he never imagined existed. They clung on to his penis every time he thrust and this made him flood into her almost instantly.

'That really was a quickie,' Deborah said as he flopped down on her breasts. 'Your first time, I'll bet.'

Christy didn't answer. He felt so empty, so unfulfilled.

'I thought as much. God, the noise you made! Now it's your turn to do a bit of work and make me come, horse man.'

They rested there, kissing and gnawing each other's faces and bodies, waiting for Christy's penis to rise again. The moment it stirred into life, he rolled straight on to her. She cupped her hands around his balls, stroked the strengthening penis with her fingers until it was quite rampant, then steered it back into her vagina, telling him with lips brushing against his ear, 'Start slow, build up a rhythm ... gently, gently does it ... no, no, slow down ... think about something else, think about horses, about King Midas, about anything except this, you great Irish potato....'

He tried very hard this time to exercise control over the surge in his groin. For a couple of minutes he succeeded. But, as Deborah began to get looser and wetter and abandon her own rhythm, he couldn't prevent himself thrusting harder and faster, until he was plunging into her wildly again, his tall body thrashing hers on the hay.

She started to stiffen beneath him, gaping in his face; her breathing stopped, her nails gored into the backs of his shoulders; she shuddered; then she shuddered again and again. He forgot everything now except the violent need to flail her insides as hard as he could, every muscle tensed, until his body was overcome by the warm release seeping through him into her and which this time was followed by an icy clean sensation in his brain.

Half an hour or so later they had another bout. Immediately after, with his penis still nestling inside her, all energy drained by the loving and the tension, sleep came to him and, moments later, to her.

A mild breeze wafted into the barn with the dawn.

Christy's first sensations on awakening were of light-headedness and numb thighs. Then he felt the warmth of Deborah's breasts against his face and he heard her light regular breathing. The air around him was full of the scents of her perfume and of her body.

He raised his head and gazed at her. Fast asleep, with her mouth half-open, her breathing was regular and deep. Her blond hair lay in wild tangles on the hay and her black blouse was rucked up around her neck. He stroked the breasts which had pillowed him, his eyes going down to her crutch. In the middle of the untanned triangle, some strands of her fine brown pubic mesh fluttered in the breeze.

His lust swelled again and he put his hand on her shoulder to jog her gently awake. She opened her eyes and looked around. 'God, what time is it?'

'Time for some more you-know-what,' he leered. He tried to part her thighs.

She pushed him away. 'God, I'd better get back to the hotel before I'm missed.' Brushing away bits of hay which stuck to her bare thighs and legs, she slipped on her pants and miniskirt, and started down towards the barn door.

'Oh, I see!' Christy yelled after her. 'You've had your oats and you're off now, is that it?'

She took no notice; just hurried out.

The tension in the saddling enclosure was almost unbearable. Everybody in the Grange team believed King Midas had a chance, but at the back of everybody's mind remained the doubt about the colt's finishing problem.

'You'll do the business out there, won't you, King?' Christy said soothingly. He'd been in a daze ever since he had come to the racecourse this morning. The feel of Deborah all over his body and the satisfied tingle in his prick wouldn't leave him.

Just before the colt went to the parade ring to be shown off to visiting royalty, Brendan Byrne produced the leather tongue strap. Christy watched with bewilderment as the trainer carefully put the thin hooped leather affair on the horse's tongue and tightened it.

'O'Donnell's done some good work with King Midas,' the trainer explained to Charles and James Greville, 'but I've realized the King has a problem with his tongue shaking itself out when he's under pressure and him then losing composure. This strap will hold the tongue in.'

When the horses rode out to the starting post, Christy had a moment alone with Byrne. 'Why did you keep the tongue strap a surprise from me of all people?' he said. 'And why did you say to me back at the Grange that the tongue business wasn't a problem?'

Byrne's response was like a slap in the face. 'You're a bloody cretin if you expect me to let you in on secrets it took me years of hardship and failure to learn.'

Because of the long fine spell, the racetrack was at its hardest that Derby Day for as far back as most punters could remember. As the horses came around Tattenham Corner in a tight group, King Midas didn't lose pace in the last couple of furlongs, but surged to a powerful finish to win the Epsom Derby Stakes by a short head.

James Greville was ecstatic: it was the family's first Derby win, and it had happened under him. Charles Greville praised the trainer Brendan Byrne for spotting and putting right the colt's finishing problem. In acknowledgement of the fine victory, he handed over to Byrne the keys of a brand new MGB GT sports car in addition to the ten per cent of the prize money.

'I know why you kept the tongue strap a secret, you know,

Mr Byrne,' Christy said bitterly to him that evening. 'Even though I did all the work, and found out what the horse's problem was, you wanted all the credit for yourself, didn't you?'

Byrne's teeth came off his lips as he gloated: 'And what of it? I've been a trainer for nineteen years now, almost as long as your whole life, and this is my first Classic victory. And the Derby at that! Your chance will come one of these days. Then you'll have your moment of glory too.'

1.3.79

Why wasn't she here yet? She should have been here long ago....

Greville glared out at the Park with impatience.

Finally, more than an hour later than expected, the sky-blue Renault 5 with the legend 'Le Car' inscribed on each wing turned in from Boucherett Street. It tore around the square, screeched to a halt in front of the House and the driver's door swung open. Lady Sarah McGonagle got out. She slammed the door.

Too bad she's upset, Greville thought. But anger did so heighten her beauty. At thirty-something, Sarah was no longer in the first flush of youth. But she retained her wonderful physical attributes, and knew exactly how to set them off. Blonde, with long willowy limbs and breasts which stood firm and high, she had on a cream cashmere sweater, jeans and suede boots.

She stomped up the wide exterior steps, clutching the large brown envelope. Her lips trembled.

'... Smile ...'
'... Though your heart is aching ...'
'... Smile, even though it's breaking ...'
'... When there are clouds ...'
'... You'll get by ...'

Greville went and switched Nat King Cole off.

'Mrs Thorpe,' he said into his desk intercom. 'Lady Sarah's not to be allowed in here, but leave the intercom on, will you? I want to hear what she has to say.'

'Very good, sir.'

Winchester tried to mind his own business by riffling through a sheaf of computer printouts on his desk, in search of something useful to do.

She strode down the wide corridor from the Great Hall, a trail of Arpège de Lanvin wafting along behind her.

Two men followed, alerted by Mrs Thorpe's urgent internal call. They were Milton Diamond the senior butler, and a uniformed static guard from Group 4 Securitas. A large black alsatian towed the guard along as if against his will.

Mrs Thorpe sat at her desk in the high arched vestibule which gave on to the ballroom. Beside her were the double mahogany doors to that den of Greville's. Lady Sarah headed straight for the doors but jiggled in vain with the handles. The doors were locked. The duke's secretary, a small middle-aged woman with tiny eyes and thick bi-focals, said, 'I'm afraid his Grace is in a meeting. Can I be of help?'

'Tell him it's me ...' Sarah's voice quivered. 'He's bound to want to see me....'

The uniformed guard and dog now took up position by the doors; Diamond wheeled up beside the visitor, ready to be useful.

Mrs Thorpe gazed at the brown envelope in Lady Sarah's hands. 'If that's for his Grace, you can leave it with me. I'll see he gets it. Or perhaps you want to make an appointment?' She gave a helpful smile.

Sarah laughed with incredulity. 'An appointment? Don't you know I'm his ...? I'm his ...?'

The secretary raised her eyebrows. She could imagine Sarah McGonagle in bed with James Greville in their love-nest in Horncastle....

Mrs Thorpe knew all about the place, of course. The detached house in Moresby Road was rented in Sarah McGonagle's name, but the rent was paid by Greville, and it was she – Mrs Thorpe – who wrote out the monthly rent cheques. It was the secretary, too, who had arranged earlier today for that brown envelope to be sent to Lady Sarah's London flat by motorbike courier. In it were the deeds to the

Horncastle house. Its purchase had been completed today, and in the name of Sarah McGonagle.

Greville had attached a note to the deeds: *'For you, Darling Sal, to remember me by. We may never stoke the fire together again at Moresby Road, but the inner light will burn forever.'*

Lady Sarah burst out crying. 'He thinks he can just buy me orf with a house ... A house worth £86,000 ... He's discarding me like ... like ... a common *prostitute*!' She said this last word in such a strangled tone that the alsatian barked loudly. The guard had to tug at its chain to calm it. 'Just because he's become the duke at last....'

Diamond tried to take Lady Sarah gently by the elbow. 'It might be best if you left, milady.'

She shook him off and flounced back down the corridor towards the Great Hall, still holding the precious brown envelope.

'She's gone sir,' said Mrs Thorpe into the intercom. 'She kept the deeds.'

'I have news Liz,' Greville said brightly as he came in on Friday night.

Elizabeth was at the far end of the table in the dining room at Condrieu Hall, the fine bones in her face clearly etched in the chandelier light. The stare from her intense blue eyes scorched into him. 'You're late again.'

'It's over between Sarah and I.' Greville raised his jacket flaps and sat down. 'I've given her the Moresby Road house.'

She arched an eyebrow. 'You'll start up with her again. Or with somebody else.'

The blotches on his face spread. 'That's typical! Just typical! Nothing I do will ever satisfy you.'

Elizabeth said, 'I read in the Nigel Dempster column on Tuesday that you and Pamela Gray "feasted their eyes on each other during the whole of the Charity Gala, and then left together in the duke's newest and smartest Rolls Royce," unquote.'

Greville spread a linen napkin across his lap. He and the American television star were long-time lovers. 'I gave the lady a lift to the Dorchester that night, yes. What of it?'

'Did you sleep with her?'

'No,' Greville lied. 'And even if I had, so what? You're hardly in a position to complain. I know it's not the most elegant way of putting it, Liz, but you've proved you're a bloody whore yourself.'

She sighed. 'Eat up your hare soup before it gets cold.'

'That's right! Change the subject as and when it suits you.'

'I have nothing to say to you when you're in this sort of mood.'

'Well, I do have something to say to you.'

She was distressed by the fraught way he stared at her across the table. It signalled he wanted something, and that he wouldn't take no for an answer. She felt defenceless. 'If only Charles could be here,' she muttered.

'Charles bloody Charles!' he shouted. 'Always Charles. What about me? I thought I'd make you happy by getting rid of Sarah. But nothing satisfies you.'

Elizabeth said sadly, 'I placed my whole life before you James. I married you, didn't I?'

'It's the family you married. The name. The money. But it was Charles who was always your god. You couldn't stay out of his bed, could you?'

His barrage would lead ultimately to violence, she knew. After a similar argument the weekend before Charles's death, he had gone to one of the estate farms and shot dead two pigs. He was determined to destroy Condrieu, where he'd never managed to be master.

'What do you want, James?' she said wearily, knowing the answer.

'You know what I want.'

Elizabeth noticed the maids hover uncertainly before the pantry door. They wanted to continue with the service. She shook her head at her husband. 'No. Never. I won't raise a penny against Greville International's assets for you to buy any more silver.'

He grinned in disbelief. 'Oh come on Liz. There's no need to keep the torch alive for Charles. What difference can it possibly make to you if we sell off one or two of the GIC properties? They're all dead losses....'

'Hardly,' she said, arching an eyebrow. 'GIC made over a hundred million pounds profit last year.'

He changed his tack. 'Look, if you like, the silver we buy with GIC money can be kept apart from the silver in my control; you can sell it whenever you want to. The thing is, I just need to buy more to shore up the price, don't you see? We have to protect the family assets. Won't you help?'

'If I sell even one Greville International property then Charles will have died for nothing.' She nodded at the maids, who busied themselves clearing the soup things and setting the next course.

'Why do you keep bringing up Charles's death?' he bellowed. 'It has nothing to do with this!'

She said firmly, 'It has everything to do with this. Your explanations about what happened just don't wash.'

'Nothing washes with you, does it, Liz? Look, he fell out of the Land Rover. A wheel hit his head. That's all. It was an accident. The County Garda never even bothered to investigate it.'

'They should have,' she replied. 'And you've never explained why you rushed out to Ireland straight after.'

'I heard about the accident, dammit. I went there so I could be by his side.'

She shook her head. 'And you never told anybody at Marylebone House where you were going or why? And you didn't get in touch with anyone in England when you were in Ireland? And you only spent five minutes "by his side" in the hospital as you put it, and then hovered about outside until he died?'

'I was in a state of shock, Liz. I didn't know quite what I was doing....'

'I'll tell you what you were doing, James. You went off to Ireland, shaking with fear, like a spineless worm, to cover up whatever you could at the Grange, so that his death couldn't be traced back to you.'

'That's not true.' But his protest lacked conviction.

After the meal, Greville sat alone at the table for a long time. Sarah McGonagle would be in the Moresby Road house in Horncastle tonight, he knew. He was also certain she'd be waiting for him, even though he'd ended the affair. It would be so easy to find solace in her arms. But then Liz would again emerge as the martyr, and he the villain. The whore he'd had the misfortune to marry didn't deserve that; no number of fine superficial qualities she had could purify her rotten soul.

Greville didn't go to Horncastle the next day, Saturday, either. For the first time in years, he spent the afternoon with his elder daughter. Lady Jane Cooper came down from York with her two sons every weekend.

In contrast to her sister Deborah, Jane was small and dark, with her mother's blue eyes and all the radiance Elizabeth had had at the same age. Greville managed to unwind with her at lunch, and cheerfully took up her suggestion of a nice long walk after.

She linked her arm in his and they went with the boys through the enormous walled kitchen garden, out past the long rows of greenhouses. Camellias, flowering shrubs, tropical plants, Malmaison carnations were cultivated in these; in one grew sweet-scented flowers which were cut daily and arranged in the Hall. 'You look so much less worried than you have for a long time, daddy. I'm so glad.'

They strolled on, coming into the wilder gardens overgrown with rhododendrons, which stretched over half a mile. Jane recounted a happy tale or two about her husband Sir Michael Cooper, and filled Greville in on all the York gossip.

He lost himself so much in this undemanding business that he gave the two boys' noses playful tweaks.

They eventually arrived at the clearing which gave lovely views of the River Trent shimmering in the distance. 'How's Simon getting on with you these days?' Jane asked.

Greville growled at the recollection of his pinched-nose comptroller. 'I used to think he was pretty bright, but it's clear now that he's got no imagination at all. Nor any sort of woman as far as I know. Reads John Maynard Keynes textbooks as his night-time entertainment for all I know.'

She chuckled. 'Well, he wasn't known as Beau Brummel up at Selwyn either. Still, he is a brilliant man. A genius at chess and all that sort of thing. You probably aren't stretching his abilities, you know. Everyone says he's just your poodle in this silver business you've got so obsessed with.'

When they turned back for the Hall, Greville said to her, 'You don't know how good it's been to see you, Jane. You should mention to Deborah that she should also visit her old father here every now and then. Or doesn't she get the time, what with her divorce proceedings against that blasted Irishman?'

By supper time, Greville had got into such a happy family mood that he suggested to Elizabeth they both join the March hunt on the following day. She agreed.

They looked fine in their hunting tunics. Greville decided to ride out in front with the whippers-in; Elizabeth preferred to follow at a gentler pace near the back, riding side-saddle on her favourite mare.

The hounds caught the fox's scent and led the party into the Haldon Woods. There was much horn blowing before the head of the posse re-emerged into open country with the fox clearly in sight. Rider after rider followed in a flurry of leaves and branches. As the last group came out of the wood, someone just ahead of the duchess let a branch swing back as he rode past it and it struck Elizabeth in the face. The skin on her cheek split open and blood spattered out all over her tunic.

Norman Willet, one of the indoors staff who was riding beside her yelled out that she was hurt. The hunt was stopped and horses champed about as Greville rode back and demanded, 'Now which bloody fool is responsible for this carelessness?'

The young man who confessed contritely was Dennis Whyte, the orphan gardener.

'In better times, I'd have been able to have you flogged,' snarled the duke. 'Nowadays, the best I can do is throw you out on your ear. I want you and your belongings off the Estate before dusk. You'll get whatever wages and severance pay you're legally entitled to. Now get out of my sight.'

The hunt was abandoned.

Back at the Hall, one of the huntsmen, a Dr Matthews, put five stitches in Elizabeth's wound. As she felt groggy, he advised her to rest. Lady Carole Markeston had driven out by now, having heard of the incident, and went to sit with Elizabeth in her bedroom.

Later that afternoon, Greville went up to see how she was.

The bedroom was full of the scent of fresh lavender, and amber rays from the sun setting beyond the woods to the southwest dappled the furniture. Elizabeth half-sat up on the bed with a pile of cushions behind her back, listening to Carole Markeston read out Irish jokes from a book.

'I was expecting you,' Elizabeth said when he entered. Lady Carole put down her book.

'I thought I'd see how you were, Liz.'

'Oh, I'm all right, James. But I'm very concerned about young Whyte. I expect you to rescind your decision to dismiss him. It could have happened to anyone.'

Greville shook his head firmly. 'He'll remain sacked. He was bloody careless. Next time around, he could do something infinitely worse.'

'Hmm,' she said. 'And yet John Early killed Charles and you promoted him.'

Carole Markeston giggled nervously as Greville snatched at the bait. 'Early didn't kill Charles!' he cried. 'It was an accident, do you hear? Early drove the Land Rover across that ditch under Charles's own instructions. Won't you ever let up?'

'I may when the truth comes out.'

Greville tried to force from his mind the recollection of his father's crumpled head, with his eyes bulging monstrously out of their sockets, then he cried, 'Charles had no reason to be at the Grange. It had been my responsibility for years before that. I won the Derby for us....'

He broke off, feeling suddenly dizzy, and his eyes flickered. He rubbed his chest. Oblivious of Lady Carole, he dropped on to his knees by his wife's bed. 'I never told Early to hurt him. Believe me, Liz, please....'

Elizabeth caressed his blotchy face. 'I want to James. But I can't. Just listen to what they're saying.' She nodded at her friend. 'Tell him, Carole.'

Lady Carole looked from husband to wife and back again, detesting the one, adoring the other. The last time she had spent a night here at the Hall, as she had often used to do, Greville had come into her bedroom and begged her to have sex with him so that he could revenge himself on his wife for sleeping with his father. She had told him to leave the room, but he had tried to force himself on her. She had screamed and fortunately Elizabeth had come in. She hadn't spent another night here since. Now, her voice rising in pitch with her nerves, she said, 'Well, frankly, they say in Ireland that you called the Grange that morning, James, and told John Early to make Charles have a *fall* of some sort. And Early did it from the Land Rover. Deliberately. Some say it's because you couldn't stand him going to the place; others that you wanted Prospero's prophecy to come true....'

'Rubbish!' He got up. His dizzy spell already a distant memory, he addressed Elizabeth: 'Don't listen to her. She always exaggerates. The only tragedy with Charles is what happened between you and him.' He departed with: 'I hope Whyte's stupidity doesn't leave a scar on your face.'

When he got back to London early the next morning, he discovered that silver had dropped further in trading in the Far East. The down-trend continued on the London Minerals Board and, later, in Chicago.

Spot silver closed eventually at $6.09 an ounce on the Chicago Grain and Metal Exchange.

'Its value's eroding every hour now,' Simon Winchester said, examining the telexes. 'And that's not to mention all the warehousing charges, the insurance....'

'That's enough! You don't have to remind me.'

'You may not like bad news, but we really do have to do something about this situation.'

Greville gave his reply the following day. 'What we're going to do about this situation is buy more silver.'

'But we can't....' Winchester began with frustration.

'We can. All we're short of is money, and the family's got plenty. What we're going to have to do is to get hold of GIC's assets through the courts.' He buzzed the intercom and told Mrs Thorpe, 'Get me our solicitors, Anthony Amory & Co.'

July 1968 – February 1970

The Derby win by King Midas meant bonuses for everyone at the Grange. Christy, as assistant trainer, received £750 for his part in the victory. Brendan Byrne also negotiated an increased salary of forty pounds a week for Christy with James Greville. It was a much bigger pay rise than normal.

Christy accepted this gratefully, though remarked, 'It wouldn't be because you're feeling guilty about the tongue strap business that you're going to all this trouble, would it?'

From the way Byrne's weasel eyes shifted about, the assistant trainer saw he'd hit the mark. 'You deserve the rise for your work, Christy. Lord James has also decided not to race King Midas as a 4-year-old, but to put him to stud straight away. He's worried that the horse won't perform as well again and might lose his stallion value. And I want you to be looking after all that side of things, seeing how you've got a mathematical brain.'

Christy knew that as a Derby winner the horse could stand at stud for a nomination of at least £10,000 serving another owner's mare. The trainer was bound to get a cut out of that. 'And would I be getting any share of the stud fees?'

'Now don't go asking too much, Christy. I've already stuck my neck out far enough, and you should be very satisfied with your forty pounds a week.'

Christy realized that, just now, he wouldn't get any greater financial rewards from working at the Grange. He'd just have to be satisfied with that.

With the benefit of his new high salary, Christy O'Donnell had savings in the Irish Linen Bank by January 1969 already in excess of £4,800. It was a formidable achievement in the space of only six years. And he was still only twenty-one.

On the day in February when his bank statement revealed he had reached the magic five grand figure, he took the afternoon off and drove down towards Cashel in County Tipperary in one of the Grange vehicles. On his way, he stopped to look at the castle up on Leprechaun's Finger. He had been down here a dozen times in the last couple of years, to observe from this same spot the place which would be the domain for him and his ma.

At Cashel Town, he went into Donald Smitherson's Estate Agency on the High Street. 'I'm interested in the castle up by Leprechaun's Finger. What could you tell me about it?'

Smitherson, a small man with horn-rimmed spectacles, looked him up and down. 'Castle Kirkpatrick? You're looking to rent it, are you?'

'Could be,' Christy replied nonchalantly. 'Is it a Mr Kirkpatrick that still owns it now?'

'That's right. Mr Seamus Kirkpatrick. Lives in Dublin. Lets the castle out for sixty pounds a week in the off-season, and a hundred pounds a week from May to September. Servants and maids are extra. Maids go from twelve pounds a week, and butlers eighteen. The exact rates depend on the hours worked, naturally. On top of that, Irish music evenings can be laid on for overseas tourists....' The estate agent noticed the young man was barely listening to all this. 'There are other details if you're interested. But one thing you should know is that Mr Kirkpatrick doesn't negotiate.'

Christy asked, 'And what if someone wanted to buy the castle?'

'Buy? Oh, no-one's ever asked to buy it before.' Smitherson took off his horn-rimmed glasses and polished the lenses. He was a man who needed a lot of thinking time before answering any unusual question. He muttered, 'The building itself, well, who would know how to put a value on something like that? But the grounds ... There's a lot of land with that property. At least a thousand acres. To buy, eh?' He put his glasses back on and peered hard at Christy. 'Would it be for you?'

'It might. If the price was right.'

Smitherson allowed himself more thinking time. 'So ... It couldn't be worth less than, say, er, seventy to seventy-five thousand pounds. No, not less than that. And Mr Kirkpatrick, well, he would want more than the going rate. He always does.'

Christy had expected it to be that kind of money. And it would still be many years before he could make a serious approach to the owner. But a thousand acres! That was much, much more than enough for his own stable and gallops and everything else....

During 1969 Christy and Deborah Greville made love whenever they could. It wasn't easy at the Grange. They were conscious of mansion and stable staff watching them every time they chatted or rode together.

But chances did come.

Farmer MacBride's field was a favourite place during mild weather. They used to do it under the oak tree where they'd kissed for the first time.

Deborah also gave him a key to a side door into the Grange. She would put a Union Jack in her bedroom window to tell him it was all right for him to come that night.

Everyone working at the place knew of the affair. Almost no-one dared say anything to Christy for fear of incurring Deborah's wrath and getting sacked.

Johnnie Early, still a good friend of Christy's, was the only one to whom Christy sometimes mentioned some of the more wondrous acts Deborah performed on him.

'God, but she's so bloody gorgeous,' Christy would tell him. 'Those long legs of hers, the way she wraps them around me. Those tits ... And the way she sucks me. She calls me her creamy Irish potato ... Oh God, Johnnie, but I love her.'

Whenever Early knew Christy and Deborah had been out to Farmer MacBride's, he would say 'Been growing potatoes again then?'

They would both have a great laugh.

Sometimes, after their lust had been fulfilled, Deborah would look warmly into Christy's eyes and he would have the urge to tell her, 'I love you.'

But whenever the words welled up in his throat, he was

unable to express them. He knew in his heart that whilst this aristocrat girl was happy enough giving him those looks and that joy to his body, she wasn't waiting for him to come out with those famous three words.

Then, one night in December, as they clutched each other tightly under her blankets after a long and satisfying joining, she came out with a different set of three words. 'I'm pregnant.'

'What about the bloody pill?' he said, unable to believe it.

'Those were my exact words to the doctor.'

'And?'

'Apparently not even the pill is completely foolproof. Not yet at least.'

'What are you going to do, Deborah?'

'I think you'd better leave me to think about it. Go back to your dormitory.'

Molly O'Donnell had often said to him, 'Two and two will always make four, son. You can't imagine how many times I said that to your father. But you know how your da was. He tried to add one and one and come up with ten! "Forget the horses, Stephen," I used to tell him. But he wouldn't. He was sure he'd be getting rich any day now. That was always his reply: "Any day now!" And so there would be good old Stephen O'Donnell, going out to the races like a king, always promising to come home with money and everything the world had to offer, and then always coming back penniless.... Two and two will always make four Christy. Don't you ever forget that.'

As Christy tried to find sleep in his room the night after Deborah announced her pregnancy, the idea came to him. It was crystal clear in its simplicity. As simple as two and two.

Could the answer to both problems – Deborah's pregnancy and his getting the castle sooner – be solved by one question? he wondered.

In February 1970 he asked it.

He had wanted to do it as soon as he next saw her but, though Deborah came to the mansion a couple more times in January, she didn't visit the stables complex. Nor did the flag go up in her window. Christy wasn't able to get near her. He started to get desperately anxious.

That Friday in February, though, he saw her walking out by the paddocks by herself. He knew this meant she wanted to talk to him. So he went up to her boldly. But in her normally confident face was a lost look.

'Deborah,' he said, taking her hands in his. 'I love you. Will you marry me?'

The lost look changed to one of surprise. 'Marry you?'

Christy was shaken by her reaction. The idea was so right for him that he hadn't even paused to consider if it was right for her. Gamely, though, he saw his intention through. 'Yes, Deb, will you marry me?'

She sneered, and he'd never seen that gorgeous face turn so ugly. Snatching her hands out of his, she said, 'I couldn't imagine you'd be such a moron that you'd propose. Just because we had a bit of bouncy-bouncy. What a laugh! I'm not even sure the baby was yours.' She paused at the mortified expression on his face. 'And you didn't really think you were the only one, did you? You didn't think I could have that baby, did you?'

Christy's head was spinning.

She laughed. 'I forget, you're Catholic, aren't you? Very god-fearing, the Irish. Though even they forget the "Thou Shalt Nots" when it suits them. But the biggest laugh of all ... You really imagined I could marry you ... An Irish stable boy!'

Christy turned and walked back towards the stable buildings, trembling to his core. Hearing her follow, he quickened his pace.

Not able to catch up, and refusing to run after him, she called loudly to his back: 'Mother had me engaged last week to Earl Patrick Spencer of Limerick. He's got an absolute fortune, I'm told. You couldn't expect a Greville to do less, could you?'

Now he stopped and turned. His voice icy with anger he said, 'You weren't worried about any bloody fortune when you were hungry for a good fuck with an Irish potato, were you?'

She didn't answer. She was trying to laugh again but there were tears in her eyes.

Two and two makes four ... Aye, ma, I understand now. But I was still stupid enough to think that an Irish stable boy and an over-sexed milady could add up to a marriage. Just as we thought a few quid profit out of over-priced turf could add up to anything more than a poor grave in Killertoon....

Christy knew now he couldn't continue at the Grange. The earnings here were no longer enough. Byrne might arrange better-than-average pay rises for him now and then, but Christy knew he'd never be let in on the real money: the shares in the winnings and the percentages in stud fees from horses like King Midas.... The trainer would always keep that kind of income to himself.

'You should demand some of it, you know,' Johnnie Early said.

'Byrne's dead against me having any share. I'll have to kick up a fuss with Lord James, and then there's no knowing what kind of crooked tricks Byrne'll try. It'll eventually have a bad effect on the horses. There's not much point really. It's best I move on.'

But Christy knew in his secret heart that his argument didn't hold much water. If he really insisted, Byrne *would* have to cave in. He knew that, in many ways, he had become as important as the trainer himself, even though Byrne would always keep the glory. The stable lads, for instance, always came to him, not Byrne, for advice these days; even the Grange accountant consulted him instead of the trainer on deals. No, the real reason he had to leave now was Deborah. He loved her, but had discovered that, when the chips were down, she didn't feel the same about him. And that was something he couldn't bear.

His next step would have to be as trainer on his own account; he'd work with owners who operated differently from the Grevilles. The Marylebone family was moneyed all right, there was no doubting that. But, as bloodstock owners, they weren't adventurous, preferring to breed and train their strings themselves, while allowing Byrne only the occasional foray to Goffs. What Christy needed now was work with owners who splashed out big at the major world auctions. These characters paid their trainers big too when their horses won.

He'd be keeping his eyes open for the right opportunity from today onwards. He'd look very hard indeed around the circuit.

13.3.79

Sir Timothy Bryant QC, Britain's busiest and best barrister, had lost three cases in ten years and won four hundred plus. The secret of his success was simple: he had a nose for a winning case which was unparalleled amongst his peers, and he only took on those which he estimated had at least a ninety-five per cent chance.

'I'm not an altruist,' he would say. 'I don't see why I should damage my reputation no matter how worthy the cause. If I can't win with a brief, I won't take it on.'

His chambers were in Gray's Inn. The consulting room was stacked to the ceiling with statute books, bound volumes of All-England Law reports, scrolled documents fastened with wax seals and ribbons, archives, journals, back numbers of *Hansard*, Inland Revenue bulletins.

He swung open the wide polished oak door in a hurry, took off his wig and gown, and hung them on the coat stand. Also hanging there were the coats of James Greville and Anthony Amory, solicitor.

'Sorry to keep you waiting,' he said to the two men. 'It's all Justice Peacock's fault for taking longer than he should have to decide on damages in Morrison versus the Coca Cola Corporation.'

Amory said in his nasal tone, 'It's kind of you to break from your heavy caseload for us. But you do realize how important this matter is?'

'Every matter is important,' the barrister muttered with ill-concealed irritation. A big, beefy man with flushed cheeks, he sat at his desk, and his clerk placed a file in front of him. He didn't bother to open it. 'I've had a good butcher's at this brief,' he said to Greville. 'And you haven't got a hope in hell.'

The duke spluttered. 'That's ridiculous.'

Amory, evidently Jewish in both appearance – with sallow skin and tightly curled iron-grey hair – as well as in his cannily insistent manner, and thus an entirely different style of lawyer from British bulldog Bryant, carefully flicked a speck of dust off the razor-sharp crease of his trouser leg. 'His Grace was counting on making a case against Charles Greville's having created Greville International Corporation outside the aegis of Robert Greville....'

Sir Timothy waved away the charge. 'GIC is an offshore trust domiciled in Monaco. It's outside the jurisdiction of the UK Chancery court.'

'Pleadings against overseas concerns in equity matters take place every day,' Amory retorted.

The barrister pointedly addressed Greville. 'I repeat, you haven't got a hope in hell. Your main problem is that Greville

International's performance in the last five years has massively outstripped that of your company, Greville Holdings. Silver's proved to be a pretty poor investment, I'm afraid.'

Greville's eyebrows bristled.

Sir Timothy continued, 'If the matter's dragged through Chancery, any half-decent lawyer will advise your wife to make a counter-claim. With someone like Brewer around, she's got the firepower to wrest Greville Holdings out of your grasp and under GIC's umbrella. That's hardly what you'd want, I'd imagine. *Non sine pulvere palma.* I shouldn't get into a fight which is bound to be bloody, and certainly not without more cards stacked on your side.'

'What do you know about Brewer?' Greville said.

'We had him investigated quite closely.' He flicked the file back and forth with the forefingers of both hands. 'He'll fight tooth and claw for your wife. And her grounds are immensely stronger than yours.'

The barrister was too wise to give full voice to his thoughts. He'd already successfully defended Greville against the old duke. That had been different. But now, if Elizabeth Greville tried for control of Greville Holdings because of the diminished responsibility of this brainsick husband of hers sitting opposite, he'd be quite happy to take on *her* brief; in contrast with James Greville's case, hers would have a one hundred per cent chance of success.

The vault was cold. The rows upon rows of bars of gleaming metal didn't make the place warmer.

But Greville didn't feel any cold. Nor did he notice the vibrations from the Northern Line tube trains passing nearby through the London clay, at the same level.

The vault was under Cornhill in the City. In it were around 20 million troy ounces of silver, or 20 thousand of the one-thousand ounce ingots.

A vault security guard had unlocked one of the cages to let Greville in, then locked it again behind him. Greville was known here. Had been since 1974. He spent ages in a cage, staring at the ingots, often running his hand smoothly along them in loving caresses. They were stacked in perfect piles, lustrous white trapezoidal bricks more than a foot long and six inches wide, weighing a massive sixty-two and a half pounds, each stamped with: *The London Minerals Board*; the assay mark: *Minimum Fineness 99.99 Parts Per 100*; the weight: *1000 oz*;

the serial number.

Stewart, James Greville's driver, sat patiently in the lobby upstairs. He sometimes wondered why his boss spent so long in the vault. The sight was always the same, after all.

Greville eventually came up by the lift and Stewart got up and put on his cap.

'John Early,' Greville muttered as they stepped out into the street. 'John Early's the solution.'

The meeting took place in the Blue Drawing Room at Condrieu Hall.

Greville and Elizabeth sat side by side on comfortable chairs by the bigger of the Robert Adam fireplaces in the room. A third chair stood opposite them, empty. A maid set the tea things on an adjacent ormolu table.

Elizabeth had a wry expression. 'I'm not sure what you expect this will achieve.'

'I just want you to satisfy yourself, once and for all, Liz. You can ask him anything you like.' He nodded at the maid. 'Send him in.'

John Early entered as Elizabeth was pouring tea. The Eden Grange trainer wore a smart blue suit. She glanced up at him and struggled to contain her revulsion. Everything about this man who now ran their stable was anathema for her. He looked ridiculous with his unkempt red hair, like a child's, and had huge apprehension in his face as he tried to smile, but failed. She wanted to shout, 'Murderer!' but restricted herself to, 'Would you like some tea, Mr Early?'

He sat down, shaking like a leaf and trying to control it. 'No, Ma'am, no thanks.'

Greville cleared his throat. 'You're to answer any questions my wife asks you.'

Early nodded stiffly.

'Fire away, Liz.'

'Don't be so nervous, Mr Early.'

'Oh, I'm not nervous.'

'Indeed,' she said. She knew the truth, or had guessed it after reading Prospero's prophecy the day after Charles's death. It would be so easy to nail this man down. But she knew she mustn't, or she'd incriminate her husband too. She could just imagine Greville telephoning Early at the Grange with words to the effect of: *'It's important that he fall from something, a car, a horse, do you understand? Nobody must know. I'll make you the trainer....'*

She said, 'My husband felt you ought to tell me personally what happened on the 5th of January.'

Early, reassured by her non-accusing tone, nodded. 'I was chatting with his Grace, the old duke, you know, and I mentioned that we used Farmer MacBride's field, and he got very angry at that....'

Elizabeth interjected, 'Why *do* you use Farmer MacBride's field?'

'Well, it's got other uses besides growing potatoes,' he said automatically, and leered. The duke and duchess gazed blankly at him. He stammered, 'What I mean is, the soil is different, harder. It was Christy's idea in the first place, you know, Christy O'Donnell? Well, we used to work King Midas down there sometimes, because that was the King's favourite type of going....'

Elizabeth said, 'But why, on the 5th of January, when his Grace demanded to go there and see for himself, did you drive across the ditch into the field, and not take the road?'

'Oh, the track across the ditch was all right. In good weather, you could drive a lorry over that track.'

'But the weather hadn't been good, had it Mr Early? Hadn't it been wet for several days?'

Greville said quickly, 'A Land Rover's hardly a lorry, Liz.'

Elizabeth nodded. 'Go on, Mr Early.'

The Irishman's voice was thick with tension. 'Well, the vehicle skidded, see, ma'am, and lurched to the left much more sharply than anyone could have expected, and his Grace fell out....' The voice dried right up.

'And the back wheel went over his head? And the vehicle was in four-wheel drive?'

Early nodded at each question. Tears beaded his eyes.

Elizabeth said softly, 'I know you did whatever you had to.'

Greville said, 'He rushed dad straight down to Dublin.'

Elizabeth asked, 'And is that where you telephoned my husband from?'

'Well, I did go back to the lodge first ma'am, to get help, and I called from there.'

'Yes,' she said sadly, 'he would have needed help. Everything was against him. Well, thank you, Mr Early, I don't think I need to know any more.'

Early departed quickly. 'So you see, Liz?' said Greville. 'It *was* just an accident. You'll help me now, won't you?'

'No, James,' she said, 'I can't do anything at all unless you admit you called Early that morning, and told him to give Charles a fall.'

'I didn't make a phone call about giving dad a fall, do you hear?' Rage darkened his face. 'But all you want is false admissions. Doesn't that prove that *you're* the one guilty of something?'

The portrait of the third Duke of Marylebone was unveiled at Sir William Butts's Chelsea studio the next day.

A life-sized James Greville was portrayed standing by the lattice windows in the ballroom, a curious half-smile – almost a sneer – on his lips, his pale eyes expressionless, his hand on the left side of his chest.

Greville grinned instinctively at the sight of himself the moment the curtains were drawn apart in front of the canvas but, another moment later, his smile disappeared. In the unerringly accurate picture he appeared not even one-tenth of the man Charles Greville did in his.

Butts said jovially, 'I thought I'd give you a sort of Napoleonic stance, what, James.'

Greville detested the fake joviality. He instantly decided to have another one done by another artist in a year or so, representing him in a stronger light. Butts wasn't the be-all and end-all of portrait painters. But this would have to do for now. The only person who would really understand his dissatisfaction with the portrait was Elizabeth. But what did her opinions matter? 'Send it along to the House tomorrow,' he said.

He tried the portrait in different parts of the ballroom, and finally settled on a position in the middle of the wall opposite the windows. But he continued to feel uncomfortable with it.

That afternoon, after he had gazed at it for the hundredth time, he finally grasped the nettle about silver.

Standing by the windows in virtually the same pose as in the picture, though not realizing it, he said to Winchester, 'So you say the price now is lower than the average price I've paid for the entire hoard?'

'That's right. That's because you bought so heavily at the top.'

Greville nodded with irritation. 'There's no need to keep rubbing that part of it in.'

Winchester said gravely, 'I'm afraid I do feel it's part of my job not to weasel out of telling you the truth.' Then more cynically: 'Pointing out the facts is all I seem to have left to do nowadays. So, here we go. One, the carrying charges of all the silver have become horrendous. Two, the best thing you can do now is to get into property. Three, Margaret Thatcher is guaranteed to get in at the next General Election, and she'll be doing everything to stimulate business confidence, and so property should rise. Four, Thatcher's also determined to combat inflation, so the trend for the precious metals can only be downwards....'

Greville shouted, 'That's enough! Why don't you stop giving me your smug theories and think of a way to force the silver price up! You're earning £90,000 but you just sit there reading out telexes. Since we can't get hold of cash, can't you come up with some idea how we can use the bullion we already own to get the price up? We've got enough of the stuff.'

Winchester sighed. He wondered why Greville had taken so long to get around to this obvious idea. Considering the 80-million-ounce bullion stack which the holding company possessed, considering the doldrums in the price, considering the way the commodities markets allowed the purchase of futures contracts on 'margin' – putting only a fraction of the value down – Greville would never have a better opportunity to try a manipulation of the market to squeeze the price upwards. But, since the risks involved were immense, it was hardly a course he could propose off his own bat. He said cautiously, 'Many people have tried many times to corner many different markets, and the failures have been well trumpeted.'

'So you're saying it's not possible?'

Winchester shook his head. 'There have been successes too. Quite a few, in fact, though these have never been publicized, for the obvious reason that if they had become known, everybody would try it....' He paused, wondering how much to reveal. Then he made a decision. His tone very low, he said, 'In fact I've done it myself. I've cornered a market in a commodity.'

'What?' cried the duke in disbelief.

Winchester nodded. 'I did it while I was with Macintyres. In bismuth.'

'Bismuth? What's that?'

'A metal, your Grace, mined by and large in South America and the Pacific Rim. It's used in pharmaceuticals, mainly by the French, for suppositories.'

'And you actually managed to squeeze the price upwards in this thing?'

Winchester gave a quiet smile.

'How? How did you do it?'

'It wasn't difficult. A certain amount of inside knowledge was required. And a lot of money up front.' He bared his teeth in a gloat. 'But lots more was made.'

Greville came and sat in a wing chair opposite the comptroller's desk. 'But can it be done in silver?'

Winchester flopped back in his chair to escape the stink of stale cigars on his employer's breath. 'I have given it some thought over the last few weeks, and while it would certainly be more difficult than cornering bismuth given the huge world-wide profile of silver, I came to the conclusion it could still be done.'

'And you never thought to mention this before?' bellowed Greville.

'There was no point. We don't have the money. And there are risks ... Huge risks....'

'You're my comptroller, dammit! It's your duty to inform me about ideas like these which come to you!' He rose, trembling with excitement. 'You're to forget about whether we have the money just now. What I want is to know exactly how to go about cornering the silver market. Step by step. I want you to produce a blueprint. Fast. Before I lose any more money.'

September 1971 – December 1975

Christy had to wait nearly two years for the right opportunity.

On a late summer day in 1971, Earl Patrick and Lady Deborah Spencer came to Eden Grange with their bonny baby, a boy of seven months called Thomas. Also with them was the Maharajah of Bhojalpur – who was a great friend of the earl's – and the maharajah's servants. They made the customary tour of the stables complex. Christy counted twelve Indians in the maharajah's retinue. One carried a portable telex machine around with him, as though urgent calls out here to Irish stables were the norm.

Deborah and the nanny set back off, after the tour, for the Grange mansion with the baby, while Patrick Spencer and Bhojalpur spent more time examining the horses. When Spencer eventually turned for the path to the mansion too, the Indian potentate excused himself for a moment. He'd noticed Christy giving orders earlier to one or two of the lads by the barns, and came up to address him now.

'You work here in some position of authority, I presume, young man?'

'Yes, sir. I'm the assistant trainer.'

The maharajah nodded. 'Ah very good. You're Irish, I see. I can tell by your accent.'

The cheek of the man! Christy thought. Some kind of nabob or something, coming here to Ireland, and commenting on *his* accent! 'You'd be right again in your presumpt*uousness*, sir,' he said.

The fat brown man, who wore a seersucker jacket and big jewel-encrusted rings on every finger, beamed. 'Excellent, well, then, you're the man whose help I need. I am looking for a new trainer. My present one is a good man, or rather, I should say, he's not bad. But unfortunately ... (and he pronounced this 'un-fart-you-nately') ... he's also Irish. The kind of Irishman all those jokes are made about; you know, not too bright up here.' Bhojalpur tapped his temple with a finger bearing the gaudiest ruby Christy had ever seen. 'He knows how to get good performances from my horses – I'll give him that much. But he's very limited when it comes to the rest of the matters concerning the stable, like the bloodstock buying and selling, wheeling and dealing with stud farms and syndicates and the what-nots ... In other words, he's not the most brainy type of chap you could hope to find in Ireland, if you see what I mean....' The maharajah shook his head sadly. 'I am telling you all this Mr ... Mr ...'

'O'Donnell, sir. Christy O'Donnell.'

'Yes, I am telling you all this because maybe you know someone in the training game who has got a bit up here.' He touched his temple again. 'So that I don't have to be always crying out with raging ruddy frustration. I am very reasonable, you know. I don't expect anyone to work out in their heads, say, seven and a quarter per cent of $66,000....'

'That'd be $4,785, sir,' Christy interrupted.

'Pardon?' The maharajah was baffled.

'$4,785. You wanted to know what seven and a quarter per cent of $66,000 was, didn't you, sir?'

The maharajah's eyes turned suspicious. 'It was the general idea I was trying to express, young man. The actual sum is hardly important. What I'm interested in is finding the right man to train my horses....' He broke off, his curiosity getting the better of him, and reached into a pocket of his seersucker jacket. He drew out a bulging leather wallet and flipped it open. Christy saw set into the left flap a little black machine. He didn't know then that it was a prototype LED pocket calculator presented by Clive Sinclair to the maharajah in London a couple of days earlier.

The fat Indian hit a few buttons on it. Then he looked impassively in Christy's face. 'Hmm. Not a bad guess. What did you say you do here, Mr ... Mr ...?'

'I'm the assistant trainer sir. And the name's O'Donnell.'

At that moment Earl Patrick Spencer arrived to explain to the maharajah that they'd be late for lunch, and ushered him away.

A little later that day, one of the dozen Indian servants came out to see Christy. 'His Highness would like to talk to you about working for him. He is staying here at this Grange place tonight, but he will be in Dublin tomorrow. He would like you to come to the MacBeith Hotel. Ask for him at Reception at seven tomorrow evening.'

'I have a proposition for you,' said the maharajah in his hotel suite.

A servant served gin-and-tonics.

Christy took a sip.

Bhojalpur elaborated. 'I need a new trainer, as I told you yesterday. I know you are an employee just now, and that you don't have your own training facility. But I'm prepared to set you up as a free-lance trainer, working with my horses of course, and also those belonging to other owners.'

Christy did his utmost to keep his interest off his face. 'Er, that's very interesting, sir. And how would that work out in practice?'

Another servant produced a large-scale map of southwestern Ireland and spread it on the table. Bhojalpur pointed to a spot on it. 'A man who owed me money gave me some farmland here instead, near Ballyporeen.' It was in County Tipperary, less than thirty miles from Castle Kirkpatrick.

He explained there was an existing house and barns on the

land; he would further provide prefabricated stable buildings and boxes, and arrange the necessary enclosure and exercise facilities for up to thirty thoroughbreds.

'I myself have nineteen. In lieu of rent at the new stable, I will pay you no training fees. But I will meet all the feeding, veterinary, tack and other out-of pocket expenses for my horses. Your income will be made up from taking ten per cent of winnings and of syndication and stud fees.' He added that Christy could also train eleven other horses belonging to outside owners, on whatever fees and terms he could agree with them.

'If you accept this offer,' the maharajah concluded, 'you will be running your own fully equipped stable within three months.'

Christy accepted. Over an Indian meal prepared and served up by servants in the suite, he chuckled wryly, 'It's funny what rewards a bit of mental arithmetic can bring, isn't it?'

Bhojalpur shook his head. 'Oh, Mr O'Donnell, if you think I made you this proposition because you did a quick sum in your head, then you are sadly mistaken. You see, when I asked the wife of my very good friend, the Earl Patrick Spencer, if she too could recommend a possible trainer, Lady Deborah had no hesitation. She named you as the best potential trainer in Ireland. She said no-one else could hold a candle up to you.'

In December of that year, Christy moved his belongings out of Eden Grange and into Twelve Pins Stables – which is what he called his new place, after the mountains in his native Connemara.

The maharajah had good horses, and prize money seeped in to such an extent that by the middle of 1972, Christy's income was an average of £650 a month after deducting all overheads, including the wages of the four lads who were working for him by then.

He managed to get seven horses for training at Twelve Pins from other owners, including one belonging to Crown Prince Ahmed of the Arabian Kingdom of the Hejaz. This country was second only to Saudi Arabia in importance as a world oil producer.

In 1973, Christy pulled off a feat which established his renown, with Atilla, a thoroughbred belonging to British breeder and banker William Lemon. Under Atilla's previous trainer, the 4-year-old horse had shown a tendency to lose pace just before the finish of races. Christy watched it carefully out on the gallops, then told Lemon, 'I reckon a tongue strap might fix it.'

The horse won the Eclipse Stakes at Sandown with the strap in, and continued to do well with it for the rest of the season.

Lemon brought his two other horses across to be trained by Christy too, and offered him the best interest rate possible if he banked at Wardle Spyers, his bank in London.

By 1975 Christy's earnings far outstripped that of Johnnie Early, who was assistant trainer by now at Eden Grange.

On the tracks, Christy's successes became more frequent. He produced his first Irish Classics winner in the 1,000 Guineas at the Curragh, with Sunita, running in the Maharajah of Bhojalpur's colours. 1975 also yielded nine Group One winners and fifteen Group Twos for the stable, including a couple for Crown Prince Ahmed of the Hejaz.

Throughout, Christy maintained his intention of never betting himself, even when he was certain his charges would win races. In September 1975, he used £23,000 out of his savings – which had gone up to £35,000 now – to buy a smart semi-detached Georgian house in beautiful tree-lined Ailesbury Road in Dublin 4.

Property, Christy decided, was a very good investment; it gave a better yield even than the deposit account at Wardle Spyers, whose special interest rate Lemon had fixed for him at twelve per cent. Houses in the capital, on the other hand, were advancing in price at twenty-five to thirty-five per cent per annum. The property market had been thriving since Ireland's entry into the Common Market. A number of European companies had opened offices in Dublin, and good quality residential accommodation was at a premium.

Christy named the house Joyce Villa after his mother's maiden name, and let it furnished to a commercial attaché from the Brazilian Embassy. Called DeSouza, he had impeccable references. The best reference of all was, of course, Mr DeSouza's signature on his cheque: he paid Christy seventy pounds a week. In advance.

Christy attended midnight mass that Christmas Eve at Killertoon in Connemara. Also there were Farmer and Mrs Regan, whom he showered with gifts. After mass was over, he went out to the simple grave and said to the granite gravestone, 'It won't be long now, ma.'

2.4.79

Winchester delivered his final draft of the blueprint to James Greville that evening at the Scimitar Club.

The duke studied it into the early hours of the following morning. When Winchester arrived at the ballroom at 8.30, Greville was sitting in one of the sofas in a distracted mood. The comptroller went around to his own desk, and started busying himself with the morning's work.

'Twenty-five dollars an ounce, eh, Simon?' the duke said.

Winchester gave a firm nod. Doing the blueprint had made him feel a real commodity man again. 'Yes, the price can go all the way there if we hit the Chicago December futures contract in the way I've outlined.'

'Twenty-five dollars an ounce....' Greville repeated.

Winchester explained: 'The actions we'll take will ensure that the price stays above the $20 level for several months after December. It'll give us more than enough time to sell all your silver slowly back and close out a profit of eight to twelve hundred million dollars.'

Greville nodded, still trying to absorb the implications. 'And these CFTC watchdog people ... You're quite sure they won't be able to intervene?'

Winchester warmed further to his task: 'Theoretically, the Commodity Futures Trading Commission have draconian powers against funny goings-on such as insider trading, manipulations and corners. In practice, the commission is a beached whale. It's hampered by a shortage of operational funds, hostility from the market pros, and procedural loopholes, of which there are loads. Here's a taster of the sort of technical detail which forever trips them up: In the US Commodities Exchange Act of 1936 – the charter under which the commission operates – you'd be interested to know that there is no definition of what actually constitutes a 'squeeze' or a 'manipulation' or a 'corner'. So how does it establish if one is going on? Then if the CFTC does overcome that hurdle, it's obliged – according to the decree passed by the US Senate Agricultural Committee in 1974 – to prove *intention* to corner the market. In my scheme, we'll be working through 400 different nominee accounts, carefully screened to avoid any inference of collusion, and thereby eliminating the chance of the commission proving any such intention.' He beamed happily at the duke.

Greville stroked his silver moustache. This would show Elizabeth. 'That's good, Simon, very good.'

Winchester picked up the reins again: 'While preparing the blueprint, I approached individuals for the use of their names to set up the nominee accounts in brokerages in London and Chicago, in case we somehow manage to get this scheme into action quickly. There have been plenty of takers. With your 80 million ounces of silver bullion to hand, we've also got the foundations for an attack on the price.' He cleared his throat. 'But of course, there is that one thing missing from it all.'

Greville nodded slowly and lit a cigar. Then he read out loud the all-important detail Winchester had given in the blueprint: '$1,000 million dollars in cash is needed to be able to buy the necessary amount of December futures contracts....' His voice almost gagged on the amount.

'Yes,' said Winchester. 'Just exactly where on earth do you think you can lay your hands on that kind of money?'

June 1976

A muffled crack split the air.

In the darkness, the animal thudded to the ground. Its throat torn out, it whined horribly as its blood pumped onto the grass.

There was a low savage growl as the other pricked up its ears and bounded across the field.

A second crack. Another bullet sang through the air.

Christy woke with a start and sat up in bed. Something was wrong.

Through the open window, the smell of hay wafted in on the

balmy breeze. High to the west, the moon smiled benevolently over Counties Tipperary and Cork.

But something was missing.

Of course. Samson and Delilah.

They weren't snuffling or growling out in the yard.

Christy swung his legs off the bed. Pulling on his dressing gown, he hurried downstairs. The stable yard was eerily silent. The dogs should be yapping at his feet by now. In the moonlight, he saw that the gates which led to the road and to the paddocks were swinging lightly to and fro in the breeze.

That was wrong. The gates should never be open like that....

He feared he knew why. There could only be one possibility. He went straight as an arrow past all the horse boxes to her one. 'Fucking hell,' he mouthed. But no sound emerged from his lips. She was gone. Miss Fortune was gone.

Christy ran to the garage, got in the Land Rover and headed for the perimeter fence. Three hundred yards out he saw Samson and Delilah in the vehicle's lights. The two German sheepdogs lay lifeless on the ground some yards from each other. That was why he hadn't heard the poor darlings outside his bedroom. The poor dead darlings.

But he couldn't stop to see to them now. He reached the perimeter track and drove along it. The headlights scanned the twelve-foot high mesh fence. Half a mile out, he screeched the vehicle to a halt. A gaping hole had been cut out of the fence. He jumped out of the Land Rover in rage, the cord of his dressing gown almost tripping him up.

'What about the damn electrification?' he cried.

Nobody heard him. He poked a fingertip gingerly against the mesh. No sting. He touched the fence again. His touch was bolder.

'Dead,' he breathed. The fence was dead.

So why hadn't the murthering alarm gone off?

Somehow, those fucking thieving bastards had nobbled the generator. When he found out who they were, he'd break their legs. He looked through the gap in the fence, searching the distance for some hint to where they'd gone. But there was only black night all around. In any case, after they'd killed the dogs, they'd clearly let themselves out through the gates. That was why they had been open. He clambered back into the Land Rover and steered it off the perimeter path. It would be quickest to cut straight across the gallops. A couple of hands were hurrying up. He slowed to shout: 'Miss Fortune's been taken! They've killed the dogs. One of you see if you can work out which way they went. But don't follow. They're armed. The other get the dogs back to the stables.'

He spurted off again in the Land Rover. The sooner he phoned the Garda the better. Then he'd have to call the maharajah. The increasingly bloody pompous Maharajah of Bhojalpur.

'You couldn't possibly name her Miss Fortune,' Christy had said. 'That's bound to bring you misfortune, see now?'

'Oh, but I must,' Bhojalpur replied. He had become unbelievably high-and-mighty since buying the charcoal grey filly by Seattle Slew six months back in Kentucky. It had been his biggest ever purchase. 'You see, Miss Fortune is the nearest English translation for Lakshmi. The Hindu goddess of wealth.'

'Then call her Lakshmi itself,' Christy had suggested, hating the idea of having a horse with such an unlucky name here.

The maharajah's eyes opened very wide, accentuating their whites. 'Oh no, it would be sacrilege to call her Lakshmi itself.'

'So call her *Dame* Fortune.' This was said desperately.

'Oh, but no. I want to think of her as virginal.'

Three million pounds and virginal. Now he and the maharajah were fucked.

It was Bhojalpur who had had the electric fence and alarm system installed at Twelve Pins when he had bought Miss Fortune.

The security system was hooked up to mains electricity, and also by a trip wire to a secondary generator in an out-house. If mains power was cut off for any reason, the generator took over, keeping the fence live and automatically setting off the alarm. An extra feature was that the alarm would also be triggered if anyone tried to tamper with the generator while it was dormant.

But hand-held 'gas guns' for squirting polystyrene foam had been developed a mere three months earlier.

Within a couple of hours of Miss Fortune's kidnapping, local Gardai were trying to examine the generator at Twelve Pins. But they couldn't open the control panel flap. A specialist Garda technician was sent for. He managed to unhinge the flap. Inside the generator's control area, every vacant cubic millimetre was clogged with solidified polystyrene foam.

By 11 a.m., the maharajah was at the stables, having

hastened out of his apartment in London's Berkeley Square at dawn to fly across the Irish Sea in his private plane.

Inspector Doherty explained: 'Somebody injected polystyrene through the flap yesterday. Someone who was obviously familiar with the MacDougall Webb A344 generator, and who knew exactly how much to use. The polystyrene expanded, filled every nook and cranny, including between the circuit breakers and contacts, and completely disabled the generator. Then, during the night, these rascals brought down the main power lines. After that, cutting open the fence and shooting the dogs was child's play ... Now, who was here yesterday, Mr O'Donnell?'

Christy searched his memory. 'The vet, a couple of jockeys, the hands and apprentices obviously, and four busloads of sightseers.'

'Sightseers?' queried the inspector.

'Oh yes,' said the maharajah brightly. 'It was my idea. We charge fifty pence a head, and we get publicity for our great filly. We get forty people in a bus you know, and three or four buses a day in the summer.' He beamed with pride.

Christy gave Bhojalpur a narrow stare. *He* had not approved of the idea. And he was supposed to be the master of Twelve Pins. But the big chief liked to show from time to time just who was boss. And when he had hit upon the sightseeing idea, he had refused to listen to Christy's objections. So Christy had gone along with it with the best grace he could muster, deciding it wasn't worth having a showdown over. Now, because of it, villains had got into the grounds, bunged up the generator, and stolen their star thoroughbred.

Inspector Doherty went down to question the travel agent in Clonmel who organized the bus tours. Had the travel agent taken the names of the tourists who visited the stables yesterday? No, of course not, the travel agent replied, his job was just to take their fifty pences.

That afternoon, the ransom demand came. By telephone to the stable. The maharajah listened, the jewels on his rings knocking against each other. The voice wanted £1 million, Irish. Used five pound notes, to be packed in a watertight suitcase and dropped in a certain part of Cork Harbour at two in the morning. If any Garda officers were seen in the district for six hours before or after the time of the drop, there would be a terrible retribution: Miss Fortune's right foreleg would be found in the streets of Cork the following day. But if the money was delivered, and in perfectly dry condition, Miss Fortune would be returned unharmed.

Bhojalpur himself supervised the wrapping of waterskins around the suitcase.

For days after the money drop, nothing more was heard from the horse-nappers. And there was no further sign of Miss Fortune. The English press blamed the kidnapping on the IRA. The Irish press blamed it on the Moslem fundamentalist-separatists who make up fifteen per cent of the population of the territory of Bhojalpur in northeast India. Eventually, the Garda gave up their inquiries. They could make no progress. Soon after, public interest in the story was dead. So too, it seemed, was Miss Fortune.

Two months after the crime, the Maharajah of Bhojalpur collected £4 million in insurance from Lloyds. In October he went with Christy to Longchamp in Paris for the Prix de l'Arc de Triomphe race. At the auction at the Polo de Bagatelle after the race, Bhojalpur used his £4 million to buy a dozen more horses. Supreme amongst this new batch was another glorious filly, this time by Northern Dancer.

'What are you going to call her?' Christy asked.

'Miss Fortune the Second,' replied the maharajah automatically. 'And, for her, we will charge £1 a head for visitors.'

'If you do that, I refuse to train her at Twelve Pins,' Christy said, determined to stand his ground this time.

Bhojalpur's lips took on a savage curl. 'Do you know who you are talking to? I'm your landlord and your most important owner. If you don't train this horse, you won't train *any* horse of mine, and you can't stay at Twelve Pins!'

Christy had rights of course. Bhojalpur couldn't sling him out of Twelve Pins without resorting to the courts. But the maharajah did take all his horses to another stable and eventually got a writ for Christy to quit the premises.

Christy contacted the other owners and told them they would have to transfer all their horses temporarily to other stables too, as he no longer had tenure of Twelve Pins. He said he would provide them with a list of the stables most suitable for their particular needs, emphasizing that the change was only temporary and that he would soon have new premises of his own. He would then be delighted to offer his services again should they be required.

'Where will you go?' asked William Lemon on the phone.

Castle Kirkpatrick would be ideal now, Christy knew. But, according to Smitherson it was still way out of his reach. So he'd looked elsewhere. 'I've seen some land out in Punchestown in County Kildare. I'm negotiating with the landowner. Hopefully, I'll be operational again in three or four months.'

Christy didn't add that the loss of the maharajah's business was a grievous blow and he'd need many more months – years even – to get back on to his previous footing. Lemon understood nevertheless.

Somebody else who understood was Crown Prince Ahmed of the Hejaz. Shortly after Christy had given the unfortunate tidings to the Arab prince's secretary Iqbal, Ahmed, to the Irishman's surprise, telephoned back in person. 'What is this, Sheikh O'Donnell? Leaving Twelve Pins and asking me to send my horses somewhere else? How come?'

'It's only temporary, your Royal Highness.'

'But why? Suppose I choose not to come back to you afterwards?'

'I'd hope you would, sir. I trust in my track record and I'd hope you'd bear that in mind. But if you didn't, I couldn't blame you.'

'It's that Hindu, isn't it? He ordered you to quit Twelve Pins, didn't he? You've fallen out with him, haven't you?'

'Since you're asking, sir, yes, I have. But everything'll sort itself out. I've been looking at other property just now, and....'

The crown prince interrupted him. 'Iqbal tells me that Bhojalpur's horse Durga is running in the Gallinule Stakes at the Curragh. Iqbal also tells me it'll be the simplest of things to nooble her, wouldn't it?'

Christy wondered what Ahmed meant. Then he realized and corrected him. 'You'd be meaning *nobble,* I suppose, your Royal Highness?'

'The word is of little significance, isn't it? But the deed will be of a much greater one, won't it? In repayment for Bhojalpur's shabby treatment, I will give you the great satisfaction of watching Durga come in last at the Curragh....'

'Oh no. I can't be any party to that sort of thing.'

Ahmed sounded offended. 'Why not? Do you think you are above jiggery-pokery going on in the horse buckets?'

'Oh no, your Royal Highness. I mean, I do have to say I personally can't condone any cheating with the horses. But, apart from the moral side, word does get around about that sort of thing. Bent trainers don't get good work. It's as simple as that.'

Ahmed grunted and rang off.

The next day, the secretary Iqbal telephoned Christy. 'His Royal Highness has bought Twelve Pins stables from the Maharajah of Bhojalpur....'

'Bloody hell!' Christy said.

'He wants you to stay and keep all the horses you have there, except of course those belonging to that stupid Hindu. You will be charged £100 a week rent, which, according to my enquiries, is a fair price....'

'Very fair,' he breathed. The income he lost by not charging Bhojalpur training fees was more than four times that.

' ... His Royal Highness will also be moving other horses he has in training in Ireland to Twelve Pins by the end of the week.'

'But why is he doing it, Iqbal?'

'His Royal Highness says this blood-sucking maharajah has already brought misery to half a million Moslems in the territory of Bhojalpur; there is no need to add your suffering to that of our co-religionists. So he made the stupid man an offer nobody could refuse....'

Christy knew that, for the crown prince, the cost of Twelve Pins was peanuts. But moving more horses to the place for him to train?

' ... And as for giving you other horses of his: his Royal Highness is intrigued by your behaviour. You act as if you are incorruptible. He has never yet seen a man who doesn't have a price. So he wants to see how long you will last purer than the blown sand, and he's decided to give you enough rope to hang yourself with.'

Christy laughed: Iqbal could be so funny. He was also so relieved he could stay on at Twelve Pins. Obviously, a few more owners had to be found to make up for the loss of the maharajah's business. But things had taken such a terrific turn for the better; he was sure he'd have no problem.

17.4.79

'I used to be a great admirer of the old dook's,' said Tusker Horatio Brunt.

'So we can count on you to join us?' Simon Winchester asked hopefully.

They sat on tall stools in air-conditioned comfort at the bar in Brunt's Bad Dude Ranch fifty miles north of Houston, Texas, sipping highballs. Outside the vast windows, women in bikinis swam in the brightly lit swimming pool or threw big colourful plastic balls at each other across the floodlit terrace.

In the hands of Brunt's younger brother Julius Stillgoe Brunt, and of the family's attorney Vance Reisman, who were also seated at the bar, were copies of Winchester's blueprint to corner the world's silver markets.

Tusker, 290 pounds in weight and a wearer of thick-rimmed spectacles, scratched the stubble he cultivated on his four chins. 'Now don't go misunderstanding me, Mr Winchester. It's no reflection of you or the new dook. In fact I'd say you're mighty enterprising folk to have come up with such an ambitious scheme in the first place....'

The Texan's tone was so discouraging that Winchester felt secretly relieved he had declined to travel here first class.

' ... Oh yeah,' Brunt went on, 'it shure is ambitious. But....' He shook his head sadly. ' ... it's just that we don't go into anything, Mr Winchester, and I mean nothing, that don't spark the spirit of the wildcat in us.'

'You must be joking!' Winchester protested. 'It's a high adventure, risky plan, and I would have thought it was just down your street as 'wildcatting' oil men. You put in 1 billion dollars – one English billion, that is, 1,000 million – watch the market go haywire, and come away at the end with 3 billion. Two billion dollars' profit. And all you have to do is invest the cash and sit back while it triples.'

'Mighty temptin', mighty temptin',' Tusker Brunt drawled. 'But if you really want to hear the truth, then I'm sorry to say the idea's just too uninspired for us. Every avenue's been thought out just that bit too well. There ain't no human factor in it, I'm afraid. It's just too, too clever. And I just can't believe anything can ever be quite that easy.'

Easy indeed, thought Winchester. Despite the huge show the man put on, he probably lacked cash flow.

Julius now remarked, 'Where you are right, Mr Winchester, is to go to people from the oil business to help you. Where you are wrong is to go for real oil men. Now me, personally, I'd try that guy from the Kingdom of the Hejaz. Their crown prince. He's their Minister of the Interior now, but he used to be their Oil Minister. We used to grease his palm with more boodle than you can ever imagine, and we sent him rock sample after rock sample, but he never once granted us drilling rights. Probably thought the rocks were something to throw at his wives.'

Tusker nodded. 'Yeah, Julius is right. Crown Prince Ay-med's your man. Dumb enough and rich enough. I've met the guy lotsa times at the Longchamp races and over at Royal Ascot. My hunch is that a gamble like this is just what he's been waiting for.'

Vance Reisman handed back the manila files. 'Thank you Mr Winchester for having considered us and having come all the way out to Texas. You have my word that we'll not divulge a word of your proposal to anyone.'

Tusker Horatio Brunt grinned. 'No, we shure as hell won't. But you can rest assured, sir, that if you *do* get yourselves a partner, and we *do* see the price go up as you say, we'll put our five cents worth in and buy silver ourselves.'

The two other Texans laughed, 'Yeah!' All three nodded their heads in unison.

March 1977 – May 1979

Crown Prince Ahmed was the most impulsive man Christy ever knew. He loved casinos. If he ever got a hunch on a number, he would stack his chips as high as house rules permitted, and for as long as his pocket money lasted.

During one five-night casino crawl he lost more than £2 million. It started at the Clermont Club in London, where he blew £460,000; then it was £375,000 at Aspinall's, 3 million francs in Deauville in France, 4 million francs in Monte Carlo and 2 billion lire in San Remo. On all five nights – in about thirty hours of gambling altogether – he stuck to the same play on the roulette wheel. Number 25. Only his secretary Iqbal knew why. Ahmed's favourite wife – his third one – had just attained her quarter century in years. 'Raisha is the luckiest thing that ever happened to me,' the crown prince said to intrigued onlookers at the end of his binge.

The horses he bought, and those belonging to other owners that he bet on, were always of the same ilk: proud and skittish and only colts.

'I want to win the Derby,' he said to Christy shortly after he took possession from the maharajah of Twelve Pins.

Christy groaned. Everybody only and always wanted to win the Derby.

'No other trainer I've used has given me such a prize. Buy whatever horse is necessary, and as many as you want, so that I can win the Derby. I ask only that of you.'

So Christy went to the Keeneland Sales in Kentucky and bought a few thoroughbreds. But amongst his haul, there was only one he held dear. This was a horse which responded to his words and gestures, and had everything in its physical make-up that he liked. Crazily – in his opinion – hardly anyone else at the auction was interested in the animal. The reason was that the horse's sire was King Midas. Not one creature produced by the King had ever won a Group One race in the British Isles. And track records counted for so much.

Samuel Davidson, a bloodstock adviser with an office on Wall Street, engaged by the crown prince to assist Christy, explained: 'Many of King Midas's offspring look great in the parade ring, but fail on the track. This is just one more beautiful donkey.'

But Christy bought the horse, bidding $52,000 to secure it. It was his cheapest buy at those Kentucky sales.

'So, I've got a few horses for your string,' he told Ahmed on the telephone that evening. 'But there's only one which will be a champion. What's more, she was the cheapest.'

'She?'

'Yes, your Royal Highness. She's got quality written all over her. I'm confident she'll be a strong contender for the Oaks in two years' time.'

'But I expected you to buy colts, didn't I? It's the Derby I want to win, isn't it? And a Triple Crown, no?'

'Only miracle horses win Triple Crowns!' Christy laughed.

'Miracles are what I expect from you, aren't they?' Ahmed replied. 'That's why I bought Twelve Pins, wasn't it? And that's why I've moved more of my horses there for you to train, no? But then this is how you thank me for my kindness, is it? You go and buy a filly, do you? What use is it talking to me about the Oaks, tell me now? What filly can ever win the Triple Crown, I want to know?' He sounded really woeful. Christy had come to know that when the crown prince lapsed into putting those awful question tags at the end of every sentence, it meant he really wasn't very happy.

He retorted: 'Aha! So here's something you didn't know, your Royal Highness. A filly can get a Triple Crown too, by winning the 1,000 Guineas, the Oaks and the St Leger.'

Ahmed's woes disappeared. 'All right, very good Sheikh O'Donnell. Get me this Triple Crown then and I won't complain about having this creature in my string.'

'Now, wait a minute,' protested Christy. 'I said she was good, and that I could make her a contender for the Oaks. I never said she could win a Triple Crown.'

'Aha, you mean you don't trust your own judgement?'

Christy realized that by buying a filly against Ahmed's wishes he had got himself into deep waters. The Arab was a die-hard gambler, and would expect Christy to back himself to the hilt on the issue. If he didn't, he would lose Ahmed's respect.

'All right then. She cost $52,000. Let's add her training fees and so on. If you like, I'll calculate every penny spent on her throughout her career, and we'll make a balance sheet. On the one side her winnings, on the other side her costs. I guarantee you she'll make at least double what she cost. If she doesn't, I'll make up the difference from my own pocket.'

The crown prince wasn't impressed. 'Do you think I go to all this bother just to double my money on what you consider to be a star horse? I am disappointed in you. Nor do I want any money out of your pocket if the horse doesn't deliver. If she doesn't win at least the Oaks, then I'm afraid that'll be the end of the road for you and me.'

Christy nodded into the mouthpiece. 'Fair enough.' He had already decided to ensure the filly would do more than that. It would have to be the Triple Crown or nothing now as far as he was concerned.

* * *

During the winter of 1978-9, Christy often drove up to Dublin in an ageing Mark 10 Jaguar which he'd bought as a twenty-ninth birthday present to himself. In Ireland's capital city, he would look in on Sally Murphy. Other times, he would motor down to Cork, Ireland's second city, for the company of Maeve O'Sullivan.

Sally had long black hair and a degree in anthropology from Trinity College. She would concoct French dinners for Christy, heavy in garlic or wine, put Chopin on the stereo and get into candlelit baths with him.

Maeve was chestnut-haired and hazel-eyed, a fisherman's daughter. She matched Christy glass for glass in Guinness-drinking binges in the Cobh waterside pubs. Drunk as two hogs, they'd then go back to her place and rut on her sheepskin rug.

Both girls would hint in the early morning hours to the tall and square-shouldered horse trainer that he should think of settling down. Wasn't thirty the age when a man should take life more seriously, have a family?

Christy's brown eyes would twinkle. He would say 'Ah, Sally, (or Ah Maeve,) my sweet, just call me the cod. C. O. D. It stands for Christy O'Donnell, see now? And don't try to lumber me with a codpiece!'

Then he would silence their protests with his irresistible combination of rough kisses and gentle caresses under the eiderdown. When he was finished, he would hurry back to Twelve Pins and Desert Princess, the only 2-year-old in the British Isles which had remained unbeaten the previous season.

Approaching the final furlong marker, he judged the moment, squeezed the horse's flanks with his thighs, and thrashed the reins downwards crying: *'Haeeeyah!'*

The glossy brown filly responded with furious delight. Lowering her head, straining the blue bridle to near-bursting point, she surged forward. The racetrack thundered by in a blur beneath her hooves and she flashed past the reflector on the winning post.

It was May 1979. The afternoon sky over Suffolk was cloudless. Britain was enjoying fine late spring weather and the temperature was in the mid-70s Fahrenheit.

A group of men were clustered under parasols by the parade ring at Newmarket racecourse. They watched Christy wheel Desert Princess around in their direction. He drew her up by Crown Prince Ahmed's table, savouring the salt taste of blood in his mouth.

'Excuse me Mr Winchester,' Ahmed said to the man with the long pinched nose sitting next to him. On the table was a manila file and documents which he'd been examining. Karim Jamal, Ahmed's financial adviser, was still looking at a copy with interest. The crown prince addressed Christy with a broad grin, his teeth great white clackers in his hatchet face. 'Brilliant. Why don't you ride her on Thursday yourself?' In spite of the grin, his tone was half-serious.

'Oh, it's the weather, not me,' Christy laughed, patting the filly's sweating shank. 'She loves a firm going, just like her sire. You'll see, with Scobie on her on Thursday, she'll murder the opposition.'

Ahmed saw her prospects in a different light. 'She is capable. Oh yes, she is capable. Only $52,000, but if she wins the Triple Crown, you will not be able to count all the bonuses I will give you! *And* ... ' His eyes shining, he raised a forefinger skyward. ' ... And, Sheikh O'Donnell, I will pay your tax for the year! The world will be yours!'

Christy grinned. He knew that the three Classics the filly was entered for had prize money totalling £350,000. Ten per cent of that would mean £35,000 for him. Then Desert Princess was entered for other races, not classics, but again with huge prize money, like the King George VI and Queen Elizabeth Diamond Stakes at Ascot and the York Gold Cup. On top of that he had other top horses running in the crown prince's and William Lemon's colours at other meetings....

His tally before this season was already £97,000, and his income base had been in a constant state of expansion. He'd increased his training fees, had got better at selling shares in successful racehorses to syndicates, and he demanded higher prices for stallion coverings. Taking his percentage from all these activities as well as from average winnings by September, he should pass the £130,000 mark. If he could pull off the Triple Crown and some other events, his total could be in the region of £170,000. And that was not to mention the additional bonuses Ahmed had talked about.

Plus the crown prince would be picking up the taxes.

Donald Smitherson had told him a couple of weeks earlier

that Castle Kirkpatrick was worth around £200,000 at current market values....

'Let's just worry about the 1,000 Guineas on Thursday for now, your Royal Highness,' he said.

He had to stay calm, keep his wits about him. So much was riding on the Princess.

19.5.79

The Scimitar Club was quiet that evening, which was just as well.

'Ahmed wouldn't bite either,' Winchester said.

'But why not?'

'He was keen when I told him the general idea, but when we got down to the specifics, he said I'd have to talk it over with his Lebanese adviser. Now this chap was something else; he understood all about how the futures markets function, but seemed not to want to grasp the fine details of my scheme. It might just have been a problem of language....'

'Get an interpreter tomorrow!' Greville barked.

Winchester chose his words carefully. 'No, I think that wasn't the problem really. This Jamal character said that, before we could even begin to talk turkey, I was to supply him with some 'fanny'. Well, I told him that an organization such as the Duke of Marylebone's was hardly likely to have links with prostitutes....'

Greville was livid. 'You bloody fool! Why didn't you just procure whatever the man wanted and take it out of petty cash?'

'Well, I'm afraid I said I couldn't. And he just walked out on me.'

'I'm not ruddy well surprised! You'd better contact him again straight away and tell him that whatever he wants in the "fanny" line can be made available.'

At around 9.30 Greville went across to the dining room for some supper. He was still glowering over Winchester's dim-wittedness.

At one of the tables in the Scimitar's lavish dining room was Roger Wellington, attacking a tray of pink matter. Greville knew that Wellington did a lot of business with Arabs. Approaching, he saw that the platter which the fellow was munching happily from was heaped with king prawns.

Wellington waved Greville to the seat opposite and asked him about his daughter Deborah; they were members of the same trekking club, and they'd been up to Scotland a couple of times together.

Greville mouthed things about her forthcoming divorce, her children and so on. Then he said, 'You're a chap who ought to have an answer to this, Roger: how does one win a business contract with an Arab royal?'

Wellington stuffed a suitably majestic prawn in his mouth. 'A business contract with a top Arab, eh? Well, the Arabs in general are unpredictable buggers. Fickle, some say. My definition is: "volatile". Their approach to business matters is quite unlike yours or mine. F'rinstance, when you talk to the princes and sheikhs about money, you *mustn't* present them with hard data straight away. They just freeze. Most of those I deal with don't know which way up to hold a balance sheet. They've either all got Lebanese advisers or they let characters from a tribe called the "Hadhrumis" – who have a special art with numbers – look after their financial dealings. The essential thing about your Arab is that, when it comes to doing business, he'll go by his gut reaction. Basically, if he likes you, if he can think of you as a friend, he'll go along with you. Then there'll be no holding him back. It's really as simple as that. But, whatever you do, don't fall out with him once you're in. He'll turn on you like a rat if he feels you've let him down. Now, if you haven't eaten yet, I can recommend the prawns.'

Winchester, who could act swifter than an arrow from the Tartar's bow when the need arose, provided a turnkey titillation package for Karim Jamal that same evening which the Lebanese found highly satisfactory. This consisted of the company of a gorgeous young woman from an escort agency for however long she was desired, a cabaret dinner for two, then "whatever".

Winchester clapped his eyes on the gorgeous young woman the next morning in Jamal's suite in the Dorchester Hotel. Blond, tall, with beautifully proud breasts filling her shirt, and lovely thighs moulding her leather trousers, she gave Jamal a longing kiss and departed.

'Well,' Winchester said hopefully, watching the door shut behind her. 'Well, what about our silver business now?'

Jamal, still aglow from his experience, grinned. 'She was called Daphne.'

'Daphne?' Winchester remembered a lady he'd gone out with who had the same name.

'Yes, and I want to thank you for your excellent choice,' added Jamal. 'But you can't seriously think that I can be bribed into investing 1 billion dollars because of one night of sex, can you?'

The Lebanese added that it had been non-stop, wickedly satisfying, and invited Winchester to Beirut so that the compliment could be returned. Shortly after, he flew off to that Levantine city on urgent business.

James Greville shook his head with frustration at hearing the sorry conclusion. He was at a total loss as to how else he could go about getting the billion from Crown Prince Ahmed, or anyone else for that matter.

September 1979

The St Leger line-up was not strong. Sceptics said that better horses had been withdrawn from the race because Crown Prince Ahmed's hirelings had gone around doing a bit of bribing. They claimed that after the arduous season Desert Princess had had, Ahmed wanted weak opposition to ensure he won this last Classic of the season, and the Triple Crown with it.

There were others who recognized her supreme qualities and who made big bets on her winning this race purely on merit. She'd performed brilliantly all year. Back in May, the odds against Desert Princess taking the coveted Crown were 500 to 1 against. One punter had had a rush of blood to the head and staked £10,000. He would be richer by £5 million if the filly won today's St Leger....

When she was led into the winner's enclosure after the race, Ahmed clapped her on her shank, clapped jockey Scobie Flynn on the back, clapped head lad Matthew O'Brien on the shoulder and clapped all the stable lads all over their bodies. Iqbal followed with a cheque-book and wrote out bonus cheques ranging from £500 to £10,000 in accordance with how hard the team members' anatomies had been clapped.

While the secretary performed this solemn duty, Ahmed took Christy out alone to the car park. The crown prince's voice quivered with emotion. 'Oh, Sheikh O'Donnell, you really have reached the top of your tree. Isn't that how they say it here?'

'Something like that.' In a bit of a daze, he waited to see what extra bonus Ahmed had in mind.

The crown prince took a deep breath. 'You have given me what I demanded two years ago. So, you deserve a small token of my gratitude.'

Christy's mind screamed, *How small?!*

'I hope, Sheikh O'Donnell, you will not be offended by an award of One Hundred Thousand Pounds?' Ahmed actually said those last four words in capital letters.

23.9.79

Greville was thankful the telex machine would stay silent that day. He didn't need to be reminded that spot silver still languished in the $5.95–$6.05 range as it had done since May.

Milton Diamond brought the Sunday papers into the ballroom in mid-morning, and Greville first opened the *Sunday Times* to the racing pages. It was his token way of keeping in touch with Eden Grange. When he first glanced at the article, he didn't take much notice of it. Only after he had put the paper aside and picked up the *News of the World* did it dawn on him there was something in the *Sunday Times* he should look at again. This was the article:

Saturday 22 September

ST LEGER TRIUMPH FOR DESERT PRINCESS

Versatility is the key requirement for landing the Triple Crown.

Very few horses are capable of winning top-class races from a mile to almost twice that distance in the span of a single season so Desert Princess's achievement in becoming the first filly since Meld (1955) to triumph in the 1,000 Guineas, Oaks and St Leger cannot be over estimated. Unfortunately for Desert Princess, the Maharajah of Bhojalpur's crack filly Miss Fortune II carried off Racehorse of the Year honours as a result of a brilliant run in prestigious international events. Desert Princess, however, was certainly the Classic queen.

Trainer Christy O'Donnell is Champion Trainer for 1979 and Crown Prince Ahmed ibn Talal Aziz is the Leading Owner. Prize money for the crown prince so far this year totals £843,927.

Christy O'Donnell's rise to the top honour is noteworthy. Starting life as a hand at the Greville family's Newbridge stable, he was assistant trainer at the time of King Midas's Derby win in 1968. He went on to join the Maharajah of Bhojalpur, with whom he enjoyed superb success. Now he has achieved a Triple Crown. Aged only thirty one, his future as a top trainer looks assured for many years to come....

Greville looked up and folded the paper. Fresh clean springs of thought flowed through his brain. He remembered the Irishman working for him under Byrne and doing the spade work with King Midas. And he had heard, naturally enough, about O'Donnell joining Crown Prince Ahmed. But he had never thought to make the obvious connection before.

Roger Wellington's words at the club all those months ago returned to him now:

When it comes to doing business, your Arab will go by his gut reaction ... if he likes you, if he can think of you as a friend, he'll go along with you. Then there'll be no holding him back. It's really as simple as that.

Greville was sure there was one person whom the crown prince would like, and would think of as a friend....

Perhaps, just perhaps ... He buzzed the Sunday auxiliary assistant. 'Get me a number in Ireland, Miss Singh, will you?'

23 September 1979

Christy O'Donnell eased his foot off the accelerator. He would be by the spot in a few seconds. Rain slanted down in great sheets across the windscreen of his old blue Jaguar and the wipers struggled to cope. He rounded the final bend and let the car come to a standstill. A quarter of a mile further along Leprechaun's Finger, at the cliff edge, the road fanned out into a car park with scenic views over the rolling pasture lands of County Tipperary.

The first thing to do would be to get rid of that bloody car park. No! That would be the second ... The first would be to move his mother's body to the grounds of her own castle. He got out of the car and gazed beyond the dripping green embankment. The spot was still there. Of course it was. It had to be. You couldn't take a place away!

The spot was a gentle dimple in the terrain a hundred yards from where he stood. The grass there was tinged with yellow, and sheltered from the gusty westerlies by a row of tall beeches. Today they were swaying in the wind, away from the castle, back towards the cliff edge.

Christy looked beyond to Castle Kirkpatrick rising baronially into the leaden sky. His heart raced. £200,000. That was its market value, and he had more than £300,000. Even if Kirkpatrick wanted more than it was worth ... even allowing for the stable and training facilities ... he just had to have enough now.

He gunned the Jaguar's engine into life and drove along to the car park. Here he circled his machine round before heading back down the road. His brown eyes remained on the castle, welded to it by dazzling fires.

Seamus Kirkpatrick was a small man with an over-sized face and thick puce-coloured veins in his neck which throbbed constantly. He had the eyes of a toad.

The castle had become a Kirkpatrick possession through

marriage many generations earlier, but, too expensive to maintain and its lands too demanding to farm, it had been left abandoned for the best part of a century. It became a popular site for succeeding bands of gypsies until, in 1949, its current owner drove the undesirables out once and for all. An entrepreneur to his core, Seamus Kirkpatrick realized the money-spinning potential he had in his hands given the increasingly numerous and affluent Americans who came every year to Erin's shores in search of their origins.

Under the caption 'DISCOVER YOUR ROOTS', Kirkpatrick advertised the castle for weekend, weekly and monthly lets in classified ads across the USA: from small ads in the obscure *Seattle Examiner* to even smaller ads in the more widely circulated *New York Times*. His income rose into thousands of pounds every year.

When Donald Smitherson telephoned him at his Dublin flat on 22 September to say that someone working with an Arab oil sheik was interested in buying his castle, the veins in his neck throbbed vigorously.

'Arabs is it?' Kirkpatrick leered.

'I've been doing work for an Arab, aye,' Christy replied.

They stood in front of the great stone fireplace in the banqueting room. Like many of the rooms in the castle, it was high-vaulted, massive and draughty. Christy knew he'd have his work cut out over long years to make the place really comfortable. But none of that mattered just now. All he wanted was possession of the castle. Immediately.

'Tell me lad, how much are they prepared to pay for this then?' Kirkpatrick stared at him closely.

'You tell me, how much do you want for it?'

Kirkpatrick didn't hear the question. 'If we can get them to pay their topmost figure, I'll put a couple of hundred pounds aside for you, I promise. So, how much can they afford?' His toad-like eyes bulged with greed.

Christy said patiently, 'It's not for the Arabs, Mr Kirkpatrick. It's for me.'

Now Kirkpatrick's expression turned sly and knowing. 'Loyal type, are you? Not wanting your masters to pay too much, eh?'

'The castle is for me,' Christy repeated. 'How much would you be wanting for it?'

The veins in Kirkpatrick's neck thickened and pulsed at such a rate that Christy was sure they'd burst. 'Siding with the bloody Arabs instead of your own folk, eh? They pay you a lot, do they? Want to buy up Ireland do they, like they've done the other side of the water?' His voice rose to a shriek. 'Well they'll not do it here! Not cheap, that is! You can tell your Arab masters that if they want the most beautiful castle in Ireland, I'll not take a penny less than a million pounds!'

That man is mad! Christy thought furiously, as he steered the Jaguar back through the blinding rain in the direction of Twelve Pins. Completely bloody bonkers. A million pounds? Anyone could buy 10,000 acres with that kind of money *and* build a castle five times the size of Kirkpatrick's Folly. Aye, Christy now understood why the locals had named the place 'Folly'. The fool didn't realize how easy it was for him to buy another castle with his £300,000.

But, his mind screamed, *I don't want any other castle!*

Then he reasoned with himself, maybe, just maybe, if he left the matter alone for some time, then went back to Kirkpatrick with an improved offer, the man might see sense?

He shook his head. It would take some doing to get that bastard old toad to see sense.

The rain hammered down and he remained confused about what best to do now. When he reached Twelve Pins, he parked the Jaguar and hurried through the rain into the homestead.

As he took his coat off in the hall, the phone rang.

'You probably won't remember me, Christy, but you knew me well enough once,' the voice said.

'Who is this?' Christy replied. There was something familiar about that voice. Distantly, distantly familiar. But he couldn't place it. The accent was slurred. Irish.

'I thought you wouldn't recognize me, Kit. It's your da. It's Stephen O'Donnell.'

Christy was numb with shock and couldn't answer.

The voice continued, 'I've been reading all about you in the papers again, see now. I've been following your progress ... I wanted to tell you I'm proud of you, son....' The voice faltered, 'I heard about your Ma too ... my poor Molly....'

Christy was still struck speechless, his heart welling up and ready to burst. This was the man whom he had always believed was an enemy. And now, here he was, on the phone, his own father, and Christy couldn't think of a word to say.

And still the man continued, 'I was hoping maybe I could

meet you, son, but I know you'd be ashamed of your da ... I wasn't a very good father, was I, lad?'

Nor a good husband to my ma! Christy wanted to yell. But what was the good of that now? Would it bring her back?

After a couple of seconds of silence, which felt interminable, Stephen O'Donnell said, 'I thought so, I thought you wouldn't want to meet your old da now.' There was a click and the phone went dead.

'No wait, da!' Christy shouted. But it was too late. And, even if he came back on the line, Christy knew that the long strung-out years they'd spent apart – twenty-seven of them – would weigh too heavily on him again. He put the phone down.

It immediately rang again. Christy stared at it, frightened. The telephone bell pealed and pealed. Courage began to grow in him. What did he have to fear? he ultimately asked himself. He'd let it ring one more time, he decided, then he'd answer it. But the ringing stopped. There was a lump in Christy's throat so big now that he had to have a drink. As he turned to walk to the kitchen, the phone started to ring again.

He raced back and grabbed up the handset.

'Is that Mr Christy O'Donnell?' a woman's voice said. She had the brisk efficiency of a telephone operator.

'Yes, yes it is.'

'Will you hold the line please. I have a call for you.'

Another voice came on the line, a man's. 'Christy you probably won't remember me, but you once used to work for me. This is James Greville, the Duke of Marylebone.'

'Oh yes, of course I remember you, Lord James, I mean, your Grace,' he mumbled, trying to pull thought and emotion back together.

'Look, Christy, I don't want to beat about the bush, and anyway I can't go into any details on the phone. What I want to know is, how would you like to earn a million pounds?'

Book Two

23.9.79

Pat Fogarty sat at the corner table of the Dublin pub, staring at a glass of stout. Cloth cap on his head, toothless mouth working as if he was chewing the cud, old Pat was calculating: he'd made the first half pint last over forty minutes by the bar clock, and he'd try to make the second take an hour if he could.

A human shadow fell across his glass and he looked up. His toothless face lit up in an instinctive smile. Stephen O'Donnell, body bowed, his hair lifeless and grey, sat down next to him. Pat shook his head sadly. 'Not tonight.' His words were poorly articulated. 'Not even for your filly. But you could try Percy Phelan. He made a right packet on that horse in the English St Leger.'

'Percy?'

'That's him. He went down to the Crown some while ago.'

Stephen O'Donnell got up and trudged towards the door, his grease-splotched trousers too long for him and making crumpled folds at the ankles.

24.9.79

I

That Simon Winchester was unhappy was plain to see. 'But why a horse trainer of all people?' 'Horse' was emphasized with some venom.

'I don't care if he's a horse trainer, a circus acrobat or a professor of Swahili. There can't be anyone in the British Isles whom Crown Prince Ahmed would like more than him just now.'

Both Greville and his comptroller sat at their Chippendale desks, waiting for the Irishman. The duke fingered the replica of the Derby trophy they'd won back in 1968, the little silver horse with a golden globe on its back. He'd had it brought out of the trophy cabinet in the Great Hall.

The ballroom was filled with the Platters singing:

' ... Only you ... '
' ... Can make this change in me ... '
' ... For it's true ... '
' ... You are my destiny ... '

'No horse trainer can be capable of getting silver out of this hole.' Today spot silver stood at its lowest that year. $5.88.

'One billion dollars will get the price up. Crown Prince Ahmed's got 1 billion dollars. And O'Donnell's the key to our getting hold of that money.'

'I can't imagine anyone parting with a billion dollars because some horse has won a race or two.'

Greville stared knowingly at his comptroller. 'You don't understand their psychology. Your disastrous handling of Jamal back in May proves that. All you've got to do today is what you're good at: explain the whole thing. Then we'll just have to hope he takes the bait.'

Traffic was heavy that Monday morning on the M4. During the long taxi ride from Heathrow, Christy had a great deal to reflect upon.

A million pounds.....

So that was how much the madman wanted for the castle, the castle he had worked for since 1963, and which should by rights have been his yesterday....

Then, his da ... His da suddenly coming forth from the dead like Lazarus. Not that anything would bring his ma back from the dead again, even though he had wanted her out of that sorry grave ever since she'd gone there. Sixteen years she'd lain in Killertoon churchyard, and not a peep from his da in all that time, even though he'd admitted yesterday that he'd heard of her fate.... It was, of course, the money Christy now had, he understood, which had brought his da out into the open....

The taxi came on to Knightsbridge. The driver quipped, 'You'd need a couple of bob in your pocket to go shopping around here, wouldn't you guv?'

'Yeah, looks like you would.' Christy took in the swanky stores, the great yellow-bricked façade of Harrods, the handsome cars crawling alongside them. The intriguing question filled his mind yet again: *What the bloody hell could the duke want him to do for a million pounds?*

Milton Diamond opened the double doors into the ballroom at Marylebone House, and Christy took in the blue ceiling with cherubs cavorting about amidst the stars, the heavy crystal chandeliers, the lattice windows in the opposite wall.

He sensed the tension inside the place as he followed the butler in.

'Christy!' boomed James Greville, rising from his desk and coming across to him as if he was Jesus bringing loaves and fishes. There was another man seated at the other desk, staring at him with hostility. Christy couldn't understand why.

'Your Grace.' He shook Greville's hand. The duke's hair was whiter than he remembered, the blotches on the face darker and more spread.

'Not too bumpy a flight from Dublin, I hope?'

Christy laughed. 'Oh, it was all right. In any case, you got me so excited I wouldn't have minded if there had been a bit of turbulence.'

'Come and meet Simon Winchester.'

They crossed the ballroom, Christy taking in the rich smell of leather, the trees out in Marylebone Park beyond the tall windows, their leaves turning brown. 'Beautiful place, your Grace. Beautiful view.'

Greville nodded. 'True.' He wanted to get on with it. 'Now, this is Simon, our local financial wizard.'

Behind Winchester, a message chattered up on the telex. Half-rising, he held out a reluctant hand and Christy shook it across the desk. 'Pleased to meet you.' The face was familiar, he realized. 'And haven't I seen you before?'

The comptroller turned to get the telex message, muttering, 'Our paths crossed briefly at Newmarket in May.'

What was bothering the man? wondered Christy. 'Oh aye, that's right.' He remembered those tiny eyes now. 'It was at the time of the 1,000 Guineas, wasn't it? You came to meet Crown Prince Ahmed and Mr Jamal. In the parade ring, under the parasols, wasn't it?'

Winchester gave a brisk nod and sat again, studying the message with a certain degree of concentration. He couldn't have made it clearer that the last thing which interested him was friendly chit-chat with Christy.

'Remember this, Christy?' The duke held aloft the Derby trophy, trying to get the mood upbeat.

Christy gazed at it. 'How could I ever forget, your Grace?'

Greville grinned, 'Brendan Byrne did a marvellous job that day. And he was helped a lot by you, I seem to remember.'

'Quite a lot I'd say,' he chuckled, remembering the tongue strap, aware that Greville would never know who was really behind the victory. 'It was a marvellous day for you and the old duke and all the family, wasn't it, your Grace?'

'Indeed.' The duke cleared his throat. He'd got the preliminaries over with. 'Well, I know Simon's bursting to explain a thing or two to you. Make yourself comfortable.' He gestured at the button-backed wing chair he'd had placed opposite Winchester's desk for this meeting.

Christy sat down. 'I expect this'll concern the million pounds you mentioned?'

'Absolutely. Fire away Simon.'

Winchester continued to be interested in his telex message for several more seconds. Then he looked up and scanned Christy's face, despising him, not having forgotten the confidently intelligent manner in which the Irishman had chatted from the saddle of a horse with the crown prince at Newmarket. 'You're a trainer of thoroughbred racehorses, I believe?' he muttered.

'I am.'

'Well, it's unlikely you'll be familiar with what I've got to explain, but I expect you'll do your best to follow. You've no doubt had a university education?'

Christy said, 'I left school when I was fourteen.'

'Oh?' Winchester looked quizzically at the duke. 'I'd assumed he'd have *some* education.'

Greville growled, 'Is all this necessary? Just tell him what we want him to do.'

Christy interjected helpfully, 'I suppose you've called me in to talk about business? So rest assured that I've got a fair amount of background knowledge in that.'

Winchester faced him again. 'I'd hardly call training horses a business. Closer, perhaps, to what a blacksmith or shepherd would do?'

Christy said easily, 'I didn't say training horses was a business, Mr Winchester, but buying, selling and syndicating shares in horses is. I have to deal with bloodstock traders and brokers all the time. Some even have offices in the City of London and on Wall Street....'

'I've heard of those characters,' Winchester interrupted. 'Hardly reputable.'

Christy retained his easy manner, though he continued to wonder why this fellow was so determined to give him a rough ride. 'You're probably a bit prejudiced, Mr Winchester, and getting some fine folk mixed up with shady bookies or something. The people I'm talking about represent the owners of racehorses. You probably know that all kinds of royalty and celebrities from around the world are racehorse owners? That top thoroughbreds are worth millions of pounds? Maybe your business – it's silver dealing, I seem to remember – is more successful ... I wouldn't know. But don't fool yourself that top-level training is only something to do with blacksmiths and shepherds.'

'Well said!' exclaimed Greville.

Winchester cleared his throat. 'But trainers aren't the same as the celebrities they work for, are they? I mean, there's just so much sleaze about the whole thing. Aren't they compulsive gamblers, always backing their own horses? Don't they get involved with all the doping and fixing of races and so on which goes on? I notice you cleverly avoid talking about all that when you describe your "business", as you call it.'

Now Christy felt his annoyance begin to rise at this piggy-eyed man's relentless denunciations. 'I had no idea I was called here to London to justify the world of horse racing. All I can say is that not everything which goes on in any field, including racing, is as pure as driven snow. But that doesn't mean that every trainer is bent, nor that we all gamble. Some of us are more prudent than you would probably imagine, and there are even those like myself who invest in property rather than in more dicey things like stocks and shares, or even silver.'

'A man after your own heart, Winchester!' exclaimed the duke.

The man with the pinched nose, lost for words, looked away and folded his arms.

Greville said, 'Come on, Simon. Stop irritating our Irish friend and tell him why we got him all the way out here.'

Winchester grudgingly took a manila file out of his desk drawer. 'I object to letting all and sundry in on something so important and delicate.' He nudged this half-heartedly across the desk toward Christy's side, making it painfully obvious he didn't want it to go any further if he could help it. 'It's all down in this, but I expect you might need some help in understanding it.'

Christy stared at the file without touching it. 'Before I look at it, I'd just like you to tell me briefly what it's all about.'

Winchester appeared not to have heard him. 'As you seem to know, we've invested in silver. Rather heavily, in fact.' He cast a quick, damning glance at Greville. 'The problem is, the silver price remains far too low. In this file is our scheme to get it to rise. To make that happen, we need the involvement of an outside party. You have been called in because you work for the Crown Prince Ahmed of the Hejaz.'

Christy nodded. 'And what is it that you'd want him to do?'

Winchester said, 'Put up a billion dollars.'

Greville said: 'We'd like *you* to be the one to put the proposition to him, you see.'

Christy laughed, 'You must be joking if you think that he'll put up that kind of money just on my asking him to. I mean, I'm only his horse trainer.'

Winchester smiled thinly across at the duke. 'I told you this character would be a waste of time.'

II

'He likes you,' Greville said. 'That's what's so important. Arabs do business with people they like, I'm told.'

Christy nodded briskly without looking at him. He'd opened the file and was scanning its contents hungrily. It all looked very complicated. The language used in the commodity and futures trading world is pretty quaint.

Winchester said, 'The crown prince may like him, but I would have thought it would have helped if our Irish friend had at least one 'O' Level.'

Christy looked up at the comptroller. 'I suppose this was the same thing you were talking about with Ahmed at Newmarket?'

'Yes. But unfortunately there was a problem with his adviser Jamal....'

Christy nodded. He knew Karim Jamal was very shrewd. 'The crown prince probably hasn't got that kind of money.'

Greville said, 'Oh, but he has. You probably wouldn't even know it, but he's richer than you'd ever imagine. Simon researched it all before approaching him. He's worth over $6 billion.'

'Never!' said Christy, wide-eyed.

Winchester rose to the challenge. 'What you and most of the general public just don't realize is the amount of funny money that there is out there in the real world. I mean, everybody knows oil sheikhs are rich. But so few people have a clue about just how sundry individuals in the oil-producing countries actually get their personal hands on the national treasure. Let's take your Crown Prince Ahmed as a specific example. As a member of the royal family of the House of Jayed, he has an annual stipend of $2 million. Then, as Minister of the Interior, he receives a further 3 million. Five million dollars a year in total officially. Nice work if you can get it, naturally, but, in today's world, as you pointed out earlier, that'll barely get you one champion thoroughbred....'

Christy nodded. He didn't further point out that Desert Princess cost only $52,000.

The comptroller went on: 'His *real* income is derived from the perks of being the Interior Minister. Kickbacks and "gifts" on an unimaginable scale pour into his lap from construction and engineering companies eager to secure and retain contracts in the Hejaz. Remember, the country is the world's second biggest oil producer and has embarked on a huge programme of modernization. Now, it's normal practice in the Middle East for any contractor making a tender to put a down payment – all hush-hush, of course, and going into numbered Swiss accounts – of two to five per cent of any proposed contract. The contracts themselves can be worth anything from a hundred million to five billion dollars. There are often a dozen tenders for any one project. I know for a fact that the recent Al Aksum dam contract went for $1.2 billion, and that there were ten tenders. Now, if we do some sums....'

Christy had already worked it out. 'So about four hundred and twenty million dollars went into his pocket from just that one deal alone, is that what you're trying to say?'

Winchester nodded, surprised at the Irishman's mental arithmetic facility. 'Yes, if we took an average down-payment of three and a half per cent, then that's the sort of figure we'd be talking about.'

Greville laughed, 'Just a horse trainer, eh, Simon?'

Winchester ignored his boss. 'Now, we know he's got at least three billion dollars in cash alone, which he's stashed away in banks in Switzerland, the Channel Islands, the Caribbean. Then he's got stocks, bonds, real estate, works of art and so on in the USA and Western Europe....' He grinned wryly, 'And, of course, racehorses. Well, all that's worth between two and two point five billion more. Add to that whatever he's got in the Hejaz itself, of which we're short of exact details, though I've pieced together published facts and things that private informants have told us and come up with an estimate in excess of one and a quarter billion dollars. So, his total wealth adds up to around six-and-a-half billion dollars.'

'Simon's very thorough,' said Greville.

'I knew he was rich,' commented Christy. 'But not that rich.'

Greville said: 'Quite. So before we discuss it any further, it's probably a good idea for you to take a close look at Simon's plan, don't you think?'

The blueprint ran to seventy pages of intense detail, but it was well written and not over-hard to follow once Christy got over the hurdle of some of the technical words.

He went over it a couple of times in the House library where Greville deposited him, realizing that Winchester may be a condescending know-it-all but he obviously knew his stuff and was very thorough. Towards the end of his second reading, Christy began to realize that, though it was all in an alien field and had more noughts than he was used to, some of the tricks Winchester had thought up were really no different from what bloodstock owners did to get a horse's price raised at an auction. But the fine details of exactly what went on in the world of silver dealing were nevertheless clearly very important.

Christy eventually put the blueprint back in its manila file and rose from the library table. For a million pounds, he'd certainly try this thing out on Ahmed. But he knew he'd have to understand it all properly, and then go and see the crown prince in person in the Hejaz. He couldn't talk to him about it by telephone, and Ahmed wouldn't be in Britain again now until the next flat season several months away.

A valet named Hutton was waiting for Christy outside the library door. The valet had instructions to call Mrs Thorpe from an internal telephone in the corridor as soon as the Irishman emerged from his reading. Hutton did this, completing his conversation with the duke's secretary with a: 'Very good, Mrs Thorpe.' Then he said to Christy, 'Will you follow me, sir?'

He led the way along a different corridor and down a flight of stairs into the basement area.

'Well I'm not sure, James,' Elizabeth said on the telephone. Greville had called her immediately after leaving Christy alone in the library.

The duke said nicely, 'It'll only take you three hours to get here. That's ample time. The show doesn't start until eight. I've booked a box. It would be rather sad if I listened to Pavarotti in a box all by myself at Covent Garden, wouldn't it, old girl?' He hadn't called her 'old girl' for years. But Winchester wasn't here in the ballroom. The comptroller had gone off to the City, needing to 'mingle with people who perform a useful service to the country's economy,' he had said.

Elizabeth sighed, 'Well, all right. I'll leave in a couple of hours. I should be with you by six. I'll have to stay down at the House tonight, of course.'

'Of course.' Greville looked forward to that. If she thought he wanted her here just so that he could get hold of Greville International's assets, she'd soon be stripped of her illusions.

The Banham strong room was in the basement.

Greville was in the process of turning the last of the combination wheels on its steel door as Christy arrived. 'Got something to show you,' he grinned. He unlocked the door at the top and at the bottom with a very long key and pulled its handle with both hands. The foot-thick door glided open with a hiss.

Greville switched on the interior light and entered the shining steel room. He beckoned at Christy to follow. The safe was sixteen feet deep and eight feet wide. Set into its sides were lockers with keyholes.

Greville opened one at random and drew out some sheets of paper. 'This is what the whole thing's about,' he said, handing them to Christy to look at. They were silver warrants from the London Minerals Board. Each warrant was for one 'lot', or 5,000 ounces, of silver, and these documents were the titles of ownership. 'The boxes are filled with them.' Greville waved around at them. 'I've got 80 million ounces, you know.'

Christy nodded. He knew. He'd read the blueprint.

Greville grinned. 'You're probably more interested in this.' He went to the far end of the strong room, where a burgundy suitcase sat on a low metal table. He snapped off the catches and raised the lid. Christy stared at the contents, mesmerized. He'd helped the Maharajah of Bhojalpur pack a million in a suitcase, but that hadn't been the same. It hadn't been for him.

'It's all here,' Greville said. 'Count it if you like.' He stood aside.

Christy came up and riffled quickly through the money. It was in bundles of one hundred crisp twenty pound notes secured by white stickers bearing the legend: *'BARCLAYS BANK LTD. TWO THOUSAND POUNDS.'* The bundles were stacked neatly across the case in five rows of five, and Christy counted that they went down twenty bundles deep.

Short of checking every single note – and there would have to be 50,000 notes, he realized – it had to be all here. One million pounds.

He turned to look at the duke. 'I'm convinced.'

'Thought you'd be.'

They went back up to the ballroom. Winchester hadn't got back yet.

'Well,' said Greville, 'do you think you'll be able to persuade the Arab now?'

Christy chose his word carefully. 'No.'

'What?' barked the duke.

'The problem is Jamal, your Grace. He's very shrewd.'

'But I'm told that doesn't matter. If Ahmed likes you, that's enough. These oil sheikhs are volatile, fickle. They go by gut reactions, not logic.'

Christy smiled. 'It's pretty likely that Ahmed *does* feel well disposed towards me just now because of our success with Desert Princess. But that alone wouldn't be enough for him to part with $1 billion, no matter what anyone's told you. It's a lot of money, your Grace, and he'll want the whole thing properly checked out. The man who'd do that would be Jamal.'

Greville scowled. He remembered last May's 'fanny' episode.

'But Jamal's not a fool either,' Christy said reassuringly. 'If a profit of $2 billion can be made, as Winchester claims, then Jamal will want to make it. There will be at least ten per cent in it for him, don't forget.'

Greville nodded. 'All right then. Just remind him of that, and we'll be all right.'

Christy wasn't to be hastened along faster than he wanted to go. 'There are two conditions I'll need fulfilled before I go any further with this.'

'And what are they?' Greville said impatiently.

'The first thing is, I need to study all the details very closely. I want to visit the London Minerals Board warehouses and trading floor, read up everything I can on the subject, etcetera. In short, I need to go over everything with a fine tooth comb because I know Jamal will bombard me with five hundred questions. I want to be able to answer every one.'

'We're short of time if we want to hit the December contract in Chicago,' Greville said. 'But a couple of days lost won't matter, I suppose.'

'I'll need at least a month.'

'But that's far too long!'

'My second condition,' Christy said calmly, 'is that you give me half a million pounds now, in advance.'

Greville growled, 'I'll give you 20,000 in advance, no more. The rest only if this chap puts up the billion dollars. They're very fickle, you know, these Arabs.'

They talked for several minutes and eventually agreed that Christy could have a maximum of two weeks to study the scheme closely, because after that they'd simply be too late. Greville proposed that, in order to save time, Christy stay in one of the guest flats at the House, with a car provided, and that he was to go to Harrods that afternoon and buy whatever clothing he needed during his stay, on Greville's account. On the money front, Christy agreed to an advance of £100,000, and not five, to be kept by him whether or not the crown prince joined in.

The sum was handed over after they had lunched. Christy drove down in the Mercedes provided by the duke to his bank, Wardle Spyers & Co in Threadneedle Street, where William Lemon put it in his account. Then he went to Harrods and selected a couple of jackets, some shirts, trousers, underclothes and shoes. The accounts department there had already been rung up by Mrs Thorpe, and all Christy had to do was sign the bills. When the valet Hutton showed him up to his luxurious self-contained third-floor flat back at Marylebone House, he felt like a king. Success breeds success, he reflected.

Before he went back down to the ballroom, he called his head lad at Twelve Pins, Matthew O'Brien, and told him to take care of things until he got back, which should be within the next two to three weeks.

'Well now, we'll be fine here, Christy,' O'Brien reassured him. 'We'll start working the yearlings and get on with the painting of the boxes. If there's any problem with any of the horses, I'll call you, don't you worry, now.'

27.9.79

In the dark barn, Stephen O'Donnell scooped the pulpy, foul-smelling droppings into the filly's two drinking buckets. These he emptied in the stream which ran behind the burned-out farmhouse, then washed and filled them with fresh water. The stream was abundant in calcium, since the springs which fed it percolated through the limestone escarpments south of the Wicklow Mountains, and this 'hardness' in the water was beneficial for the horse, though these were details of which Stephen O'Donnell was unaware. Equally uninitiated in veterinary matters, he didn't know that Miss Fortune's diarrhoea was caused by the red worm which infested her, bleeding her abdominal cavity and bowels dry and slowly killing her.

The charcoal-grey filly, a magnificent thoroughbred at the time of her kidnapping three years ago, was by now hopelessly emaciated and out of condition, but the only exercise Stephen O'Donnell could give her was a walk in the fields whenever he came down to this abandoned property. These were the only times Miss Fortune ever saw daylight, spending the rest of her life tethered in the perpetual gloom of the barn.

At first, she had used to bite and kick at him in her rage, confused by the lack of constant schooling and race practice, demoralized by the niggardly feed and the infrequent supply of water, driven berserk by the dark and the loneliness. Her mouth ached constantly because her frustrated grinding of her back teeth had caused them to break, and their jagged edges cut her cheeks and tongue. It was only because she was basically a 'good doer', with deep resources of will-power, that she survived a severe bout of strangles a few months ago. She had coughed and wept for weeks, but Stephen O'Donnell, blissfully unaware of the disease, had believed she had contracted nothing worse than a cold.

The farm was forty miles outside Dublin. It had been set on fire some years before the kidnapping of Miss Fortune by the same gang, the McDaids. The farmer had squealed to the Garda about one of the gang members, and his punishment was to be incinerated along with his wife and three children. The place had never been reoccupied. The locals, knowing it was used periodically by the gang, warned any prospective buyers that there was a curse on it.

One barn, which was set some distance from the rest of the farmstead, had escaped the blaze, and it was here that the kidnappers had brought the horse while they waited for the ransom money. It was also here that they had intended to kill her when they got it.

When Stephen O'Donnell took her from Harry McDaid in return for his cut from the ransom money, he knew the place was ideal for his purposes. Not only did the barn provide shelter for the horse, but sometimes, when he had no digs, he'd sleep here himself. The village of Cloonbarry was only a mile and a half away and had a bus service from Dublin. It also had a feed merchant, and here Stephen O'Donnell bought hay and oats. Earlier today, he had spent more than usual at the merchant's on maize flakes which he had mixed with oats and chaff in an attempt to check Miss Fortune's diarrhoea.

Money for her keep was the hardest thing to come by, but he occasionally won on the courses, or managed to scrounge a pound or two from old Pat Fogarty or Percy Phelan, or eventually resorted to working with the McDaids. Whenever he had cash in his pocket he'd come down to Cloonbarry from Dublin, buy half a hundredweight of feed, and walk down to the farm with the bag on his shoulder, aglow with happiness that he was doing something to please the filly.

Miss Fortune pawed the straw forlornly as he came into the barn now and set the water buckets down before her. As she drank, he stroked and patted her scrawny neck. 'So I finally tried to get in touch with the lad, as I know you wanted me to. To tell him I never knew it was his place that we were going to that night when we took you. To tell him I'd sacrificed my £5,000 from the job just so that they wouldn't kill you. But the lad didn't want to know me, see, pet. He wouldn't talk to me.

He's never forgiven me for leaving his ma behind.'

When she finished drinking he untied her from her tethering post and walked her out in the field. The burned farmhouse remained a constant reminder of what Harry McDaid was capable of if ever the law found out about her. She stopped to graze in a thickly grassed patch and he stroked her neck again. 'I don't want to do this next job with the McDaids, see now, pet, but I've no choice. I've nothing left, and I owe Percy twenty-three pounds. If the lad had been a bit more forthcoming, I wouldn't need to. He's got plenty of money, but he doesn't care to let me have any of it because of the past. So I've got to work with Harry McDaid again. If the takings are good, I'll perhaps get a vet out to see to your diarrhoea.'

24.9.79 – 4.10.79

Christy learned.

He went to Hanseatic House and Plantation House and saw in the grand old Victorian buildings, redolent of tea clippers, how the world's precious and non-precious metals, foodstuffs like coffee, sugar, cocoa and wheat, and other commodities were bid and offered for on the trading floors.

He visited commodity brokerage houses and saw dealers working with price screens and phones, and became familiar with the curious language.

He read books, newspapers and everything he could get his hands on and got to understand how the same thing went on, but differently, across the Atlantic in New York and Chicago.

In the study Greville gave him to use – the one which had used to be Winchester's before the comptroller moved into the ballroom – he went over and over the ingenious and not strictly illegal scheme spelled out in the manila file. He learned who the nominees were – friends, family and associates of the duke, all prepared to have accounts opened in their names at virtually no risk, for 2 per cent of the proceeds; where these accounts had been set up; how Crown Prince Ahmed's money was to come in and be used if he agreed to invest; and how the profits would be returned to him. As the mechanics of it all gradually got locked into Christy's brain, the conviction grew in him that it would work.

The comptroller gave him a wide berth at the House. 'You're wasting your time and ours,' he'd say whenever Christy had to check details with him. 'The way you're carrying on, we'll miss any chance we've got left to hit the December futures contract.' That wasn't strictly true, and both knew it.

Winchester's unceasing antipathy towards the Irishman was the sole nuisance for James Greville during a week in which the duke had otherwise been in excellent spirits. He was confident as never before that his silver would rise in value to the level at which it should be by rights, since O'Donnell would undoubtedly persuade the Arab to bring in this billion dollars. Greville's domestic life had also perked up. At the beginning of the week, Elizabeth had come down for that marvellous *Rosenkavalier* at Covent Garden and there had been a cordial atmosphere between them. When they had got back to the House after the opera, he had wanted to sleep in her bedroom; but, though she had been too tired for that after her long day, he had nevertheless remained encouraged by her coming down. She had made no mention of Charles throughout, and he had believed he might begin to forgive her for her conduct with his father.

By the end of the week, Greville was looking forward to going up to Condrieu and seeing her again. Also Jane. Late on the morning of Friday 28 September, he suddenly had an excellent idea. He spoke to Winchester, then spoke to Christy, and, having secured their agreement, made a phone call to Condrieu.

'Yes, James,' Elizabeth said into the mouthpiece. She stood by the satinwood console in the Blue Drawing Room.

'I'm bringing two chaps up to the Hall for a working weekend: Winchester and a fellow called Christy O'Donnell, who used to work with us at the Grange. I'd like you to make sure Jane's there tomorrow. She went to Selwyn College with Winchester. They might like to chew the fat together about their Varsity days.'

'Jane's here every Saturday,' Elizabeth said. Hanging up, she became even more intrigued about her husband's curious recent behaviour. First, asking her down to London on Monday for the opera. Then, wanting to sleep with her, something they hadn't done for years. Most intriguing of all, not broaching business matters, or asking her for money, or berating Charles. A fairy godmother had obviously visited him. It was unlike him to behave quite so decently on his own initiative.

She felt like speaking to Jane now, even though her daughter was due at the Hall the following day, and so she called her in York. 'Be sure to come in good time tomorrow,' she said, explaining that the two men would be there with James, and that he was in remarkably good spirits.

This last piece of news pleased Jane, since her father had been in the doldrums for several months. When she finished talking to her mother, she remembered him wishing Deborah would also come to see him from time to time at the Hall. What a jolly thing it would be, she thought, if her younger sister were to join in the gathering tomorrow too; her divorce matters had almost been settled, and she might like to get away. So, Jane rang Deborah in Limerick to suggest she come to Condrieu for the weekend.

'Simon Winchester'll be there,' she explained. This didn't exactly set Deborah on fire, so Jane added, 'Plus there'll be someone else along who used to work at the Grange.'

'Oh?' Deborah was only marginally more interested.

'Yes, some Christy O'Donnell person. You might remember him. He was the assistant trainer when we won the Derby. They're coming up for a working weekend. So, do you think you'll make it?'

'Yes,' Deborah said, much more interested now. 'I think I probably will.'

Winchester couldn't avoid Christy at Condrieu Hall on the Saturday, and the two worked through lunch. They didn't break before tea, which was taken, inevitably, in the Blue Drawing Room, with Greville, Elizabeth and Jane.

While Christy chatted with the duchess about horses, Jane and Winchester reminisced about their Selwyn College days.

'And the expression on Jack Goodall's face during that economics lecture,' Jane said, 'do you remember, Simon?'

Winchester nodded. Members of the Selwyn College Dummy Suckers Club had used to wear babies' dummies on strings around their necks, hidden in their shirts; the rule had been that if any member produced his dummy in public and sucked it, you had to do the same or pay a shilling fine, which went to charity. Jane was referring to a day when a Dummy

Club member had spotted them through a lecture room window and had pulled out and sucked his dummy. Jane and Winchester and the six other Club members in the room at the time had done likewise, and the jaw of Jack Goodall, their lecturer, had dropped. 'I'll have you know this isn't kids' stuff!' he had shrieked.

Jane clutched her sides, laughing at the recollection, and Christy saw Winchester grin for the first time. It wasn't an attractive sight.

Later, they all wandered down to the Condrieu stables and looked at the horses. Christy gave Elizabeth and Jane the benefit of his wisdom as he looked over the animals, then the two women mounted their favourites and went off for a ride.

The three men strolled back to the Hall with Jane's children, with Greville asking, finally, 'So Christy, when on earth are you going to the Hejaz?'

He answered: 'It's almost all sorted out in my mind, your Grace. I'll probably be ready by Wednesday, or at the very latest, Thursday.'

Winchester sniggered, 'And I bet Ahmed will still say no, despite all your efforts.'

Greville was livid. 'I expect you to do everything you can to help Christy before he goes, do you understand, Simon?'

Deborah appeared at dinner. The duke, duchess and Jane were delighted, Winchester a little awed by her animal presence, and Christy somewhat overcome by his memories of what they had used to get up to. She said hello to him, shook his hand, made some banal remarks about Ireland and had very little more to do with him, though she did sit directly opposite him at the dining table.

She chatted incessantly with Winchester who was next to her, while Christy's gaze inevitably fell on her numerous times during the meal. He observed that she hadn't changed much … Those grey eyes so beautiful but still without warmth. And that blond hair hanging loose and wild like on the first day he had seen her … How he had used to love burying his head in that, and to smell the perfume behind her ears….

After dinner, he worked some more with Winchester, then retired to his suite. He undressed and washed in the bathroom, which was carpeted in green and had an antique Victorian bath standing on little brass feet, his mind chewing over the vision of Deborah across the table from him earlier. He had known a number of women since his days with her, and nowadays there were Sally Murphy and Maeve O'Sullivan to give him company. But there was no getting away from the fact: not one of his other lady friends had ever made him feel the way Deborah had.

He got into bed in the high-vaulted bedroom and did some background reading on the Chicago Grain and Metal Exchange before finally switching off the bedside light. As his mind floated away from wakefulness, he had a hazy notion of the door creaking open, then a light footfall on the carpet as someone came in. There was a rustle of clothing, and he had a dreamlike impression of some ancient blend of perfume and body scent. His blanket came off him, then fingers glided up his thigh and sought out his penis.

Christy opened his eyes. In the darkness, he saw her head, with its long fair hair, at his midriff. Completely awake now, he realized Deborah had actually come to him as he had desired, and was taking him in her mouth. Moaning, she swallowed and withdrew, swallowed and withdrew.

Christy dropped back on his pillow, paralysed with pleasure. As she continued working on him, his mind filled with the overpowering need to pound violently into her and spray the back of her throat with his semen. Succumbing to the urge, he raised himself on his elbows and thrust wildly. Then, suddenly, some hidden rage darkened his mind.

What the bloody hell was she doing here?

He didn't want her here! Who did she imagine she was, thinking she could just pick up the pieces like that after she had thrown him on the rubbish heap?

He raised a foot on to her hip and thrust her roughly away with it. Then he switched on the light. The bedclothes were thrown right back, and Deborah was crouching at his legs, naked. Her fine lace négligé was strewn on the floor. She stared back at him with her large faint eyes, her mouth wide open. Then she blinked and licked her lips.

'Hello, Christy.'

'What the bloody hell are you up to?'

'Well, I wouldn't call it giving Thomas his supper, would you?' she chuckled.

His libido diminishing with every second, Christy said, 'Don't you think it's time you stopped playing games with people's emotions?'

'Who's the one playing games? I'm not ashamed to take what

I want. I'm just about divorced now. I can do this without any feeling of guilt.' She bent her head down to take his prick in her mouth again, but he swung his legs off the bed.

'Go away, Deborah. I'm not interested any more.'

She smiled with understanding. 'Oh, come on, Christy. You can't still be hurt after all these years?'

He didn't answer, so she got off the bed and pulled her night dress over her. Shaking her head sadly at him, she went into the bathroom. A few minutes later she re-emerged and left the room, blowing him a kiss.

He would discover in the morning that his underclothes and socks had been stuffed in the toilet pan, and all his shirts and trousers immersed in the quarter-full bath.

James Greville silently let himself into the duchess's bedroom, which was in another wing of the Hall. He wore pyjamas.

Elizabeth was in bed, reading, but she put her book down on the bedside table and watched him ease the door shut behind him. She didn't quite know what to do about this visit. Last night, he had asked her if he could come to her bedroom as he had wanted to do down at Marylebone House, and she had again replied she was too tired. Tonight, he had evidently decided to take the law into his own hands.

'Not sleepy, James?' she said.

'Felt like having a bit of a cuddle, old girl.' He padded round to the other side of the bed and crept in under the sheets.

She unhooked her reading glasses from around her neck. 'Business must be going well.'

He made love to her that night for the first time in six years, and for the first time since Charles Greville had moved more or less permanently to Condrieu Hall. She didn't enjoy it, and told him so in the morning. 'It's too soon after all the hurt, James,' she said, meaning the constant barrage of vilification he had subjected her to.

He, however, believed in silent rage that she still kept some infernal torch alight for Charles, that she wouldn't ever forgive him for his father's dubious death. But, because he had been physically intimate again with her after such a long time, he didn't make one of his usual ugly remarks. His uncharacteristic silence on this occasion was, ironically, what would lead to his ultimate undoing.

On the evening of Wednesday 3 October, after a week and a

half of solid indoctrination in the silver scheme, Christy said to James Greville, 'That's more or less it your Grace. I'm ready to go to Khurbah by Friday.'

Greville beamed. 'Excellent, excellent.'

'There's just one thing, though.'

'Oh? What is it now?'

'I want Simon Winchester to come along too.'

Greville remembered Jamal. 'I hardly think that's sensible.'

Christy was quite firm. 'I believe it's essential. I've learned as much as I can about this thing, but he's the only one with the inner knowledge which might matter most when the chips are down.'

The duke harrumped. 'Very well. I'll put it to him.'

Christy called Iqbal from the flat at the House that night to say he wanted to come to Khurbah to speak to Ahmed, and that he'd be bringing a colleague with him.

'If it's for the Khurbah Champions Cup, Sheikh O'Donnell, please be warned that Arabian turf conditions are very different from what you're used to in your damp islands....

Christy grinned. Iqbal managed always to be so amusing. 'No, Iqbal, it's not for that. It's for something completely different. Karim Jamal will need to be there too.'

The next morning, two first class tickets to Khurbah were delivered to Christy at Marylebone House by an agent for the Crown Prince Ahmed. Attached to the tickets was the message: *'Welcome to the Hejaz, my wonderful fellow. And I am intrigued that you are bringing along a certain Mr Winchester, but please tell him that he too is welcome in my home.'*

7.10.79

'Oh what a miserable existence I have, Sheikh O'Donnell, except when I witness the sun rise in the desert. Then I know life has its better side.' In the darkness before dawn, Crown Prince Ahmed turned to grin at Christy across the rear compartment of the Daimler limousine, and his eyes and teeth glimmered. To Christy he looked like a devilish *djinn* silhouetted against that car window. Miserable existence indeed, reflected Christy. The man was worth six and a half billion dollars!

The limousine was heading westward, its tyres crunching over the coarse sands which had been swept on to the main highway overnight by the dry desert winds. Three other limousines followed. They were all going to Talal's Wadi, thirty miles west of Khurbah, the capital of the Kingdom of the Hejaz.

'We do this twice a year,' Ahmed explained.

Christy was conscious that the crown prince had honoured him by letting him ride in the leading car, and also by sitting beside him in the back seat instead of in his customary position next to the driver. In Arabia, leaders of tribes tended to ride in the fronts of carriages.

In the other cars were Simon Winchester, Karim Jamal and some of the crown prince's sons and cousins.

The Daimler turned off the highway and on to the narrow track which had once been the country's main east-west route. They rode downhill for several minutes over bumpy, stony ground. Then the car slowed and eventually pulled off the track in a great flurry of dust. 'We have arrived,' the crown prince said.

Waiting boys glided up to open the doors. They bowed low as the passengers stepped out. Christy noticed campfires burning in a hollow a hundred yards away. He could make out the shapes of tents in the flickering firelight.

Back along the track, other cars drew up. The young princes got out, smoothed down their *thobes* and stretched their limbs in the light chill of the air. Winchester was one of the last to emerge. He wore a neatly pressed khaki safari suit he'd bought at Dunn and Co's store in the Strand three days earlier.

The crown prince put an arm around the Irishman's shoulders. 'Come Sheikh O'Donnell.' They made their way down into the hollow. Here, the sand was gritty and had just become tinged with the blue which indicated that night was about to end. A patchwork of rugs was spread out on it before the tents, and everyone sat down on these facing east. They had come all this way specifically to see the sun rise. Christy took care to tuck his feet under him and not insult anyone in the party by pointing his toes in their direction.

Ahmed addressed Christy and Winchester. 'This place where we sit today is a most revered one for the people of the

Hejaz. It was in this wadi that my father, the great Talal Aziz ibn Jayed, camped on the night forty-nine years ago before he made his triumphant entry into Khurbah. He was to be the first king of the Kingdom which was to be inaugurated the next day, and it was from this very spot that he and his followers witnessed the sunrise which gave birth to our Kingdom.'

A hush fell on the gathering as light cracked open the rim of the horizon. Christy watched with amazement how rapidly the pink light brightened. A sense of awe became fused with the silence as the pale circumference of the sun edged its way up and warmth seeped across the sands towards them. By the fires, where the boys were preparing coffee, the air filled with the aroma of coffee pods roasting, and with ringing and scraping sounds as the roasted beans were pounded into powder with brass mortars and pestles.

Crown Prince Ahmed took a deep breath and mumbled '*Allahu Akhbar!*' (God is most great!) and Jamal and the other princes repeated the invocation. Then all the gathering turned their backs to the sun to prostrate themselves towards Mecca in the west.

Christy mimed the action, though Winchester remained stiffly upright. Then the Imam led the chanting of the morning prayer. When it was over, little cups of bitter coffee came round on silver trays, and these were followed by large glasses of sweet tea. Winchester couldn't stomach his coffee and had to refuse the tea. This provoked some disgruntled muttering and one or two eyebrows to be raised.

It was now that Prince Turki, one of Ahmed's sons by his first wife Jauhara, came up to the Englishman as if in response to a pre-arranged signal.

'Sheikh Winchester,' he said. 'Will you accompany me on a visit to the waterhole in which Talal Aziz cleansed himself before setting off to Khurbah on that famous day forty-nine years ago? The spot is well worth a pilgrimage.'

Aware now that this was something he mustn't refuse, Winchester got up and slunk off behind the young prince as if he was being led away to have his throat slit.

Ahmed watched with a grin, and turned to Christy. 'Now, let me take you to a much more interesting place. It is where my father was almost assassinated the night before his entry into the Kingdom, and might never have been proclaimed king.'

With the light brightening all the time, they walked up the far side of the wadi, heading towards a spot marked with rocks.

Ahmed recounted some of Talal's history, and Christy, seeing him delight in his role of story-teller, listened patiently.

'My father was very clever. During the Great War against the Ottoman Turks – which your people call the First World War – he offered his uncontested allegiance to both the British and the Germans, knowing that each of these powers needed his backing, because he had united the Ikhwan bedouins to fight for him under the flag of Islam. Now, both the great powers knew of his double-dealing, but of course they still needed him more than he needed them. Talal Aziz, with three armies in his hands, easily drove the hated Ottomans out of our land. Then the Americans came in, and he quickly abandoned the Germans. Indeed, he helped the Yankees and their Britisher brothers to send the Hun packing! It was after this that Allah himself intervened, rewarding Talal for his boldness, by allowing the Americans to discover the black fossil fuels in our eastern sector.' Suddenly overcome by a sense of Allah's greatness he declared, 'Oh, *Wallahi!*'

Christy felt he should make some useful remark here, but couldn't summon up the right words.

Ahmed, however, hadn't finished. '... And even the discovery of oil, Sheikh O'Donnell, was used by my father towards the establishment of our Kingdom.' Another grin spread across his face. 'He made promises of cheap oil to the Americans, and these turned them against their British allies. After that, it was easy for us to gain back all those parts of our land which had been under British dominion.' The two men had by now reached the top of the slope. 'He was both a fox and lion as Machiavelli said a prince should be. Do you not think so?'

'Oh aye,' said Christy. 'He certainly knew how to play all the powers off against each other.'

Ahmed nodded. 'So, it is to pay homage to him that we are here today.' In his eyes was such a wondrous, proud glow that Christy was a little taken aback when those black eyes suddenly swivelled back on to him. 'But now, my dear horse trainer, I want to know why *you* are here today. Naturally, I am very pleased you have honoured me by coming, but why, please tell me, has this Greville duke chosen *you* to come here to talk to me about this silver business? Did he not tell you that Jamal already looked into it on my behalf with your colleague Winchester, and decided not to proceed?'

He answered carefully: 'Winchester did tell me about their

previous meeting. He believes Mr Jamal was interested, but that some silly personal misunderstanding made Mr Jamal back off. It wasn't the scheme itself that Mr Jamal didn't like.'

Ahmed nodded. 'It is possible. Jamal can be temperamental. But you still don't answer why this duke chose *you* to come out here?'

Christy, sensing the crown prince's skittish mood, chuckled. 'Oh, that's simple enough, you know. The Duke of Marylebone thinks you will listen to me because you probably *like* me, because Desert Princess won the Triple Crown.'

Ahmed looked at him in amazement. 'So, this Greville tries to get money from me by using my own horse trainer. And why? Because he thinks I *like* my horse trainer! Priceless! Oh yes, that's priceless.' He clapped Christy on the back. 'Yes, I think I *like* your James Greville actually. He has got style. Sending me my own horse trainer indeed. Yes, despite whatever problem Jamal had with Winchester, I approve of your James Greville. He has vision. Yes, I think I'll send him a billion dollars just on a hunch. Tell me, does he think there's a secret Ali Baba's cave here, whose door will open when I utter some magic words, and be full of crates of dollar bills inside, which you will stuff in a suitcase and take through the green channel at Heathrow Airport?'

Christy retorted: 'He might accept a cheque.'

The Arab's hatchet face carved into a grin. 'He-might-accept-cheque! Well, that is very decent of him, I must say.' He thought for a few seconds, then asked wryly, 'And no-one in the financial markets would find it fishy if a billion dollar cheque suddenly appeared and was used to buy millions upon millions of ounces of silver?'

Christy laughed, 'I wasn't being serious....' He broke off, understanding now that what Ahmed wanted was reassurance that what was being proposed by Greville was legal and above board as far as the markets were concerned. He chose his words with even greater care. 'Everything's legally watertight, your Royal Highness ... why should anyone find anything fishy? The duke wants to catch a whale. Even if the Americans look for the hook for ten years after it's all over, they won't find one.'

Ahmed led the way to a group of tall stones. 'I know that you, Sheikh O'Donnell, are an honourable angler, and wouldn't take me into murky waters. No fish I work with must have any kind of stink.'

Christy smiled. His instinct had been right. He kept the game going. 'The English shark who sent me here smells clean.' He certainly hoped Greville *was* clean.

'That is most important. Smell counts for much. When you're not sure if a man is fragrant or stinking, then take a note of his father's odour. My own father always used to tell us that.' The crown prince nodded briefly at the wisdom of Talal Aziz's words. 'And I remember the father of this Greville Emir. Now *he* was someone quite marvellous. I met him a few times on the racecourses and in Monte Carlo. Our yachts used to berth near each other ... We used to laugh a lot. He used to call me crazy because of my gambling....' He shook his head. 'A shame he died so tragically.'

'I agree.' Christy had heard that his old friend Johnnie Early had been driving the Land Rover out of which the duke had fallen and died.

'We have reached,' Ahmed said. He gestured at the stones. 'That is where my father was almost killed by the Jaluwis – they were the only bedouin tribe not to join him. That night forty-nine years ago was their last chance to stop him entering Khurbah and assuming power. My father came here to relieve himself after the feasting, and three of them leaped at him, daggers drawn, as he squatted in the act of emptying his bowels....' He paused, visualizing the scene.

'So, what happened?' Christy blurted, imagining it all too.

'He saw them coming and broke wind very loudly. You know, farted. The attackers thought a cannon had gone off, and hurled themselves to the ground. My father got up and ran, shouting for his bodyguards. They were waiting just up here on the crest of the slope. In seconds, they finished off the Jaluwis. This spot, Sheikh O'Donnell,' he said gravely, 'is known to the Hejazis as the Place of the Royal Fart.'

Christy, conscious that he stood in a place holy to the people of this kingdom, struggled to keep his expression reverential.

'He was nimble minded, don't you think,' Ahmed said solemnly.

'You can certainly say that, your Royal Highness!' It seemed you needed not only a nimble mind but also a nimble backside to survive around here. At this thought, his laughter swelled right up in his throat, but he controlled it, emitting only a rough, choking noise.

'Are you unwell?' asked Ahmed with concern.

Wheezing, with tears rolling down his cheeks, Christy

managed to say, 'No, it's my throat ... it's a little dry in the desert.'

A smile spread across Ahmed's face. Then he started chuckling, and then he was laughing uproariously. With relief, Christy let himself go too, and for a minute or so the two of them stood by there, weeping and shaking with laughter right down to their guts.

Then, still laughing, Ahmed put his arms around the Irishman's shoulders. 'Come, Sheikh O'Donnell. Let us return to the camp. You can drink something there to wash away your throat dryness. And we must also discuss this silver business with Jamal.'

They walked back down, Ahmed asking, 'This James Greville whom I like so much now ... how much is he worth?'

Christy gained control over his wheezing and wiped the tears from his eyes. He was very familiar with the facts: 'Greville Holdings has assets worth £350 million, taking into account all the silver bullion it owns, as well as the remaining UK properties. That's around $700 million. On top of that, Greville International has overseas property to the tune of another $600 million, and it yields annual profits of a little over $200 million.'

Ahmed raised his eyebrows. 'But Jamal tells me this James Greville has no connection with Greville International. That he concentrates only on the silver. Working apart from the rest of the family. This was one of the things Jamal didn't like. It seems this Greville had legal problems with his father when he was still alive, and that there were some problems with the wife too. Jamal couldn't understand why a man who gets on with nobody suddenly comes looking for a partner.'

Christy replied: 'He has no choice, your Royal Highness. He has a huge holding in silver and is convinced the market is undervaluing the commodity. I've studied it all, and I happen to agree that silver should go up. In the short-term, it can be made to go up a very long way. But to make this happen, he needs finance. And he hasn't got it. That's why he needs you.'

They had reached the camp. Christy saw that Prince Turki and Simon Winchester hadn't yet returned from Talal's waterhole. The other sons were a discreet distance away. Only Jamal remained sitting on a rug waiting for them.

Ahmed indicated for Jamal to follow them into a tent. They all sat down on rugs in here and glasses of iced water appeared. The Lebanese said to Christy, with irritation, 'Sheikh

O'Donnell, it's nice to see you here in the Hejaz, but was it really necessary to bring along that Winchester?'

The crown prince intervened: 'Sheikh O'Donnell, you know we have already been approached about this silver business. But Jamal decided it didn't suit us. Tell me now honestly, why should I risk so much money?'

Christy said, 'I've had some difficulties with Mr Simon Winchester myself. He's a bit over-intellectual and doesn't always understand how to deal with things on a personal basis....'

Jamal nodded.

' ... But that doesn't stop his idea being completely brilliant. I've spent almost two weeks looking at it, and I really believe it will work.'

'You are, perhaps, only saying this because you will undoubtedly earn something if I join in?'

'No,' Christy replied firmly. 'It is of course true the duke will compensate me, and with quite a lot of money, if you put in the amount they're asking for. But I wouldn't have come here unless I believed that this scheme could succeed.'

Jamal said, 'I presume then, that you yourself will be investing in it within your own means?'

Christy shook his head. 'You know I don't make any kind of gamble at all, Mr Jamal. I never backed even Desert Princess, the best horse I ever had the privilege to train.'

Ahmed said, 'But this silver business, you tell me, is no gamble. It is a sure thing, you say.'

'It *is* a gamble. It's not like investing your money in the five per cents, your Royal Highness. But the way it's been planned is to make the gamble work for you, not against you. The gamble is to make you bigger than the market, so that you can milk it for all it's worth.'

Ahmed's chest puffed up with pride at the concept of being bigger than the market. Hadn't Talal Aziz ibn Jayed made the Hejazis – and their Saudi brothers – bigger than the oil market by quadrupling the price?

Jamal said, 'This is all very well. But how do we know anyone can be bigger than the silver market?'

'It's possible, Mr Jamal. For a short period of time. The period we're talking about is between now and the end of December.'

Silence fell on them. Somewhere far up on the highway, a caravan of lorries trundled by. In the desert, sounds carried cleanly and over vast distances. When the echoes faded,

Ahmed said to Christy, 'I need to speak to Sheikh Jamal in Arabic for a moment.'

'Oh please don't mind me.' Christy's tone was casual, but his heart was racing.

The two men started to talk rapidly in the guttural language, and Christy knew that everything hinged on the next few minutes ... a million pounds ... a castle.... Not that he was prepared to pay what that madman Kirkpatrick had demanded....

'A most, er, interesting spot,' Winchester said, entering the tent just then. Prince Turki had guided him in and gone off to join the others. 'Yes, er, Talal's waterhole was certainly worth a visit....'

The two Arabs, engrossed in their conversation, took no notice of him. Christy motioned to him to sit down and be silent.

'I need a deal like this to fill my coffers,' Crown Prince Ahmed said. 'We will be bigger than the market! And we will have the chance to earn up to $2 billion.'

The Lebanese said urbanely, 'That is only what these Christians say. Like they say the silver price is too low. How do we know all this is true?'

'We shall ask them in a moment. But let us not be too cautious and lose what may be a wonderful chance. Let us listen for the advantages as much as for the flaws. After all, your biggest objection, the presence of the Christian whose name begins with W, has now been offset by the inclusion of my horse trainer. I know the curly-haired one to be a magnificent fellow who possesses, in addition to an almost Arab-like skill with horses, a truly exceptional skill with business affairs which almost matches that of the Lebanese.'

Jamal suddenly smiled. 'You are right of course, *Ya* Ahmed. It certainly is a prestigious concept. We must not allow it to go begging if it has any chance of success. Very well, I agree that we should join in, but only if they prove beyond reasonable doubt that the price will rise to the sort of levels they are talking about.'

Ahmed swivelled his fierce black eyes back on to Christy. 'Sheikh Jamal has asked me a fair question. We don't doubt your sincerity, but how can we be sure the price of silver is too low at the moment? How do we know it is sure to rise?'

The Irishman had naïvely been expecting a straight yes or no. He could only stare back blankly.

Winchester now piped in: 'Your Royal Highness, when the Duke of Marylebone started buying silver, the price was $1.47 an ounce. Today it is just under $6. Already four times....'

The Lebanese interrupted. 'But that has taken five years to achieve, as you told me at Newmarket in England. Why suddenly should the price now quadruple again in a matter of two months?'

The sun had climbed above the high dunes to the east, and the heat in the tent was already almost too intense to bear. Winchester ran a white cotton handkerchief quickly over his forehead and cheeks before answering.

'The buying we've been doing over the five years was on a slow scale, and the price rose in proportion. The buying we intend to do now will be on a much more massive and rapid scale. We will also cut off the supply. The price is bound to react much more violently....'

'Theory, Mr Winchester, theory,' Jamal laughed.

The Englishman, never having forgiven Jamal for landing such a glorious Daphne and giving nothing in return, lost patience. 'Look! The only real way then is to put it into practice, isn't it, by stumping up the cash!'

'You're right, Simon,' Christy said. 'That could be how to prove one way or another if this will work.' He turned to Ahmed. 'I think a demonstration is possible. I'll need to discuss it further with Mr Winchester here first. And then, to carry it out, we may well need you to put up just a little bit of money.'

9.10.79

The manager of the International Cayman Islands Bank in the Caribbean couldn't believe his ears.

The telephone line from Khurbah was bad enough, but the words coming down that line from the bank's biggest customer were worse.

'But I can't do that!' the manager said. 'We have a reputation to maintain. There may be an enquiry....'

The Royal voice, crackling in from the Kingdom of the Hejaz seven thousand miles away, cut him off. 'What are my daily balances as of this morning Sheikh Parribo?'

The banker looked at the statements on the desk in front of him. He took a deep breath as he said, 'Current is $94 million and deposit is 627 million, give or take a few hundred thousand dollars.'

The Royal voice was brusque. 'Give and take is what I believe in, Sheikh Parribo. If you don't carry out my wishes, you will give me back every cent from both accounts and I will gladly take it all. In cash. Today.'

The bank manager mopped his sweaty brow. The crown prince wouldn't do that really, he knew. He couldn't. Not today. Not $721 million ... And actually, come to think of it, what Ahmed was asking him for wasn't all that difficult. The banking community would protect him. It always shielded members, except when their misdemeanours became too grotesque. And this was nothing like that; it was just a small hiccup which was bound to pass unnoticed. 'Well, your Royal Highness, we shall try our utmost to oblige you this once. But I do beg you....'

The line from Khurbah went dead.

11.10.79

The market floor of the Chicago Grain and Metal Exchange was the size of six tennis courts, with a towering thirty foot high ceiling and huge electronic 'scoreboards' lining the walls. Rippling relentlessly up on to these were prices from the trading on the floor, as well as from the Chicago Board of Trade, the Chicago Mercantile Exchange, the New York Board of Trade and Comex.

The trading pits were hexagonal or octagonal recesses punched into the floor with steps around them. Large television screens, angled downward, were suspended above the pits. Men wearing different-coloured jackets were clustered around these curious arenas, waving and shouting frenziedly as they bought and sold a variety of commodities ranging from soya beans to gold.

In the din which echoed around the room in waves, Barry Turnowsky had to cup his hands to his mouth. 'The total turnover on the floor in terms of contract values can run into several billions of dollars in a week.'

Turnowsky, a bespectacled man in his late thirties, had been given the job of escorting Christy around the market. He worked for Bachmann Gardner & Co., Chicago commodity brokers. One of Winchester's broker friends had called from London and told the firm that the Irishman was the representative of some 'very influential commodity traders' in both the Kingdom of Hejaz and London.

Turnowsky added, 'Not many people know it, but the volume and turnover here in the Grain and Metal Exchange is far in excess of the share dealings on the New York Stock Exchange, even though Wall Street gets all the limelight.'

'What are all those cards being thrown across the place?' Christy asked.

'They're the buy or sell orders. The floor clerks ... that's the people over there ... ' He pointed to the rows of booths surrounding the market floor, which were manned by people talking on telephones. ' ... The floor clerks get the orders in by phone from their firms' dealing rooms, and send the order cards to the pits by runners – that's the guys going back and forth between the pits and the booths. Or they just throw them across to the floor traders.'

'And all those cards strewn all over the floor? It looks like complete pandemonium.'

'They're the orders that never got executed because there was no buyer or seller. It may look like pandemonium, but everything is actually very efficiently organized. Come with me.'

Turnowsky expertly picked a path through all the activity on the floor and headed in the direction of the soya bean pit, explaining, 'The guys in the green jackets with yellow piping are the Bachmann traders. Let's just watch a typical trade take place.'

At the Bachmann booth nearest this pit, the floor clerk swiftly shook hands before turning to answer a ringing phone. He listened with the phone cradled in his ear and wrote something down on a card printed with red rubric.

'That's a sell order,' Turnowsky explained. 'The buy order cards are printed in black.

The floor clerk handed the card to a runner, who sped off towards the soya bean pit. The runner passed the card to a floor trader in green and yellow, who glanced at it, waved his hand forward into the pit and yelled something. Another trader at the pit, wearing a maroon jacket, shouted back and made an inwards gesture to him.

'They've traded,' Turnowsky said, 'and what they're writing down on the cards now is the price and each others' badge numbers.'

Exactly thirty seconds later by Christy's calculation the runner was back at the booth with the completed card, and the floor clerk was on the line to the office to report the price they'd sold at.

Turnowsky gave a complacent grin. 'From the time a client places an order with one of our dealers in the office to the time confirmation of the trade comes through can take less than one minute, as you have just seen.'

'Very impressive Mr Turnowsky. Now, which one's the silver pit?'

'Over there. Come, I'll show you.'

There was much less action going on in the silver pit than in the agriculturals. The men in the brightly coloured jackets seemed to be hanging around waiting for things to liven up, with only sporadic bids and offers being called out.

'So why's silver so quiet now?' Christy asked.

'We-ell,' Turnowsky said. 'People are saying it's a bit unnatural. There's an English lord who's got a lot of physical stock, and no-one's sure if he's going to dump it all on the market or make a play to raise the price. So everyone's watching and waiting. It's a nervous market, particularly today. The price has been slipping all day, and the sentiment is bearish. But there are people around who think it could explode upwards.'

The Irishman nodded calmly. But inwardly, he had a shudder of nerves at what he planned to do to this very market within the next twenty-four hours.

'Let's go on up to the office,' Turnowsky said. They left the market floor, handing back their special badges, and on through to the elevators. Bachmann Gardner's dealing room was on the twelfth floor. Christy followed Turnowsky into the vast area, with numerous desks and price screens sometimes banked three high. He hadn't seen any commodity firm in London this big. The dealers were much younger too. Many were dressed in shirt sleeves and jeans, and the atmosphere, though charged with trading activity, was much more informal.

'It's a youngster's game,' Turnowsky chuckled. 'I burned out when I was thirty, and all I do now is the PR.'

Christy nodded, intrigued at seeing something else he hadn't seen in a London commodity dealing room – a woman sitting in front of a price screen and talking on the phone. Not only that, but she really was very attractive. She had on a bottle-green woollen suit, and her blouse bulged in a way to suggest big firm breasts. Her auburn hair, permed and quite long, fell in little ringlets on her collar. She wore no jewellery and only a touch of make-up around the eyes. In her right cheek was a delicious dimple.

'I wasn't expecting to see a woman here,' Christy said, unable to take his eyes off her.

Turnowsky laughed. 'There aren't many in the world of commodities. But that one's special. She's Thomas Gardner's daughter Susan. Susan Gardner.'

At that moment she put the phone down and looked across at them. She had a detached expression in her big green eyes, but behind that there was more than a hint of bottled-up mischief and sparkle. Wow! thought Christy, ready to go on looking into those eyes all day long. Especially since she seemed to be returning the compliment.

She broke the spell and turned back to face her screen.

Turnowsky grinned awkwardly. 'It'd be no problem for me to introduce the two of you to each other....'

Christy would have loved to get a closer look at her dimple ... But the context was all wrong for that sort of thing. 'Another time maybe,' he said. 'I wouldn't want to keep Mr Bachmann waiting.'

Cute, real cute-looking, Susan thought.

She couldn't concentrate on the screen straight away after an experience like that. It was that impish twist to his lips and the healthy outdoor look ... Life did have nice things to offer. Maybe she'd do a picture of him, from memory. She hadn't been at her easel since she'd failed miserably at trying to do those few of Ross from memory. With a sigh, she tapped her way through the 'pages' on the screen which gave the prices of the precious metals for future delivery months, reminding herself that art was her past. Her future was this, the commodities business. She had no more artistic inspiration. It had all died with Ross. She hadn't encountered anyone else to make her believe it was possible for her ever to be swept off her feet again.

Ross. Not handsome in the classical sense – his eyes too close together and his mouth too small, but blazing like the sun with his immense sexuality, and with such a degree of self-possession that she had utterly trusted him. He would only have to say the sky was green, and she would have painted it emerald, viridian or olive in every picture. She gave him everything she had. Just two and a half years ago their world was Eldorado. Ross, a free-lance arts editor, journalist and reviewer, had won a coveted commission to do a series of twelve big colour books on Renaissance painting. She was engaged to him, and they were making plans to go to Italy together to do the research, more plans to marry as soon as they got back, and they had bought a house out in Elmhurst. Ross's future as a front-rank arts writer was guaranteed with this project; she would be graduating from the School of the Art Institute of Chicago and had planned to launch her career as an illustrator of children's books.

Then Eldorado disintegrated.

Susan came home early from the Art Institute one June morning and found Michelle Kramer, a jealous colleague from the Institute, in her bed. Ross emerged in the bathroom doorway in his towelling robe to see what was going on, with a stupid embarrassed grin on his face.

'It was just a one-off, Susan,' he implored her that evening in her father's apartment. 'She'd been giving me the come-on for months and I thought, heck, why not just one time?'

Susan, sitting next to her father, gazed stonily at the television.

'It'll never happen again. Please believe me baby, it'll never happen again. You're the only one I'll ever love.'

'It's over Ross,' she said simply. 'I've called off the wedding.'

'We've got so much going for us,' he begged. 'Can't you give me a second chance?'

'It's just the way you did it Ross. We were at the church yesterday, making the wedding arrangements, and today Michelle's smoking a cigarette in my bed. In my bed ... I'll never be able to look you in the face again.'

There was a finality in her voice which distressed even her father. The senior partner of Bachmann Gardner & Co. was one of the two people in the world who knew how determined this girl could be when she wanted to. The other was Ross. He often called her a hammerhead. Both Gardner and Ross knew she wouldn't go back on her decision. Certainly not for a long time, in any case.

'Can't you persuade her, sir?'

The reply was given with kindness: 'Let her be, Ross, for the time being at least.'

Ross had gone to the nearest bar, got blind drunk and then driven away wailing out sad love songs. He didn't make it home. His car was finally fished out of the Chicago River three days later. He had struggled to get out, it appeared, but had been incapable of winding down the window. Susan had had to go to identify his blackened, horribly bloated, body. She had gone through worse torments about it than she could have imagined for over a year.

Casting the recollections out of her mind now, she glanced around the dealing room. Activity on the agriculturals desks was still hectic, with forecasts of cold weather causing nervous price changes in soya beans, wheat and corn. A number of the dealers frantically followed the price action on their screens and were on calls to clients and pit clerks.

But in the precious metals, where she worked, the action was the opposite. The dealers down on the floor must have all croaked or something, she decided. How she hated the whole thing. Still, at least pop was happy. He worried less about his side of the business going out of the family when he retired and it falling into the hands of that rat Mike Bachmann.

She smiled wistfully. If only that curly-haired imp had come across and swooped her away from this sad desk. She had an urge to go somewhere wild with him, like the Canadian Rockies. She suddenly had this crazy romantic notion that he'd come from Vancouver....

'You look a little lost to the world,' Barry Turnowsky said. He leaned against her chair.

Susan gave a start. 'What? Me? No, not at all....'

'Maybe it's because the precious metals are so quiet?'

'Yeah, yeah,' she stuttered, 'they are pretty dull aren't they?'

'Or maybe,' he simpered, 'you were thinking about that guy I just brought through here?'

'Guy? What guy?'

Turnowsky tapped the side of his nose knowingly. 'I can tell you he took quite a shine to you.' He laughed, then left her to chew that over.

The Bachmann Gardner & Co. board room was a few doors away. There were no price screens in it, but top-of-the-range furniture from Marshall Field's, Chicago's finest department store.

Mike Bachmann sat next to Christy on a thick hide-coloured sofa. The broker was short and well polished, wore a natty suit, and had suspicious, darting eyes. These reminded Christy of Brendan Byrne, the trainer at Eden Grange with whom he'd won the Derby. 'I'm interested in opening an account with your firm,' he said.

'That's music to my ears, sir,' Bachmann grinned. 'Would that be a speculative account or a professional one?'

'Let's just say a big account.'

Bachmann's grin widened. 'The tune's getting better.'

You just wait till the crescendo! Christy thought. 'There are just one or two questions I'd like to ask you first.'

'Go right ahead Mr O'Donnell.'

'Regarding silver ... can I place an order with you here to trade in London if I want to?' The question wasn't necessary. He already knew the answer.

'No problem at all, sir,' Bachmann replied effusively. 'We buy and sell all the time in London through our associates down there. Sheedy and Ratcliffe, they're called.'

'Good. Then this is what I want to do: at the opening of the London Minerals Board tomorrow morning, I want to buy some December silver.'

Bachmann wondered why the Irishman wanted to deal in London and not Chicago, but didn't reveal the question on his face. Probably to tie in with some Moslem rite in the Hejaz or something. He played it as if such a request was the most natural thing in the world. 'All righty, sir, all you have to do is put down the margin. The amount depends on how big a silver position you want to create. Just how much do you want to buy?'

Christy prevented a gulp in his throat. 'I want a couple more answers from you before I answer that. First, do I have your personal guarantee that the details of this trade won't be mentioned to anyone at all, not even within your own organization? And second, that you won't use this information to trade on your own behalf?'

Bachmann's darting eyes narrowed at this. 'I'll have you know it's Bachmann Gardner's policy to maintain strict client confidentiality....

Christy interrupted, 'Can I have specific yeses or noes, please, Mr Bachmann?'

The broker was clearly displeased at the way in which the integrity of both his firm and himself was being given the third degree. He nodded curtly, once, and looked away in a pained manner to indicate he wasn't going into the matter any further.

'Good,' said Christy. He leaned forward. 'Now, I want to buy 25 million ounces tomorrow.'

Bachmann's jaw went slack. 'Is this for real?'

'Perfectly real.' Christy tried to sound suitably confident. 'You see, the "very influential" person I represent in the Hejaz is Crown Prince Ahmed himself.'

He took a folded sheet of paper out of the inside pocket of his jacket and passed this across to Bachmann. It was a letter from the crown prince, typed on his royal stationery.

As Bachmann hungrily scanned the text, Christy decided that this man was very much like Byrne indeed. Ideal for what had been planned. Winchester's broker friends in London had chosen well.

'Well Mr O'Donnell,' Bachmann said, his attitude submissive again. 'So you're employed by Crown Prince Ahmed, and you have full powers of attorney to make commodity trading decisions on his behalf?'

Christy's answer was to extract another piece of paper from his pocket and hand this also to the broker.

Mike Bachmann gazed at the yellow slip of paper. It was a cheque, drawn on the International Cayman Islands Bank, and signed by a Karim Jamal. The space for the payee's name was left blank, but the amount written down was $10 million.

'I think that's the right margin amount for 5,000 lots,' Christy said, knowing it was. Twenty-five million ounces was 5,000 lots of 5,000 ounces each. The margin for one lot of silver was $2,000.

Observing Bachmann's eyes gorging on the cheque, he added nonchalantly, 'I'm staying at the Marriot Hotel in Rush Street. If you're prepared to act on our behalf, I'd like you to call me there tomorrow morning with news of this transaction in London. Will you deal for us, or should I take my business somewhere else?'

The broker cleared his throat but spoke nevertheless in a

hoarse whisper. 'Oh no, Mr O'Donnell, there's no need to talk of taking your business anywhere else. We'll do exactly what you want. Just write down our firm's name on that cheque ... sir.'

11.10.79 – 12.10.79

I

Commodity futures markets are sometimes incomprehensible even to those who have worked in them for decades. That is part of their charm. Or challenge.

'I promise to buy ten tons of such-and-such,' says somebody.

'I promise to sell you ten tons of the same,' says somebody else. Nine hundred and ninety-nine times out of a thousand, neither party will see what he is buying or selling. He will sell back or buy back the ten tons of such-and-such he promised to buy or sell in the first place, well before the time for its delivery. In the meantime, the price will have risen or fallen. A profit or loss will have been made, depending on which way the price moved and whether the somebody was a buyer or seller.

Those who wonder why these 'futures' transactions are made are told they are essential for the trade in the world's raw materials. With tens of thousands of deals going through daily, the futures markets are the best way for prices to reflect the supply-demand equation.

Professionals supposedly use the markets to maintain price stability in their dealings in the 'physicals'. Speculators try to make a buck by guessing which way the market will turn, as they do in the share and bond markets. The deals which speculators make are either fun or a nightmare, depending on how they guessed. More usually, it's just a matter of luck.

But then, there are those who say, 'You make your own luck.'

Some speculators do try to make their own luck. They devise all kinds of clever methods to predict future price trends.

Charts are popularly used. Past prices for a commodity are plotted on a graph, and certain 'signals' indicate whether to buy, or sell, or do nothing. For someone not initiated in the ways of these 'chartists', it might appear hazardous to predict future changes purely on the basis of past behaviour on a chart. A Chinese proverb found in a fortune cookie said it all: *To prophesy is extremely difficult, especially with respect to the future.* There are, however, a lot of traders, some highly sophisticated, who risk substantial sums of money on the basis of messages and trading signals they read on a chart.

Now it can happen sometimes, when a number of chartists all see the same trading signal on a chart, and the market happens to be thin at the same time, that the price of that commodity can shoot up or plummet purely in response to the chartists' activities.

At about the time Christy showed the crown prince's letter to Mike Bachmann, things were developing in the gold and silver pits which would trigger a flurry of chart-trading.

The teleprinters and telex machines were in a corner of the dealing room, and Susan had strolled over to them to look at the latest bulletins.

She scanned several inches of crop yield figures and so on, then read: *'Trading in gold and silver remains thin and listless. No sudden break is envisaged by the majority of traders, but a continuing drift downwards is likely.'*

As she sat back down at her desk, she noticed on her screen that December gold, which had been trading in a range of \$326.50–\$328 an ounce, had slipped to \$325.20. It was only fractionally above the year's low of \$325.00, which was an important 'support line' on the price charts. If the price went below that, according to the chartists, it could keep going down a very long way. This meant that many of them would start selling gold short heavily as soon as it did drop below that figure.

The impish guy and all ideas of going off to Vancouver with him vanished from Susan's head. She picked up the phone and dialled the firm's booth by the gold pit down on the trading floor. 'What's going on? Are the wire services right? They say there won't be any sudden break.'

The clerk replied, 'Looks like they've been lulled into a false sense of security, Susan, like most of the pros, because I can tell you that nerves are breaking down here. There's going to be a rush of selling in both gold and silver any minute now. I can just smell it.'

Susan glanced up at the nine clocks on the far wall, which gave the times in the four US zones: Eastern, Central, Mountain and Pacific; and in Sydney, Hong Kong, Johannesburg, Frankfurt and London. The red second hands on each clock swept around in perfect unison. On the clock marked 'Central', the time was 1.20 p.m. Ten minutes to the gold market closing.

She knew she'd better get in touch with Breimyer Gold & Platinum Inc. This was only a small gold merchant, but nevertheless the most important client assigned to her. They would probably want to sell now to hedge their physical inventory of gold against this sudden drop in the gold price.

She hit the dialling buttons fast and, as the receiver at the other end came off the hook, she snapped, 'John Cootner, please.'

The operator at the other end said unhurriedly, 'Breimyer Gold & Platinum Inc.'

'John Cootner, please,' she repeated. He was the chief trader at Breimyer Inc.

'May I know who's calling please?' the operator asked, remaining maddeningly calm.

'It's Susan Gardner from Bachmann Gardner. It's urgent.'

Now the voice was a little less relaxed. 'I'm afraid he's not at his desk right now. Can anyone else help?'

Goddammit. Cootner would choose to be out now, wouldn't he? 'Give me Daniel Breimyer himself, please.'

'He's in Miami for the Jewellers' Convention, Miss Gardner. He won't be back in Chicago till around midnight.'

Dammit! While she'd been daydreaming about the Canadian Rockies, she'd clean forgotten about the convention.

On the Reuters' screen, the price of December gold had dropped to $324.50. The crucial support line of $325 had been breached.

The Breimyer Inc. operator was saying, 'If you want a trading decision, Mr Cootner should be back in a quarter hour or so.'

Susan glanced up again at the third clock. 1.24. In six minutes the market would close. Perhaps to open way, way down tomorrow. It was quite likely that the price would continue to fall in the Far East and European markets overnight.

She would have to make a decision to trade now on this company's behalf, since she had discretionary trading powers on this account. Her instinct made her check in any case: 'You are quite sure there's nobody in charge of the trading desk at this moment in time?'

'Why, no, Miss Gardner.'

'Okay, thanks.' She rang off and concentrated on the screen. The fall was accelerating, and was already $323.80.

She knew she should sell some gold short now, before the price dropped any further. If she didn't and the price opened further down tomorrow, she could be held negligent. It was precisely for situations like these that discretion was given to brokers, empowering them to act on clients' behalf in an emergency. Susan had been nervous about this aspect of her job, but her father insisted she have at least one discretionary client. 'It's responsible work,' he had said. 'Just what you need right now.' She had already used her discretion once to trade on behalf of Breimyer's, and it had all turned out fine that last time.

But, now, some instinct nagged at her that the gold price would open *up* tomorrow. Then, if she did sell short today, there would be a loss and she would be accused of lack of judgement. One or two assholes here were sure to start crowing again that women were not fit to work in the world of commodities, that Susan was only holding her position because she was pop's little girl, and so on. Not that any of these misgivings solved her present dilemma, she knew. *Should she sell short or should she do nothing?*

Hang it, she decided, there was only one of those two awful alternatives she could possibly take. Picking up one of the grey Interphones, she called the booth downstairs again.

'Gold pit!' came back the clerk's voice. Susan could hear the tension which had developed in it during only the last few minutes. She could also hear the frantic yells of the floor traders beyond. She took a deep breath. 'This is Susan again. Sell one hundred lots Dee Cee Christmas gold at market.' One hundred lots of one hundred ounces was the minimum amount the Breimyers dealt in. By dealing in the minimum, she couldn't do a great deal of damage if the trade went wrong, whilst at the same time she couldn't be accused of negligence in doing nothing.

It took over a minute for the clerk to get back to her with: 'Confirm one hundred lots December gold sold at $323.20.'

It was done. A little transaction involving almost three and a quarter million dollars' worth of gold. When she rang through to the Breimyer Inc. offices again, she was told now that John Cootner was out until at least four o'clock, and probably wouldn't return until tomorrow morning. 'Okay,' she said, 'I just want to leave a message that we've gone short one hundred lots of December gold for your account at a price of $323.20.'

For the last couple of minutes of the gold market, she gazed at her screen, glancing every few seconds at the third clock on the wall. When the minute hand moved to exactly 1.30, she saw that the price was exactly $319. A couple of seconds later, the message flashed up on to the screen that the market had just closed. She breathed a sigh of relief. So far, her decision had been right. And as long as the market opened below $323.20 tomorrow, everything would be hunky dory.

As Christy strode back out through the dealing room after finishing with Mike Bachmann, he saw that the woman was busy on the phone now. He resisted the urge to go up to her. He should have done that when Turnowsky had offered to play Cupid.

Peeling his eyes off her, he left the dealing room and took the elevator back down, to the Grain and Metal Exchange's viewing gallery. The pits closest to the eye were the agriculturals, which seemed to have gone strangely quiet all of a sudden. No-one had informed him that it was because general speculative interest had switched, with the speed and virulence of a prairie fire, to the precious metals markets just before they had closed.

Even though Christy didn't realize it, the markets had smelled that something was about to happen; had perhaps, even, got a nose about some of the things he and Winchester had planned. Rumours had spread in London that Simon Winchester and Greville Holdings were up to something, and information trickled through from the Hejaz that one of the major princes was taking an interest in some precious metal. This scuttlebutt, tied to the chartists' activities, had made the market hawk-eyed.

The gallery gave a broad view of the entire floor, and Christy worked out from the hundreds of new dealing cards strewn about the silver and gold pits now that a huge amount of business had taken place while he had been up with Mike Bachmann.

Up on the price boards, the digital figures showed that

December silver had closed at $5.88. It seemed to Christy that the price was far too low, but he couldn't work out whether this unexpected late drop in the price would help or hinder his plans for tomorrow. But he was committed now. And so was the crown prince's $10 million.

When the corn market closed a few minutes after his arrival, Christy got up from his seat in the observation gallery and left the building. There were still a few things to be done.

In the board room upstairs on the twelfth floor, Mike Bachmann was trying to recover his breath.

Of course he had seen big accounts. But they didn't come much bigger than this one. So why was there this smell of a dead rat about the whole deal?

As his head cleared, Bachmann looked hard at the documents the Irishman had left with him. The broker had never had any intention of trading tomorrow on the London Minerals Board until he was satisfied about a couple of things. The first thing he did was to ring a special number. It was a direct line to the desk of the Chief Executive of the Norris Guaranty Bank of Illinois.

'Pete, can you clear a cheque for me urgently today?'

It was a strange request to be made to one so high as the chief executive. But Pete Simons knew that Mike Bachmann would have a good reason. 'Sure, Mike,' he replied. 'How much and drawn on whom?'

'Ten million dollars. And it's the International Cayman Islands Bank.'

'How much? And where did you say?'

'Yeah, that's what I thought. But the client is 24 carat.' Bachmann gave the details on the cheque, including the bank's head office address on Grand Cayman Island, and spelled out Karim Jamal's name. He didn't mention the involvement of the crown prince himself.

'Well,' the banker said. 'I'll have to check it out and call you back, Mike.'

Immediately after breaking the connection with the Norris Guaranty, Bachmann called the Consulate-General for the Kingdom of the Hejaz. He had discovered it was located on North Michigan Avenue. Bachmann asked for the commercial attaché.

The man had evidently been waiting for a call. When Bachmann queried him about the identities of Messrs Christy

O'Donnell and Karim Jamal, the attaché was quite emphatic. 'Yes, Mr Bachmann, both of them are engaged by his Royal Highness the Crown Prince Ahmed ibn Talal Aziz ibn Jayed. His Royal Highness has personally ordered me to assure you that whatever instructions these two gentlemen give, or documents they sign, are to be considered as if they originated from his Royal Highness himself.'

Bachmann was beside himself with joy when he hung up. His suspicions had been misplaced and everything was beginning to check out after all. Both the letter and the cheque on the desk in front of him were authentic. A $10 million account ... and *he* had bagged it for the firm. And more, this curious purchase of 5,000 lots of silver in London would have a huge impact on the price, and there had to be an opportunity for him in that....

Pete Simons of Norris Guaranty called straight back. 'Mike, two things. First, we've checked out the bank. It's good. Handles lots of big Arab accounts, and this Mr Jamal gets a "Triple A" reference for the amount stated. Seems he's the middleman for a lot of very high-ranking royals in Saudi Arabia, Hejaz and the Emirates.'

The banker paused for breath before continuing: 'But number two, this Cayman Islands bank says its telex line is down. They can't send us formal clearance of the cheque just now. Hopefully the line should be fixed by tomorrow.'

Bachmann protested, 'But the client wants me to trade for him in London first thing tomorrow morning. That's the middle of the night, tonight, here. Clearance tomorrow would be too late.'

'I'm afraid, Mike, as you probably know, we can't credit you the funds until we get the International Cayman Islands Bank's written confirmation, together with its secret interbank telex code for the day.'

There was a pause while Bachmann thought through the situation. He had a cheque for $10 million drawn on a satisfactory institution which was on the interbank network. The telephone reference for the client's ability to meet a cheque for that amount had come up as a Triple A. According to the Hejaz Consulate-General here, everything concerning O'Donnell and Jamal checked out.

The only snag was this lack of formal clearance for the $10 million cheque. Since brokers were always the principals in futures transactions as far as the exchanges were concerned,

Bachmann Gardner & Co themselves would have to carry the risks, or rewards, of 5,000 silver futures contracts if this cheque did bounce.

It took Mike Bachmann just three seconds to decide that the cheque wouldn't bounce. 'Okay, Pete, thanks for looking into it personally for me. I'll send the cheque across this afternoon and I'd like you to inform me of its clearance as soon possible tomorrow.'

The banker had already worked out that there must be a big deal brewing. 'What is it you're buying or selling for these guys, Mike? I'd like in on it too.'

'No can tell, Pete,' Bachmann replied. 'My hands are tied on this one. Can't even trade myself. But I promise to tip you the wink on a good one some other day.'

The minute he put the phone down, Mike Bachmann made a number of casually phrased phone calls to different bullion merchants around the city, and ended up buying four lakhs of silver for his own account.

When it was all done he was highly satisfied. He surely wouldn't tell anyone else about this thing as he had agreed with the Irishman, but hell, surely that dumb guy hadn't expected him to keep that ridiculous promise not to trade for himself?

II

In London, James Greville was so excited about his prospects that he didn't quite know what to do with himself while he waited.

The weekend that Christy and Winchester had observed the sun rise at Talal's wadi, he hadn't gone to Condrieu. Elizabeth had proved to be nothing more than a waste of time the previous weekend, and he also wanted to be at Marylebone House for news from the two men. On the Sunday evening Winchester rang to say the Arabs wanted proof, and that he and O'Donnell were trying to set things up to provide that. It would all take another week.

On the Monday morning, still itching with impatience, Greville went into his father's study. Henry Brewer, who came in every Monday and Thursday on Greville International Corporation business, hadn't yet arrived.

The duke sat behind the huge oak desk and surveyed his

father's portrait. It was the first time he had looked at it since his own had been painted. He didn't care that Charles overshadowed him; he just gazed at the shotgun and thought: *You shot a hole in Elizabeth's and my marriage, but you're gone now. I'm sitting here in your seat, and what can you do about it?*

When the Condrieu agent entered the room at nine o'clock sharp, he was astonished to see Greville in the chair which was now his. 'Good morning, your Grace. Was there any particular reason for your visit?'

'I fancied working in here today. Got any objections?'

Brewer's face became grim. 'As I understand it, this is the study of the Managing Director of Greville International. I would kindly beg you to be so good as to relinquish that place.'

'Fuck off,' said the duke.

Brewer left the study. Two minutes later, the phone on the desk rang. It was Elizabeth. 'James, what's come over you?'

'Ha!' he cried. 'Fine managing director you have. At the first hint of difficulty, he runs off and calls you.'

'Actually James,' she said. 'Henry wanted me to ask you politely one last time to leave the study before he has you forcibly removed.'

Greville reddened. 'You're a whore, Liz. Did you know that? You're siding with that bastard instead of with your husband.'

'Very well,' she said with exasperation. 'Stay there if you must. Henry'll work in one of the other studies instead.'

With triumph written all over his face, Greville beamed at his father's portrait. Then he rubbed his chest. That wretched ache again. But did it matter? He'd scored a notable victory.

Half an hour or so later, bored, he left and returned to his ballroom. A couple of minutes after, Brewer regained the study.

On Thursday 11 October, Brewer's next visiting day and the day Christy arrived at the Chicago Grain and Metal Exchange, Greville again took occupation of his late father's desk. Brewer opened the door, nodded at the sight of him, and departed. This time, Greville didn't leave soon after. He waited for Winchester. The comptroller was due in later that morning, coming straight to the House after flying in from Khurbah.

'Do you think it'll work, Winchester?' Greville said.

Winchester nodded, gazing about himself. *This* was what a study should be like. Not that stupid ballroom, with dated soul music on all the time. He said, 'By dealing with such a huge amount on the LMB, which is much smaller than Chicago, it could work, yes.' His tone was a little strained, Greville noticed.

'You're not a tiny bit jealous, are you, Simon?'

'Jealous? Whatever of?'

Greville grinned. He knew how Winchester had hated O'Donnell's involvement. And now it was the Irishman who had come up with this clever idea. 'Must be jet lag that's getting you down, I suppose, after your Arabian nights away. Anyway, just remember: it was you who taught him everything.'

Winchester just sighed.

Greville said, 'Well, it's a clever idea. And tomorrow morning, we'll see if it works, won't we?'

'I did insist to Ahmed that if it does work, and he makes a profit, Greville Holdings should have a share of it. He was ready to give us fifty per cent, but Jamal flatly refused to go higher than ten.'

Greville nodded, but he wasn't really worried whether it was ten or fifty per cent of tomorrow's profit that Ahmed gave them. What he wanted was the Arab's billion dollars so that they could get the price up to $25. And quickly.

III

After leaving the Exchange building, Christy went to see another commodity broker in Jackson Boulevard. Here he made arrangements for the following morning. Then he took a cab across the Chicago River to the Hejaz Consulate-General on North Michigan Avenue.

'Oh yes, Sheikh O'Donnell,' the commercial attaché said. 'This Mr Bachmann has telephoned to inquire about yourself and Sheikh Karim Jamal. I said you both had impeccable references.'

Christy was delighted. Bachmann's doubting behaviour continued to prove that he was the ideal person for the job.

The diplomat added, 'Bachmann also wanted to confirm that you were staying at the Marriot Hotel on Rush Street.'

The broker only had to carry on in this vein! But Christy knew he shouldn't get over-confident. There was a long way to go yet; lots of things still had to fall into place before the broker could be put to the final test.

That evening he strolled along the Boul Mich – one of

Chicago's evening playgrounds – then dined out on thick charcoal broiled prime steak in Rush Street. From the restaurant, he went straight back to the Marriot Hotel. At around 10.30, he telephoned the Conrad Hilton Hotel on South Michigan Avenue and confirmed a reservation he had made there. Then he packed his bag, went down to the Marriot cashier's desk, and checked out.

At ten to two in the morning, the alarm went off in the bedroom of a house on North Lake Shore Drive. While Jenny Bachmann snored on in her curlers, her husband groped to switch on the bedside lamp. Even in his sleepy state, Bachmann was aware that the London Minerals Board kerb dealings would start in five minutes, at 7.55 London time. He picked up the phone and dialled a number he knew by heart: that of the Sheedy and Ratcliffe floor broker on the LMB.

To the astonishment of the London dealer, Bachmann said, 'Buy 25 million ounces of December silver at the market opening for our account.'

The London man said, 'Can you repeat that please, Mr Bachmann?'

The Chicago broker did. Then he switched off the light and went back to sleep.

A few hours earlier in a brownstone apartment building several blocks away in Walton Street, Susan Gardner bid goodnight to the three girlfriends who had come for dinner.

Throughout the evening, Susan had tried to keep her mind on the weekend ahead, which she planned to spend with one of her friends, Jessica Hurd, in the Gardner family cabin up in Eagle River. For the last two years, Susan had often needed to retreat from Chicago. Still, the attractive prospect of a break hadn't stopped her fretting about the gold market. Her unease lingered after she left the office, and the need to know what would happen to the price tomorrow remained alive inside her.

After the last of her friends departed, Susan decided to go into the office early the following morning – at around five – to check on how the London market was behaving. Making this decision eased her mind and she went to bed just before 11.30, relatively calm. But at around 1.40, she awoke, worry devouring her now like a malignant cancer.

She jumped out of bed and quickly washed. There was no way she could wait until later as she had planned. Not even till five o'clock. The dealing room was available for use twenty-four hours a day so that the markets around the world could be followed, and Susan had a pass key. She knew she had to get to her screen right away to catch the opening dealings in gold on the London Minerals Board. As she came out of the bathroom, she checked her watch. 1.48. In seven minutes the LMB would open....

She dressed in a hurry and drove down to La Salle Street. It was 2.15 when she let herself into the premises. There was one other dealer there, a 25-year-old called Sol Goodman. Facing away from the door, his feet on the desk, he was drinking coffee out of a paper carton and talking on the phone.

The atmosphere was eerie, caused less by the darkness outside the windows than by the unnatural silence within. Apart from Goodman's Yiddish-accented voice, there was only the hum and whirr from Big Brother in the corner. This was a computerized voice recorder which captured every conversation made on the dealing room's external phone lines. The tapes were regularly monitored by the FBI and the CFTC, and provided *prima facie* evidence in legal disputes between clients and the brokerage. They were turning even now to record Goodman's words.

At the sound of her footsteps, he swivelled his chair. When he saw who it was, he waved. Cupping his hand over his telephone mouthpiece, he said, 'Precious metals have gone crazy in London,' then swivelled back and continued on the phone.

Even before sitting down, Susan switched on her Reuters screen. The monitor took an age to warm up, and she muttered involuntarily at the machine, 'Come on, come on.' The green address message glowed now, and Susan rapidly tapped out the four letters XPGA on the keyboard. The 'page' which gave the gold price on the London Minerals Board came up.

For five seconds or so, Susan's mind refused to register what the screen was showing.

SPOT	Bid 339.20	Ask 339.40	Last Trade 339.20
DEC	Bid 342.40	Ask 342.70	Last Trade 342.50
MARCH	Bid 346.00	Ask 347.00	Last Trade 346.40

She tried to focus on the flashing numbers and take in their full importance, and concluded none of it could be true. According to the screen figures, December gold had just traded at $342.50 an ounce. The price had risen by $19.30 an ounce since last night. Susan shook her head. A rise of such a magnitude was impossible. The screen had to be wrong.

But if it wasn't, and please God let these figures be false, then her decision yesterday to sell short for Breimyer's account had resulted in a position which was making a huge loss. Even as she watched, the screen flashed again. The last traded price now was $342.90. A second later the price rose to $343, and ten seconds after that, $343.40. The loss just kept increasing.

Inside her, the panic had begun to build, and she fought to control this, remembering from her short apprenticeship that she should cut a badly losing position. Fast. Before the loss got still worse. This was something she often told clients herself. But she knew now also that she mustn't act hastily. The conflicting ideas paralysed her will and the unearthly silence in the dealing room at that hour added to her confusion.

Now the price flashed up to $343.80. Already the loss was over $200,000, plus commissions. And only a minute or so had passed since she had switched on her screen.

Automatically, she started dialling the Sheedy and Ratcliffe floor broker on the LMB. Before she took any action, she had to find out what was causing this meteoric rise in the gold price.

The London line was busy. The monitor now flashed a price of $344.20, followed by $344.80.

Susan had never realized before that numbers on a screen could be so full of hostility. Furiously, she dialled the number of Sheedy's head office in London's Mincing Lane. The London number rang and rang, but there was no answer.

Cradling the phone in her neck, Susan picked up another phone and dialled another London broker occasionally used by Bachmann Gardner & Co.

'Garrett Commodities,' said a British voice on the first ring.

She breathed a sigh of relief. 'Hello, this is Susan Gardner of Bachmann Gardner in Chicago. What the hell's going on in gold down there?'

'It's silver,' said the man languidly. 'A massive buy order of 25 million ounces hit the market first thing this morning. It came from Chicago, and the silver price went straight up by 60 cents. It dragged up the gold price. Both precious metals, as well as platinum, are still rising. Speculative buying's been fuelling the rises since. They're saying gold could reach $360.'

'Thank you,' Susan put the phone down. Just then the other line answered. 'Sheedy's.'

Susan hung up on that one immediately. She had found out what she needed to know, and now she could put her thoughts in order. On the screen the price advance had also temporarily paused, with December gold dancing capriciously between $344.40 and $344.70.

Rapidly, she thumbed through her client list. Finding Breimyer Gold and Platinum Inc., she looked up the private number of Daniel Breimyer. She had to speak to him. Since she had made the trade on his behalf, the thing would be for him to tell her what to do next. As she dialled his home, she glanced up at the clocks. 2.30 a.m.

A sleepy voice answered, 'Who's that?'

'Can I speak to Mr Daniel Breimyer, please?' she said urgently.

'Speaking. Who's that?'

Susan was conscious now of Big Brother's spools turning in the corner of the room. Biting back the tension in her voice, she said, 'Mr Breimyer, this is Susan Gardner from Bachmann Gardner. I am sorry to bother you at this hour sir, but December gold is currently trading in London at $344.60....'

'And?' he retorted, fully awake and wary now.

She continued, 'Yesterday afternoon, I went short on the Exchange a hundred lots for your account, at $323.20, when the price broke through the year's low of $325....'

Breimyer rasped back, 'Why the hell did you do that Miss Gardner? I just sold the last of our physical stock in Miami, and we were waiting to *buy* in the market. You should have consulted John Cootner before selling.'

On the screen, the price leaped over $345.

'But he was not there, Mr Breimyer,' she said. She realized that desperation was creeping into her voice but was unable to control it. 'And now the price is $345.20. What do you intend to do, sir?'

'What I intend to do is ask your father why the hell he assigned someone like you to look after my account. Women always goddamn well over-react in these situations. They have no business judgement whatsoever.' He slammed the phone down.

Susan stared at the handset. He had hung up on her! The bastard wasn't giving her an answer! Then it occurred to her that maybe Breimyer hadn't hung up, but that there must be a fault on the line. She pressed the button to redial his home number. It was busy. Now, she wondered if Breimyer Inc.

would stand by the trade later in the morning. Maybe not....

Immediately, she dialled London again. The Sheedy floor broker at the London Minerals Board answered.

She said, 'This is Susan Gardner from Bachmann Gardner. What's December gold trading at?'

'Just traded at $346.40.'

Susan's voice was thick as she said, 'Buy one hundred lots at market.'

'Okay, hang on a tick.'

She waited for what seemed like hours, then he came back with, 'Right, we got in at $347 dead.'

'Thank you. We'll do the necessary cross transfers.' She put the phone down. She didn't need a calculator to work out the loss. The sums were fairly simple. $347 less $323.20 made $23.80. Multiplied by 10,000 ounces, it made a 'closed out' loss of $238,000. Almost a quarter of a million dollars.

Panic gripped her afresh. She knew she had acted in Breimyer Inc.'s best interests. But the fact remained that a huge amount of money had just vanished into the bottomless pit of the silver market. And, after Daniel Breimyer's reaction of a couple of minutes ago, she was certain now he wouldn't accept that loss.

Obviously, later in the morning, it would all come out and she'd be bombarded with a whole lot of questions. She would just have to have her answers ready. Right now though, she was totally drained. She left her desk and went into her father's office, where she lay on the couch. Within a few minutes, she fell into a troubled, overtired sleep, not suspecting what else the day had in store for her.

Earlier, while Susan had been saying goodbye to her friends, Christy had checked into the Hilton Hotel. In his room, he nibbled at a club sandwich and watched a movie channel to kill the time until the London Minerals Board opened.

At 1.56 a.m., Christy was watching Gary Cooper and Lloyd Bridges slug it out in *High Noon* on NBC when the phone rang. It was Simon Winchester from the floor of the London Minerals Board.

The Englishman was trying to keep his voice deadpan, but Christy could hear it tremble down the line. 'The buy order just came in, and silver rocketed up.'

'By how much?'

'Sixty-five cents.'

'Sixty-five cents?' he repeated breathlessly. It was stupendous. Much much more than Christy had dared hope for.

Winchester now achieved the deadpan tone he'd been striving for. 'Gold also went up in tandem, by over $18.'

This was of no consequence to Christy. 'Sixty-five cents did you say?'

'And rising.'

'All right, then, Simon,' Christy said. 'I'll try to get some sleep now. If anything unexpected happens, call me back.'

'Okay.' They broke the connection together.

A rise of 65 cents. A movement of more than ten per cent! But Christy knew it wasn't over yet.

Before dawn broke over Ireland, Stephen O'Donnell rolled up his thin mattress in the fetid air of the barn. His subsequent routine was well established: Miss Fortune's droppings – still diarrhoetic – were mucked out, fresh water was brought in and the buckets set for her to drink. Then, after he had taken her out for a walk, he heaped her feed into the metal crate he used as her manger and brushed her sides and back with the body brush – taking particular care with this, since her ribs poked out through her dull coat. Finally, he put her rug back on her.

'We'll be all right for months after this my love,' he muttered to her, stroking her neck. 'Don't you worry now. I'll be able to get you that vet I promised you, and maybe even some decent feed. McDaid will never know about the vet. I'll make sure he doesn't breathe a word to anyone.'

He kissed her on her grey forehead, carefully closed the barn door behind him and set off at a pace for Cloonbarry Village. The first bus to Dublin was at 7.05, and it reached Dublin Castle at 8.25. The job was scheduled for 8.55.

'Don't do it, Stephen,' Pat Fogarty had said at The Jolly Jockey last night. 'You'll get yourself in terrible trouble again. I've got this terrible feeling.'

'I've got to,' he'd answered grimly. 'I need the money for the horse and things.' Both knew 'things' meant betting.

'The gambling'll be the death of you,' Pat had said sadly.

Stephen O'Donnell got to Willy Wallace's flat at 8.40. It was just around the corner from Great George Street, where the jewellers was. Harry McDaid, the leader, was already there with the cloth caps, shotgun, black plastic bag and money. He handed a hundred pounds to Wallace, who would be the gun man, and fifty to Stephen. Both men had been assured of much more from the proceeds of the robbery.

All three of them now pulled their caps on well over their brows. None of them had shaved for the last week. Wallace virtually had a beard. Once the caps were off and the facial hair shaved, they would be practically unidentifiable. McDaid's methods were crude but always effective. Wallace tucked the shotgun under his coat and Stephen slipped the plastic bag into his jacket pocket. When they left the flat, it was 8.47.

The street was heavy with traffic and pedestrians. They arrived across the road from Haskins Jewellers at 8.53 by the large brass clock above the shop. It had opened at 8.30. The moment the long hand of the clock jerked up to the 'XI', the three men weaved across the slow-moving traffic to the pavement opposite. McDaid, glancing through the shop's glass door, growled, 'There are two customers in there. Both elderly.'

Wallace gripped the shotgun confidently under his coat. He knew Haskins was a frail man in his sixties and the assistant a young woman. Easy enough meat, both of them. With his free hand he pulled his cap down to hood his eyes better, then led the way into the shop. Stephen O'Donnell went in next. McDaid was last, stopping just inside the door, blocking it.

The old jeweller had a glass to his eye and was examining something one of the customers had brought in. His red-headed assistant had a tray of diamond earrings out on the counter for the other customer. Both Haskins and the redhead cast cursory glances at the newcomers advancing into the shop. Then both looked again, eyes wide open with horror.

Wallace had the shotgun barrel pointing straight at the assistant's face. 'Hand over that tray to my friend here, darling, and then I want all the trays out from under all the counters, and if you or your boss go getting any funny ideas about setting off the alarm with your feet or anything I'll let the first barrel off on to your pretty face and the second barrel on to your boss's ugly one, all right now?'

There was a long silence and one of the customers raised his hands. The other quickly did the same.

Wallace jerked the gun meaningfully at the redhead and she grabbed up the tray and held it out. Stephen O'Donnell took it and tipped the contents into the black bag he'd fished out of his pocket. Wallace said, 'All the trays, one by one.' He swung the shotgun around on to the jeweller, who aged twenty years in that very moment. 'You too, Haskins. Hand over whatever you're holding and get the trays out from under your counter as well.'

Then as Stephen O'Donnell snatched the ring from the jeweller's hand, the customer who had brought it in stammered, 'Now wait a minute, er, gentlemen, that ring belongs to my wife ... I only wanted to see how much I could get for it ... It's got nothing to do with this shop....'

Stephen, shocked by the familiarity of the voice, swivelled his gaze sharply across, and recognized Oscar McGillicuddy; he was a fellow punter always around at the Curragh, sixty-two years old, bald and with dyed black sideburns which came down to his throat. McGillicuddy was staring straight back at him, and, despite Stephen's attempt to pull his cap down to shield himself better, cried in astonishment: 'My God! It's Stephen O'Donnell!'

'No, no, you're wrong!' Stephen mumbled. Dropping the bag, he rushed past the startled Harry McDaid and out into the street.

IV

Susan awoke a lot later than she'd intended, at 8.30.

After hurriedly tidying herself up, she went into the dealing room. In contrast with a few hours earlier, it was pandemonium in here now. The room was filled with daylight, and dealers were shouting on their phones and at each other.

She was at her desk in a couple of seconds, and saw that gold and silver, which had opened by now in Chicago, were still rising. That was good news. December gold was way up at $353 now, and she had bought the metal for $347 in London, when it still been spookily dark here. But Susan knew that Breimyer Inc. would take some persuading that the actions she had carried out on their account had been with their best interests in mind. Before telephoning Cootner now, she decided she'd fortify herself first with a waffle and coffee in the ground floor cafeteria.

Mike Bachmann arrived at the office at eight o'clock.

Going straight to one of the dealers' desks to check the silver price, he was silently delighted to discover the metal was trading an incredible 85 cents up on yesterday' close here. This meant that the 400,000 ounces of silver he had bought for himself was now making a paper profit of $340,000! It wasn't short of a year's drawings, and he'd earned it in less than twenty-four hours!

Bachmann chuckled inwardly with glee at that dumb Irishman having actually told him not to trade for himself!

But he knew there was still unfinished business with this deal: he had to contact the Norris Guaranty to check if clearance of Karim Jamal's cheque had been telexed through.

When he rang the bank, he was put through to the documentary credits department. Someone there told him: 'No, sir, no telex has arrived from the International Cayman Islands Bank.'

At this piece of news, Bachmann's joy at his huge profit evaporated. The massive silver position the firm had taken earlier might be in great health just at the moment, but the bottom line remained that there were no cleared funds to back it up officially. He asked for Pete Simons, and was put straight through to the chief executive. 'Pete, how come there's no clearance yet on the cheque I brought in to you yesterday?'

'Well, I rang the Cayman Bank first thing and it seems that their telex machine is still down.' The banker's tone was hesitant, unconvinced, and Bachmann's nostrils filled with the second odour of dead rats in less than twenty-four hours. He wasn't an expert on the banking system, but he understood pretty clearly that the Cayman Bank's telex machine should have been fixed a long time ago, or that a back-up one should have been used. One way or another, the bank should have telex facilities functioning by now. How could it do business otherwise? 'Do you have this Cayman Bank's telex number?' he demanded.

'I'll have it for you in a couple of ticks.'

A minute or so later a Bachmann Gardner telex operator was dialling the International Cayman Islands Bank telex number.

The bank's answer-back number came up immediately:

6439 INTCAY

Bachmann smiled with relief. Just the fact that the answer-back had come up meant the bank's line was working.

The telex operator in Chicago punched out this message:

> This is Bachmann Gardner & Co. from Chicago, USA. Please confirm that you are the International Cayman Islands Bank and that your telex facilities are fully functional.

The machine chattered back, almost in indignation:

> We are the International Cayman Islands Bank. What is the reason for your call? Our machine operates fine, thank you.

The Bachmann Gardner operator tapped out a message of thanks and disconnected. Then he tore off the printout of the 'conversation' and handed it to Mike Bachmann.

The broker rang Pete Simons again at once. 'Pete, looks like the Cayman bank's telex is in working order now. Can you get back on to them for the formal confirmation on the cheque?'

When Simons called back three minutes later, Bachmann couldn't believe his ears. 'Mike, they insist their telex machine still doesn't work. Can't understand it.'

Bachmann now called Christy O'Donnell's hotel to find out what was happening. The Marriot receptionist informed him that Mr O'Donnell had checked out in the middle of the night.

'Where's he gone?' demanded Bachmann.

'I'm afraid he left no forwarding address.'

Bachmann hung up, remembering O'Donnell had said yesterday he wanted news of the London silver transaction to be telephoned to him at the Marriot this morning. Now he'd disappeared....

It took the broker a few seconds to put everything together before coming to the conclusion that every damn thing about this deal was wrong! The client had cut and run, the bank was playing hide and seek, and the guy in the Hejaz Consulate-General who had okayed both O'Donnell and Jamal was probably engaged in some sort of double game and lining his own nest because of it. And, in the meantime, the firm still had a 25-million-ounce position, and he held four lakhs in his own name, and the price could come crashing down any minute! The markets were the most treacherous places on earth. 'Shit!' he mouthed; neither he nor the firm could hold on to their silver ... Then it dawned on him that he couldn't sell everything back in a hurry either. If there was some kind of enquiry, it would surely come to light that he had bought bullion for his personal account yesterday, before all this had started, and made one hell of a profit....

'Shit and double shit!' These words he said a little louder. He didn't know what the goddamned hell he was supposed to do.

Christy stood nine stories down on the Grain and Metal

Exchange market floor, watching the cards fly into the silver pit. With him was a floor trader from the other brokerage he had visited yesterday. The man had a Siemens walkie-talkie to his ear.

'Nothing yet?' Christy asked anxiously.

The man shook his head yet again. 'No, sir.'

Christy's breakfast at the Conrad Hilton an hour earlier had been a big one, to help him settle his nerves. Now that same breakfast weighed heavily in his stomach. Was that bloody Bachmann fellow going to do it or not?

Upstairs, Bachmann had already decided to get rid of his own four lakhs of silver, and quickly sold it all to Manson Metals, registering a personal profit of around $375,000.

Now he had to face the other, sickening, question again. Before he could do this, he took two Valium tablets from the bottle he had stolen from Jenny's bedside cabinet. Then he asked himself for the hundredth time in the last few minutes: could he risk getting rid of the 5,000 silver futures contracts the firm was saddled with? There was no doubt that, despite all this morning's excitement, the price would plummet if the market was hit by such a huge sell order, and probably by more than it had risen earlier. It was that Irishman ... that goddamned Irishman! This was all his fault!

Bachmann got up from his desk and went out to look at the dealing room in case O'Donnell had showed up in there for some reason. All he saw, though, was that things were getting more frantic by the second. His head started to spin. *This could only be a bubble which was about to burst, leaving the firm high and dry with an astronomical loss, and it would be his fault....*

Bachmann didn't come to the decision; rather, it took him over. Jerking the door closed, he hastened back to his desk and, with shaking hands, telephoned Sheedy and Ratcliffe in London. He asked for Martin Johnson, one of the directors.

'I bought 5,000 lots of December silver at the London opening this morning. But it looks like the client can't honour the margin requirement. We'd better liquidate the position pretty rapidly. Sell it all back, Martin, at once.'

Down on the trading floor, the walkie-talkie babbled.

Christy's companion stiffened as he pressed it close to his ear. 'It just came in on the LMB Mr O'Donnell. A panic order to sell 5,000 lots of December silver ... Hold on, yeah, they're saying it's the same client who originally bought it who's now selling it all back. Some broker from right here, in Chicago....

Christy took a deep breath. If silver was fundamentally weak, then the price would have to fall right back.

Its first reaction was to drop 25 cents, as 800 fresh sell orders for a total of 12,000 lots – 60 million ounces – thundered into the Chicago pit within a minute and a half. Then buyers began to wade back in on both sides of the Atlantic, and the price rebounded and rose by 11 cents in another couple of minutes. The rebound didn't tail off; it continued. More than ten minutes after Bachmann's huge sell order hit the London market, the silver price in Chicago was actually up by 4 cents over what it had been. Fifteen minutes after that, it had risen by another 8 cents. Then it started to stabilize around $6.85 an ounce for December delivery.

'The market's holding, Mr O'Donnell,' the floor trader said. 'A full 97 cents up on yesterday. Incredible. It's bound to go on up to $6.88 and reach the daily limit ... Do you have an interest in it yourself?'

Christy smiled, 'A little one, yes.' He didn't elaborate that it was to the tune of £900,000, nor that this money awaited him in a burgundy suitcase in London. For he was quite sure that the two men in Khurbah who had asked him for proof had taken note of everything which had gone on. It had worked. It had actually worked!

He turned to leave the market floor, not hearing the man say, 'Silver held, but gold has fallen right back down to $330.'

Back up on the viewing gallery, Christy made for a row of telephones; from here he made a call to Grand Cayman Island.

Mike Bachmann was staggered. By selling 25 million ounces, he had expected the silver price to fall all the way back. Instead, it had only shaken a little, then held. Bachmann Gardner & Co. were now left with a profit of around 20 cents per ounce on 25 million ounces. Five million dollars!

It was while Bachmann was still reflecting on this remarkable piece of luck and deciding that he should quietly take the profit for himself, that Christy O'Donnell walked into his room.

At the same moment, the broker's phone rang.

It was Pete Simons. 'Mike, the telex confirmation just came through from the International Cayman Islands Bank. Your client's cheque has cleared.'

* * *

Every word coming in from Breimyer Inc. was an incendiary device.

'We do not accept the trade you conducted for us, Miss Gardner,' John Cootner declared. 'The price of gold has now fallen back to $325, and is looking to fall back still further. You had no authority to buy at such a high price of $347 in London. Mr Breimyer tells me you asked for a trading decision earlier this morning, but he gave you no instructions to buy. I have to inform you that we consider your actions highly negligent, and we certainly do not intend to carry the loss of $238,000 you incurred.'

Susan had no answer. It was the silver market which had wrecked all her efforts in gold. Whoever had been responsible for buying those 25 million ounces of silver in London, then selling them all back like that, had caused the gold price to act totally irrationally. And she would be the one held responsible for the huge loss incurred with her trade on Daniel Breimyer's account. She had actually done everything right by the book, but the book didn't allow for people playing games with the markets. And that's what some bastard had done with silver.

In Bachmann's office, Christy was quite indignant. 'Why did you liquidate our position, Mr Bachmann?'

As Bachmann stared at Christy, he had the uncanny feeling that this curly-haired Irishman knew perfectly well why the position had been liquidated. Bachmann also suspected that the events of the morning had somehow been engineered by this man. But he had no proof, so he didn't dare make accusations and offend a client who had deposited $10 million with his firm. The money had come through and was in the firm's account, after all.

He did his best to answer Christy's question. 'Mr O'Donnell, your funds weren't cleared, and the silver market has been unhinged all morning. I couldn't risk a sudden fall in the price while we were holding a large position without cleared funds.'

Christy cast a severe look at the broker. 'Am I supposed to inform Crown Prince Ahmed of the House of Jayed in the Hejaz that Bachmann Gardner & Co. feared his cheque would bounce?'

Knowing he had to wriggle out of this somehow, Bachmann said nicely, 'It's simply that until we get to know our clients better we can't be too careful. But you can rest assured, sir, that nothing of this manner will ever happen again.'

Christy struggled to control the delight he secretly felt. Since attack is generally considered to be the best form of defence, he tried to make his look as aggressive as possible. 'And what do you propose we do now?'

Bachmann clung to the slim ray of hope which remained. 'Well, look on the bright side. We closed the position with a $5 million profit. Naturally, that'll be transferred to the crown prince's account.' Saying this hurt him badly. For a few minutes he'd been convinced those $5 million were his.

Christy shook his head. 'Oh, that money will have to be transferred to his Royal Highness, that's for sure. But I don't know if it's enough. I'll just have to see what he has to say about it. In the meantime, I reckon you would be even more better off than before to keep completely quiet about the whole thing.'

'How do you mean "even more better off", sir?'

'Simply, Mr Bachmann, that any leak of what happened can only come from you. And if even the slightest sniff gets out, I'll demand an enquiry by the CFTC into your own actions during this episode. I'm sure you didn't do anything to trap yourself – like trading in silver for your own account for instance – but if you did, I'll make damn certain the CFTC finds out.'

Mike Bachmann gazed at him for a long time as the understanding sank in. Then he shook his head with a rueful smile. 'I never thought the Irish could teach us Jews anything about business, Mr O'Donnell. But it seems I was wrong.'

Just one office partition away, in the other partner's room, Susan slumped into a chair opposite her father's desk.

Thomas Gardner had a slab-sided face under his mop of iron-grey hair, and he wore wire-framed glasses. He scratched his head as he sought the right words. 'Susie, this, er, Breimyer affair....'

What are you going to say, pop? she wondered, her eyes ringed with fatigue. She had written a full account of her actions in a memo to him, and now he would pass judgement. There had already been jeers over the affair by several of the assholes back in the dealing room.

' ... There has been a loss of almost a quarter of a million dollars. And Daniel Breimyer's been on the phone. They don't intend to accept responsibility for the loss....'

Susan shook her head slowly. A bunch of bastards. That's what all these guys were. That Daniel Breimyer, with his thick gold bracelets, and that chain he showed off through his open-necked shirts....

' ... I see your side of it baby, but right now there's a big mess to untangle. I think you'd better go on down to our New York branch for a few months. Maybe six....'

Now she exclaimed angrily, 'Oh that's just great, pop! You force me to join the firm only a short while back, and now that something goes wrong, you want me out of the way, to rot in some sleepy office with only three desks and two monitors! You goddamn well know I did everything right, yet you're ready to pin this thing on me!'

Thomas Gardner raised both palms. 'Now hold on, Susie, just hold on. Nothing's being pinned on you, kid. It's just that it'd be best if you were out of the way for the time being, what with you being a woman and all that....'

'Oh thanks a lot for standing by me pop! I never thought you were as chicken-livered as the rest of them.'

'Now, Susie, you're way off the beam and you know it. This is to do with money, nothing else. I've got to make certain that Breimyer Inc. stand this loss. We have good grounds: neither of their traders was available when an important decision was required, and their account is a discretionary one. So you had every right to trade on their behalf. And the trade you made was the right one. Then, when you saw the price escalating in London, you again did the right thing. According to our "time and trade" tape, the price reached $354.10 on the Exchange at 8.17 a.m., so your second trade, when you bought at $347, can be justified too....'

She hammered out, 'So why do you want to send me to New York then, pop? Everyone here'll be sure then that I was to blame.'

Gardner smiled grimly. 'Don't bet on it. By tomorrow, everyone here will have other things on their plate. But, if you're still around, the issue will carry on, and that's because you're a woman. It'll make it a whole lot easier for me to handle with Breimyer if you're not here, don't you understand?'

She shook her head at his cynicism. 'So why don't you just let me quit the firm for good, huh? You know I'm not interested in this business anyway.'

Thomas Gardner tried harder. 'Susie, Susie, you know that's not the right solution. Do *you* want to see Mike Bachmann take over completely here when I retire in two years' time?'

She didn't respond.

'Please, baby, try to understand.'

'Oh yeah, pop, I understand all right....'

Gardner ignored the indignant tone. 'Good, so when do you plan to go to Wall Street?'

Susan shook her head. 'Never!' However he may try to justify it, New York meant demotion.

Father and daughter stared at each other, trying to figure a way out. For Susan, the image of that cute guy came to mind. Why hadn't he come and swooped her away yesterday, before all this had happened? She blurted out, 'Why don't you open an office in Vancouver and send me there instead?'

'Vancouver?' he repeated, then saw that she was being absurd just for the heck of it. 'Now you know Canada's crazy, Susie, but you have just given me an idea. How about London? You can work in Sheedy and Ratcliffe under our reciprocal arrangement ... How about that, hey, baby?'

Now that, Susan figured, was a much more appealing idea. She liked London, and what was more, when she was there she could look for the bastard who had been behind this game in the silver market which had caused all her problems. She knew the CFTC had no jurisdiction in London, but she could find things out there which might help start some kind of investigation here. Yes, she decided, London sounded just fine. 'Okay, pop, the UK it is.'

Gardner grinned. 'Good. After all, the experience can only help for the future. Even though they only deal in peanuts down there.' He nodded. 'Yeah, that's the best solution. I'll call Sheedy's right away and let them know you're coming. When could you get there?'

Susan decided there was no point going upcountry for the weekend now. She might as well pack instead. 'Tell them I'll come in first thing on Monday morning.'

Gardner's grin widened. 'I'll go one better: I'll get them to collect you at the airport.'

The dimple in her cheek deepened as she smiled. He saw she was over the worst now. 'The only thing is, pop,' she said quite solemnly. 'Will I need a bowler hat?'

Book Three

13.10.79

The old blue Jaguar swept out of the car park at Dublin airport and got into lane for the city.

'But I was just about to get supper ready,' protested Sally Murphy.

'First things first.' Christy hustled the pretty, raven-haired doctoral candidate down the stairs of her tiny flat and out into the street. 'And the first thing we're going to do is visit a pub or two.' He opened the Jaguar's front passenger door and steered her in.

'But you know I can't stand filthy pubs.' Pouting with apparent irritation, she was secretly delighted that he had just turned up after flying in from Chicago, bearing duty-free Opium perfume and a bottle of Smirnoff vodka.

'You should go to pubs more often,' Christy laughed. He was in a terrific mood. 'You're doing a Ph.D. in social anthropology, remember?'

He gunned the engine into life and accelerated away. As he drove, he removed from a jacket pocket the silver locket with his parents' wedding photograph. He flipped it open and held it out to her. 'We're looking for him.'

She looked at the two pictures. 'Your father? But didn't you tell me you'd lost him?'

'I thought I had.'

'So what's all this about?'

Christy glanced across at her. 'He tried to be in touch a few weeks back, see now, but I couldn't speak to him. It was only later that I thought maybe he was in a bad way and needed me.'

Sally gazed at the old photograph with renewed interest.

The saloon bar of The Jolly Jockey was noisy and crowded. Groups of men stood about in the smoke haze with long beer glasses in their hands, arguing or laughing. Although it was a pub Christy had visited just once or twice before, he knew much of the conversation would be about racing. The establishment was one of the favourite haunts of Dublin racegoers; racing prints and posters were tacked up over all the blue velvet walls.

With Sally in tow, he headed for the bar counter, glancing hopefully around at the men quaffing stout ale, aware he didn't have the remotest chance of spotting his father just like that. Still, you never knew....

He elbowed his way to a space at the polished wooden counter, nodding at a couple of racegoers who waved their recognition of him. 'A pint of Guinness and a vodka and orange, please,' he called out to a barman with buck teeth who was drying glasses with a cloth.

The man served up the drinks and Christy paid for them.

'I'm looking for a man called Stephen O'Donnell. Would you know if he comes in here?'

The barman thought for a moment, then shook his head. 'I couldn't say the name's familiar.'

Christy showed him the locket. 'Here's a picture. This one on the left. It was taken over thirty years ago, though.'

The barman took the locket. Christy noticed a faint glimmer of recognition in his eyes. The man turned to show it to his colleague. 'Here, Brian, d'you know this fellow? He's called Stephen O'Donnell.'

The other barman, a burly type with tattoos on his fat freckled arms, screwed up his eyes in concentration over the picture. 'I know a Stephen who comes in here. But this looks more like you than him.'

'It's a very old photo, and he's my father.'

The barman handed back the locket and jabbed a thumb over towards the public bar. 'You'll find old Pat Fogarty at the corner table in there. He knows the Stephen who comes in here.'

'Cheers.' Then, to Sally: 'Come on, my sweet.'

In the public bar, they went straight across to where an elderly man in an old overcoat and flat cap was gazing woodenly into his Guinness.

'Mr Fogarty?' Christy said. He pulled back chairs for himself and Sally and they sat down.

The old man looked up, his eyes watery. At the sight of the pretty girl he smiled and revealed his toothless gums. Then the smile faded, the expression in his eyes died and he resumed his staring match with his glass.

'Mr Fogarty?' Christy repeated.

'Who's after him?' His eyes stayed on the glass.

'Mr Fogarty, I was told you might know the whereabouts of Stephen O'Donnell.'

Fogarty raised his head again, his watery eyes defensive. 'Oh he didn't do what they're accusing him of. He's learned his lesson....'

'Mr Fogarty,' Christy urged. 'I'm not after making any problems for him, see now? I'm his son, see now? I'm looking for him so that I can help him.'

Fogarty looked Christy up and down. 'You're not from the Garda then?'

Christy passed over the locket. 'Take a look at this, now, Mr Fogarty. It's a picture of him. Taken on his wedding day thirty-three years ago. Go on, Mr Fogarty, take a look at it. You can easily make out I'm his son.'

The old man tried but couldn't focus. 'This is some trick the McDaids are playing, isn't it?'

'No, I tell you I'm his son.'

His tone was so earnest that Fogarty's toothless mouth spread into a fresh smile. Then he gave a thin cackle of a laugh. 'His son, eh? I thought you might be the minute you sat down. His spitting image you are. "My son's a great horse trainer," he's been telling me proudly all these years. But whenever I ask him for a racing tip from you, he says you won't tell him, because he's down and out....'

Sally chimed in, 'Could you tell us where we'd find him, Mr Fogarty?'

The old man glanced about at the milling drinkers. Then he muttered, 'He's gone and got himself into trouble, and there are people after him. They'll break his head if they find him.'

'Who? Who's after him?' Christy said.

Fogarty kept his voice low. 'He went on an armed raid at a jewellers with this lot, see. They're a bad bunch, no mistaking it. And then he ran out in the middle of the job. Someone in the shop recognized him. The law are after him too.'

'The law?'

Fogarty nodded glumly. 'Aye, and he's got that poor horse of his to feed, and no money to do it with now neither.'

'But these people he's mixed up with. Who are they, Mr Fogarty? Could they lead me to him?'

The old man shook his head, fear writ large on his face. 'You won't get me telling you their names now. They've murdered enough in the past.' He stared back into his beer.

Sally said gently, 'Would you have any idea where Christy's father might be living?'

Fogarty shook his head again. 'He's always changing his quarters. Last place he told me about was some boarding house in Dorset Street. But that was at least a year and a half back. He's moved more than five times since then. And they're all after him for the rent. Many's a time he's stayed where he keeps that horse of his. He may be hiding out there now.'

She didn't let up. 'And where does he keep this horse?'

'I wouldn't know. He's never said. He promised McDaid he'd tell no-one. All I know is that it's in some burned-down farm outside Dublin. Could be twenty miles away, could be fifty. I wish I could help you more.'

They asked the old man a few more questions, but it was clear there was nothing else he could or would usefully tell them. Finally, Christy thanked him and gave him a fiver for his trouble.

They went off and tried a few more pubs, but got no more news of Stephen O'Donnell. Christy was subdued by the time they dined and went to bed, more shaken then he could have imagined at the idea of his da on the run from a gang of known killers.

The following morning he set off for London.

14.10.79

It was warm and sunny that Sunday morning when Winchester arrived in the ballroom at Marylebone House, wearing a pin-striped business suit and carrying his briefcase.

Two of the house staff, supervised by Diamond, were putting up the painting of Charles Greville next to that of the third duke. James Greville had decided that having the portrait moved here would be an elegant way of killing two birds with one stone: it would annoy Liz when she heard about it from

Brewer tomorrow, and his father would be here to witness silver rise astronomically.

Gloriously light-headed with the success of events in Chicago, he was gazing out at the Park. The occasional car cruised around the square, a group of young folk strolled laughingly by and people were seated on benches in the gardens in the fine weather. Some read newspapers.

Winchester sat at his desk and consulted notes in his briefcase. 'The whole press have got hold of the story of the Chicago Exchange closing "limit up" at $6.88 on Friday, but nothing about our involvement has leaked. Thankfully there's plenty of loyalty left in the City.'

'A horse trainer,' the duke said, turning to him. 'A ruddy horse trainer. Goes out and proves what I've been saying all along. The price goes up a dollar an ounce; the value of my bullion goes up by $80 million. *All in one day!*

Winchester continued to read from his notes. 'Things have spilled over into the unofficial markets around the world over the weekend. In the souks and bazaars of the Middle East, silver bullion, coins and Marie Theresa *Thalers* have been changing hands at well over $7 an ounce.'

The two handymen had got the portrait exactly straight according to their spirit level, and Diamond showed them out. When the doors shut behind them, Greville lit a Romeo y Julieta. 'The Arab's billion's bound to come in now.'

His comptroller didn't share his enthusiasm. 'I'm annoyed O'Donnell didn't come here yesterday as planned. There are loose ends to tie up with Friday's 5,000-lot deal. Ahmed agreed to let Greville Holdings have ten per cent of any profit, remember? There was a $5.2 million profit, so he owes us 520,000.'

Greville shrugged his shoulders. 'We can wait for that money. As for O'Donnell, he called from Chicago to say he had to stop overnight in Ireland on urgent personal business. But he should be here before lunch. He's deserved a few hours off, wouldn't you say?' Observing his comptroller querulously shifting about in his chair, he weighed his next remark carefully. 'Don't forget, Simon, he's done something in one day which you didn't manage during five years of reading the silver price on the telex.'

Winchester reddened and clapped his briefcase shut.

Greville enjoyed the moment. 'That $520,000 can't come through the system until tomorrow anyway. Same as the billion.'

The comptroller's next words wiped the smug smile off the duke's face: 'I am now totally against that billion coming in.'

'What?'

Winchester nodded curtly. 'It's my opinion that we don't continue with this business.'

Greville couldn't believe his ears. 'You're talking gibberish, man. We've just had the most emphatic demonstration that the price is ready to rise, and by a long way. And, what's more, the means are now available to do exactly what you planned yourself!' His pale eyes suddenly lit with understanding. 'Ah, you're upset that O'Donnell proved something you couldn't.'

Winchester rose from his desk. For him it was Greville who was talking gibberish. 'That's got nothing to do with it. No, I have this gut reaction. You're too strapped for cash yourself; too dependent on a partner's goodwill. I've had closer dealings with the Arabs now, and they're not to be trusted.'

Greville laughed, 'But trust doesn't come into it. You've provided for that in your plan. The Arab money's to go into nominee accounts which no-one can withdraw until the whole thing's over.'

'Only $300 million are due in at first, remember? And so many things can go wrong as far as Ahmed is concerned before the remaining 700 million arrive.'

'But the price will have already skyrocketed by then. And when the banks see the riot in the silver market, they'll bend over backwards to lend me any amount I need. Plus it wouldn't be in Ahmed's interest to withhold the second lot of money.'

'All that's only true in theory.'

Greville stared at him, puzzled. He took a long drag at his cigar, and further understanding bloomed. 'Ah yes ... it's the million our Irish chum's getting, isn't it? You want the same.'

Winchester said primly, 'Not at all. If you do decide, unwisely, to go ahead with this affair, I'll be satisfied to continue on my normal salary.'

'So you *are* a romantic, Winchester. Just the adventure will be enough, eh?'

'Something like that.' The comptroller didn't add that there was something just so squalid about the way O'Donnell operated. As if money and the profit motive mattered more than carrying out a job of work simply for the joy of it.

The duke thumped Christy on the back upon his arrival. 'You'd better give up training horses and take a job in the City. They could do with men like you down there.'

The Irishman laughed. 'That's very kind your Grace, but I'm quite happy with the horses, thank you very much.'

Winchester muttered from his desk, 'Well done Mr O'Donnell. Though it was lucky for you that this Bachmann fellow panicked.'

Greville snorted. 'Lucky for all of us, surely.'

To Christy, Winchester said, 'I suppose you'd better finish off with the crown prince and get back to the horses you love so much.'

He laughed, 'In a real hurry to get rid of me, eh, Simon?'

He called Khurbah from his flat upstairs in the House.

Ahmed was equally fulsome in his praise. 'You have done wonders, Sheikh O'Donnell.'

'Oh, it was the market, your Royal Highness.' But though Christy played down his excitement, he was itching to get his hands on the burgundy suitcase and the £900,000 in it. 'The duke was right. Silver was underpriced, otherwise it would have fallen back down. Gold did, see now?'

'Whatever it was, even Jamal admits this is incontestable proof.' There was a long pause. Then: 'You can tell Greville Emir that I agree to join him in his courageous venture.'

The Irishman's heart beat vigorously.

' ... But only on one condition. And that is that you, my dear Sheikh O'Donnell, continue to work with this silver business in London on my behalf.'

Christy said automatically, 'But what about Twelve Pins? There's so much to do in Ireland just now....'

Ahmed interrupted, 'This is much more urgent. Your assistant O'Brien can handle all the work at the stable for the next couple of months. And in any case, the flat racing season doesn't start again until next spring. I need you.'

Christy was at a loss for words.

'Tell me,' the crown prince went on, 'how much has Greville Emir agreed to pay you if I put the money in?'

Christy made an instant decision that he had little to lose by disclosing the figure. 'A million pounds. Cash.'

There was another pause. 'It is a lot of money. Yes, but it is fair. I shall be just as fair. So, as I say, work on my behalf in London and, when the business is all satisfactorily completed, I will give you the same amount. A million pounds.'

Christy's hands were sweating. Another million pounds! He

said, 'Make it 10 million. You'll make 2 billion yourself.'

'Aha, you're haggling with me now. It's a good sign. There's every chance that you can yet become a good Arab. Well, I'll give you 2 million pounds, even if I don't make any profit myself. I mean, what guarantee do I have that I won't lose the billion I'll be risking?'

'You won't lose that billion, and you know it. But I'll accept 2 million if you give me 1 million now, up front. The rest can come when the job is completed.'

'I will give you 200,000 now, up front. Ten per cent. Take it or leave it. It's my final offer.'

Christy smiled grimly into the mouthpiece. Ahmed had him over a barrel and knew it. Greville wouldn't cough up the 900,000 until Ahmed agreed to join. Ahmed wouldn't agree to join unless Christy was prepared to work for him in the affair ... The Crown Prince could command any price he chose. Mike Bachmann had been Christy's pawn in Chicago; but Christy was the pawn of somebody who had more individual economic power than all but a handful of people in the world. What was more, Ahmed knew how to use it. Hadn't he done so with the International Cayman Islands Bank? So, what choice did Christy have other than to say: 'I'll take it, your Royal Highness ...'?

'I thought you would. Jamal has your bank details. Two hundred thousand pounds will be transferred into it tomorrow.'

At 2.30 that afternoon, the fourth member of the team arrived and was ushered into the ballroom by Milton Diamond. The three others were seated around the conference table, with the lunch things now cleared off it.

Diamond served coffee, wheeled a refrigerated drinks trolley to James Greville's side, then withdrew from the ballroom.

'Obviously,' Simon Winchester began, 'the fewer people involved the better. In addition to O'Donnell and myself, we'll manage with two others, who'll be based in America. Compton here is one of those.'

The portly middle-aged man who had joined them sat slumped in his wing chair, smoking a Gauloise. He had heavy red jowls and a bulbous nose which was networked with fine veins. A lifetime of sumptuous lunches in the City was indicated. But Compton Crabbe's eyes hinted at why he had been summoned. They were chips of blue ice in his fleshy face.

Winchester continued, 'I spent yesterday with Compton, explaining everything, and he also helped out in the scam I did in the bismuth market when we were at Macintyres. He'll be able to work single-handedly in Chicago.'

Crabbe leaned calmly forward to flick his cigarette over an ashtray. He had been paid £100,000 yesterday, and would get another 250,000 on 31 December when it was all over.

'In New York,' Winchester went on, 'I need the services of Jason Gilbert, who manages GIC's office building at 210 West 51st Street. He'll operate in New York, Boston and Philadelphia just like Compton here will do in the Midwest. Plus, of course, the Bank of Mexico's silver trading office is in New York.'

Everyone at that table knew, from Winchester's plan, that Mexico was the world's leading silver producer. The Bank of Mexico's New York office was commissioned to both sell new silver production into the US commodity markets, and buy whenever it was necessary to support the price. Crabbe said, 'The New York Bank Mex silver desk manager is a Señor Jorge Menendes. I've known him on and off for twenty years. A real snake in the grass. I spoke to him last night and he'll play ball.'

Winchester explained to the duke: 'From time to time we have to hit the market with extra big buy orders. We don't want these to be spoiled by Bank Mex offloading piles of silver at those times. Gilbert'll keep Menendes privately informed before these orders come in, and in return for Menendes not selling into these peaks, he'll be able to use this inside information to deal quietly for himself.'

'But what about Henry Brewer across at GIC?' Greville growled. 'He's hardly going to let Gilbert work for us.'

'I've dealt with that already.' A mirthless grin spread across Winchester's unattractive face. 'I offered Gilbert £100,000 to leave Greville International and join us immediately, and another 250 at the end of the scheme – same as Compton here – and he's agreed. Brewer will have Gilbert's resignation by telex tomorrow. I sent Gilbert a copy of the dossier by air courier on Friday afternoon, the moment it became obvious the price would hold firm in Chicago, and 100,000 will be wired to him tomorrow.'

Greville nodded. 'I'm impressed, Simon. So there are things other than twiddling about with telexes that you're good at.'

'I thought I'd put some of the $520,000 Ahmed owes us to use.' Winchester turned to Christy now. 'Have you arranged the initial transfer of funds with the crown prince?'

'Exactly as per your brilliant plan, Simon. Jamal's got the full details of the nominee accounts, which we left with him in Khurbah, and Ahmed told me the banks will start wiring the money through first thing tomorrow morning. They'll be sending only $60 million a day so as not to make anyone suspicious. A hundred million will be going through to the different London brokers, and then 200 to the Chicago ones. The first 300 million will all be in by Friday. The rest will follow from the beginning of December onwards.'

Winchester warned, 'I hope you've explained to them that once the money goes into the nominee accounts it's out of their control? No-one can withdraw a cent of it before January at the earliest, and the accounts will be managed exclusively by us to buy silver futures contracts. We'll take delivery of bullion under these contracts, and that's what the Arabs will eventually end up with.'

Christy nodded. 'Aye, Simon. They've understood all right.'

'And I hope *you* understand you'll have to write off the next three months from your life and your horses? We're going to be busy day and night, including weekends.'

'You don't have to worry about me,' he said nonchalantly, but a shaft of anxiety shot through his mind. There was that gang old Pat Fogarty had talked about. He needed to go and find his father before they did. But when would he have the time?

Greville said to the comptroller, 'I'm glad you've decided to bury your differences with Christy and give him a full role.'

'As I said, the fewer people who are involved the better. Since O'Donnell's been foisted on us by Ahmed, we might as well make use of him. I've arranged for another couple of desks, an extra half a dozen telephones, two Reuters price screens and an ADP teleprinter to be installed in my study. A couple of telephone engineers have promised to get it all in by Tuesday afternoon at the latest, for a, um, couple of bob on the side.'

The other three laughed, in admiration rather than amusement.

'Now,' continued Winchester, unmoved. 'Let's get off the overall strategy and on to the first-phase tactics.'

The talk went on for several hours into the autumn evening. It was accompanied by a pungent fug as Crabbe consumed Gauloise after Gauloise and Greville kept him company by smoking a string of cigars. Thankfully the cold drinks which the duke passed around moistened the atmosphere. When the discussions finally came to an end, the sodium lamps were blazing out in the Park. Winchester and Crabbe departed, but Christy didn't budge from his seat, and neither did Greville. They chatted desultorily for a few minutes about their chances of success, about horses and so on, looking thoughtfully into each other's eyes. Christy was sizing up the moment. Finally, he said, 'Well, your Grace, I think there's some business to be settled between us now.'

Greville sipped a whisky, all expression vanishing from his face. 'I've been thinking this afternoon about the remaining £900,000, Christy ... I'm afraid I've decided to keep hold of it until that billion dollars actually arrives.'

Christy's hackles rose. 'Now wait a minute. The deal was that the million pounds would be mine when I got Ahmed to agree to join in this scheme. And he's agreed.'

'There's really nothing to worry about, old boy,' said Greville jovially. 'The minute that billion is in, as I said, you shall have your money.'

'But that won't be until the end of December! Almost another three months.'

'You weren't planning to go off anywhere before then, were you?' Greville asked coolly.

'No. But a deal's a deal.'

Greville fished a little square key out of his pocket. 'Quite right. And here's the key to the box in the vault where the money's lying now. Box B14, and this is the only key.'

'But I can't get into that vault to use this key unless you open the main door, can I, now?'

'You will when the billion dollars comes in. As you yourself said, a deal's a deal.' He added, 'Nothing personal, Christy. It's just that now Ahmed's made it a condition that you stay on with the scheme, the money should stay here until the whole thing is over.'

The Irishman continued to bridle. 'You didn't say anything about this before I got Ahmed to join you.' He felt like the Pied Piper, who didn't get paid after he had rid Hamelin of the rats.

'I didn't need to. I would have thought it was obvious.'

'But $300 million in cash will be in by Friday. What about that then?'

James Greville raised his hands in surrender. 'All right, all right, Christy, when that $300 million is in, you can have £200,000 to add to the £100,000 you've already had. Three hundred thousand altogether. I think that's fair enough. But the rest of it stays in my safe until the rest of the Arab money comes in. Don't look so worried. You'll have the only key.'

He handed it over.

Christy put it carefully into his pocket, not liking this turn of events at all. When it came to actually parting with money, there were people, no matter how rich they were, whose hands trembled with fear. But, like with Ahmed earlier, there was nothing he could do about it except console himself with the thought that the duke, being titled, had to be a gentleman at the bottom of it.

15.10.79

'Some things are done differently in England,' Paul St John Burrowes said at noon the next day.

'Wow, I can certainly see that.' Susan followed him in to lunch. Sheedy and Ratcliffe plc's oak-panelled executive dining room was on the sixth floor of their building in Mincing Lane. A picture window from floor to ceiling gave panoramic views over Tower Bridge and a lengthy stretch of the Thames; standing before it was a long table with glittering silverware and cut glass laid on crisp white linen. Boats glided by on the river. 'You guys have a banquet every day, huh?'

Burrowes turned and smiled charmingly at her. 'The City of London functions on its stomach.' He had floppy blond hair over sparkling blue eyes, an accent which Susan could spread on toast and devour, and he was immaculately dressed. A neatly starched white kerchief stood unflaggingly in the top pocket of his black Hardy Amies suit. He took her by the elbow and led her to her chair. 'Unfortunately, we can't all eat together. The problem is the clients. They do tend to call at unsociable moments.'

Susan chuckled, 'Now what would my father say if I went back to Chicago with that attitude?'

Burrowes smiled knowingly.

Lunch consisted of five exquisite courses with three different wines and was provided by French contract caterers. Watching the directors and senior dealers drift up to and away from the table, Susan thought of the shirt-sleeved guys back at the firm who'd be gulping down a sandwich in the Exchange cafeteria later today. Wine in crystal glasses sure wasn't available there.

When the crème caramel and compôte des fruits came around on a trolley, it began to sink in for Susan that she actually was in London. First thing that morning, she had arrived at Heathrow Airport, where this hunk, Burrowes, a director of Sheedy and Ratcliffe Ltd, had met her. Smiling tiredly, she had stuck out her hand with: 'Well, hello there, Mr Paul Saint John Burrowes.'

'Oh no, that's not how you're supposed to say it,' he had laughed. 'It's 'Sinjin'. Paul Sinjin Burrowes.'

Sinjin Burrowes, she repeated voicelessly to herself, casting a surreptitious glance at him now. How wickedly quaint and British and charming both you and your name are.... He transferred a spoon of compôte de fruits to his mouth, then wiped his lip clean with his napkin. She wondered: Are you married, Mr Sinjin Burrowes? He didn't notice.

After lunch, Burrowes put her with the precious metals experts, as these were the commodities she was used to, and she found herself alongside the most physically imposing of the four gold and silver traders, a 28-year-old Yorkshireman with broad coat-hanger shoulders, who wore large square spectacles on his large pimply face. His name was Giles Clark.

He swivelled round in his chair when she was comfortably installed in front of her screen, and handed her a sheet of paper with a list of names. 'Here you go now, luv.' His Yorkshire accent was engagingly difficult to follow. 'These are the boogers you'll be looking after.'

'Okay thanks, Giles.' She glanced down the names of the small private speculator clients. 'I guess I'd better start calling them and introducing myself, huh?'

'Mightn't be a bad idea. And if any ever blame you for bad advice, or complain that we're robbing them in commissions, just pass 'em over to me. I'll sort them out for you.'

'Oh thanks.' She smiled at him, really meaning it.

In fact what irritated her that afternoon wasn't the clients but the British telephone system. Unlike the tone-activated Bell phones back home, when she hit the buttons on these ones they clicked and clicked for an eternity before she got the ringing tone. That was a drag. The market action, on the other hand, was easy enough for her to familiarize herself with.

Silver continued in a firm uptrend after Friday's shock waves, with December futures having already hurdled over $7 that morning. It was trading in Chicago at $7.10 when the London markets went to bed at around five o'clock.

Sinjin Burrowes drove her in his red Porsche to the company flat in Clarendon Place, off the Bayswater Road. Beautifully airy, with a forty-foot lounge overlooking Hyde Park, it was tastefully furnished with period furniture and expensive prints on the walls. On the dining table was a vase of fresh flowers; stacked neatly on the coffee table were up-to-date magazines.

'How thoughtful,' she said, going into the kitchen. 'Hey, there's a microwave!' she cried. 'They've caught on here, huh?'

'We do try to be up-to-date.' Burrowes followed her in.

'I bet a dog hasn't been grilled alive in one here yet. Some lady in Wisconsin put her wet chihuahua to dry....' She broke off. His blue eyes were running smoothly up and down her body.

'The fridge and larder should be fully stocked,' he smiled. 'I can rustle you up a bite of supper if you like.'

Uncomfortably conscious of the largeness of her breasts all of a sudden, she stuck out her hand. 'I had such a big lunch that I think I'll survive, Sinjin. Thanks for the trouble you've taken, but I suddenly feel all out. Jet lag, I think.'

She nibbled at coleslaw from the refrigerator after he left.

Why had she been so ill at ease with him? she wondered. Guys had been coming on at her for the last three years, but she had never felt threatened; she had just disregarded them. Now, she realized, changes were taking place inside her. Could it be that she needed some louse from the opposite gender in her life again?

When she went to bed and switched off the bedroom light, a shadow was thrown on the wall by the street light. It looked curiously like a man. Gradually establishing that it was cast by a tree outside her window, she mumbled, 'Have you come to haunt me, Ross?' She drew the bedclothes tightly over herself, adding, 'I'll get that bastard who had me burned in the Grain and Metal Exchange. I'll have his balls.' Deep sleep quickly overtook her, and jet lag wiped out all dreams.

16.10.79

In 1979, tapping some keys on a telex board was all that was required to send money from one bank to another. Account numbers, amounts and, of course, the all-important secret codes were the elements which had to be composed. It was a fairly low-noise operation, even when the amounts were huge and the banks communicating with each other were in different parts of the globe. The main thing was to have the money to send.

From Beirut, Karim Jamal orchestrated the clicking that week of such telex keys in banks in Switzerland and the Caribbean, and millions of Crown Prince Ahmed's dollars flowed silently into London and Chicago.

On Tuesday 16 October, silver surged forward again, with December futures opening on the LMB at $7.15.

Twenty-four hours at Sheedy and Ratcliffe's had made Susan more tolerant of the telephone. She got cordial with her clients and made many trades on their behalf. As the talk in the busy dealing room continued to centre on the bullish mood in silver, she took the opportunity to ask Giles Clark, 'Isn't there a lord or something here in England who's got a load of silver bullion?'

'Aye, luv,' replied the Yorkshireman. 'It's James Greville, the Duke of Marylebone. He's the one with the silver mountain.'

'So he's the guy who made that play on the LMB last Friday which started off all this buying, huh?'

'Nobody knows who was behind that,' he said, a mite hurriedly.

But Susan got the feeling from his tone that he did know. That everybody here knew, except her. 'I'll let you into a little secret, Giles?' she said sweetly. 'It was because of that business that I got thrown out of Chicago, and if it's not too hush-hush, I'd like to identify the guy responsible.'

The expression behind Clark's glasses was sympathetic.

'Well why didn't you say so, luv? Everybody suspects it was something to do with Greville, of course. But no-one can be quite sure. What's made it hard to pin down is that the order for the 5,000 lots came from Chicago....' A thought struck him. 'But hang on a minute. Wasn't it your own Mike Bachmann himself who placed the order? Yes, I believe it was, you know. And he's the one who wanted it all kept highly confidential. Martin Johnson, one of our directors, did ask him who the client was though, but just got told it was something to do with "bloody Arabs".'

Susan had heard the Arab rumours before. But Mike Bachmann had placed the order? That she hadn't known. 'Well, thanks for telling me all that Giles. You really are a sweetie.'

Taken by her frank friendliness, he lowered his voice and said, 'But apart from what happened last Friday, there *are* other things concerning Greville and silver which are really fishy.'

'Yes?' She edged her chair closer to hear better.

'When we have a minute, I'll show you.'

During the coffee-time lull in the trading, Clark nodded at her. 'Come with me.'

They went up in the lift to the administration floor. In one of the accounts offices, Clark asked the senior book-keeper, a dignified Asian named Bipin Patel, for details on three clients.

The master client list was kept in a complex card index system, with all deals recorded in old-fashioned ledgers. But a man was seated at a desk punching data into a computer terminal.

'We're finally getting computerized,' Clark explained.

'Yeah,' Susan laughed, 'Sinjin told me yesterday. You guys don't quite live in the dark ages, you're only ten years behind.'

Patel produced the requested cards, and Clark took Susan to an empty office nearby. 'Look at these. And they're just a few.'

She examined the cards. They gave account details about the Duchess of Avon, Lady Jane Cooper and Viscount Jonathan McGonagle. 'All titled folk, huh, Giles?'

'Aye, that's the first obvious link. The second is that they're all connected to the Duke of Marylebone. The Duchess of Avon is his cousin, Lady Jane Cooper his daughter and Viscount McGonagle manages some of his lands in Scotland – McGonagle's daughter is supposed to be the duke's mistress, but that's by the by. Now, look closer for the next obvious link.'

Susan gazed over them again. 'All the accounts were opened

in May this year by a Simon Winchester.' She looked up. 'Who's he?'

'I'll give you three guesses.'

'He works for this Greville guy?'

'You got it in one. He's the duke's right-hand man. Used to be an analyst at Macintyres, and it was just after he joined the Marylebone family five years back that James Greville started investing heavily in silver. Curious, don't you think?'

'Definitely.'

Clark returned the cards to Patel with thanks, and went back down in the lift with Susan. 'There are at least a dozen accounts like that here, and I'm a hundred per cent sure there are similar trustee accounts with just about every other big commodity brokerage in the City.'

'Wow.' When they got back to their desks, Susan said, 'Giles, thank you so much for letting me in on all this. But will you be a real, real sweetie and let me ask you just one more thing?'

He laughed, 'Go ahead, luv, what is it?'

'This Duke of Marylebone ... What I'd like to do is to meet him somehow. Or at least that Simon Winchester guy.'

'Well, I wish I could introduce you, but I don't know them closely enough.' He thought for a second or two, then shook his head. 'The only way I can think how you'd get in through their front door is for you to try to sell them some of our services. Not that they're short of any, that is!'

'I've got to have this business out with them, you see. Isn't there some place I could bump into one of them accidentally?'

Clark's eyes brightened. 'Now there's a possibility: the London Minerals Board. Winchester's sometimes there for the silver "ring". Do you want to try there later this morning? I'll come across with you and point him out if you like.'

'Oh yes,' Susan said, her excitement soaring. 'If it's no bother for you, I'd like that very much.'

After an early lunch, Susan and Clark went across Mincing Lane to Hanseatic House, where the 12.55 chime had just gone to end the official zinc ring and start the aluminium one. This whole 'ring' business was something Susan had found wickedly droll when it had been explained to her in Chicago. The tradition started in the nineteenth century, when London was competing for commodities trade against Liverpool, Bristol and Glasgow. The City's merchants and brokers realized that, to win world-wide business, they had to demonstrate that only in London could fair prices be obtained which didn't benefit any particular party. So the London Metal Exchange was set up in 1837; shortly after, the rival London Minerals Board was also formed and organized along similar lines, with the addition of gold and silver trading. Members daily drew a large chalk circle on the floor and shouted out the prices they offered or bid for the metals. Each metal was traded by open outcry like this for periods of five minutes. A clang of the bell by the Secretary, customarily togged out in frock coat and top hat, and a cry of 'Copper, gentlemen, copper', would commence the day's proceedings.

The frock coats had gone by 1979, and so had the chalk circle. Now, soft red leather chairs for the dealers made a ring around a brass plate on the floor, and behind these were banks of phones. The dealers' assistants kept in contact with the trading offices by telephone, and sent coded gasps, sneezes and screams to their principals who, upon interpreting the signals, did their best to out-shout the competition.

'I really hope that Winchester guy's around,' said Susan as they crossed the foyer of the Board. City gents stood gossiping by the display cases, which contained ore samples of the metals traded, though the pieces of rock were outnumbered by the golfing, cricket and backgammon trophies won by Board members.

Susan and Clark went on through to the trading floor. There were only a dozen or so dealers lounging about in the leather chairs, and the trading in aluminium was dull. Clark glanced around. 'He's not here, luv, but that's where he usually stands when he does arrive.' He pointed to a set of booths in the corner just beside the Secretary's rostrum. 'Johnson Mathey let him use their phones.'

Susan nodded. 'Okay, let's wait a while.'

Just before the chime went for the start of the silver session, dealers materialized seemingly from nowhere. In seconds, the floor was crowded. For the five minutes that silver was traded, Susan observed the men using the booths by the rostrum. One or two stared wolfishly back. Women weren't entirely unheard of in these parts, but were rare. Susan was rarer than most.

At ten past one, the ring ended. Clark shook his head. 'I'm afraid he didn't come in. But did you see how bullish silver's staying? My guess is that half these blokes here today have been buying for other nominee accounts of the duke's, too.'

* * *

Across the Atlantic that afternoon, silver futures reached an all-time high of $7.29 an ounce, with fund managers from the big institutions wading in on the long side despite powerful short selling by the major bullion merchants and refineries.

In all the commodity brokerage houses in London that afternoon, even in firms such as Czarnikow's – who specialize in sugar – the price screens were tuned to silver. At Sheedy & Ratcliffe's, Susan was constantly busy on the precious metals desk, despite her clients only trading in little parcels of lots.

As she ploughed on, the idea plagued her that she should go down to the LMB again later that afternoon for the unofficial ring in silver. But she couldn't bother Clark again to come along to identify Winchester. He'd got even busier than her.

At 4.40, when the last unofficial silver ring was over, she turned to Clark. He had paused to drink down a cup of tea. 'Giles, I don't want you to go to the trouble of coming down with me to the silver ring every time to try to identify this Winchester guy....'

'That's very kind of you,' he laughed, putting his cup back in its saucer with a clink.

'But couldn't you describe what he looks like?'

'A bit of a terrier, aren't you?' He thought how best to help her. He scratched his head, then shook it. 'I'm sorry. I'm hopeless at describing people. What I can tell you is that he hasn't got a glass eye or a harelip or a beard. At least he didn't have about three years ago when I last saw him.'

'Well could I get hold of a photograph of him from someplace?'

Clark chuckled again. 'I may not be able to describe him, but I can tell you he's no pin-up beauty. I mean, where do you imagine there'd be a photo of him? *Playboy* magazine?'

'Back home,' she said determinedly, 'there are articles and features all the time in *Time* and *Newsweek* and other magazines and newspapers about guys who are prominent in Wall Street. Doesn't that happen here, too?'

His brow creased with thought. 'Well, of course, City people here get in the news, too: in the *Financial Times,* and also *The Times,* the *Telegraph* and other serious papers. I've a friend, a lass, who works at *The Times*. If you want, I'll call her and ask if you can go along and look at what they've got on their files.'

Susan leaned across to give him a peck on the cheek. 'Did

anyone ever tell you that you were an angel, Giles?'

He grinned. 'Well then, I'll spread my wings and tell you something else that I shouldn't really. But you're such a tenacious lass, I reckon you've deserved it.' His voice dropped several decibels: 'I heard from Martin Johnson that money – in US dollars – has been coming in from Switzerland in the names of those accounts we looked at earlier.'

'You've believed all along that the duke's behind this, haven't you, Giles?'

'Aye,' he nodded thoughtfully. 'There's still no hard proof, though I'd say it's pretty obvious now.'

It was blustery and dark over London at six the next morning when Susan left Clarendon Place in a minicab. She got out by the massive Henry Moore sculpture in Printing House Square and went into *The Times* Newspaper building. To the desk sergeant she announced she had an appointment with the journalist Lesley Robb.

'Fourth floor, third office on the right as you come out of the lift,' he said.

Susan followed the directions. When she entered the room, an attractive woman in purple came up to her. 'Miss Gardner?'

'That's right.'

'Hello, I'm Lesley Robb. Giles said to give you every assistance. What can I do for you?'

'I'm doing some research on Macintyres, the big City investment house. My firm back in the States may be merging some of our activities, and I'd like any information I can get about what they've been up to over the last five to ten years.'

Lesley Robb nodded. 'Sounds reasonable. Wait here and I'll see what we've got on them in our cuttings room.'

About ten minutes later she returned, bearing a fat black file. 'You're in luck. There's much more here than I expected. You can take a seat at that desk there and have a go.'

Susan thanked her profusely and flicked through every article, looking for a photograph. There were several, and she examined each one closely, though without yet coming across Winchester. Then under a story about Macintyres making a killing in the bismuth market in 1973 there was a small picture of two men outside the firm's offices. The caption read: *'Crabbe and Winchester Cash In On Bum Bullets'*. The 'Bum Bullets' was a reference to suppositories; bismuth was an important commodity in the manufacture of these.

Susan stared at the man on the right of the photograph, thinking, why the hell hadn't Clark told her about that goddamn nose? It poked right out of the picture!

She looked on through the file for another ten minutes, but the only other story referring to Simon Winchester was a short article about him leaving the company to join James Greville.

She took the file back to Lesley Robb. 'Can I have a copy of this picture?'

'Yes, I don't see why not.' If Lesley Robb was puzzled about what this photograph could have to do with a merger of investment houses, she didn't show it.

Five minutes later, the photocopy in her briefcase, Susan was on her way across the Square Mile to Mincing Lane and the offices of Sheedy & Ratcliffe.

Giles Clark's 'confidential' information about funds being transferred from Switzerland was now being openly talked about. But today's rumour was that it was Arab money, being channelled out of Beirut, and nothing to do with the Duke of Marylebone.

All morning, December silver futures continued to rise slowly but relentlessly, sucked up by an invisible magnet. At 11.40 Susan left her desk to go over to Hanseatic House in time for the 11.50 silver ring. She had the photocopied picture in her hand. As she hurried through the foyer of the LMB, she collided with a man who was just terminating a conversation with another man, and who stepped casually into her path. He had mousy-brown hair.

He turned to look at her, but she had already recognized him by the profile of his nose. It was Simon Winchester, and she had literally bumped into him.

His gaze went to the picture of himself in her hand and she crumpled it up immediately. Winchester now scanned her face with his piggy eyes, a question mark in them.

'I'm sorry,' Susan said sweetly. Then, with pretended surprise, 'Why, you're Simon Winchester, aren't you?'

He blinked as he took in how attractive she was, and straightened his tie. 'Yes, that's right. But I don't think we've met?'

Susan followed her instincts about the best way to hook him: she uncrumpled the photocopy and let him see it. 'I recognized you from this picture. I also know you're six years older now, but I see you haven't changed.'

Winchester's curiosity was more marked now, and red tinges

crept into his cheeks.

'I was so hoping to meet you and be able to talk to you.'

The man with whom Winchester had been chatting glanced at his watch and said, 'Must rush, Simon, the silver ring's about to start.'

Susan's own interest in the ring had vanished, and she thrust out her hand. 'I guess I'd better introduce myself, huh? I'm Susan Gardner from the States.'

Winchester took it limply, wondering what this was all about.

'I believe you work for a duke?' she said.

He cleared his throat. 'Yes, that's common enough knowledge.'

She smiled gaily, and the dimple in her cheek was very pronounced. 'It's just that we in the States are completely fascinated by royalty....'

He glanced beyond her towards the trading floor and it was obvious that he wanted to tear himself away.

'You see I've just come from Chicago, and um, I'm at Sheedy and Ratcliffe's, and it would be a feather in my cap with the folks back home if I could land an account with someone royal....'

'We already have accounts with your firm, Miss Gardner.'

'Yes, yes, I know,' she said hurriedly. 'But I think you probably don't know of all the other services we offer. I mean I'd just love to have lunch with you and ... '

Winchester glanced up at the foyer clock, 'Well I'd like to help and so on, but lunch is simply out of the question any day of the week, and as it happens I'm already late just now and ... '

'Dinner then,' she said firmly. Then she added, in as meek a voice as she could muster, 'Please? On Friday, for instance? When you've no work to distract you? You can't imagine how much I'd appreciate that.'

He fiddled with his tie again. 'Well, er, all right then. I think I'll manage dinner on Friday. You'd better call me at Marylebone House to confirm....'

'I've got a better idea. She dug into her pocketbook and fished out a Sheedy and Ratcliffe card. On the back she scribbled her Clarendon Place address and handed it to him. 'Here's where I'm staying. Why don't you come by when you've finished work Friday?'

'Well, all right then, I suppose I could make it 8.30-ish.'

Smiling, she held out her hand again. 'That'll be just fine.'

19.10.79

By nine a.m. that Friday, the study which Winchester and Christy were working in was again a sea of paper. The LMB had been open just an hour, but computer printouts, telex messages and buy orders were strewn over the floor. The cleaners had done their best earlier, and would do so again tomorrow morning; just now, it was impossible to tell that they'd been.

The desks were pushed together to form one large work area. Price screens faced both directions and numerous phones were to hand. Both men were busy on these. Billowing out of the telex machine was an unbroken roll of printouts which curled on to the floor five yards away. There were messages from Karim Jamal and Swiss banks of funds which had gone into the brokerage houses; confirmation that the $520,000 bonus had been wired through; information from Crabbe and Gilbert about the shipment of bullion from the certificated warehouses of the Chicago Grain and Metal Exchange and the New York Board of Trade to vaults in Zurich and Geneva; bookings of space made by the two men across the Atlantic in silver refineries; price updates, confirmations of trades and so on.

More information chattered up non-stop. Christy or Winchester glanced at the machine whenever they could, making use of any relevant data. Otherwise they were permanently on the phone to brokers and traders in London, Zurich and Frankfurt, monitoring the kerb and ring and 'round the back' prices, and buying silver in every dip. Winchester slipped off to the City once a day or so to confirm the arrival of monies at some brokerage house, check the execution of some of the larger trades, and just get a feel of the sentiment on the floor of the LMB. He hadn't been back to the Board since his encounter with Susan.

In late morning, when the duke looked in, December futures had long since passed seven and a half dollars and taken the value of his bullion stack over $600 million. Now, Winchester glanced up from something just coming up on the telex. 'That's it, your Grace: confirmations from Manufacturers Hanover Trust and Geneva Credit Reserve. The last of the funds have reached Chicago. That first $300 million is all in now.'

It was almost twelve o'clock when the duke finished counting out £200,000 to Christy in the basement.

The Irishman checked the money twice, withdrew ten bundles – £20,000 – which he tucked into his inner pockets, and clicked shut his briefcase. Then he drove off to his merchant bankers in Threadneedle Street and handed the 180,000 over to William Lemon as before.

Two hundred thousand pounds had also come in for him from Switzerland as Ahmed had promised, and Lemon was so impressed by all this money inflow that he added an extra tick on to the interest terms which he had already made very advantageous for his beloved horse trainer. There was now around eight hundred thousand pounds of Christy's here.

When he returned to Marylebone House, he paused by Mrs Thorpe's desk to ask her to make a reservation with Aer Lingus. He knew Winchester wouldn't like him taking leave, with all the work piling up, but he absolutely had to go to Ireland this weekend. It would be his last chance before December.

In Clarendon Place at 7.30 that evening, Susan was seated in front of the dressing-table mirror with a hair dryer, shaking her auburn ringlets in the hot-air blast. Wanting her hair to be perfect tonight, she ended up wetting and redrying it twice before she was satisfied.

She then searched the wardrobe for a suitable outfit. She tried four, and rejected each one out of hand. Then she tried the second one again. This was an $1,800 Bill Blass creation: an amber cotton top which wrapped her torso in soft cocoon-like swathes, and sage silk trousers which made her legs longer. A cummerbund raised her waist and attention was focused on her upper body. Ross had used to say the outfit made her look like Goya's 'Clothed Maja.' It certainly accentuated her breasts. Too much? she wondered, as she examined herself in the mirror. Then she muttered, 'Well, hang it, why not?' It took a sprat to catch a mackerel, and she really wanted to hook this Winchester guy tonight. While she was at it, she might as well enjoy it, she decided, rummaging about among her bracelets, brooches and earrings to find the right combination. It had been a long time since she had taken so much trouble about her appearance.

The entry-phone buzzed as Susan was clipping on her earrings. She squirted a burst or two of Chanel No. 19 in the right places and went to answer the door. When Simon Winchester emerged from the lift, his eyebrows shot up in admiration. Then he noticed her breasts. His Adam's apple bobbed in his throat.

'Come on in, Simon.' Hooking her arm in his, she made sure he got a good whiff of her perfume through that long pinched nose.

'You're, er, looking very nice, Miss Gardner.'

She said sternly, 'Now no more of that Miss Gardner stuff.' She led him to the dining table. 'It's Susan, okay?'

'Er, yes, all right.' He was clearly flustered.

'Here are some things I'd like you to look at.' She indicated brochures spread out on the table, knowing it was a flimsy pretext for getting him here. With a bit of luck, though, he'd be sufficiently distracted to swallow the bait.

Winchester quickly flicked through the handouts, which had glossy colour pictures of copper tubing being loaded on to ships and pigs crammed in an abattoir yard – thereby demonstrating that the world's commodities were being well taken care of by Sheedy and Ratcliffe – while Susan fixed them both a drink. A minute or two later, he shook his head with embarrassment. 'I'm afraid it is all rather tame stuff.'

The reaction was not unexpected, so she tried her next card. With a sorrowful shake of the head, she cleared the brochures off the table. 'Oh well, I guessed you were too high-powered. So no aristocratic client for me to tell the folks about, huh?'

Winchester watched her, embarrassed by her disappointment. Clearing his throat, he said, 'Well, perhaps, if it will help you so much, perhaps I can put a tiny bit of business your way.'

She was suddenly ecstatic. 'Oh can you! Really?'

'Anything to help the "special relationship" with the Americans.' He bared his teeth at her in one of his best grins, and she gave as sincere a smile as she could muster to show that she had enjoyed his little joke.

Winchester jiggled his tie knot. 'But it will be tiny. You see, I look after a small investment fund for one of the duke's daughters – Lady Deborah Spencer. So why don't I open one of your firm's offshore managed accounts and transfer, say, £30,000 for you to play with?'

'Oh Simon, that's wonderful!' She threw her arms around his sloping shoulders and gave him a peck on his pale cheek.

He turned crimson and stuffed the relevant brochure into a side pocket. 'Come on. My minicab's waiting outside.'

They went, inevitably, to the Lemonia Restaurant in Regent's Park Road. Kostas's jaw dropped lower than the Grecian urns in a recession, while Winchester proudly wheeled Susan to his favourite table for two.

'Nice place,' she said when they were comfortably installed. Then, aware that every direct stare of hers into his eyes got him warm under the collar, she said sweetly, 'So, Mr Simon Winchester, mystery man of power and influence, tell me all about yourself. And I mean everything, from A to Zee.'

Kostas served up retsinas on the house and slyly winked his approval at the comptroller. Winchester didn't notice. He was trying to think how best to please her and feeling a bit scared at wining and dining quite such a lovely woman.

'Just tell me everything,' she urged. 'From when they weighed you in the delivery room till you came up to my flat tonight.'

'Oh, but it's all so boring,' he protested.

'You let me be the judge of that.'

So the poor, charmless Simon Winchester did the only thing he was capable of in the circumstances: he took her words literally and stuttered his way through a factual history of his life. It was lengthy, detailed and utterly dreary, but Susan sat through it patiently, feigning interest, and never questioning him in case he went on the defensive. But if she thought her patience would be ultimately rewarded, she was disillusioned.

They had gone through the starters (his education, sprinkled with illustrations of his native ability in economics), the main course (his career up to his time with Macintyres, peppered with hard details of business problems he'd overcome), and were into the baklava stage (his reasons for joining Greville during the 1974 property slump), when he clogged up with, 'And so, that's about it really.'

She raised her hand, 'Whoa, Simon. You can't be finished yet. Your precious duke's sitting on at least 20 million ounces of silver, and there must be some pretty good reason why.'

'It's no big deal,' he mumbled, not revealing that Greville's hoard was four times that. 'Silver's just a good investment.'

She decided to throw a more direct ball at him. 'And I guess that mysterious purchase and sale of 25 million ounces on the LMB last Friday couldn't have hurt him none, huh?'

His reaction was to eye her suspiciously. He had already worked out that she must be linked with Bachmann Gardner in Chicago, and was some relative of Thomas Gardner's. So she may or may not know something. It didn't matter. He answered non-committally, 'Well the price has been shooting up since then proving what a great investment silver is.' He turned and waved at Kostas for the bill.

Susan wondered whether to press it further. Probably not, she wondered. He'd just get really cagey and clam right up, and she might lose all chance of closing in on the truth; it was probably best to try again on another occasion. So she excused herself and set off past a crowd of happy young diners to powder her nose.

Kostas now materialized with the bill on a plate, smirking and cupping his hands in front of his chest suggestively. 'A bit better than the last lady's, eh, Mr Winchester?'

The Comptroller of Greville Holdings allowed himself a smug grin, and declined Kostas's offer of a free raki as he settled up. All the way back to Clarendon Place in the cab, he worked himself up to popping the question; when they arrived in front of her apartment block, he blurted: 'Can I come up for a coffee?'

Her evening had been so dull and unproductive that she was about to say no. But what did she have to lose? she reflected. He might still let something slip. She nodded, 'Okay, why not?'

In the lift going to the third floor he stared blankly at his shoes, giving no hint that he'd make a pass at her. Inside, he hung his grey overcoat on the hall coat-stand as if he was at home. 'You know, Susan, I've had a wonderful evening.'

She stared at him in amazement. He'd actually had a wonderful evening? 'I'll fix the coffee,' she said. 'Make yourself comfortable.' She watched him through the kitchen hatch. He put a record on the hi-fi, an old Nat King Cole song. When she came through, he cleared a space amongst the magazines on the low table for the tray. She sat next to him. 'That's pretty ancient mood music you've put on, Simon.'

'I suppose I'm in a funny old sort of mood.' He looked solemn. 'You know, I gave you the history of my life earlier, but I never mentioned that I'm quite a romantic sort really.'

'Huh! You talked about everything tonight but the women in your life.'

'That's because there have hardly been any women in my life. None have found me interesting enough, I suppose.'

She poured the coffee. 'Well, I find that strange. You're right-hand man for a duke, and a very rich one at that, and you're pretty highly thought of yourself in the City. There should be dozens of women taking an interest in you.'

'Is that why you're interested in me, Susan?'

She looked at him thoughtfully. 'To be perfectly honest, I suppose that who you represent was why I wanted to meet you, yes.' She wondered whether to go the whole hog and ask him directly now if he'd been behind that 25-million-ounce business. No, she decided. Not yet. She held out his cup and he shuffled closer. Instead of taking it, though, Winchester put an arm around her shoulder. 'Hey,' she laughed. 'We hardly know each other.'

Wordlessly, he pressed his lips against hers, and she let this happen without responding for a moment. Then she moved her face away and put the cup down on the table. 'I guess you're not thirsty. So I'd better call you a cab.' She made to get up, but his other arm came around her and he forced his mouth back on to hers. An uncertain hand groped her breast.

She shook herself clear of him easily. 'Now come on Simon. That's enough.'

He looked up at her. 'When I saw you with my photograph in your hand, I couldn't understand it. I thought you might be interested in me personally, not just in who I represent....' He got up off the sofa and smoothed down his suit. 'I'm not proud of what I've just tried, Susan, but neither am I sorry. If you're honest with yourself, you'll have to admit you've been giving me the come-on ever since you bumped into me, and especially this evening.'

His wretched manner gave her the creeps, but she said kindly, 'I do quite like you as a person, Simon, honestly.'

He held up his hand to silence her. 'I'll go now. There's no need to call a cab. I'll find one at Marble Arch. And you can come around to Marylebone House on Monday to pick up the account forms. Good night.'

He took his coat and let himself out.

'Thank you for dinner, Simon,' she called down the stairs as he disappeared from view.

20.10.79

Christy got his first piece of news about his da at the nineteenth bookie he tried on Saturday morning.

Paddy Mahoney's shop was on St John's Road, near Dublin's Heuston Station. The bookie, a thick-jawed man with a stick of yellow chalk behind his ear, was scrawling the latest prices for that afternoon's races on the blackboard behind the counter. Mahoney recognized the champion trainer straight away and was eager to help.

''Tis sure that I know Stephen O'Donnell. He's always in here for his betting, though I haven't seen him for over a week now. The law are after him, for that job on the jewellers. Try up the Tannery Arms on Bangor Road, and ask for the McDaid brothers.'

McDaid. He'd heard the name before. Hadn't old Pat Fogarty mentioned it? 'Thanks, now, Mr Mahoney.' He leaned forward and said softly, 'If I were you I'd put a stake on Sir Michael in the Cesarewitch next week.'

The bookie knew the ante-post quote for the horse in the Tote Cesarewitch Handicap was 50-1 right then. It had to be worth a £20 punt on a tip from the champion trainer himself. 'I'm very obliged.' (To Mahoney's delight, Sir Michael would romp home an easy first in the race in seven days' time, and allow him to reward himself with £1,000.)

Seamus Kirkpatrick stared right through Christy. 'Half a million pounds you're offering is it now?'

Christy sat on the other side of the little parlour, observing the wild eyes. The converted flat was on the top floor of a meagre terraced house in Oxmantown Road. Kirkpatrick, though clearly still insane, seemed less so here than at his Folly up on Leprechaun's Finger, where he no doubt had as much space as he needed to vent his delusions of grandeur. 'Half a million pounds, Mr Kirkpatrick, and not a penny more. You can take it or leave it. It's the very best offer that I or anyone else'll ever make, and you know it. You can have the money in cash by Tuesday.' He withdrew the ten bundles of cash from the inside pockets of his jacket, and put them on the table. 'Here's a sample. Twenty thousand pounds. Go on count it.'

The avarice throbbed in the veins in Kirkpatrick's neck. He slowly picked up a bundle and flicked through it, then did the same with another bundle.

'You can keep it all, whatever your decision. If you agree, there'll be 480,000 more in cash like that. If you don't agree, that 20,000 there will be my loss. But I'll never come back to you again with another offer.' It was a gamble, but the only way to play it. He had learned a thing or two in dealing with Greville and the crown prince.

The old man stuffed the money into his pockets. When he had safe possession of it all, he suddenly shrieked, '*But you can't force my hand like this!* I need time. You don't know how much I'd suffer if such a great family treasure like the castle was wrenched from me....'

It was obvious to Christy that he would try his hardest to see if he could sell it for more. 'How much time do you need, then?'

'It's my property, but there are a couple of cousins in America who'd be heart-broken if it went out of the family. I'll have to write to them, and break it to them gently. Then I'll have to wait for their reply. They're never very quick in writing back....' He was so clearly ad-libbing.

'How much time do you need?' repeated Christy.

'Give me three months, and don't go looking for anything else in the meantime, all right now?'

Christy knew he wouldn't have the time to hunt for castles before January anyway. Not that he wanted to. 'A month. You can have a month. Then you can give your answer direct to Mr Smitherson in Cashel. If he or I don't hear from you within a maximum of six weeks, I'll take it that you're not selling, and I'll just buy something else.'

The blind violinist sat on a raised platform in the Tannery Arms, coaxing a melancholy strain from his ancient instrument and silently mouthing the tune his trembling hands created. His music was drowned out by the early evening hubbub in the saloon but, lost in this world of his own, he didn't hear anything else.

When Christy came in, he had just drawn his bow across the

strings for the last chord. Now he launched into a lively jig, smiling through his stubble. The change of tempo got one or two of the drinkers clapping along in time.

Christy trod carefully across the sawdust-sprinkled floor and said to the barman. 'I was told I could find the McDaid brothers here. Do you know them?'

The fellow spun away from him as if he was a leper, and a powerfully built man in black leather gear at the far end of the bar perked his head up with interest. The barman threw him a nod. Setting his glass of stout down on the counter, the man in black leather made his way over. He was as tall as Christy, though much broader, and had long black hair which was oiled back behind his ears.

'You O'Donnell?' he said. His lips were thick and they had taken on an ugly twist.

Christy said easily, 'What is it to you who I am?'

The man's hands bunched into meaty shillelaghs. 'I've got business to settle with Stephen O'Donnell.'

'What business would that be, then?'

'He robbed my brother Harry. Took his money and disappeared in the middle of a job. You're looking for him, they say. You're his son. Is that right?' He bore forward.

Christy edged away along the bar. 'Are you one of the McDaids?'

'Are you always after answering questions with more questions? I said, are you O'Donnell?'

'You tell me where Stephen O'Donnell is first ... '

His words were choked off as an arm from behind the bar gripped his neck in the crook of its elbow. The arm was the barman's. Christy wrenched it violently off, and as he did, Martin McDaid – for that's who it was – slammed his right fist into Christy's ribs. He fell sideways onto the sawdust, and the music and clapping stopped abruptly.

The pain throbbing in his chest, Christy laboured to get on to his knees. He kept a wary eye on McDaid's steel toe-caps, which were not more than eighteen inches from his face. Their owner glowered down at him, fists still bunched.

Christy slowly raised himself on to his feet. Brushing the sawdust off his trouser legs, he said, 'How much does he owe you, McDaid?'

'A hundred pounds that bastard stole of ours.'

Christy took his wallet out of the breast pocket of his jacket. From it, he drew five twenty-pound notes and handed these over gingerly. 'Will you tell me where he is, now?'

McDaid stuffed the money into his back pocket. His face split into a smile. 'If I knew where he was, I'd have finished him off already, wouldn't I?' The smile vanished as he shook his fist in Christy's face. 'A hundred pounds is nothing. We had to abandon a job worth thousands because your dad did a runner. What about that, eh?'

Christy turned to walk away but McDaid grabbed his shoulder and spun him round. In the same moment Christy hooked a leg around McDaid's and tripped him up. The man fell against the counter and groped out to grab the nearest object. It was a quart bottle of cider. Christy threw a punch in the direction of his face but McDaid ducked out of its path easily. He smashed the bottle against the counter. Cider sprayed everywhere and Christy was momentarily blinded by a splash in his eye. McDaid got his balance and turned the jagged edge of the bottle towards Christy.

The other drinkers who were clustered at the bar dissolved away from the vicinity.

McDaid lunged forward with the bottle a couple of times, but Christy managed to weave out of the way each time. The third time, the broken bottle end came at him with more violence and he ducked back only to find himself hemmed in by the bar counter.

An evil grin crossed McDaid's face. 'How far do you think you can go now, eh, O'Donnell?'

Christy held up his hands. 'All right, McDaid, all right. There's no need for this to go any further.' He reached slowly into his jacket for his wallet. He fished out another hundred from it. 'This should settle it for any trouble you had. And I want no aggro against my da either, all right, now? It'd be best for everyone if the matter was finished off here and now for good.'

'Sensible fellow, aren't you, now?' McDaid leered. He took the money with his free hand and made to put it in his back pocket.

Christy relaxed and at that moment, the man in black leather slashed the bottle at him in a vicious arc. Christy, whose gaze had only momentarily flickered to the people around, saw it coming late. He tried to swerve out of the way, but the bottle struck him a couple of millimetres below his right eye. His world exploded into blinding white light and brutal, searing pain. He staggered about against the bar counter, his ears ringing with the sound of his own shriek. As he tried to focus his gaze, he found that the blood spraying from his face obscured his vision. He groped along the counter trying to steady himself, and his hand came across a bar cloth. He held this up to his face to staunch the blood flow. All the time, he could hear McDaid's laugh echoing around the pub, and he wanted to kill the man. But McDaid was still holding the bottle.

Keeping the cloth to his face, Christy stumbled out of the Tannery Arms. As the saloon bar door swung shut, he heard the violin start up again inside.

They put seventeen stitches into Christy's cheek at St Vincent's Hospital. The right side of his face was monstrous – black and so badly swollen that he could barely see out of that eye. He passed the night in Sally Murphy's arms, but the pain kept him awake for much of the time.

The following day he continued his search for his father. He drove by a number of villages around Dublin, enquiring if there were any burned-down farms in the vicinity. But either nobody knew, or didn't want to get involved with him. By dusk Christy had discovered nothing, so he returned to the city and The Jolly Jockey pub.

Old Pat Fogarty observed his smashed-up face. He had already heard of Christy's encounter with Martin McDaid. 'They're a nasty murthering bunch of so-and-so's, lad.'

Christy nodded bitterly. He gave the old man the telephone number of his flat in Marylebone House. 'You're to call me any time, reverse charge, if you hear anything about my da.' He handed across a twenty-pound note. 'That's for a glass of stout or two for yourself.' Then he produced five more twenties. 'These I want you to give to my da as soon as you come across him. They're for his own use. And you're to tell him he's to call me too the minute you see him.'

Pat put the money away. 'You've nothing to fear from me. I'll not spend a penny of your da's money on myself.'

'Remember now, Mr Fogarty. Call me in London the moment you have any news at all.'

21.10.79

Over two hundred petitioners gathered in Ahmed's palace before the noon-day prayer that day for the weekly majlis. The usual number was about fifty. Most of the petitioners wanted to know about what was going on in the silver market, though the petitions they brought along didn't necessarily reveal this.

The crown prince sat on one of the three gold velour conference chairs in the majlis chamber. In the hall outside, the petitioners sipped coffee from cups without handles, waiting their turn to be summoned by Ahmed's chamberlain. Since custom ordained that bare-footed bedouin tribesmen enjoy the same right of access to the crown prince as wealthy city merchants in gold-trimmed robes, they were from all walks of Hejazi life.

Ahmed drew the petitions one by one from the chamberlain's hands. Not all were elegant documents. Some were sheets of paper torn from exercise books and scribbled on in fine traceries of Arabic.

'Faisal bin Tariki,' the chamberlain called out.

A 40-year-old man with a handle-bar moustache, wearing a striped mishlah, came into the majlis. He kissed Ahmed on the right shoulder and sat beside him in one of the gold chairs. The crown prince knew he was the owner of the largest general store in central Khurbah.

Bin Tariki said gravely, '*Ya* Ahmed. I must protest against the outdated censorship in our country. The censor blacks out the naked shoulders of women in the European magazines I sell, even though they wear swimming suits. The censor himself goes to the French Riviera every year and sees women brazenly flaunting their naked breasts on the beaches. But what I object to most of all is the felt pens he uses on my magazines. They leave an awful smell of spirits. It is harming my sales.'

Ahmed's eyes blazed. 'The tenets of Islam are clear on the subject of uncovered women. Go from here in repentance or I shall ban *all* magazines from your store.'

Bin Tariki went off, though whether in repentance remained unclear.

The chamberlain called, 'Nasir al Mansour.'

This was an old man with a straggly beard. He fell on his knees and grasped Ahmed's hand to kiss it.

The crown prince yelled, 'I ask pardon of God for this outrage! You may kiss on the shoulder but not on the hand. Shake hands, old man, shake hands!'

Nasir al Mansour got to his feet and mumbled, 'Two of my wives are in hospital and I have no money to pay the huge bills. I seek guidance, *Ya* Ahmed. Should I buy silver? They say everywhere that you are buying silver and making huge profits.'

'Send me the infidel who dares to say I am buying silver! I will have his tongue out for speaking nonsense. I have your paper and the names of the hospitals. We shall tell them to be moderate with your bills. Now go from here, Nasir al Mansour.'

All enquiries about silver were treated in the same way. However, certain bedouin and businessmen favourites, selected because each had several millions of dollars in loose change, were invited to lunch with Ahmed later on roast sheep and brown rice. To these worthies he gave this advice: if they wanted their loose change to double, triple or quadruple, they should get hold of a commodity broker in the West and invest in December silver futures. Many hastened straight off, and middlemen on yachts in Marbella, Cannes and Monte Carlo received frenzied phone calls to buy silver when the markets opened the next day.

It didn't take long for news of the hullabaloo to filter back to King Musaid, and Ahmed was summoned to his brother's palace for an audience that same afternoon. Musaid was only two years older than the crown prince, but acted so grave that he might have been Ahmed's grandfather. 'You've been telling people to invest in silver. Why?'

Ahmed shrugged. 'Someone recommended it as a good investment. I passed the message on to anyone interested.'

Musaid's black beady eyes stared flatly back. 'They're saying you'll have profits in billions. That kind of money cannot be made without a monkey's tail being twisted.' It was an old Hejazi expression for fraud.

'There is no monkey business,' Ahmed protested. 'Everything is being done officially, in the silver markets of the West.'

Musaid nodded, but remained sceptical. 'They say you have an English partner, and that his father died in suspicious circumstances, and that fingers were pointed at your partner?'

Ahmed laughed. 'Oh, people always point fingers. But this Greville's father merely died in a motor accident.'

The king contemplated all this for several seconds before making his conclusion. 'All your casino-going and merry-making with horses, all that sort of thing is not really objected to by anyone. If anything, your doing it while you are crown prince makes you a sporting hero in our subjects' minds, and creates the idea of a cheerful future. It may, therefore, almost be encouraged. But this silver business, and this Duke of Marylebone, are a different sport. Millions around the world are involved; some will win, some will lose. But if this Greville makes a lot of money, fingers will point at him afresh; then, like it or not, the names of our Kingdom and our family will be dragged along in the gutter with his. That is something I will not countenance, and so I will demand the Council to review the succession for the House of Jayed. Walid is proving to be a very capable Minister of Oil.'

The warning was clear. Ahmed, next in line for the Crown, risked being thrown out on his ear, and Walid promoted over his head. Strictly speaking, the succession had been pre-ordained by their father Talal Aziz: it was to pass from brother to brother, from eldest to youngest, and no heir was to be missed out. In practice, whoever was king had total sway, and the Council would ratify any proposal he made. Such was the power of the absolute monarch in the Hejaz, as well as in many neighbouring kingdoms.

Ahmed said, a lot less happily, 'I repeat, there is no monkey business going on, nor any need to point the finger at Greville Emir. So the Council will not need to review the succession.'

'Yes. I would prefer Walid not to be king before his time.'

That evening, Ahmed lay on a divan by the pool in the inner courtyard of his palace. From the mouths of four solid gold lions in the pool's middle, refrigerated water shot up. Ahmed's favourite wife, Raisha, massaged his feet and ankles.

'I don't want to lose the chance of making billions of dollars because of Musaid's silly old-fashioned views, do I?' he said thoughtfully. 'But at the same time, to be king in the footsteps of Talal Aziz is without price, isn't it?. And then there are the $300 million that have already gone into this thing, aren't there?'

'Tell me everything,' Raisha said.

He did. When he finished, she gave him her opinion. He grinned. She was so wise. It was no accident that he loved her quite so much. He clapped his hands, and told the servant who appeared, 'Fetch me Prince Turki.'

When his son appeared, Ahmed said, 'Turki, you know all about the silver business and the huge profits which are promised. But problems may arise so I want to be prepared. You will fly tomorrow to Beirut, and work on my behalf with Karim Jamal, sticking closer to him than a postage stamp and keeping your eyes and ears open to everything. I want you to be ready to act in an emergency if I need you to.'

22.10.79

The bears struck for the first time on the wettest day that autumn. At 8.15, the Met Office reported a fall of already almost an inch in London. Much more was forecast throughout the day. The duke was in Winchester's study as the rain drummed remorselessly against the window.

'Ever since the kerb dealings started, a network of London bears have been trying to hammer the price down,' the comptroller explained.

Greville was alarmed. 'Is it serious?'

'Not for the moment. But Crabbe called last night with the news that bullion merchants from Dubai, Zurich and London flew into Chicago to meet with local dealers and major investment houses. Including, supposedly, the Morgan Guaranty Trust. All these are parties who are, for one reason or another, short in silver, and they're being crucified by the price rising and rising. Apparently, they've made a cartel to counter ours and force the price back down.'

'But what does it all mean?'

'It means we've got a fight on our hands. For today at least, and possibly for some time to come....' Winchester raised his eyebrows at the deepening anxiety on Greville's face. 'Are you ready for a fight, your Grace?'

'We've made contingency plans for this haven't we?'

'We've got $300 million physically sitting in brokerage accounts now, don't forget. When used as collateral margin, this money has a buying power of four and a half billion dollars, and I calculate the Chicago cartel won't dare try to match it. All we need to do is go on absorbing everything that they throw at us. It'll be rocky throughout the day, especially when the Grain and Metal Exchange opens, but we should be all right as long as we've got all hands on deck. What we don't need is O'Donnell disappearing like this. He ran off to Ireland on Saturday, and isn't here now when he should be.'

The girl at the reception desk in the Great Hall buzzed just then to say that a Susan Gardner had arrived to see the comptroller.

Winchester took up the account form and cheque he had prepared and went out to reception with them. There was an awkward atmosphere when he came face to face with Susan.

'What an amazing place, Simon,' she said breezily.

He steered her away from the reception desk. 'Susan, I'm so sorry.'

'Oh don't be silly.'

'No. No. I should never have touched you. My hopes just made me blind to the reality of your feelings.' He gave her the forms and the cheque. 'Here's everything, including the £30,000 I promised you.'

'Oh, you are such a sweetheart.'

He smiled sadly. 'Well, I'd better get back.'

She said, 'We can meet again you know. Honestly, it wasn't just this account I was interested in.'

'Do you mean that?'

'Of course I do.' She stroked his hand lightly with the tips of her fingers. 'Look, call me at Sheedy's sometime. We'll get together. Okay?'

'Okay.' He hastened back along the corridor.

With the rain absolutely bucketing down, Susan stared out of a window in the Great Hall for over twenty minutes, hoping for a cab to arrive. Just when she was about to ask the girl at the desk to call again for one, she saw a black taxi sloshing its way around the square. It pulled up outside the House.

Clutching her briefcase close to her chest, hugging her Burberry tightly about her, Susan dashed out and down the broad steps. As she reached for the handle of the passenger door, it opened by itself and a man stepped out.

Susan was mesmerized. He had the most awfully injured face: a terrible gash running across his cheek and a huge shiny bruise which puffed his eye into a nasty little slit. He'd clearly just had a mauling by the lions in the Colosseum. Her gaze locked with his for a couple of seconds, then he said in an Irish accent, 'Haven't I seen you somewhere before?'

'I don't think so,' she stammered, 'I'm sorry, I'm getting drenched.' She pushed past him into the cab and pulled the door shut.

'Where to, Miss?'

Susan settled back in her seat, her Burberry raincoat dripping. 'Mincing Lane.'

As the taxi diesel-rattled away, she saw the beat-up guy with the nice Irish accent standing on the steps of the House in the downpour, staring after her. She quickly put him out of her mind and reflected on her mission: Simon Winchester still had the hots for her, and that made her flesh crawl. But it was important she meet him again, even though it meant leading the wretch on still more. There was a feeling about Marylebone House which convinced her that it was the place where she had to keep digging.

'Shocking weather, innit, miss?' the cabbie said.

'Sure is that,' she replied.

Horror was written large on Mrs Thorpe's face.

'I bashed into a car windscreen,' Christy mumbled.

'Oh my goodness, you poor thing.' She shook her head, feeling desperately for him. 'Will you be all right? Can you see?'

'Oh aye, the doctor said it'd be just fine. It just looks worse than it actually is.'

She was still shaking her head when he changed the subject: 'That woman who just left here ... '

'Susan Gardner?'

Of course, thought Christy. That's who she was: the woman in the dealing room in Chicago. 'That's right now. What was she doing here?'

'She came from Sheedy and Ratcliffe's on some business with Simon Winchester.'

'I see. Thanks.' He strode straight off to the study.

James Greville rose from his seat. 'Good heavens, man! What on earth have you done to yourself?'

Christy grinned sheepishly and gave the windscreen

explanation again. Then he pulled off his jacket. 'Best be getting back to work then.'

'If it's not too much pain,' remarked Winchester.

Christy couldn't fully concentrate that morning. Winchester explained the situation about the bears, but Christy's mind kept harking back to the meeting at the taxi earlier. That Susan whom he'd taken such a fancy to was here, in London....

With constant, unspectacular buying under the comptroller's direction, they managed to keep the price steady around $7.73 until noon. Then the sell orders became fewer, and the lunch period marked a complete lull. There would undoubtedly be another, heavier assault on the price at the opening in Chicago.

Before that, Christy finally asked the comptroller, 'That American woman who was here earlier ... what did she want, Simon?'

'I don't really know what business it is of yours, but she's been trying to sell us some of Sheedy and Ratcliffe's services.' He smiled. 'If only she knew how much business we're already putting through them via the nominees.'

Christy left the office and went up to his flat.

'Susan!' somebody cried across Sheedy's dealing room. 'Line 4. Mr O'Donnell.'

'O'Donnell?' She couldn't think of a client by that name. Puzzled, she flicked up the phone tab. 'Hello.'

'Is that Susan Gardner?'

A charming Irish lilt again. Was it Saint Patrick's Day? 'Yes, what can I do for you?'

'I saw you this morning. At the taxi.'

Of course. It was the same voice. 'Do I know you?'

He chuckled. 'No. But I hear you're selling your services to the Duke of Marylebone's company. I just called to let you know I work for him too, see now?'

Now she was interested. 'Oh really?'

'So I was wondering if we could meet and talk.'

Susan flicked open her diary. 'Okay when would you like me to come to Marylebone House?'

'No,' he said. 'Not here. Over a bite to eat.'

'Okay.' Her mind flashed back to dinner with Simon Winchester the previous week. 'Let me see which days I'm free for lunch.'

'Lunches aren't possible. It'll have to be dinner.'

With a sinking voice, she said, 'Dinner?'

'Aye, it'll have to be very late too. I'm very busy, right up to at least ten o'clock every night.'

'I see, Mr O'Donnell,' she said drily. 'And are there any other conditions?'

'Just two more. First, let's make it this evening, at 10.30. And second, just for tonight don't try to sell me any of your services. It's best if I come to your place, so you'd better let me have your address.'

'You guys who work for the duke sure don't let the grass grow under your feet, do you?' she mused.

Powerful waves of silver selling hit the Chicago Grain and Metal Exchange from all corners of the globe that afternoon. But there was always enough demand for everything on offer to be picked up.

In Sheedy's dealing room, like in every other commodity brokerage house in the western world, phones jangled incessantly. Trading instructions yelled by dealers down lines to Chicago generated the flight of tens of thousands of order cards to the silver pit at the heart of all the action. In every country the price screens flashed the frenzied signals of the battle over control of the world's silver.

Through all the activity, Susan willed the clock to go round faster, so that she could return home. In her experience, most things that were out of the ordinary one day proved to be banal another day. Also, she was getting more and more intrigued by the prospect of encountering again that face which looked like a piece of lion's chewing gum. 'The Gladiator', she mentally nicknamed the Irish-voiced man. What tickled her about him, and what she found just so engaging, was the way he had stood getting soaked in the rain, gaping at her.

The last ten minutes of the market were the busiest. Over 2 million contracts changed hands in that short spell, and the price for December silver futures see-sawed violently between $7.80 and $7.90. It was just before the close that hordes of previously uncommitted speculators and investors in every major trading centre from Los Angeles to Tokyo, Dubai and the European seats came in on the long side and pushed the price over $8 an ounce. December silver closed at $8.03.

For brokers and dealers around the world, an ominous victory was signalled. The bears had fought hard all day, but the bulls had established another bridgehead.

* * *

Susan laid out all the brochures again on the dining table at the apartment that night. Who was that Irishman to tell her he didn't want to bring business up this evening? Supposing *she* wanted to talk business?

After the last incident, though, she didn't make herself look like the Clothed Maja again, but wore a grey and white flecked smock-like dress which played down her figure and let her green eyes sparkle. She looked at herself in the mirror thinking, *Let Spartacus stare at those instead of at my boobs.*

When the entry-phone went at exactly 10.30, a little spring crept into her step as she went to answer it. She buzzed the downstairs entrance door without bothering to check who it was.

As Christy stepped out of the elevator, Susan gave a little start at the sight of his smashed-up face again. 'I've been wanting to ask you ever since you called ... did you hit a car windshield or something?'

He laughed. 'That's the exact bloody explanation I've been giving people all day.'

'Isn't it true?'

'It's true I had an accident.'

'Well,' she said. 'You'd better come in.'

She led him to where she had laid out the brochures.

'Aha!' he cried. 'You forgot my condition.'

'*I* make the conditions in my apartment, Mr O'Donnell.'

He wagged a finger. 'Now, no more of this Mr O'Donnell business. It's Christy. And I hope you don't mind me calling you Susan. And as for the paperwork, I'll look at it all later.'

I know this guy, thought Susan when she got in the Mercedes. It was that profile ... the undamaged left one ... She'd seen that before ... But where? If only she could put her finger on it.... 'Everything's so quaint in England, isn't it? I mean, I can't get used to you guys driving down the wrong side of the street.' In the light from passing street lamps she saw that he really was quite appealing to look at.

He nodded. 'Yes, when I saw you in Chicago I wondered if you'd ever end up going the wrong way.'

'You saw me in Chicago?' Now she remembered him saying that morning: *'Haven't I seen you somewhere before?'*

'When was this, Mr O'Donnell?'

'It's Christy, Susan. Don't you remember?' He turned to look at her and she was startled by his injury yet again. 'I was chatting with Barry Turnowsky, and you were on the telephone....'

'My God!' she shrieked. 'You're the man from Vancouver!'

'What?'

'Oh never mind, never mind.'

'I'm from Connemara, actually.'

She was lost for words. Then she managed to say, 'I've heard it's a beautiful place.'

He smiled sweetly, and all erotic intentions towards this goddess went into temporary suspended animation as he thought of the bogs, of Farmer Regan's cottage, of the market square in Galway, of the grave in Killertoon, of his castle.... 'Ireland is paradise on earth, Susan. There's always a piece of it in me wherever in the world I may be. It never leaves me.'

There was such a sense of vast longing and deep tragedy in him that chords were struck in her and she felt her heart open. Goddammit, she was happy. 'Where are we going, Christy?'

'Well, there's this nice Indian restaurant in Mayfair ... '

'I don't like Indian food,' she said straight away. It was a lie. She loved Indian food. 'Can we go back to my apartment? I'll rustle us up something.' She didn't quite know how she would handle things from here on.

He looked across at her with wonder in his eyes. His injury seemed to have disappeared.

She said quickly, 'But no funny business, okay? The last time somebody came back, he tried to jump me. If there's going to be a romance, it just has to take its slow patient course.'

When they got back to the Clarendon Place flat, she made spaghetti, over which she poured olive oil and crushed garlic.

'But that'll make my breath stink,' Christy protested.

'I won't complain.' Susan smiled. Her dimple was very pronounced and he had no option but to kiss it.

She thrust the bowl of spaghetti at him. 'I said this romance has to take its slow patient course, remember?'

He put the bowl down on the kitchen worktop and scooped her up in his arms, with Eros by now working overtime inside him again. 'All right then, I'll take you slowly and patiently to the Garden of Eden.' And that was how he carried her into the bedroom – slowly and patiently – while she laughed, and giggled, and pecked him on his nose, and on his chin, and on his ear lobe, and finally, and most gingerly, on the huge black bruise on his cheek.

* * *

Later, as she sat naked in his naked lap at the table, scooping up forkfuls of cold garlicky spaghetti for him, he purred between mouthfuls, 'There's nothing to feel shy about, Susie, my sweet. The romance between us has been going on for ever. You knew it, and I knew it when we saw each other back in Chicago. For ever is long enough, isn't it, Susie?'

'Yes,' she said, stroking him where it tickled. 'It's plenty long enough.'

26.10.79

'Love is such a curious thing,' Elizabeth said.

'You aren't answering the question, Liz.' Carole Markeston took a sip from her cup. They were in a tearoom in Horncastle. 'Do you love him?'

Elizabeth looked dreamily away. 'Charles was a mountain of love. Such *give* ... And the other one in the family as gifted is Jane. She's utterly devoted to Michael and the children. They are such a close family, and she can never give them enough. Now as for Deborah, love equals unhappiness, dissatisfaction. She demands too much ... invests too much passion. She'll throw herself at people and want them to do the same. When one of them withdraws out of boredom or whatever, the other is terribly bruised....'

Lady Carole waited patiently for an answer. She knew James Greville was coming to Condrieu this evening for the first time in weeks. Liz had been in a strange mood since her husband's last visit when, she had said, Greville had slept with her.

Elizabeth tuned back into here-and-now. 'All right, Carole, let me answer your question. I've realized how much *he* loves *me*. Looking back over events, that's the only explanation that makes sense. The insults, the rage, the fits ... all these have just been pleas for help. I know I certainly *used* to love him, despite his moral cowardice – the sleeping around, the refusal to knuckle down decently to the family's business, and so on. But then, all the things that have happened this year, starting with Charles's death ... ' She gazed deeply into her friend's eyes. 'You see Carole, he did want Charles out of the way.'

Lady Carole nodded. Everybody knew that.

Elizabeth's gaze wandered off again. 'But it wasn't because of the silver. It was for me, I think. I can tell now from the way he tried so hard to win back my favour: getting rid of Sarah McGonagle; bringing John Early across in that ridiculous attempt to prove his innocence ... '

Her friend interrupted, 'But wasn't all that because he wanted money from you?'

She thought hard. 'Yes. And no. He knows me well enough to realize that I wouldn't sell Charles's assets whatever tricks he pulled. No, what was interesting was his behaviour when his business prospects started to look up. He begged me to go to the opera with him, and he insisted we sleep together....' She didn't add that she hadn't minded lying beside him but hadn't wanted him to take her sexually just yet.

'So tell me, Liz. Are you pleased he's coming tonight?'

The duchess nodded slowly. 'Yes, I think I'm rather looking forward to it.'

He arrived early for a change, and found Elizabeth, as always, in the Blue Drawing Room. She was reading, in the window embrasure, and she put her book down and smiled as he strode across to her. 'Well, the return of the all-conquering warrior. I'm so pleased silver's picked up....'

He grinned, 'Vision, old girl. That's what I've got. Vision and judgement.'

Her smile tailed off. 'Yes, well, I wouldn't go quite that far, but you do seem to have been doing rather well.'

His blotchy face mottled with contempt. ' "Doing rather well", indeed! And it's no thanks to you! I had to do it all off my own bat, you bloody bitch. You and Charles plotted my downfall. Neither of you helped when I needed it. No, you tried to destroy me through the courts. But you failed. And don't think I'm coming to your bed again. You can go down to the vault and spend night after night squealing with delight with him for all I care. You did it enough times when he was alive.'

He turned on his heel and marched out. Within moments, Stewart was speeding him back to London, his heart thumping so hard that he hardly noticed the pain in it. He'd tried everything in his power to please her, but never, not once had she ever shown either appreciation or concern for him.

For hours after this fresh, totally unexpected, outburst, Elizabeth wept.

'He's rotten through and through,' Charles had used to say. *'Not even you can bring out the good in him.'* And yet, she had believed that the good in him had finally come close to surfacing. But now she knew it never would. Charles. She needed Charles. If only he were here to tell her what to do.

27.10.79 – 7.11.79

Silver continued its meteoric rise into November.

In the shops, the effect was already apparent. Articles from baby spoons to tea sets and photographic film had been marked up in price and would be marked up again and again. Ilford and Kodak started muttering about worker redundancies in their factories if this trend continued. There was talk of cutbacks by hospitals in their purchase of X-ray film because of the spiralling price of silver.

In the half-light his eyes glimmered. She clung to his thick curly hair with both hands and he plunged his lips down on to hers. Then he moved his head down to her breast and his tongue flicked repeatedly against her pink nipple. It hardened and she felt it tingle unbearably, and she raised her knees up around the outside of his hips and squeezed him in more tightly; his tumescent, warm penis rubbed against the little bulge of her tummy.

She lifted his head off her breast and kissed his face hard and ran her fingers along his shoulders; those broad firm shoulders, with the hard nodes at the joints. His fingers sought out her sex and began to stroke it gently and she grasped his shoulders tighter. Then she let her hands glide down his back and on to his muscular buttocks, and she squeezed them and felt the ring on her finger eat into his flesh.

He worked his head further down, then his tongue plunged in and out of her opening, flicking again and again against her tight wet button until she couldn't bear it any longer and had to tug at his head to pull it away, but he resisted, continuing to stroke her sex with his tongue until she was crying out softly, 'Oh God, Oh God.'

Just when she was about to shatter into a million fragments, Christy was up kissing her face, her mouth, and she could taste her own juices on his tongue and lips. She raised her knees higher to grip his face with them and, his weight crushing down on her now, he prodded his thick hard penis into her.

He thrust and thrust and Susan, unable to move under his tremendous weight bearing down on her body, was overcome by the rough texture of his face against her knees, the velvety sensation of his foreskin rolling back and forth as he gouged her insides, and the shortening raspings of his breath.

'Come on then, Susan my sweet, come, come, let it go, let it go,' he panted violently, shaking his head clear of her knees and forcing them wider apart.

She gasped as every nerve in her body began to vibrate, then the vibration amplified into a delicious tautening and relaxing of every nerve ending, until the tautening and relaxing became so intense that there was no difference between the opposites, and then she was wailing out repeatedly as the sensation swamped her body in waves which grew bigger and bigger while Christy savagely chewed and kissed her neck, and continued to plunder her below with all his force. Then she felt the head of his penis bulge inside her and squirt and squirt, and then his body collapsed on to hers and his weight was no longer a crushing thing but a vast moist and all-enveloping blanket under which she drifted for a long long time, out of herself, away from that room, that building, that city, that country....

Susan opened her eyes. Christy was rolling off her body, his eyes closed and every muscle in his face relaxed. He was so goddamn handsome, she thought, even with that dark scar which ran across his cheek. The bruises were gone. So much more handsome than Ross....

Why am I still comparing? she wondered. There's no need to compare. I've known you only two weeks, you goddamn leprechaun, but that's been long enough. I never believed in love at first sight but if the thing I felt in Chicago when I first saw you across the dealing room wasn't love, then it must have been something else as near as dammit.

'What's the matter now, Susan, my sweet?' Christy said, opening his eyes. 'What are you staring at me like that for?'

'Just thinking what a lousy lover you are. I mean, falling asleep just when I was starting to get aroused.'

Christy yawned. 'It's a question of getting too used to good things, see now. The Chinese have a saying: if, during your first year of marriage, you put a grain of rice into a bowl every time you make love, and then after that you take a grain of rice *out* every time you make love, that bowl will never get empty.'

'But I've only known you two weeks, not one year, and we're not married!' She gripped his penis. 'Now stop giving me the wise saws of Confucius and start putting in some more rice where it's needed instead.'

The Lex Column on the back page of the *Financial Times* is enjoyed for its insight and for the ironic note it sometimes strikes. This article appeared in it in the first week of November 1979:

ODDS ON BET IN SILVER

> The odds have shortened on the identity of the mystery buyers in December silver futures. The leading runner is James Greville, getting close support from the bottomless pocket of Crown Prince Ahmed of the Kingdom of the Hejaz. The involvement of Desert Princess's owner is widely suspected because Christy O'Donnell, his trainer, has taken up residence at Marylebone House. The Duke of Marylebone is known to possess warehouse warrants on the LMB, NYBOT and the Chicago Metal Exchange for over 30 million ounces of silver bullion. Add to this rumoured holdings of another 40 to 50 million ounces in Switzerland.
>
> It's not illegal to hold so much silver, but if the value just keeps going up the way it has, the Commodities and Futures Trading Commission in Washington will eventually have to investigate, particularly since silver's strength cannot be justified by the normal supply-demand equation. But the CFTC is notoriously short of manpower and funds, and we're betting they won't discover in time if a manipulation is going on in the silver pit. Our money, with the price of December futures now over $9, and with the odds so strongly in their favour, is on the bulls.

Susan put the pink newspaper down on her desk in the dealing room. Should she ask him to explain? How many had been the times that she had wanted to ask him why he really was in London, working for the duke; why he had been in Chicago. But she hadn't been able to. She didn't want the answer to be spelled out. She already knew it. Had known from their very first night together that he had been the one who had played the game in the market. It was so obvious. The day he'd been there was the very day it all happened. He'd been to see Mike Bachmann, who'd been the broker involved. And now he was involved with the Duke of Marylebone. 'I'll just have to have it out with him sooner or later,' she muttered aloud to herself. Otherwise, their relationship would remain built on pretence.

Her face flushed. She couldn't wait for tomorrow evening. Was it only a couple of hours ago that she had last seen him? It already felt like a very long time. God, but she wanted him. Every minute of every day....

She got busy on the phone with clients, but couldn't put Christy out of her mind. They'd only seen each other six times in total, and only late at night, he'd been so busy, but she lived through every one of them all the time – *Jesus Christ Superstar* at the Palace Theatre; an Indian meal (she had admitted to him by then her love of Indian food); a drive around London in the moonlight; a Thameside pub at Mortlake, and fish and chips after; twice just staying in and sending out for food: once a pizza, once Chinese. And never any talk about their pasts, nor what they did when they were apart in the present, nor why he couldn't see her at weekends. All that mattered was the *now*-ness whenever they were together. His company was the only thing in the world that mattered for her.

'Susan!' Giles Clark called across to her. 'Simon Winchester for you, luv, line 7.'

This made her snap sharply out of her reverie.

'Um, hello Susan,' said the Comptroller of Greville Holdings. 'I know you've been busy settling in and so on, but I had rather hoped we could, er, go and eat Greek again one evening....'

'What a nice idea,' she lied. 'Let's do that one of these days. Now I'll just get the details of the latest positions we've taken in Lady Deborah's managed account. Hold on.'

'No wait, Susan' he called out, but though she heard it she laid the phone on the desk and went to see Brian Fletcher, head of the managed accounts section.

A couple of minutes later she was back. She said quickly,

'Well, Simon, we went short five lots of LME aluminium last Thursday at £643 a ton, and it's trading today at £639. And then long ten lots of New York January cocoa at $2,076 a ton. It closed on Friday at $2,093. Rest assured that both positions are performing fine.'

'I'm very pleased,' he said, not giving a damn, 'but what I really wanted to know was which evening you'd be free.'

'Well, things are still kind of hectic right now, but as soon as I've got everything cleared out of the way I'll give you a call.'

'Oh, thank you, Susan. That would really be lovely.'

9.11.79

The second bear raid hit the market on the second Friday in November. Christy and Winchester had been sure it was coming. The evening before, the price had closed perilously near the all-important $10 mark in Chicago, at $9.83. Crabbe and Gilbert had also told them the US market buzzed with rumours that the short sellers who had failed on 22 October were coming back stronger. But, even with the advance notice, none of them expected December futures to open on the LMB 22 cents down at $9.61 an ounce.

Christy and Winchester bought furiously all morning, but the weight of selling was enormous, engulfing their efforts. The price fell steadily, and by eleven o'clock, silver was down 10 cents more. 'What the ruddy hell's going on?' Greville demanded. 'Why can't we fight them off this time?'

'Some big bullion merchants – Mansons and De Angelis – have joined the sellers to stop the price getting to $10. They're playing on investors' doubts about whether silver should be in double figures. We should be able to see them off by tonight.'

At 7.30, after the busiest day they'd had so far, Greville turned away from the Reuters screen. 'Nine dollars forty-seven. I can't believe it. Thirty-six cents down on yesterday. And you said we'd see them off by tonight.'

Winchester held his ground. 'They'll run out of steam as long as we go on absorbing the pressure.'

Christy said, 'We bought more than ever today, but it made no difference Simon; plus it's Friday, and that's pretty important.' It meant they'd be going into a weekend with their tails down.

Winchester said, 'They'll lose heart by Monday, you'll see.'

On the line from Khurbah, the crown prince sounded troubled. 'Such a big fall today.'

Christy replied, 'I agree it looks serious. But all we can do is keep soaking up the pressure by buying.'

'But Jamal tells me there is no provision for such a setback.'

'Don't forget, you're still showing a huge profit. Almost a hundred and fifty million dollars.'

'But this $2 billion profit looks improbable now, doesn't it?'

'I still say it's too early to worry, your Royal Highness.'

However, when Christy finished talking to Ahmed his instincts told him it was wise to worry a little. Just in case.

He had no worries when he arrived at Clarendon Place that evening, and Susan didn't confront him with anything other than her arms around his neck. They kissed from the lift door all the way to the pillow, undressing each other while their lips remained clamped together. When they finished making love, Susan lay her head on his bare chest. Her dishevelled auburn hair tickled his lips and nose and he blew at the vagrant strands. She could hear his heart thump vigorously and this gave her strength. They lay there for some time, Christy stroking her back and she pecking his nipple from time to time. Then she got up and went to the refrigerator in the kitchen. It had to be now or never. She poured juice for herself and a lager for Christy.

He had just started to snore lightly, so she tilted his glass to let a drop of beer strike him on the nose. 'Hey!' he cried out, sitting up in the bed.

'No dropping off now.'

He took the glass, grumbling, 'No need for rude awakenings....'

'It's not even ten o'clock, lover boy.'

He took a swig. 'Good. Dinner time. Is it ready?'

She tweaked his nose. 'Not yet. I just wanted to tell you how proud I am that your fame has spread so far that even the *FT* is writing about you now.'

'Oh yeah?' He was suddenly wary.

'Yeah,' she answered.

He drained the glass and swung his legs off the bed. 'I think I'll get another beer.'

She put a hand on his chest to stop him. Looking steadily into his eyes, she said, 'I think it's time we levelled with each other, don't you?'

'I don't know what you mean, Susan.'

'You never asked me why I was in London, Christy.'

'That's simple!' he laughed. 'You came to find me!'

She smiled mysteriously. 'Yes, actually, that's true. I came looking for a bastard. A bastard who had me burned in Chicago. I wanted his balls.' She reached into his crutch and stroked his testicles. 'And I found them.'

Christy didn't like this. 'What do you mean, "burned"?'

She kept smiling and caressing his balls, and his penis started to stir in a northerly direction. 'This bastard, you see, my darling with the Irish-eyes-that-aren't-a-smilin-no-more, this bastard bought 25 million ounces of silver and then sold it all back at about 20 cents higher.'

'Sounds like he was a good businessman,' he said warily. 'But what's that got to do with us? Let's get back in bed and put some more rice in the bowl.'

She gripped his erect penis. 'It *has* got something to do with us. You see, I was short in gold for a client that day, and ended up losing a quarter of a million dollars for that client's account because this bastard had been playing around with silver. And that's why I'm here in London. Pop threw me out. So I came looking for that bastard.'

His erection fizzled. 'I'm sorry to hear about that, my love,' he mumbled, looking so mortified that her anger subsided.

'Your love?' she repeated, homing in on the word.

He didn't want to make a big issue out of it. 'You know what I mean,' he said simply.

'Are you trying to say you love me?' she persisted.

He nodded.

'Then say it, you bastard. Just say it in so many words.'

He took her in his arms, and mumbled, 'I love you, Susan.'

She whispered, 'I love you too, Christy.'

After that, her pressing need to have the truth out about what had gone on in the commodity markets faded. Both could only think of making love, and they did this over and over, only snatching a couple of hours of fitful sleep the whole night.

Some time after dawn, Christy dressed, shook her awake and told her he couldn't see her again until the middle of the following week.

'But it's Saturday,' she complained sleepily. 'I thought we could have a weekend together at last. To go to the countryside ... wheel a cart around a supermarket....'

'Too much work, Susan, my love.' He kissed her long and hard and left. When he got back to Marylebone House, he didn't go out that whole weekend, his conscience racked by what he had inadvertently brought upon Susan back in Chicago. Winchester was surprised at the way he buried himself in work, tying up every loose end from the preceding week's activities, so they'd be as fit as possible to fight off the bears on Monday.

December futures opened 4 cents higher than Friday's Chicago close in a flurry of nerves on the LMB on Monday 12 November, because of unexpected bullishness in Tokyo and Hong Kong.

But it was down at $9.48 by lunchtime and, when Chicago opened, really big waves of selling came in. Crabbe called from there, telling Winchester, 'It's Mansons and De Angelis again.'

The comptroller repeated this to Greville, who muttered with exasperation, 'Who else?'

Immediately after, there was another call, and Winchester stiffened as he listened. Then he hung up and fiddled with his tie. 'That was Jason Gilbert from New York. There's been an unexpected development: Señor Menendes, Bank Mex's silver office manager, has been fired for insider trading, and Manson Metals have persuaded the bank to offload silver in huge quantities.'

'Does this mean we've had it?' said Greville in alarm.

Winchester tried to remain calm. 'We'll survive if fresh buying interest comes back in. That'll force Bank Mex to hold back from selling....'

Christy interrupted: 'But fresh interest will only come in if the price goes over $10 and the millions of small investors enter and create the tidal wave we need.'

The comptroller, a little more rattled now that the truth had been voiced, could add nothing. He had budgeted for Menendes doing insider trading, but not for being caught at it. The duke's men kept buying all afternoon, but the selling pressure was too great, and Bank Mex waded in short regularly. The price moved inexorably down to close in Chicago at $9.32.'

This is twice now that we have failed to reach $10, Sheikh O'Donnell. Jamal tells me we are running out of time. Unless we can get the small investors in straight away, this business will fail.'

Christy knew the crown prince was right. 'Jason Gilbert's gone to Mexico City to talk to Bank Mex officials, but it does look like we've lost the upper hand.'

'You'd better get it back quickly, otherwise I will have to find a way to get out of this scheme.'

Before the markets opened the following morning, news leaked through that there would be the biggest attack yet by the bears. Bank Mex was certain to offload millions of ounces.

Greville called the two men into the ballroom for a conference. 'I've decided we should use every penny we've got and bid the market "limit up" to get it over $10. Before Bank Mex start selling.'

'That's ridiculous,' Winchester said. 'To suddenly try to buck the trend in this bearish mood would be too suspicious, and the CFTC would be forced to intervene.'

'But you've planned to bid the market up, Winchester. It's in the blueprint.'

'Yes, but only when the tide is in our favour. If we do it now, in this negative climate, it'll draw enough attention for the CFTC to suspend trading in the commodity and investigate. And that really would be the end. The investigations could drag on for days and weeks, and then we'd have no market to corner.'

Christy suddenly said, 'You're so scared about the CFTC investigating, Simon, so why don't we actually give them something to investigate?'

'I don't know what you mean,' said Winchester.

An idea began to germinate in Christy's mind and he let the words flow by themselves. 'Let's think about this now. Let's say, for argument's sake, that his Grace and the crown prince start buying loads of silver futures in their *own* names.'

'But that'll give the game away if anything will,' Greville protested. 'The CFTC will then surely do what Simon says!'

'Just hear me out, sir ... I think part of the game *should* be given away now, without it looking too suspicious. Let's say you and the crown prince start buying silver openly, and also make a public announcement that you believe silver is a good long-term investment. And then let's also say that you announce a little later that you intend to take physical delivery through the futures markets of whatever you are buying and that you intend to hold on to the bullion.'

There was a long silence in the ballroom. Then Greville said, 'I can't see what good that will possibly do.'

Winchester stared intently at Christy. 'I think I do. You're working on the assumption that open knowledge that his Grace and the Arabs are putting money in will lead to fresh buying?'

'Exactly, Simon.'

Greville looked with mystification from one man to the other.

Winchester tried to explain: 'Remember, your Grace, only a few people outside the trade suspect that you are already involved. If you come in openly, there's bound to be a new wave of buying, and Bank Mex may well stop dumping until the price gets higher.'

'That's right,' said Christy. 'And if a public statement is made that we're buying purely for investment, that should kill a lot of the rumour that anyone's trying to corner the market. And also, with a bit of luck, the CFTC will start investigating the purchases by his Grace and the crown prince, which we'll make sure aren't big enough to force them to close the market; in the meantime, we'll just keep up our main buying through the 400 nominee accounts, which the commission will be too tied up to look into.'

Greville scratched his head. 'What do you think, Simon?'

The comptroller nodded grudgingly. 'Under the circumstances, it seems worth a try.'

'No, Sheikh O'Donnell,' said Crown Prince Ahmed later on the telephone, 'you may not use my name publicly for any silver buying.' He didn't explain just how hungrily Walid was waiting in the wings for a blunder on his part.

Christy had been prepared for a negative answer. He asked, 'And what if we did it in Jamal's name?'

There was silence on the line. Then Ahmed understood. 'Aha, I see. The market will say, 'Jamal may be fronting for Crown Prince Ahmed or he may not. What is certain is that Jamal is connected with other Saudi and Hejazi princes; so, even if Crown Prince Ahmed himself isn't involved, some very rich Arabs most certainly are.' Isn't that it, Sheikh O'Donnell?'

'That's it.'

Ahmed laughed, 'Very well, go ahead and use Jamal's name. I'll see that he doesn't mind.'

The bears forced the price down below $9.23 that day, while Christy and Winchester did all they could to absorb the pressure. They were busier setting up the new accounts with London and Chicago brokers, and preparing a press release. That afternoon, the statement was issued: the Duke of Marylebone and a Mr Karim Jamal of Beirut were entering the silver market to buy large quantities of the precious metal. This immediately caused the price to rise sharply and close eventually at $9.51.

Ahmed and Jamal, a lot happier that evening, were prepared to give silver another day or two to pass the $10 mark.

Christy didn't finish work until 1 a.m. When he finally went back up to his flat, the phone was ringing.

A woman operator said, 'There's a reverse charge call from Mr Pat Fogarty in Dublin. Will you take it?'

'Yes, put it through.'

The old man came on the line. 'I've got some news for you, lad. Your da was nabbed by the Garda a week ago.'

'A week ago?'

'That's right, but I only had the news this morning. Someone told me Stephen was coming up before a beak at Malone Road magistrate's court this afternoon. I went along to the court, and he was there all right. In a sorry state he was, lad. The McDaids were there, too, and they said they'd bail him out, but he refused their offer. He told the beak they'd do him harm, and he'd rather stay inside....'

Christy said at once, 'Well, I'll get one of my assistants out there to offer bail on my behalf....'

'No, lad,' Fogarty said. 'I already put the idea to him that you should post bail, but he refused. He'd heard about the attack on you and didn't want you to go to any more trouble. So he was remanded in custody at Collystone Prison....' Fogarty's voice sounded very old now. 'I think you should come to visit him as soon as you can, lad. He's in a bad way.'

Christy had half a mind to say he'd be there tomorrow. But how could he miss even one working day, what with everything going on in the silver market just now, with all these new accounts, and the bears ...? 'I can't make it right away, Mr Fogarty. Things are too complicated here just now. But I'll do my best to get across as soon they're sorted out.'

Fogarty said, 'Now look, lad, there's something else too. That filly I told you about, remember?'

He did remember Fogarty telling him that his da kept a horse in some burned-out farm where he was hiding out himself.

'Our Stephen finally told us where she was – near Cloonbarry in Wicklow – and he begged me to go and feed her. I went down there this evening and found the old farm and saw the horse. There was some hay there which I gave her, and some water, and I'll buy some feed for her tomorrow out of the money you left for Stephen. But I can't do it for ever, see, lad?'

Christy said, 'All right, now. I'll call my head lad at Twelve Pins, and tell him to meet up with you at the pub and get this horse out to our stable. We'll look after it. Don't you worry now. And tell my da the same: not to worry, now. I'll be along to see him as soon as I can. Tell him I've got great prospects for him and me. Tell him we'll both be living in a castle soon.'

But, until Christy fell asleep that night, he wondered if he was doing the right thing in not going to see his da straight away. He reassured himself that at least the man couldn't get into any more trouble now, not with the McDaids nor anybody else. Not while he was safely locked away in Collystone Prison.

14.11.79

'It's on all the services,' Winchester said. 'Bank Mex's President has just confirmed they don't intend to release silver on the market at this time, pending developments in the price.'

'I'm not surprised.' Christy gazed at the Reuters' screen. 'What did you expect when the December contract opened at $9.90, and is trading right now at 97?'

Greville said, 'Brilliant idea, Christy, announcing it publicly like that. And the real stroke of genius was to use Jamal's name instead of the crown prince's. Everyone's now thinking the Saudis are in this too.'

The numbers on the Reuters' screen flashed again. Christy shouted, 'It's just hit $10. We can't fail now.'

'Ten dollars,' Susan said into the mouthpiece of her telephone, staring at the Reuters' screen on her desk in the dealing room.

'Okay then,' said a speculator who had been content until now to trade in pork bellies. 'Buy one lot at that price.'

'All right, Mr Wilson, I'll call you back as soon as we've traded.' She pressed a button which connected her direct to the floor of the Chicago Exchange. 'Buy one at 10 dead.'

'Too late,' the Bachmann floor clerk replied. 'It's already up to 10.08 and rising.'

'Hold on,' said Susan, and called Wilson back. 'The price is rising sharply. I'm afraid we've missed $10. It's already 10.14 and going up fast.'

Wilson's voice was thick with excitement. 'Still rising? How much more is it going to go up?'

'The mood's very bullish right now. Don't quote me, but people are talking about $25.' What, she wondered, were the Duke of Marylebone and this Lebanese up to, making this announcement? She had to find out, and she knew who would have the answers.

'Buy,' Wilson was saying. 'Just buy at any price!'

The intercom buzzed in Winchester's study. The receptionist said, 'There's a call from Miss Gardner.'

Winchester smiled. At last. 'Good, put her through.'

'I'm sorry, but it's Mr O'Donnell she wants to talk to.'

Christy picked up the receiver. They'd agreed right at the beginning never to call each other at work, and that only he would call, from home, when he was free. So this had to be important. 'Yes, my love, what is it?'

The colour drained from Winchester's face at hearing that.

Christy listened for a few seconds, then said, 'Calm down Susie my sweet. I'll tell you all about it later. I'll be over tonight, okay now, my love?'

Winchester was unable to face Christy for the rest of the day, or communicate coherently with him. In Chicago, silver closed at $10.22. It was the first news item on all the US networks. Brokers awaited the onslaught from tomorrow with bated breath.

After cheerful conversations with Khurbah and Beirut that night, Christy went in the Mercedes to the block of flats in Bayswater. He sprang out of the car and pressed the button for Susan's flat. As he waited for her to answer, he noticed someone standing in the entrance way of the adjacent block.

The man had his back to him, but wore a familiar grey overcoat. Susan's voice came loud and clear over the entry-phone. 'So you're here, huh, lover boy? Well, come on up and face the music.' Christy, half-sensing the man in the overcoat turn his head, put him down as a nosy neighbour and pushed open the buzzing door.

Upstairs, Susan's expression was graver than he'd ever seen, and she obviously wanted to have a serious talk.

'Look, Susie,' he said, forestalling her. 'We'll talk later.' As he grabbed her in his arms saying, 'The bedroom's too far, let's do it here on the sofa,' she wanted to protest but didn't. But nor did she particularly enjoy it, for the first time since they'd become lovers.

Their arms entwined together, they emerged an hour later into the night air and headed for the Mercedes.

This time Susan noticed the man in the grey coat as he stepped out of the lighted doorway of the next-door block, into the darkness of the street. She didn't see his face, just registered something vaguely familiar about him. Also putting him down as one of the neighbours, she got in the car. But when Christy drove away, she looked back and he was standing heavily on the pavement, staring after them, a sense of menace reaching out from him. She wondered if it was Ross, come to punish her for being happy. Then they were swinging on to the Bayswater Road and the man vanished from sight.

They liked the look of the Hindenburg Disaster in the Fulham Road and took a booth in here. Christy ordered Guinness and Susan white wine.

'So, now you've had your sex for the evening ...'

'Nice, wasn't it, Susan my sweet.' He stroked the inside of her thigh under the table in the booth.

'Wonderful. Well, now we're here, comfortably installed, maybe you'll answer the question I asked you on the phone. Just what the hell is James Greville up to?

Christy's eyes twinkled. 'And I thought we'd come here to talk about us. About our future.'

'This is connected with our future. I haven't until now asked just what 'financial work' you, a horse trainer, are doing at Marylebone House with the duke. But now I want to know.' She looked straight into his face, unaware that her hands had bunched into fists.

He withdrew his hand from her thigh and clutched one of these fists. 'Susie, why can't we just enjoy whatever time we can manage to spend together? Forget all about business ...'

But she was determined. 'Please, Christy, can't you just trust me and tell me what the hell you're up to? Are you guys really trying to corner the silver market?'

He took a long drink of Guinness. Then, softly: 'Are you interested in listening to a fairy tale?'

She nodded, sensing those deep, ancient stirrings in him again, as she had when he had first talked about Ireland long, long ago in his car, on their first night. Could it have been only twenty-two days ago?

He twirled his glass about on the little cardboard beer mat. 'All right then, once upon a time, there was a young lad who worked on a farm ...'

'Yo ho ho,' she laughed. 'Was his name MacDonald?'

'No, he was Irish, not Scottish. Now, he lived with just his mother, because his father had disappeared when he was very young, and the funny thing about his mother was that she had used to dream of living in a castle, because that was what her husband had promised her, and she had clung to that belief for ever, trusting her husband, right until the day she died....' Conscious he sounded illogical to say the least, he found his words dry up.

'Wow!' Susan exclaimed. 'They say the Irish have the gift of the gab, and now I know you're no Wall Street gunslinger in disguise as I thought you were. No, you're just a really corny romantic who hasn't left his mother's womb yet.'

He smiled, 'And so I have this dream, you see, Susie, that my mother should spend the rest of eternity in the grounds of her very own castle, and when that dream's fulfilled, I want to spend the rest of eternity with you.'

She shook her head in disbelief. Could this guy be for real? 'Is that a proposal of some kind?'

He smiled sheepishly. 'Well, it's not a quote about the price of silver, is it?'

She had to admit: 'No, it sure isn't that.'

Summoning up the courage, he said it: 'So, will you marry me Susan?'

Not comprehending how they had suddenly gotten on this, the thing she probably wanted more than anything else in the world, she said uncertainly, 'Christy, honey, we've only known each other four weeks.'

'So?'

'So, we still haven't reached that point of truth between us where I can say 'Yes' with confidence. I mean, honey, you've told me about this fabulous dream you've got for your mother, but you still haven't answered my question.' Her eyes moist, she kissed the hand which still gripped her fist. 'I understand that you've done everything so far out of good intentions.'

He nodded.

'No. Don't nod like that. Answer me first. Is the duke trying to corner the silver market, and are you in it with him?'

'Yes,' he said simply.

'Oh God, Christy. Oh God. If only you'd said no, at least to your being in with him.'

'There's a lot of money involved.'

'I know there is. But it's wrong Christy. I feel it here, in my innermost soul. This duke's an evil man.'

'There's £3 million in it for me, Susan. Only one million of that's coming from the duke.'

'Three million pounds?'

He nodded and gestured for more of the same drinks.

Susan did some mental arithmetic. 'My share in pop's firm's worth $4 million. That's just under £2 million. And I thought that was a fortune.'

'So maybe now you understand.'

The drinks arrived and Christy paid for them. When he looked back at her, she was shaking her head. 'No, I don't understand. I would give up my share tomorrow if pop told me that I had to cheat and hurt people before I could have it.' She had spoken loudly, and customers in other booths looked across in their direction.

'Susan, won't you just try to see? It's for my ma, and my da....'

'Your da now! You've resurrected him too! How convenient!'

He shook his head. 'It's not like that, Susan. You see, just before I met you, I found out he was still alive. And that he still needed me.'

She was incredulous. 'And you haven't thought to say even one word about him these last four weeks?'

'I only heard last night where he was, see. He was spotted in the middle of a robbery and the police have now caught him. He's in prison in Dublin.'

'I just don't believe this. In prison?'

'Aye.'

'And you haven't been to see him?'

'I can't, Susan. There's too much work....'

She stood up. 'I thought so. Your mother, your father. Convenient excuses while you hunt glory for yourself. You say you love me. But all you're doing is using me too.'

Lots of people were staring at them now.

'Sit down Susan.'

'Not till you promise you'll stop working with the duke.'

'I can't do that.'

'I knew it. You don't care about anything except you and your glory.' She turned and walked out of the Hindenburg Disaster.

He rose to follow, but knew it would be a waste of time, having been aware for several days now just how determined she was to stand her ground over what had happened to her when he'd been in Chicago. So he downed his glass and waved for another. Before it arrived, he realized he should at least see her home. He tossed down some money and went out. But she had already disappeared in a cab.

At the Scimitar Club, Roger Wellington said, 'I see you've managed to get the Arabs to join you, eh, James?'

Greville deftly clipped the end off the Romeo y Julieta with his cigar cutter. 'You were quite right back in May, you know, Roger. It needed the personal touch.'

'Everybody's crying out that the Grevilles are finally back in business. That Charles Greville's feats during the forties, fifties and sixties may even be matched.'

Greville held the cigar before his eyes and applied a match. When it glowed a little he drew on it. The action helped him to hide his delight. 'Really?' he said casually.

'I know that at least half the members here have started buying silver.'

Greville glanced around the reading room at other members reading or engaged in muted conversation. He blew out a stream of contented grey smoke. Now he noticed that Collins, the head steward, was standing by the doorway and gazing discreetly in his direction. The man obviously had news to convey to him.

'Just a second, Roger.' Greville nodded at the steward, who trod soundlessly over.

'What is it, Collins?'

'A Mr Winchester wishes to have a word, your Grace. He is waiting downstairs.'

Greville said, 'Very well. Send him up.'

Roger Wellington rose. 'Well, I think I'll go down to the games room. By the way, could your secretary call mine tomorrow with the name of a good commodity broker?'

The duke pulled out his diary and pencilled a note for Mrs Thorpe. 'Consider it done.'

Wellington crossed paths with Winchester near the door. The comptroller was in a hell of a hurry. There was a rage in those piggy eyes which Greville had never seen before. 'What's the trouble, Winchester? It must be pretty bad if you couldn't wait until tomorrow at the House.'

Winchester, who had had the confirmation that he didn't want that Susan and O'Donnell were lovers, had difficulty expressing himself. 'It's O'Donnell, your Grace ...'

'What about him?'

Words gushed out in an angry torrent. 'Well don't you think he's out of place with what we're doing? He's just a horse trainer. What knowledge has he really got about the commodities business? I've been involved in it for years. Who does he think he is, muscling in on other people's territory?'

Greville was flabbergasted. 'What on earth's come over you, man? O'Donnell's been doing marvellously well. It's thanks to him that we've got the price into double figures. And quite apart from anything else, we have to have him around until his wog friend stumps up the rest of the cash.'

'He may be friends with the Arabs, but we don't need him any more. He could wreck our plans if he remains. We should get rid of him. Jamal can come here to look after Ahmed's interests if necessary.'

'You're talking gibberish. Have a drink and pull yourself together.'

Winchester straightened. 'No thank you, sir. I have to go now. I apologize for having bothered you.' He gave a curt nod and strode out and down the sweeping staircase to the lobby. Collins was already waiting for him with his heavy grey overcoat.

By the time Susan reached Clarendon Place, she was a mess of confusions. So now Christy had finally admitted what he and Simon Winchester and the duke and the rest of them were up to ... The bastards. But yet again she'd walked out on the man she loved ... Had she been right to have been so utterly unforgiving with Ross? Poor dead darling Ross, who'd had a stupid fling and ended up dead....

'One pound thirty, miss,' said the taxi driver.

Susan focused on this more immediate problem and handed a pound note and a fifty-pence piece across the glass partition. 'Keep the change.' She got out and glanced cautiously around the square. Was the man in the heavy coat still here? She saw no-one, and realized she was being silly. But she had felt threatened, and there had been something familiar about him.

The taxi drove away and she crossed the road to go up to her block. As she opened her pocketbook for her keys, a hand shot out from behind her and clapped roughly on to her mouth. Before she could think, her head was forced back on to her assailant's chest. A hard point pressed against her spine and her heart stopped. It was a knife ... she was going to be killed....

The thought overwhelmed her and she lost all sensation in her legs. She felt an all-encompassing need to sink to the ground, to rest on the pavement and drift away from reality, but the man gripped her too tightly. And the hard knife-point pressing against her back was only too real.

'If you don't want to die lady,' a muffled voice breathed against her ear, 'take your keys nice and gently out of your bag and hold them up.' The face, touching her cheek now, was covered with a smooth nylony fabric.

She tried to nod but her head was too firmly held. She was also unable to see her pocketbook over the hand which was clapped over her mouth. The hand reeked of cigarette smoke and was black. She could tell this even in the dark because black people's palms are not black and she could make out the sharp contrast along the side of his finger. Quaking with abject terror, she groped about in her pocketbook, managing to fish out the keys and hold them up. They were whisked away by another man who stepped out of the shadows. He wore a nylon stocking over his head, but she could see he was white. He jiggled different keys in the door until he found the right one.

The entrance door swung open.

Susan was driven forward. The black man said, 'Right, lady. I'm going to let go of your mouth. But one sound and I'll use this.' He prodded her in the back with the hard point, then released her mouth.

Relief flooded over her even though she wasn't free yet. Her mind yelled, *'Christy, where are you Christy?'* as she waited, trembling.

The white man pressed the timer light switch which lit up the lobby and stairwell. He said softly through the mask, 'What floor do you live on?' The accent was Cockney.

She tried to mouth the words but they wouldn't emerge.

'Hurry up, hurry up,' the man said. 'Unless you want me to beat it out of you.' He raised a threatening fist.

'Third floor,' she mumbled.

'And who else lives there?'

'No-one else, I'm alone.' She instantly cursed herself for her stupidity.

The black man hissed, 'Right, let's go. No, not in the lift.' He grabbed Susan's shoulders and pushed her beyond the lift to the staircase, and up the first couple of steps.

Wild ideas about escape sprang in her mind. But the knife which she knew was behind her smothered any hopes of that. Even if the black guy didn't kill her, he could maim her for life with it. Bile came up in her mouth at the thought, and as he shoved her again, she had to keep from vomiting.

Between the second and third floors she stumbled. The black man grabbed her dress and jerked at it. It ripped from her shoulder down to the middle of her back with a loud tearing sound. The white man whispered harshly, 'Sshh, Eric! Don't fucking spoil it by starting now.'

A new chill seeped into Susan's heart. My God, why did I leave Christy? Please God, don't let them hurt me ... please God, send Christy to me now....

The black man, stinking of stale sweat, gave her another violent shove. On the third-floor landing, there were four doors. The black man turned Susan to face him and poked his knife into her throat. 'Just point at your door. Otherwise you'll see your vocal chords all over this nice clean floor.'

She pointed to the one directly opposite the lift.

'If that's not yours, lady, I'll cut you all the way down from your neck to your cunt. Are you sure it's yours?'

She nodded.

'Good. Clever honky lady who understands. All right, Keith, open it. Quick.'

'Yeah, all right ... there's no alarm, is there?

Susan shook her head.

'Thought not. There's no key here for an alarm.' He swiftly unlocked first the Chubb, then the Yale, then pushed the door open and let himself in. Eric shoved her in straight after, and slammed the door behind them.

He whooped as he switched on the light. 'Whoooo, man! We're in.' Then he pulled off his stocking mask. His face was round, his lips thick and his eyes beamed almost kindly. Susan drew in a breath of surprise; she'd imagined a vicious, hateful face.

'Right, honky lady. Get everything you've got here in silver. Antiques, cutlery, everything.'

'Silver?' she repeated, not really hearing the rest, her mind spinning around the idea of bullion bars. 'Well, of course there's not much of that here, but there are a couple of valuable works of art ... prints....' She thought of the two Hockneys on the walls of the corridor to the bedroom. 'I mean, the silver cutlery and stuff aren't worth all that much....'

Eric guffawed. He was lighting a cigarette. 'Hey, Keith. She's got an American accent, but she doesn't read the papers. The silver's not worth much, she says. White women have only shit between their ears and dry rot between their legs. Maybe now you'll understand why I keep telling you to get yourself a black woman.'

Keith had pulled off his stocking and was runtish-looking. He didn't share Eric's sense of humour. 'Stop fucking around and get the silver, Eric.' He stuffed his stocking into his pocket and went across to the dining area where there was a glass-fronted cabinet in yew wood. 'Here, look. That fancy silver plate, and those soup bowls and all those other bits and pieces of silver.'

He tried the delicate cabinet door but it was locked. 'Come and open this, will you, darling?' An ugly grin spread over his yellow teeth. 'Otherwise I'll open it my own way.'

She couldn't think where the cabinet key was. She decided that looking for it would give her time. 'Just a minute. I'll have to find the key.' She went to put her hand on top of the cabinet. After groping there for a few seconds she said, 'No, it's not there.' Then she affected to think where else it might be.

'What are you trying to do?' Keith shouted at her. His face was livid. 'You trying to waste our time?' He struck her violently across the face with the back of his hand. The force of it stunned her and sent her staggering back against the table. She tried to get her vision back into focus, conscious only of salty blood in her mouth.

'*Please!*' she screamed. 'Please don't hurt me!'

The black man came across to Keith. 'Stop it, you arsehole! I don't want her smashed up yet. Just fucking break the cupboard open, all right?'

He dragged Susan to the sofa and lay her down. Then he sat beside her, put his knife into the tear in her dress and ripped it all the way down. She had no power to resist. Keith's blow had sapped her strength and will. In her daze she heard Keith shout across, 'Oi, Eric! Who says you're first? I'm not putting mine in after your nigger one's gone in.'

'Fuck off, you white shit, and get the silver. That's what you came for, isn't it?' He tugged her dress away, stuck his knife into her panties, and ripped these open too.

Her mind numb with horror, Susan heard the glass in the cabinet door smash. But her arms were paralysed and she was incapable of fighting back. Eric now snipped her brassiere in between the two cups and thrust them apart.

'God!' she tried to scream, 'Please, God, kill me instead of this....' No words came out.

'God in Heaven,' Eric said. 'What fucking amazing tits.'

He jiggled his knife about at the entrance to her vagina and then his lips slopped on to her left nipple. The rough tuft of hair under his lower lip scrubbed her breast. One of his hands unzipped his trousers, while the middle finger from the other groped into her vagina.

The entry buzzer sounded.

Eric got straight up on his knees. His penis stuck up out of his flies. 'Who's that?' he demanded.

She mumbled the first thought that came into her mind, 'It's my boyfriend.' It had to be Christy. She knew that. She raised her hands to hide her naked breasts. 'He's got a key.'

The black man sprang off her as if he'd been scalded. 'Get the silver, quick.' He crammed his prick back into his trousers and hurried to the dining cabinet to help Keith with the silver.

The buzzer sounded again.

Eric turned to look at Susan, puzzled. 'If he's got the key then why's he ringing the fucking bell?'

Susan was trying to draw her ripped dress around herself. 'Sometimes he forgets his key and has to be let in.'

A slow grin crossed Eric's lips. He walked back towards her. 'If he's forgotten his key, then all you've got to do is not answer, eh, honky lady? So he'll go away.'

She shook her head, knowing that hesitation would lose her the initiative. 'He knows I'm here. He's just finished work and is coming up for dinner.'

The black man paused to consider this.

Keith piped up, 'Hurry up, Eric, I can't carry all this gear by myself.'

'Shut up,' he growled back, staring at Susan's naked crutch.

His face was smeared with lust.

The buzzer went a third time.

Eric ignored it, his eyes still fixed on her. 'Maybe he'll think you're out? That you haven't come home yet? All you've got to do is not answer. Yeah....' Satisfied with his vast logic, he pulled his prick out of his flies again.

'No,' she said, her mouth open in horror. 'He can see the light up here from the sidewalk. That's why he keeps buzzing. If I don't answer he'll know something's wrong. Then he'll buzz my neighbour, who's got a key.'

Keith had now come up, carrying a number of silver articles. 'Let's scarper, Eric. The longer we spend here, the more chance we've got of getting nicked.'

The buzzer sounded twice in quick succession.

'That's the last time he'll call ...' she went on inventing.

Eric stood there uncertainly, his penis a seventy degree ebony ramrod.

' ... then he'll try the next door apartment, and the first thing he'll do from there will be to phone 999.'

'Right,' he said, tucking his staff back in for the last time and zipping himself up. 'Let's go, Keith.' He jabbed a warning finger at Susan. 'But don't worry honky lady. We'll be back. I've tasted your tits, and they're delicious.' He went to grab a few more things from the cabinet. Then the two slipped out of the apartment.

The moment the door shut Susan rushed across to put it on its chain. She picked up the entry-phone, praying that Christy hadn't gone. In the earpiece she heard the faint tread of footsteps.

Whoever it was, was going away.

'Christy!' she cried into the mouthpiece, hoping that if it was him, he was still in earshot of the downstairs speaker.

There was silence.

Then the footsteps started up again, getting louder. Christy's voice came over. 'Susan?'

Relief surged through her. Then she remembered Eric had a knife. And they'd undoubtedly be going back down by the stairs.

She gasped, 'Come on up, Christy, come up. Quickly. And take the elevator.' She was sure they wouldn't emerge into the lobby if the light was on and if somebody could be heard waiting for the elevator.

'What's wrong, Susan?'

'Just come up right away and take the elevator. You *must* take the elevator!' She pressed the buzzer to open the downstairs entrance door, praying Keith and Eric would hear that too and not go into the lobby.

She waited by the door, her ear pressed to it, whimpering, 'Please Christy, come up quickly, please.'

She heard the elevator go down, the doors open, the doors close, and then the elevator come up. The doors opened again. There was a gentle knock on the door. Then Christy's voice: 'Susan can I come in?'

She took the chain off and opened the door.

'Jesus Christ!' He stared at her, at the blood on her mouth, at the torn dress she was clutching about her, at the damage beyond in the dining area. 'What the hell's going on?'

'They've just gone,' she whimpered, nodding at the window.

Christy darted across and looked down. It was difficult to see into the darkness from the lighted room, but he glimpsed two men scurrying away down the street.

'They mugged me,' Susan whimpered. 'They tried to rape me.'

'Jesus Christ!' he repeated. 'Why didn't you tell me through the entry-phone? I'd have gone after them.'

'They had a knife, Christy.'

Now he grasped her to him. 'Are you all right, my love? Are you hurt?'

'They hit me, Christy,' she bawled. 'Call the police. Please.'

They were alone again an hour and a half later. Two police officers from Edgware Road CID had been and gone.

When they arrived, Susan had been in the middle of a long shower, scrubbing every part of her body. But she couldn't rid herself of Eric's lips on her breast, nor his filthy finger inside her.

The police took a full statement from her, including detailed descriptions of Eric and Keith. Eric had left behind his stocking mask, and they put this in a plastic bag and tagged it.

'Make sure you're accompanied home every evening, Miss Gardner,' they said before going. 'And don't let anybody into the flat whom you don't know.'

Susan was sure Sinjin Burrowes would drive her back after work daily. As for not letting anyone in, that was the most unnecessary piece of advice anyone had ever given her in her life.

Now, as Christy fixed her a very stiff whisky, she said, 'I'm very pleased you buzzed when you did you know.'

He held her and tried to kiss her. 'I was hoping we could make up. You don't know how much I missed you after you went.'

She wormed her way out of his grasp. 'Have you had second thoughts, Christy?'

He said, 'The truth is, I was hoping you'd have cooled down. But you didn't really get a chance, did you, now?'

She shook her head in disbelief. 'I don't believe it. You haven't even *thought* about what those two guys were after, have you? You didn't even listen to my statement to the police....'

'Now don't go upsetting yourself again, my love.' He tried to take her again, but she thrust him away firmly this time.

'They were after the silver, you son of a bitch. Do you hear? The silver! And why? Because the value had gone up, they said. They read it in the papers, they said.'

'But Susan,' he protested, determined not to let her have it all her way just because she was hurt. 'They didn't turn to crime just because the silver price has gone up. If it wasn't silver, it'd have been something else. A pair of petty, opportunistic little roughs, the cops said.'

She unleashed all the pent-up rage from her trauma. 'Well, you're wrong! There *is* an artificial price on silver, and people *are* being tempted into crime because of that. Suddenly, there's a whole new target for that kind of petty criminal ... all that silver that's sitting in ordinary people's homes. It's worth so much more now, isn't it, and why? Because you and the Duke of Marylebone and some other smart asses think you've got the right to play with the price!'

He said woodenly, 'I've got to do this thing, Susan, don't you understand?'

'Then I don't want anything more to do with you,' she said. 'Please go. Please Christy, just go.'

He went. When the door clicked shut behind him, Susan put it back on the chain. Then she turned the key in the Chubb lock and let a thousand silent tears flow.

15.11.79

The excellence of the Fortnum and Mason breakfast rashers was disregarded by Greville the next morning. He was furious. What could Winchester have in mind, shoving his oar in like that at the Scimitar? How could he even think of having O'Donnell removed, with the Arab's $700 million not in yet? He rolled a rasher with a fork and dipped it in the yolk of an egg. 'Call Winchester here, will you.'

The ever-available Diamond, who was busy preparing the toast, left the ballroom saying, 'Very good, sir.'

The comptroller was a little less tight-lipped than the night before. A night's sleep had temporarily eased his torment over Susan. Greville indicated a nearby chair. Winchester sat.

'About last night ... your charging into my club ...'

'I had a piece to say and I said it. The incident is buried now as far I'm concerned.'

Greville raised his eyebrows. 'Really? And would you care to explain what prompted your outburst?'

Winchester stated coolly: 'O'Donnell's a wrong sort, your Grace. Everyone's been seduced by his flashy successes including, I'm afraid, yourself. But you'll see, he'll bring this business crashing down. I just know it. There's a self-seeking arriviste aspect of his nature which always emerges when the chips are down. That's all I have to say, really.'

Greville chewed all this over. 'I see. And do you plan to inform Ahmed or Jamal about your grievances? Or ask them as you asked me to remove our "self-seeking arriviste" from the affair?'

'O'Donnell can go to hell,' Winchester said irritably. 'And he'll probably end up there under his own steam. I certainly haven't got any more time for him.' A different thought occurred to him. 'And speaking of time, I'm glad you called me in. Crabbe isn't going to have enough time out in Chicago now to do all he has to with the new accounts in your and Jamal's names. So there's another ex-colleague of mine ...'

Greville waved him to silence. The man had given him the solution to stop all this bickering between him and O'Donnell. 'Are you saying you need somebody else to go out to work in Chicago now?'

'That's right.'

He nodded. 'I've the perfect idea. We'll send O'Donnell out there and have your other friend work here in his place. There should be no more idiocy after that.'

The comptroller thought about this. Thought about Susan … 'Yes, that's not a bad idea. In fact it's not bad at all.'

Greville rose. 'I'll come across to the study and put it to him. I'm sure he'll agree.'

Paul St John Burrowes shouted across the Sheedy dealing room, 'Susan. Line 6. Mr Wilson.'

Susan flicked the switch on her console. 'Hello, Mr Wilson.'

'What's December silver this morning?' he demanded.

She glanced at her screen, deciding he probably hadn't slept all night because of his silver position. 'It's up to $10.39.'

Wilson calculated aloud. 'I bought one lot of 5,000 ounces at $10.16 yesterday, so that's a profit of 23 cents … that makes $1,150 already! And I only put up $2,000 for that.'

'That's right.'

'Right then, buy another lot. At the current market price.'

Susan hung up and placed the order. It was, according to her daily record sheet, her forty-second buy order for the metal already that day. She knew there would be many more, especially when the Exchange opened in Chicago in around three hours' time. And she would just have to go on executing them; just have to go on helping James Greville.

All right, sir,' Christy said. He knew someone was needed across the Atlantic at once, and it might as well be he. Susan didn't want to know him any more, and his da was safe enough behind the high walls of Collystone. 'I'll go tomorrow.'

All the funds necessary for the operation of the new accounts in the names of James Greville and Karim Jamal were re-allocated by that afternoon. The other colleague Winchester had mentioned – Edward Bowman – had already arrived at the House and was quickly in the swing of things. A well-tanned man with fair hair and blue-grey eyes, Bowman was a metals dealer with Benner Schwarz Ltd. He had started working in the

City in 1962, the same year as Winchester; the two, after meeting at a livery company dinner given by the Lord Mayor, had remained friends ever since.

'How did you manage to get away so quickly to come to work with us?' Christy asked him.

'It was easy. I confessed to my boss that I had a "Coke" problem and that I needed to go to a detoxification centre for a two-month cure. My boss told me to go immediately. Today.'

'So you take cocaine, eh?' Christy had heard the drug was snorted all over the City.

'I don't know about cocaine,' Bowman grinned. 'But the Coke problem I have is that I can't stomach Bacardi without it.'

Mrs Thorpe came into Winchester's study just then and announced to Christy that his flight to Chicago tomorrow was on TWA at 10.15 from Heathrow, and that Stewart would have a car ready from 7.30 onwards.

Paul Burrowes dropped Susan off at the Clarendon Place flat that evening. She sat alone watching television until half-past eleven, when she checked her watch. It was 5.30 in Chicago. Pop would have got home by now and would be watching Dan Rather read the CBS News. You could set your watch by that.

Susan picked up the telephone and dialled. Across the Atlantic, her step-mother answered. Susan wondered whether to tell Florence about her mugging yesterday, but decided not to. As for pop, she certainly wouldn't tell him. He'd be on a flight over tomorrow. She chatted with Florence about the British weather before asking if her father was there.

'Sure,' said her step-mother. 'I'll just go get him.'

When Thomas Gardner came on the line, Susan let fly. 'Do I have news for you! You remember that business in silver which caused the Breimyer fiasco? Well, I know for sure now that the Duke of Marylebone was behind it. What's more, he's trying to corner the market. One of his henchmen told me himself.'

'Oh yeah?' Gardner sounded unconcerned.

'Pop, you're not interested?'

'Sure I'm interested, sure. I'm just worrying about your phone bill.'

'Phone bill! You're grouching about this phone call when your office phone bill is a half a million dollars a year?'

'Now listen, Susie. Don't worry your sweet head about silver. There's no problem at all as far as I can see.'

'No problem? They're trying to corner the market, pop!'

He chuckled, 'Well if they are, it's fine, just fine. Do you know the volume of business we've done these last few weeks? It's been phenomenal. The commissions are pouring in and that'll boost our profit figures no end for the year.'

She was amazed. 'Aren't you going to do anything about it?'

'You bet,' he said happily. 'I'm going to sit back and let the commissions keep flowing in.'

She was speechless.

Gardner muttered, 'Anyway, there's nothing else I can do.'

'Yes, there is!' she snapped. 'First of all that scam back in October. The buy order to the London Minerals Board came from our own office and Mike knows all about it. You could get the details from him and pass everything on to the CFTC so they can investigate. Then, I can dig out some hard facts about the accounts that the duke has opened in Sheedy's right here....'

He intervened quickly, 'Now, Susie, I don't want you making any waves in London. We've a fine relationship with Sheedy and Ratcliffe. They put an awful lot of business through us, and there are fewer and fewer really big British brokers like them. We don't want to go rocking boats which have been steady for years. Now you just forget all about what's going on in silver. You could switch to cocoa trading. Or potatoes ...' His voice brightened. 'Yeah, I've heard a lot of action goes on in London potatoes. Look, I'll call Paul Burrowes in the morning and ask him to move you to the potatoes desk.'

'No you goddamn well won't. I've had enough of you pushing me around whenever it suits you.'

'Okay, okay, just simmer down Susie. Look, in a few months this'll all blow over and you'll be back here and soon running the show. So just enjoy yourself down there. London must have lots of interesting things to offer. I'm sure you've made nice friends down there ... probably even a man friend at last, huh?'

'No!' she blurted. 'I mean, yes. I mean, I do have friends, but no man in the sense you're thinking of. Not just now, that is ... Anyway, getting back to this silver business ...'

'No,' he cut in firmly. 'Let's not get back on that. There's nothing we can do except go along with the market. Look, tell you what, if you like, you can leave London and come back here sooner than we had originally planned. Daniel Breimyer's getting around to seeing sense and he's on the verge of swallowing the loss. What do you say to coming back say next month, huh?'

Susan replied automatically. 'No. I'm going to stick it out here for the full six months as we agreed.' She hung up and knew she'd again got exactly nowhere. Except to discover that she hated the idea of leaving London. Then she remembered Eric approaching with his disgusting penis sticking out of his flies, Keith striking her across the face. They were still out there and Eric had warned her he'd come back. Last night, Christy had come to the rescue; next time, there'd be no-one to do that.

Earlier, Christy had telephoned Khurbah with details of the day's trading. He also informed Ahmed he was going to Chicago to help out with the extra work. After a late solitary dinner in a nearby restaurant, he returned to the House around midnight, brooding about Susan being all alone in Clarendon Place. It may be what she wanted, but that fact gave him little comfort.

When he let himself into his flat, he heard music playing down in the lounge and saw that lights were on in there. 'That's funny.' He was sure he'd switched everything off. He went in, and there was Deborah, Lady Deborah Spencer, sitting curled up on the sofa, a drink in her hand, humming gently to herself. He threw his keys on the coffee table. 'Deborah! What do you want here? Haven't you got children to look after or something?'

She looked at his face for a long time. 'You're in love with someone aren't you, Christy?'

He pulled his coat off. 'If I am, what's it to do with you? Do you think that because your father owns the place you can visit me uninvited whenever you feel like it?'

She got off the sofa and came to him. She was very beautiful. Her blond hair was tied in a pony tail by a simple blue silk ribbon and her normally cool eyes glowed like living rock. 'You don't know how much I've missed you.'

Christy snorted, 'So you haven't found anyone else to take Patrick Spencer's place in your bed, I take it.'

Deborah said softly, 'I'll admit, Christy, that it was just sex between you and me at first. You had – still have – this enormous sexual pull ... Then the years rolled by without you and I realized how deeply I really care for you. I came here today only because I heard you were staying and I needed to see you. Like I came to Condrieu when I heard you were there.' When he didn't respond, she added, 'I wish now that I'd had your baby.'

Feelings which had hardened against her over the years

thawed in his breast. He shrugged his shoulders. 'You said at the time you weren't even sure it was mine.'

'Did you really believe that, horse man?' She reached a hand up to stroke the scar on his cheek. 'I only said that to make it easier for you to bear. But I knew. A woman always does.'

He moved away towards the bar. 'But you were doing it with a different man every night, you told me.'

Deborah followed him. 'There was only Peter Callaghan around that time besides you, Christy. And he had been away in South Africa for three months just before it happened. So it had to be you, don't you see?'

Christy pulled a glass out for himself, knowing he didn't want a drink. What he wanted was Susan. Deborah was right, he did love someone else ... But here was his sweetheart from his youth, telling him she had wanted his baby, offering herself to him – and not just for sex – in a way he had never dreamt possible before. 'So why didn't you accept when I asked you to marry me?'

She clasped her hands together. 'Christy, you know I couldn't. I had to marry someone from my own class. My father's a duke, after all.'

He waved away her pleading gesture. 'So go and find someone from your own class now. Why do you keep coming back to me?'

Deborah went back to the sofa and curled up in it again. Her gaze wandered off into the distance. 'I'm older now. I've realized what the important things in life are. Not money. Not position. What counts is someone who cares for you.'

Christy laughed without humour. 'You sound like an empty tin drum, Deborah. Do you know that?'

She said coolly, 'Probably.'

There was nothing he could add to that. Scratching his head, he realized that whatever her drawbacks may be, the one thing he had always admired about her was that she was cool. Like the way she didn't even ask how he had got the scar on his face. She had real class. The sort of class which came with good breeding....

He unbuttoned his shirt and went towards his bedroom. So why shouldn't he take what she was offering? She had never tried to stand in the way of what was precious to him, not like Susan ... On the contrary, wasn't it because of her that he'd got the job with Bhojalpur? And now that she needed him, did he have a right to refuse her? Aware he was being fickle with his emotions, but carried away by his memories of the wonderful times with her in his youth, he said over his shoulder, 'All right, so if you've come all this way for me, you might as well have me.'

Deborah waited until the record ended; then she undid her pony tail, shook her hair free, and went into the bedroom after him.

At six the next morning, Christy rang Hutton with instructions to bring in breakfast for two.

As they drank coffee in bed, Deborah said, 'I really am yours for life, Christy. All you have to do is click your fingers, and I'll come running.'

Christy kissed her on the lips, then reached for the rest of her under the bedclothes. He wondered if her father knew what she was up to just a couple of doors away, and whether he'd be putting the Union Jack up in his bedroom window. At exactly eight, he boarded the waiting car and set off for Terminal Three at Heathrow Airport.

Trans World Airlines' flight TW 242 left on time for Chicago. Christy hoped he would leave all memories of Susan behind too. But he suspected he wouldn't. He had used Deborah's body last night to avenge himself on both of them, and the sex had been great. There was no-one like Deborah for that. But as he gazed down from 30,000 feet at the Severn estuary, he realized it was Susan's body he had made love to, and not that randy bitch to whom he had lost his virginity in a barn in Surrey.

19.11.79 – 26.11.79

Every day for a week, Simon Winchester called Susan at Sheedy and Ratcliffe's to ask her out to dinner. Each time, she put him off. In the markets, silver continued to rise.

At the opening on the LMB on 26 November, December futures went up to $11.25 an ounce. Then, around noon, one of the dealers shouted across the Sheedy dealing room to Susan that Simon Winchester was on line 7.

'Susan, I'd really like you to make it to dinner tonight,' the Comptroller of Greville Holdings urged her. 'Please.'

About to say no as usual, she suddenly thought, why not? Christy hadn't called for ages, so why shouldn't she enjoy someone else's company? 'Yes, Simon,' she said. 'I think I will be able to manage it this evening.'

He was waiting outside her office at 7.30 when she emerged. They went to a steak house in Leicester Square and managed to get through the meal without too many awkward silences. Susan found him more at ease with himself than she had expected. They nattered about films and books they'd loved and hated. Winchester revealed himself as a great fan of Peter Sellers and of Ian Fleming novels, but declared he couldn't stand the Bond films. 'The work of a superior literary craftsman has been trivialized by all those bimbos and that technological trash.' They took a cab back to Clarendon Place and, when they arrived, he leaped out and raced around the back of the taxi to open her door.

'Very dashing, Simon. Thanks.'

'Can I come up for coffee?' he said shyly.

She laughed. 'I thought you'd never dare ask again. Sure you can come up. I need escorting ...' Wagging a finger at him, she added, 'But only coffee, not like the last time, okay?'

'Okay.' He paid off the cabbie.

In the apartment, she went into the kitchen to get the coffee on the boil, and he came up behind her.

'Susan ...'

She spun around. 'No funny business, okay? Just coffee, remember.'

'All right,' he said, going back into the living room. Already less relaxed than at the restaurant, he didn't even put any music on. When she brought the tray through to the low table before the sofa, she noticed he was on edge, as if he wanted to get something off his chest.

She wondered if he knew about Christy and her, and the thought made her uncomfortable. 'Drink up, Simon, then you'd better leave me to my beauty sleep.'

He sipped from his cup in silence. Then he got up and made awkwardly for the front door. She let him out and he called for the lift. 'Can I just kiss you goodnight?'

'All right,' she smiled, turning her cheek at him.

Instead, he just stroked her lips with his finger.

She stepped back behind the safety of the apartment door. The lift arrived and its doors glided open. 'The problem is, Susan,' Winchester said with an awkward smile, 'that I want you really rather badly. If only I knew how to make you feel the same towards me....'

She said gently, 'Simon, I am quite fond of you. Honestly. But I'm not drawn to you that way. Do you understand? Now go home and get a good night's sleep.'

He made no move to get into the elevator. Its doors closed behind him. 'Is it because there's someone else more important to you?'

She nodded. 'Yes, there is. I mean, there has been. But that's not it, Simon. It's just that I can't feel for you what you want me to, and I know that somehow I never will.'

A dark, frustrated need to hear O'Donnell's name on her lips made him ask, 'Who is it, Susan? Will you at least tell me that?'

'It doesn't matter now, Simon. It's over between him and I, and now I've just got to get him out of my system.' Then her bitterness about Christy spilled over: 'He's got too much on his plate which is more important than I am or than any other person is. All he cares about is money. His father's in prison, but he's more interested in making £3 million and getting some castle in the air....'

'Won't you tell me his name?' asked Winchester, badly needing confirmation.

She shook her head. 'No, Simon. Good night.' Fed up with him also now, she closed the door with a sigh.

28.11.79

Crescendoes of noise rose from the trading floor of the Chicago Grain and Metal Exchange. From the observation gallery, Christy watched the price boards on the walls. December silver ranged between \$11.93 and \$11.96 an ounce.

Compton Crabbe glided up to Christy's side. 'The last load went off exactly on cue this morning.'

'Good,' muttered the Irishman.

The final consignment of Greville's Chicago bullion stocks had been dispatched on a Flying Tigers 747, destination Zurich. The silver had been air-freighted out so that the Exchange stock figures would reveal a shortfall when published at the end of the month. The panic would be heightened, and more buying sparked.

Crabbe lit a Gauloise. Observing one of the floor traders, he took a long draw on the cigarette. 'Any minute now.'

The price didn't in fact hit $12 an ounce for another quarter of an hour. As the figure rippled on to the board, the first of the fireworks went off. The dealer commissioned by Crabbe to act for them made the familiar inwards gesture and yelled above the din, *'Buy at twenty!'*

There was a momentary pause as traders registered the bid. $12.20. A leap of 20 cents. There was a thunder of sell offers, all of which were taken up by Crabbe's dealer, whose name was, appropriately enough, Martin Hornblower. He followed this with another spectacular bid, this time of $12.30, and there was the same reaction; then, in the brief lull which followed that, he bid $12.40. More offers, and again everything taken up. By the time he yelled out, *'Buy at 50!'* only three minutes had passed, but speculators around the world had got the message, and the pit was barely discernible to the observers in the gallery for the blizzard of trading cards streaking across from the booths. Silver was going wilder than ever, and everybody wanted to be part of it.

The buying pressure escalated for the next hour. Then, at exactly ten o'clock, Hornblower made a bid of $12.83 for 100 contracts. The moment it was supplied, the pit buzzer went. The price had gone 'limit up', a full dollar higher than the previous day.

30.11.79

The party at Condrieu Hall that Friday night was Jane's idea. It was a black tie affair, and she had thrown it in her father's honour. England was abuzz with his achievements just now. He was being generally praised for having guessed right in 1974, when he had chosen to get out of property and into silver. The *Daily Mail*'s leader column the previous morning had commented: *'James Greville is one of that rare number to be blessed with the level of certainty about his actions that only saints and madmen possess.'* Other newspapers, most notably the *Financial Times,* suggested darkly that the silver market was being secretly manipulated.

But that night, every light in the Hall blazed. In the great saloon, an orchestra played waltzes, swing music, ballads by the Beatles and Tamala Motown soul numbers. Strippers performed in one of the drawing rooms for those who were partial to that sort of thing; in another drawing room, cribbage, poker, blackjack and whist went on; in the smoking room, there was cocaine on tap for anyone who desired it.

Hundreds came from Horncastle, Lincoln, York, the surrounding counties, the Midlands, Scotland and London. James Greville, the toast of the party, behaved through it all like a Roman emperor receiving a triumph. It was a performance which made Elizabeth sick. Still, she joined in by waltzing a couple of times with Matthew Brown, the ex-Mayor of Horncastle.

It was only when Lady Carole Markeston finally arrived, later than expected, that Elizabeth felt at ease. They hadn't seen each other since their tea-time meeting six weeks ago. It was Elizabeth who hadn't wanted to. But they had spoken almost every other day on the telephone, though, as Elizabeth had never mentioned James, her friend had desisted from doing so too.

This evening, Carole had come deliberately late. Since Elizabeth had gone into a shell over the past few weeks, Carole thought that if she made Elizabeth look forward to her coming, the duchess might finally open up about what was so obviously bothering her.

It didn't take Carole very long to broach the subject. 'You haven't said a great deal about James lately, you know, Liz.'

Elizabeth arched an eyebrow at her. 'Let's just say I wouldn't have thrown this party on the basis of his recent behaviour.'

Carole frowned. 'Do you want to tell me about it?'

'Yes.' They went into the kitchens. Elizabeth sought out a quiet corner, and Carole nibbled at a canapé she'd picked up from a tray on the way. 'I've heard he's taken up with Sarah McGonagle again, Carole. But, apparently, they only meet in London. At her flat.'

'I don't want to believe that, Liz, not after what you told me the last time we saw each other.'

Elizabeth nodded. 'It's true. It's been going on for a couple of weeks now, I've been told. I haven't seen him since the day you and I had tea in Horncastle. It was that same day that he turned utterly hateful again.'

'I knew,' said Carole, 'that something had obviously gone terribly wrong. You haven't wanted to speak about him to me, nor have you wanted to see me.'

'I've been under an awful cloud, Carole. I haven't known what to do. He seems to get away with everything. He killed Charles, using the trainer as his instrument, and got away with it. Then he promoted John Early, and got away with that. And he's been manipulating the silver market ever since, and been getting away with that too. It's all so wrong.'

Her friend gazed upon her in sympathetic silence.

'That last time he came here, he brought up all that rubbish about my adultery with Charles again, and you can't believe how all that dismayed me, even though I had thought I was fairly inured against it by now. Do you remember that discussion we had about love, you and I, earlier that day?'

Carole nodded. 'I do.'

'I told you I was convinced he loved me, and that's why, later, I was utterly shocked by his behaviour and realized that, really, he probably didn't. And then, some time after he had gone, I came to the conclusion that the problem wasn't about whether he loved me, since I'm convinced again that he does. No, the problem was – is – that he can't believe that *I* love *him*. He just can't. Do you know what he told me that last time? He said I should go into Charles's vault and squeal with delight with him in there!'

Carole raised her eyebrows in horror. 'How mean he's always been. If only you *had* had an affair with Charles. I often wish you had. At least then all this torture he's put you through might have been worth it.'

'He can't even leave Charles in peace in his grave.'

Carole, bitter on her friend's behalf, muttered, 'Well, I don't know how you've put up with it. How you go on putting up with it.'

'Noblesse oblige, I suppose,' Elizabeth said wryly.

'Noblesse oblige my foot! If I were you I'd just go and do exactly what James suggested. I'd go down into the vault and spend the night in there with Charles.'

'The idea!'

'Do it, Liz,' Carole said mischievously. 'I mean it. Do it. Go down into the vault one night. Spend the whole night in there, and let out a squeal. You'll feel so much better after. I'm absolutely sure of it.'

'Huh!'

'In fact, do you know what? I think you should do it tonight. While James is here. So that tomorrow, when he asks you where you've been, you can say, "Why, in the vault with Charles, of course, squealing with delight." ' She clapped her hands and laughed uproariously at the expression she imagined James would have on his face.

Elizabeth smiled. Carole had just come up with the finest suggestion anyone had made since Charles's death.

While the party went on, Norman Willett, Elizabeth's most trusted butler, took blankets, an oil lamp and a chair out to the mausoleum, where the two women waited, giggling. They had already sworn him to secrecy. Colin Badcock, the head gamekeeper, and his three sons also arrived here now, having been summoned by telephone by Willett, who in his turn had sworn them all to secrecy too.

In the light thrown by the oil lamp, the five men shifted the marble slab of Charles Greville's tomb to one side. One of the gamekeeper's sons jumped into the hole and they passed the blankets, the chair and the lamp down to him. Ricky Badcock had to push the coffin a little to the side to make enough space for the chair to stand properly, but this wasn't too hard since the coffin rested on steel struts and slid across fairly easily.

Finally, Elizabeth was lowered into the grave, with the gamekeeper's boy below taking special care not to manhandle her in any way. Elizabeth sat on the chair and drew the blankets over her while Ricky Badcock climbed out.

'Goodnight, Liz,' Carole called.

'Goodnight, Carole.' She turned off the oil lamp.

Just before she fell asleep, Elizabeth remembered she had to squeal, and did so; though, being rather self-conscious about exactly where she was, she didn't do it very loudly. When, some time later, the coffin opened and Charles came out to talk to her, Elizabeth realized how much she'd missed him.

In the early hours of the morning, all five men and Carole returned to reverse the process, and Elizabeth was wide awake, waiting for them.

'The party's still going on,' said Carole Markeston with a grin as the duchess came out of the grave. 'But I don't think you were missed.'

Elizabeth smiled happily. 'Oh Carole, you were right. You can't believe how liberated I feel. Charles spoke to me, you know. And he told me exactly what I must do. You understand, don't you, Carole?'

'I do,' said Carole Markeston, with perfect understanding. She always understood Elizabeth Greville. That was why they were the best of friends.

In the Hall, the orchestra had stopped playing by now, but a disc jockey put on record after record. The party continued until three o'clock in the afternoon, though both James Greville and Elizabeth had gone to their separate beds long before then.

1.12.79 – 2.12.79

On the morning of that same Saturday, a man wearing a pin-striped suit arrived in Dublin on a British Airways flight from Heathrow. He signed the hire papers for a car – a medium-sized Peugeot – at the airport desk of Hertz Car Rentals, and drove to the nearest police station.

His enquiries there were treated with the utmost respect, and he was eventually directed to Collystone Prison. Here, he spent some time talking to a prisoner who was awaiting trial for his part in a failed armed robbery attempt. When he left the prison, he consulted his Philip's Road Map of Ireland and took the N81 down into County Wicklow. At Baltinglass he turned left on the R747 and drove along this for several miles before taking the narrow country road to Cloonbarry Village. He located the burned-out farm a mile and a half from here, and inspected the one surviving barn. When he left the place, he was deep in thought. He finally decided to drive across country, and ended up staying at the Rosemount Hotel in Galway.

After an early breakfast on the Sunday, he drove to the village of Killertoon a dozen miles away, and talked at length to the parish priest there. He decided to make one more stop before heading back to Dublin airport. This was at Twelve Pins stable in County Tipperary, and here he found the final piece of the jigsaw.

3.12.79

Susan boldly entered Edgware Road police station early on Monday morning. She was led by Inspector Hallam into a dark room, on one wall of which was a broad pane of glass. Through it, another, more brightly lit, room could be seen.

The inspector said, 'That, as you may have guessed, is a one-way mirror. One of my officers is going to bring a few men into that room through there, and if you recognize your assailant just speak out. No-one in there can see or hear you.'

She nodded, ill able to conceal her fear. Hallam pressed a button on the wall and she stared through the glass. A door in the lit room opened noiselessly and a policeman came in. Then a black man entered. He was followed by another. The policeman waved them along to the end of the room, where they turned and faced the glass, backs against the wall. Susan shook her head. Eric came in next, followed by a couple more men.

'That's him,' she said, pointing at him. He was just lining up alongside the first pair, and stared ahead with an unfocused, bland gaze. 'The third guy.'

Inspector Hallam nodded. 'Eric Cato. We were sure it was him. Now there are just a couple of formalities to be taken care of, Miss Gardner....'

He broke off. Her hands were trembling like leaves in the wind and her face was completely white.

Later, in the dealing room, her nerves steadier, she found two messages on her desk. Both were from Mr Wilson. She rolled her green eyes up to heaven.

This guy had been trading in silver for just two weeks and

was already the world's greatest expert in the commodity. He regularly informed her that he read the *FT* every day, the *Wall Street Journal* 'for balance' thrice a week, and watched *The Money Programme* 'to get an overview of big business'. He had three lousy lots of silver, and used to have one in pork bellies; but, since he was a client with Sheedy and Ratcliffe, holding open commodity positions, he was entitled to call up for information. It was a privilege Mr Wilson didn't neglect. He was on the line every ten minutes, it seemed, to assume 'hands-on management over developments' in his silver contracts.

With a sigh, she dialled his number. 'You called, Mr Wilson?'

'Yeah.' He was angry he'd been made to wait. 'Your Mr Clark told me some US company called Manson Metals is trying to get the silver market closed. Should I get out now and take my profit?'

She wanted to say that he should get out. Get right out of her hair and shove his precious silver up his ass. Mustering up some patience, she said, 'Let me look into it and get back to you.'

When she was rid of him, she gave in to what she'd wanted to do since she'd seen Eric in the identity parade. She called Marylebone House, hoping somehow to get on to Christy. If not, she'd chat about the managed account portfolio with Simon Winchester – who was sure to want to talk to her – and try to get news of him. Why the hell hadn't Christy been in touch for so long?

The receptionist at the House put her through to Winchester's study, and Edward Bowman came on the line. 'Hello.'

'May I speak to Simon, or even Christy, if Simon's busy?'

'I'm afraid neither of them are here. But Simon telephoned from Dublin airport earlier to say his flight last night was cancelled due to fog and that he'd be here by mid-morning.'

'Dublin airport? Oh, you mean Christy I suppose....'

'No, no,' said Bowman. 'I mean Simon. He went to Ireland over the weekend. Christy's in America of course.'

Susan thanked him and hung up. So that's why that selfish son-of-a-bitch hadn't been in touch: he was in the States. But what was he doing there?

The kerb dealings on the London Minerals Board had been going fifty minutes when Simon Winchester arrived. James

Greville was in the study with Bowman, who was busy on the phone.

'Caught the disease of running off to Ireland, have you?' Greville snapped.

The comptroller replied with cold dignity: 'I'm not going to give you any fictions about car accidents.'

Greville didn't like the tone. 'What do you mean?'

The comptroller went around behind his desk and snapped the catches off his briefcase. 'I've discovered a few things about your dear Mr Christy O'Donnell.'

Greville's face darkened. 'Now look, Winchester, I don't want a repeat of your performance at the Scimitar the other week.'

Bowman looked across at the two of them with curiosity, then busied himself with another phone call.

Winchester drew papers from his case. 'I warned you about his background, remember? Well, you just listen to what I've got.'

'Now look here!' bellowed the duke. 'You've got to stop all this character assassination. You and O'Donnell were put together to do a job, not carry on vendettas.'

'All right, only I thought you'd be interested to know that his father's a criminal and in prison....'

Despite himself, Greville repeated, 'Prison?'

The comptroller cast an eye rapidly over his papers. 'I went to Collystone Prison in Dublin on Saturday ... Here we are....' He read out: 'Stephen O'Donnell, prisoner number 3461, awaiting trial on charges related to an armed raid on a jeweller's ...'

'This is a joke isn't it?' Greville broke in. 'O'Donnell's got no father. I remember that from when he worked at the Grange.'

'I'm afraid there's no doubt that he has.' Winchester delved with malicious glee into his fact sheets again. 'You see, I went to a place called Killertoon in County Galway and got details of O'Donnell from the records of his baptism in the local church. His father's name is down as Stephen O'Donnell of the same village, and his mother was Molly O'Donnell, maiden name Joyce, of Clifden, also in County Galway. The Stephen O'Donnell who's in Collystone prison was also married to a Molly Joyce in the same church on 16 August 1946, and they had a son, Christy, on ...'

Greville tried to appear disinterested. 'You are much too well informed for my liking.'

The comptroller fiddled with his tie. 'I found out by chance about the father's being imprisoned, you see, and took it further with the Dublin police. They're known as the Garda Siochana....'

'I know what they're called,' growled Greville.

Winchester cleared his throat. 'It also appears that this Stephen O'Donnell has been bound over to keep the peace after drunken behaviour on numerous occasions, and served a previous two-year prison sentence.' He looked up from his notes. 'Hardly surprising his son pretended he was dead.'

James Greville felt the rage well up in his breast. 'But who was it who put you on to all this?'

'That hardly matters.'

Greville rose. *'And none of this matters either!'* He walked heavily to one of the windows. His initial anger quickly abated, but those talons clutched at his breast. He needed to rub the spot, but didn't want Winchester and Bowman to see him in pain. He turned to face Winchester. 'Now look, you're to forget all this rubbish. It's got nothing to do with us or the business.'

Winchester jiggled again with his tie. 'Unfortunately, it's not as simple as that.' He consulted another sheet of notes. 'O'Donnell junior, whom Crown Prince Ahmed "likes" so much, has also been involved in a crime.'

'Well, go on, don't keep me in suspense.'

'A horse in his keeping was kidnapped.'

'D'you mean Miss Fortune, man?'

'That is correct.'

Greville sat opposite him with a relieved laugh. The pain in his chest was gone. 'Oh, that had nothing to do with him. It was the IRA.'

'Actually, the Garda weren't able to solve the crime. But I have no doubt that Christy O'Donnell collaborated in it with his father.'

'Rubbish. If the Garda couldn't solve the crime, then you can't possibly have proof.'

Winchester gazed self-assuredly across at him. 'I have circumstantial evidence which I believe adds up quite convincingly. First, do you remember those injuries to his face some weeks back? Well, I heard he got them in a barroom brawl with a man suspected of at least six murders, including that of some old drunk called O'Fogarty or something last week. Now that may or may not tell us something. But this certainly does.' He handed a note across his desk.

Greville studied it. Then he looked into the piggy eyes staring expectantly back. 'So the father has signed a statement that he was part of the gang which kidnapped the racehorse.' He thrust the paper back. 'But where's the mention of the son?'

'I could hardly have expected that. I was lucky enough just to get this out of him: he was only permitted to sign it because he was on remand, and not actually convicted.' Winchester put the papers away in his briefcase and said with quiet satisfaction, 'The one final thing which settles the matter is this: O'Donnell senior told me that the horse was in a barn in a burned-out farm in County Wicklow. So I went there to look for myself, but when I got there, there was no horse. So I took a chance and went to visit Christy O'Donnell's stable – Twelve Pins – in County Tipperary yesterday. And do you know what? The horse was there. One of the stable lads showed her to me ... Miss Fortune herself....'

The duke bellowed, 'That's quite enough! It's deplorable the way you've been snooping on these people. Not to mention the time you've lost over the weekend and this morning. You're to forget all about O'Donnell and his father, and do what you're being paid to do. And what's most important, you're not to bring the matter to the Arab's attention. Is that clear?'

Winchester bridled. 'I should have thought he was the very first person who needed to be told just what kind of a man he's got looking after his interest. Ahmed's smart enough not to back out of our business just because of that.'

'That's a chance I'm not prepared to take.'

The comptroller put his papers away in his briefcase. 'It's obviously best that you and I don't discuss this matter any further.' He glanced at the screen on his desk. 'December silver has just traded at $13.75. I'll need to work it out, but I suspect you've become the richest man in Europe again.'

'Now you're talking, man!' cried Greville.

3.12.79 – 6.12.79

Trading in the Chicago Grain and Metal Exchange silver pit

grew daily more delirious. On one day, panic flared when the Exchange stock figures were published, revealing a sharp decline; on the next, a big bullion merchant, thinking he'd scare the buyers off by going short in futures for five times the quantity of physical silver he possessed, was put on the rack for delivery; on the third day, rumours were rife that the pipeline for fresh silver stocks had been choked. Short sellers who couldn't meet margin calls were wiped out as the price frothed higher and higher, but the efforts of Christy and Crabbe were rewarded.

They had taken a service bureau in the Mercantile Exchange building on West Jackson Boulevard, adjacent to the Merrill Lynch suite. It was equipped with desks, ADP Comtrend screens, telephones, a coffee vending machine, a water cooler and, most vitally, total discretion. A telex had also been installed on Crabbe's instructions, and he had hired a desk-top computer.

From this nerve centre, the two men kept up their hounding of the silver market. They purchased in the pit at every dip, and they paid on the nail for all bullion delivered to their brokers; in tandem with Gilbert in New York, they kept the silver refineries tied up melting down into ten ounce bars the thousand ounce ingots which they were taking delivery of. These bars would not return to the CGME or NYBOT warehouses in exchange for warrants, but be sent to Dubai for eventual handing over to Jamal. Thus, recently mined silver ore, as well as the tableware and jewellery which poured out of people's homes as the price rose, were blocked from entering the market, keeping it in a strangle-hold. By close of trading on Thursday 6 December, spot silver looked down on a breathless world from a towering $16.82 an ounce.

'There's a manipulation going on,' thundered Nick Jasuwecki in the press and on the networks. He was president of Manson Metals. 'Trading should be suspended immediately.'

'Impossible,' replied Marvin Berendt, the Chairman of the CFTC. 'We can't justify any intervention. What we are doing is following closely the purchases of some big players, namely, the Duke of Marylebone in London and a Mr Jamal in Beirut. It *is* unorthodox for parties to take delivery of physicals through the futures markets, I agree, but the rules allow them to, and the rules must be upheld if free enterprise is to prevail. There is, or will be, enough silver to meet the demand.'

The unspoken fact was that Berendt didn't dare close the market. Apart from the prohibitive expense of investigating affairs in London and the Middle East, the CFTC would face crippling law-suits. The majority of CMGE and NYBOT members were brokers and floor traders, and daily commissions and scalping profits were running into tens of millions of dollars right now. Any cutting-off by the CFTC of this free-for-all would result in court battles lasting years.

Berendt concluded a commission 'star chamber' meeting with the following statement: 'No one individual is buying enough to manipulate the market; there is nothing to substantiate allegations that several hundred different individuals are acting in collusion. We can only take the drastic step of suspending trading when we have incontrovertible proof.'

But Winchester had seen to it that there could be no proof.

In the service apartment on South Wacker Drive which Christy shared with Crabbe, he watched the debate rage on television. He told Ahmed in his daily call to Khurbah, 'We've got them over a barrel. The CFTC are powerless.'

'Jamal tells me I have contracts for almost 200 million ounces, with an average profit of four and a half dollars an ounce.'

'That's right. A paper profit of almost a billion already.'

'And this will rise even faster as the remaining 700 million of my money starts to come in from tomorrow?'

'By the end of the month, all the silver bullion you own will be worth 4 billion dollars. The price will go down slightly as you slowly sell it back over January and February, plus there will be the small percentage to pay to the nominees, but you'll still end up with over 3 billion cash. Not a bad return for your billion, eh, your Royal Highness?'

'If it happens like that, then I will be very happy, Sheikh O'Donnell.'

'It has to happen like that. Unless they find some way of turning grass into silver in the next two and a half months.'

7.12.79

Twenty miles north of Khurbah, the Barabbut mountains rise majestically from the flat desert plains. At their base are many watering places where the mountain springs emerge. Crown Prince Ahmed's camp had been set up by one of these springs, and his hunting party arrived there before dawn.

Outside the royal marquee, hooded falcons perched on tasselled staves driven into the sand. An old poet sat on a clump of rugs by the entrance, shouting out his verses.

> *'A king has been here,*
> *Who lions hath slain.*
> *The fox has escaped,*
> *Now crows are his prey.'*

The scouts departed to search the hills for game, while Ahmed went in to sip at coffee. 'My profit in silver is already three times what I have invested so far,' he announced proudly to the sons and friends gathered about him as the cups were passed around. 'And this uptrend is continuing unabated.'

Many of the party also recounted with satisfaction how much they too had made in these marvellous goings-on in Chicago.

The first of the scouts' reports came in soon after dawn. Ahmed and his companions put on their gauntlets and took their birds on their fists, before lurching off across the sands in their specially adapted Range Rovers. These had sawn-off tops and plush velvet chairs which were fitted with hydraulic lifts.

When the beaters saw them approaching, they scared up a covey of sand grouse roosting in the rocks. Ahmed, in the leading car, grinned happily at the flurry of wings. He pressed a button on his dashboard and his seat rose above the level of the windshield. Perched above the desert like this, swaying about as his vehicle accelerated, he loosened the jesses of the falcon on his fist. When he took off its hood, it streaked away downwind after the grouse, easily gaining on them. Selecting a plump slow-flying female, the falcon swirled away high above it, then came tearing down with a shriek.

The marquees were struck after several more forays and the hunting party set off back to Khurbah in their Daimler limousines. Bedouin victory chants were sung out over the CB radio link between the cars, and these continued right up to the time Ahmed's Daimler went through his palace gates.

To the crown prince's surprise, parked in the compound before the palace entrance was one of the king's limousines, a white stretch Mercedes. As Ahmed got out of his Daimler, Iqbal came out to meet him on the marbled steps. He was followed by the secretary of his brother King Musaid. The two secretaries cast black looks at each other, and had obviously been squabbling.

Iqbal got his words in first, 'A European has just come from your brother's palace, *Ya* Ahmed, and he is waiting inside to talk to you....'

King Musaid's secretary thrust out a white envelope he was holding. 'The man brought this letter. His Majesty has read it and has given the European a hearing. There are some terrible incriminating details about the man you have working with you, and His Majesty is distressed you didn't heed his warnings....'

Iqbal squealed, 'His Majesty is calling a Council meeting for tomorrow to propose your removal from the succession, *Ya* Ahmed!'

The king's secretary gave Iqbal the vilest glare yet, then addressed the crown prince again: 'If you want to explain yourself to the king after speaking to the European, *Ya* Ahmed, he will be free this evening after prayers.'

'I'm afraid the game is up!' cried Iqbal to an increasingly bemused Ahmed. 'But at least you have one more chance to choose: it is either the crown, or those billions of dollars.'

By this time, the next $100 million had already flowed into various Chicago brokerage houses, destined for accounts in the names of Greville, Jamal and a myriad nominees.

Christy and Crabbe were busy all morning switching the funds amongst the different brokers to pay for the silver warrants as they were delivered up. They amassed 6 million ounces of bullion, and the prices of spot and all the futures months went above $17. When Christy called Khurbah that afternoon to report the good news, Iqbal answered instead of the crown prince.

Christy's surprise at not getting Ahmed directly for the first time in two months was brushed aside by Iqbal's explanation. 'His Royal Highness is engaged on matters of state. Let me know your business and I'll relay it to him at the appropriate time.'

Christy had his second surprise when trying to get Karim Jamal in Beirut immediately after. There was no reply from the Lebanese's number. That had never happened before either. The following day, Saturday 8 December, there was no trading on the Exchanges. But Christy tried Ahmed again. Iqbal's under-secretary answered and said neither Iqbal nor Ahmed were available. He tried Jamal again, but without luck. Nor were there replies to a couple of telexes he sent to Jamal and to the crown prince's palace.

Christy could only think that an important national crisis or something else serious was taking place in the Hejaz, and this was keeping everybody there tied up. But the newspapers and television didn't mention any such thing.

'The good news,' Compton Crabbe said ebulliently in the service apartment the following evening, 'is that despite tons of bootleg silver coming into Dubai from India and Pakistan, the price in the Arabian souks is holding firm this weekend.'

Christy nodded, remaining quietly concerned about not being able to speak to either Ahmed or the Lebanese for two days now. Something was wrong; he just knew that. Into everybody's life come moments when dreadful inevitability leaps into hard focus, and this was one such for him. But he wouldn't alarm Crabbe with what might yet prove to be unfounded fears....

The first shock came early in the morning of Monday 10 December.

'No, sir,' said Jake Roberts of Sherman Luther Commodities to Christy on the telephone. 'No overseas funds have come in to us by telegraphic transfer overnight.'

The Irishman scanned a telex from Jamal a week ago. 'Are you sure? Five million dollars should have come in for each of these accounts: Sir Colin Thompson, Hussein bin Mahfouz, Lady Adela Wilde and Soroya Gani.' He then reeled off the names of the different banks in Switzerland and the Caribbean from which the monies were due.

Everything was meticulously taken down by Roberts, who then said, 'I'll have to check it out and call you back, I guess. But I'm the chief accountant here and transfers of this size would have to cross my desk. Nothing has done so yet.'

'Please get back to me quickly, Mr Roberts.'

Crabbe stared at him. 'I've just called Midwest Brokers and they've had no money in either.'

'There must be some mistake. Let's see what the other three brokers due to get money in today have to say.'

But none of the others – Prudential, Sharps Pixley and William Guinn – had received funds either.

'I don't know what your Arab friends are playing at,' Crabbe said. 'They must understand how crucial it is to pay for the bullion on the nail?'

Christy wondered whether to reveal his doubts of the night before. Deciding it would be pointless, he said instead, 'Right, Compton, start ringing round the brokers and find out how much bullion we've got to pick up today. There's still a fair bit of Friday's money left.'

That was when Jake Roberts of Sherman Luther called back. 'There's been a development you may want to hear about?'

'Yes, yes,' Christy said impatiently.

'I called the Chicago branch of Commerciale Suisse about the 5 million you claim is due in for, er, Sir Colin Thompson?'

'Yes.... ' He was getting irritated at the way Roberts phrased everything like a question.

'Well, the bank had no information about the transfer, so they got in touch with their head office in Geneva to find out what was going on? In the meantime, my assistants contacted the three other banks about the amounts and beneficiaries you stated?'

'And?'

'I'm afraid they lucked out too ... but I just had a call back from the Commerciale Suisse thirty seconds ago? They tell me their Geneva branch did receive instructions last Wednesday to make a transfer to the account of this Sir ...'

'Oh, that's all right then.' Christy was unable to keep the relief out of his voice.

'No, no, hear me out completely, sir ... Those instructions of last Wednesday were cancelled in Geneva over the weekend....'

'Cancelled? But why, in Mother Mary's name?'

'I'm afraid the Commerciale Suisse gave no reason. Simply that the remitter rescinded the original paying instructions. I wondered if you knew something else?'

Christy hung up on Roberts, his head spinning. He didn't know what to say to Crabbe, who, having heard his side of the conversation, was waiting for an explanation.

Instead, Christy dialled the crown prince's number in Khurbah. Iqbal replied. 'No, Sheikh O'Donnell, I know nothing of any funds for Chicago. If his Royal Highness has anything to communicate with you, he will be in touch himself.' The phone clicked back on its hook.

Christy stared back at the handset, then tried Jamal's number. All he got this time was a recorded announcement in Arabic, repeated over and over again. It seemed this number was no longer in service.

Crabbe read off from his computer screen, 'We've only $16 million of last Friday's hundred left, and over thirty lakhs of bullion to pick up already today.'

Christy didn't need a calculator to work out the sums, nor the implications. Thirty lakhs was 3 million ounces and the silver had been bought at between $7 and $15, so well over $30 million was needed in cash just now, and they only had sixteen. And this was only mid-morning. Several more lakhs of bullion were sure to be delivered up before today's close. But it seemed like the Arabs no longer wanted to play ball. He said, 'Well, let's not mess about, Compton. You start paying for everything we can straight away. I'll try Khurbah on the telex one last time, then speak to London.'

The smell of decay in the buyers' positions had already permeated the floor of the Grain and Metal Exchange. The market was so leery, mistrustful of the abnormal rise, that rumours of shortage of funds kept the price depressed into late morning. Towards noon there were fresh reports that silver depository warrants hadn't been paid for. This caused the sporadic waves of short selling in the silver pit to become more frequent. Heavy selling had started in the meantime in the adjacent gold pit too.

By one o'clock, the sharpest of the scalpers on the floor had already made dozens of quick turns on the short side. 'It always smelt like a bubble,' they said. 'We knew it couldn't last.' Many had forgotten that only a couple of hours earlier they'd been convinced silver would streak up to $25.

When the pit buzzer ended the day's trading, delivery month silver stood at $16.78. It had fallen 34 cents on the previous trading day, an inconceivable amount in light of the recent bullishness.

'What on earth's going on there, O'Donnell?' Winchester cried down the London line. 'Brokers have told me you can't take delivery of bullion. Is it true?'

Christy said slowly, 'Yes, Simon, there's been a hitch. The 100 million due in today didn't arrive.'

'I suggest you get straight on to your Arab horse owner.'

'I have been trying all weekend and today, but neither he nor Jamal are available.'

There was an ominous pause. Then: 'So what do you propose to do now?'

'We need about $30 million transferred by TT from London, straight away if you can, to stave off the hungriest suppliers.'

Winchester snarled, 'Bah!' and rang off.

A few minutes later, he was back on the line. 'You'll have to make your friends in Khurbah and Beirut understand they'd better pull their fingers out. I couldn't get through to them either. It's impossible to get that kind of money out to you just like that. I'll need at least three days.'

Christy was incredulous. 'You're joking. Thirty million dollars is peanuts to the duke. He's holding a billion and a quarter dollars' worth of warrants just now. All he has to do is pledge a few of those with a big London broker, and their associates on this side could make funds available immediately.'

'What you don't realize, Mr O'Donnell,' Winchester replied tersely, 'is that his Grace won't part with even one warehouse warrant to raise cash. It's your business to get the money in, not his. You're being paid a million pounds for it, remember?'

And 2 million from Ahmed, he thought grimly. It all seemed like a pipedream now. 'But I can't get anything out of the Arabs. We need *some* money before tomorrow....'

'Get a grip of yourself,' Winchester interrupted. 'You were brought in because of your connection with the Arabs. So you'd better find some way to get us out of the mess. And fast.'

Christy tried the two numbers in Khurbah yet again, and discovered that the crown prince's line now replied with a recorded message similar to Jamal's. He sent numerous telexes to the Lebanese soliciting money, but never got a reply. In the late afternoon, the telex line became unobtainable.

In the meantime, Crabbe managed to raise four and a half million dollars after countless calls to London investors, and after making deals pledging local warrants with Chicago and New York brokers. Winchester weighed in with another 3 million. Christy got William Lemon in London to TT through $500,000 on a pure investment basis by the bank, though he himself flatly refused to pledge his own money held in Wardle Spyers against any more funds.

By evening, every cent of this $8 million had been exchanged for new bullion warrants.

'It's nowhere near enough,' Crabbe said to Christy over a hurriedly taken supper. 'Quite apart from the bullion which is still hanging over our heads from today, I'm expecting over sixty lakhs to be delivered up tomorrow. There had better be something from the Arabs over tonight or we're well and truly stuffed.'

Both men suspected no money would come; each dreaded tomorrow.

First thing next morning, Tuesday 11 December, Crabbe went off to see a dozen more brokers to procure money. Christy got straight on to the brokerage houses again at which the $100 million should have arrived yesterday. Each one said there had been no overnight transfers of funds.

By this time, the market had opened. Silver was trading right down at $16.50. The wire services chattered out that a stampede was expected out of the precious metal. They also remarked on a parallel weakness in gold.

Christy refused to believe the bewildering speed at which sentiment had switched in the market, and began calling the brokers due to receive funds today.

The first one, Cargill Inc., told him no funds had come in from overseas banks for the names he had given. Then the Cargill man asked him, wasn't he the representative for an account held by Lady Jane Cooper?

'Yes,' Christy replied, his heart leaping even though he knew no money was due in for her account. 'What about Lady Jane Cooper? Have funds come in for her?'

The man from Cargill's said, 'No, sir. Manson Metals have just sent in depository warrants for fifty lakhs of bullion in her name, and are demanding $42 million by return. Will you make your remittance this morning?'

Fifty lakhs! All in one go! Mansons were trying their scare tactics again. And this time they'd probably succeed!

It was then that Compton Crabbe burst into the service office. His face was flushed, his eyes were popping and his bulbous nose was a bright purple. 'This'll make you jump: one of our dear Crown Prince Ahmed's sons, Prince Turki, flew in from Beirut yesterday, and has been around loads of brokerages with which we don't have accounts instructing them to sell as much gold as they can. About $200 million is rumoured to have come in. My hunch is that it's the money we should have had which is being diverted to some other game. It looks like they've sold us down the Swanee, old son.'

11.12.79 – 13.12.79

It took three days of unrelenting deterioration in the situation for James Greville to finally do the unthinkable: he asked Henry Brewer for money.

At first he made insistent phone calls to Chicago demanding that Christy and Crabbe get hold of Prince Turki and find out what that 'Moslem Judas brat' was up to. Then he ranted and raved against those 'cowardly turds with circumcised pricks who run off and leave their partners high and dry'. This was followed by a period when he thought Crown Prince Ahmed must be trying some sort of test on the market again. When Winchester explained that couldn't possibly be the case, and that they sell out the silver in the nominee accounts as fast as possible, his reply was an uncompromising: 'I'm not selling an ounce of my silver.'

Winchester further explained it wasn't 'his' silver they were talking about, but that of people like his daughter, Lady Jane Cooper, who could be wiped out if they didn't get out of their positions at once.

Greville's response to this was: 'They didn't object to the accounts being set up in their names when they thought there would be only profit. So tough luck on them now that the thing's turned.'

Winchester followed this up by saying he would resign at once if they didn't try to salvage the nominees' positions.

Up against this threat, Greville relented, but on a condition: 'I'll establish a priority list of whose accounts can be sold from, and whose can't. There are some family members I'd quite like to see go to the wall.'

It was now that Bowman got up from his desk and announced he'd had enough and was going back to Benner Schwarz.

'Abandoning ship, eh?' Greville sneered.

'With all due respect, your Grace,' Bowman retorted, 'When I came on board, I didn't realize I was on the Titanic, nor that the captain was a reincarnation of Martin Bormann.'

Edward Bowman's departure was followed by the arrival of Mrs Thorpe in a state of bother. She announced to Greville that a man had come from Garrett Commodities and was demanding half a million pounds' variation margin immediately, in cash, or, failing that, silver warrants for double that amount to provide sufficient cover for a plummeting position Greville held with them.

'I refuse to part with even one ounce of my silver,' Greville reiterated. However, he did remember there was £700,000 in one of the lockers in the strong room. The problem was that O'Donnell had the only key.

Then he had a fiendish idea. 'Tell the man from Garrett Commodities to come back in a couple of hours, Mrs Thorpe, and I'll have the cash for him. In the meantime, get me a locksmith competent to work on the boxes in the Banham.'

When this little problem was got out of the way, his next phase was heavy whisky drinking and going to the London Minerals Board silver vaults for hours on end.

Unfortunately, none of these acts by Greville had any effect on the silver price. It closed limit down in Chicago at $15.78 on Tuesday 11 December, $14.78 on Wednesday 12 December and was certain to close a dollar down again on Thursday 13 December.

It was during the morning of that Thursday that Greville went into his late father's study.

The Condrieu Agent and Managing Director of Greville International Corporation tried to look impassive at the condition of the duke.

'You're a man of sense,' Greville said. 'That's why Elizabeth chose you to be managing director. I know I objected to your getting the job, but that was only because I didn't want it to go out of the family. I need money, Brewer, and if you've got even this much feeling for the Grevilles ...' He held up a thumb and forefinger, showing a very narrow gap between them. 'If you have even this much feeling for the Grevilles, you'll let me have some. Quickly. To stave off all those bastards in Chicago who are trying to destroy us.' He grinned lamely, 'I take this as your big chance to prove your mettle to me.'

Brewer replied cautiously, 'I'll look into it, your Grace, and let you know in due course.'

When Greville left the study, Brewer rang Condrieu Hall. 'It's about your husband, ma'am. He's coming apart at the seams. I've never seen anyone look or act quite as ghastly as he's doing right now.'

To the relief of professional traders around the globe, hordes of small speculators were holding on to their long positions, and also, incredibly, were still prepared to buy.

Mr Wilson in London was a case in point. After pestering Susan endlessly for advice when it wasn't needed, he hadn't wanted to take any when she actually had some to give.

'Sell, Mr Wilson. I'd get out as soon as I could if I were you.'

'No! I was making over $15,000 profit only three days ago. It's only $8,300 now....'

'It's still a fine profit! Sell and take your profit before it gets still less.'

'No! The price is bound to recover. Buy another two lots.'

By the close, Wilson's profit had dwindled to $3,000, but he nevertheless declared his intention to 'stick to his guns' until the market came back to its senses.

13.12.79

The undercarriage came down with a grating noise and the Pan American DC9 began its descent into Khurbah International.

Christy gazed out at the distant minarets and high rises

beyond the city walls. He had managed to get a telex through to one of the crown prince's sons known by one of the Chicago brokers to say he was arriving, but he wondered if the message had been received by Ahmed himself.

The aircraft's wheels bumped and skidded on the tarmac, the reverse thrusters boomed to slow the forward rush, then, a minute later, they were taxiing on to the apron before the modern terminal building with its graceful Moslem arches. The plane came to a dead stop and a stewardess levered open the port-side door.

Christy was the first out and into the air-conditioned arrivals hall. He tried to remain optimistic, but felt totally out of control. It had all been going so well, and now this. Why? And, worst of all, why the lack of communication?

Five armed National Guardsmen in green and gold uniform stood by the Customs desk. As Christy approached, the commander said, 'You are Sheikh O'Donnell?'

'Aye that's me.'

The soldier put his hand out. 'Your passport.'

Christy had hoped Iqbal or someone would be here to whisk him through the formalities. But this wasn't the moment to protest about his reception; he produced the passport silently from the inside pocket of his jacket. The commander flicked through its pages and slipped it into his own jacket. 'Come with us.'

A National Guard jeep transporter with a dozen seats and a flimsy canvas canopy waited at the kerb. Christy was ushered into one of the middle rows of seats with a guard at each side, the commander and another in front, and the rest behind. The vehicle careered off towards the city walls. The heat was unbearable and Christy was quick to take off his jacket.

'So where would you be taking me?' he said to the commander. The guard on his right gave him a dig in his ribs with a rifle butt. It hurt. Christy remained silent for the rest of the journey. He would find out soon enough.

For an age, and in heat which came at them like the sharp end of a sabre, they crawled through the city. Finally, the jeep pulled up outside the Ministry of the Interior building in Khurbah's Baghdadi Beit street.

Christy was escorted into the vast marbled entrance hall. On either side were sweeping staircases and in the centre tinkled a fountain. He was led up the right staircase, into a small waiting room, in which portraits of Talal Aziz, King Musaid and Crown

Prince Ahmed in full ceremonial dress hung on three walls. The commander pointed him towards one of two small chairs behind a table, and left the room.

Christy sat there waiting, trying to fathom out the meaning of this reception. About a quarter of an hour later, a Ministry peon, dressed in a grey thobe and skull cap, entered with two glasses of water. He left these on the table and left.

Christy swallowed down both glasses and continued to wait.

Five more minutes later the door opened again and the peon came in with two more glasses of water. He was followed in by the crown prince's dapper secretary. Iqbal had on a cotton suit with large lapels, and looked like one of Al Capone's henchmen in a mural Christy had seen in the Saint Valentine's Day Massacre bar in Chicago's Rush Street.

'Salaam al-ey-qhum.'

Christy rose from his seat. *'Salaam al-ey-qhum,* Iqbal.' They shook hands. Iqbal sat opposite Christy. The Irishman said, 'So, you probably know I've come to see his Royal Highness....'

Iqbal steepled his hands in front of him. 'He will not be able to meet you.'

'But it's essential that I talk to him. There's hundreds of millions of his and James Greville's money at stake....'

Iqbal continued as if he hadn't heard. 'He asked me to thank you for all the work you have done for him, both with his horses and in silver. As a token of his esteem, he wants you to have this.' He handed a cheque across the table. Christy stared at it. It was for £100,000.

'His Royal Highness wants to remember you by your marvellous triumphs with Desert Princess and he wants you to have the same bonus again. You have deserved it. The crown prince apologizes, but he will have to move all his horses to new stables in England, which will take place in the next seven days.'

Moving his horses to England? A cheque for a hundred thousand pounds and Ahmed's thanks? It was the sack! But why in God's name?

He cried, 'Now wait a minute, Iqbal. There's a lot of things I've got to settle with the crown prince first. He can't just leave his partner in the lurch ... If there's something wrong, he should at least tell me. I mean, we've never had any problem in the past....'

Iqbal's look was quite relentless. 'Let me make everything completely clear on his Royal Highness's behalf. He no longer wishes to be involved in your silver scheme. He can also no longer continue having you train his horses, though you can stay at Twelve Pins for as long as you want.'

'But what about the £2 million he said he'd pay me....'

Iqbal clapped his hands loudly and the five guardsmen marched in. 'It would be a good idea for you to drink your last two glasses of water before you are taken back to the airport. It is very hot outside. In about two hours, you will be on a Swissair flight to Zurich. At Zurich airport, you will be provided with an open ticket to any destination in the world. Now, where do you want to go? Back to Chicago?'

Christy shook his head. There were only two possibilities. London or Dublin.

'I'll need to make a phone call,' he said.

Iqbal nodded and graciously took him to a room with a telephone.

He called Marylebone House and got through to Winchester.

'The whole thing's fallen apart,' the comptroller said. 'If you can't get hold of several hundreds of millions of dollars out there in Khurbah, there's nothing you can do here.'

Christy decided that in that case he would go to London second. To Iqbal, he said, 'That ticket from Zurich you were talking about? Make Dublin the destination.'

The first thing Christy said to Matthew O'Brien at Twelve Pins when he arrived there late that night was: 'I'm afraid I've got bad news.' He explained briefly that they were going to lose the crown prince's custom.

O'Brien blanched. It was a terrible blow. But he checked his flagging morale by saying, 'Oh well, we'll survive. We've been turning owners away because of lack of space since we won the Triple Crown. We'll just tell them that we *can* take them on now. In fact, I reckon that, even without Ahmed's horses, we'll need bigger and better facilities than we've got here.'

Christy nodded. His head lad had great resilience at difficult times, and that raised his own spirits no end. 'So, how have the horses been while I've been away?' he asked.

'No problem at all, now. And I can tell you that the filly you had us collect is in fine fettle now, too.'

He was puzzled for a moment. 'Filly?'

'The one I went and got with old Pat Fogarty from The Jolly Jockey, remember?'

The top door of her box was closed in the cold. In the dim

lighting in the yard, O'Brien fiddled with the latch, which rust had rendered difficult to undo.

Christy waited, gazing at another box a little distance away. Desert Princess ... She'd be gone in a week.

The box door creaked as O'Brien swung it open. Then he drew back the two bolts on her lower door and opened that one too. Going into the box, he switched on the light.

Christy gazed at the horse. A charcoal grey, drawn and weakened in appearance, but he saw straight away that she was a thoroughbred. A certain majesty about her bearing ... and something familiar ... He had definitely seen her before. But he couldn't put his finger on the where and when. If he hadn't been so preoccupied with so much else, he might have been able to.

O'Brien patted her head. 'You should have seen her when we found her. She really was in a sorry state. She had red worm, was hopelessly out of condition, skinny as hell. She'd have died in a couple of weeks if we hadn't got her.'

'Well, my da'll be pleased she's being looked after,' he said.

O'Brien said, 'Aye, Pat Fogarty said she belonged to your father. I expect he races her at pretty low-grade meetings in the counties. Judging by her condition, though, he can't have won much prize money with her.'

'Yeah, you're very probably right.' But he was thinking she was too good a horse to have been owned by his father. Conformation and bearing like she had would fetch hundreds of thousands of pounds at auctions, if not millions. Yes, that's where he must have seen her before, he decided. At an auction. Tomorrow he'd find out. Tomorrow he'd ask the man concerned personally. 'Okay, Matt,' he said, 'You can shut everything up. I need to turn in now. I'm bloody shattered.'

As Christy wrote his name in the register, the warder eyed him with interest, recognizing the name. The warder, a muscular, greying man, had won some money on Desert Princess over the season, but found it curious that the champion trainer should come visiting here, at Collystone Prison. He pointed to a door with translucent wired fire glass. 'Go through there now and wait in the waiting area. They'll call out your name and table number.'

The waiting area was half-full of people glancing doubtfully around at each other. Christy sat and stared patiently at a clock high on the wall. The names of visitors came regularly over the tannoy, and they'd get up and go into the visiting hall.

After about half an hour came the announcement: *'Christy O'Donnell. Table Seventeen.'*

A tremor went through him as he got up and went into the visiting hall. Prisoners in brown outfits sat at tables, talking to the visitors. His heart missed a beat as he scanned the room for table 17. The numbers were written on stiff folded card standing in the middle of the table. Then his eye fell on it.

Sitting on the far side of it, on one of the four chairs, was a man with a bowed, grey head, looking anxiously at him.

His legs leaden, Christy went to the table. He sat down opposite Stephen, unable to look directly at him, gazing woodenly instead at the number card.

'So you came at last, eh, Kit?'

Christy raised his head and said, 'Hello, da.'

Stephen smiled weakly. 'Hello, son.' He'd aged so much. His face was lined in every possible place, his teeth were rotten and his shoulders drooped. But there was no doubting it. It was his da. 'I'm glad you could make it, Kit. So, how's it going?'

He nodded. The words were hard to mouth. 'Oh, I'm all right, da. How's it with you?'

'I'm all right too. I couldn't really ask for more. I've got a bed here, food ...' He leaned forward. 'You knew Pat, didn't you?'

'Pat?' he said with surprise. 'Pat Fogarty?'

'That's him. They did him in, you know.'

'Did him in, who?'

'The McDaids, Kit. They killed old Pat.' He started to cry.

Christy's throat tightened. 'What? Old Pat? Why?'

Stephen shook his head. 'They're a bad lot, Kit. They wanted to hurt me, but couldn't, because I was here, so they took it out on old Pat instead. Someone had to pay for the job that got fouled up ...' He lowered his head and sobbed. 'I hoped your friend Simon would have told you....'

'Simon?' Christy said, puzzled.

'The English feller, you know, Simon Winchester, wasn't it?'

'Simon Winchester?' he said. 'You know Simon Winchester?'

Stephen nodded. 'Aye. Didn't you know he came here? A couple of weeks back?'

Christy was shaking his head in disbelief. 'Simon Winchester came here? *Here*?'

'He said you'd sent him, Kit. Didn't you?'

'No, da. I can't imagine how he even knew you were here....'

'Oh God!' said Stephen. 'I was so shit scared about the McDaids because of what they'd done to old Pat that I told him everything. Told him because he said he'd tell you....'

'What did you tell him, da?'

'About us, Kit, about your ma, about Miss Fortune.'

'Miss Fortune?'

Stephen passed a hand back and forth across his mouth a few times, uncertain what to say. 'You don't know, do you, Kit? I've got Miss Fortune. She's mine, I'm looking after her. I told Winchester to go and feed her....'

'You've got Miss Fortune? Is that the filly old Pat told me about?'

Stephen nodded. 'Your friend Simon knows all about it....'

Christy interrupted savagely, 'You kidnapped Miss Fortune? You, da?'

Stephen babbled, 'It wasn't like that, Kit. I told that Simon all about it. I told him how I hadn't known it was your stables the McDaids were taking me to. I swear it on my poor Molly's head....'

Christy tried to get his thoughts in focus. 'So you told Simon Winchester that you'd kidnapped Miss Fortune?'

'I had to, Christy. Pat had been killed. Somebody had to go and feed her. He asked me, would I sign a paper if he put it all in writing, and I said, yes, I would, I'd do anything just so that he'd go down there and feed her....'

'You signed a piece of paper for Simon Winchester that you'd kidnapped Miss Fortune, da?'

He nodded. 'You see, Harry McDaid wanted to kill her the next day after the kidnapping, but I said no. I'd realized by then that she was your horse, Kit. I thought of her as mine. As part of my family. I decided to look after her, to make it up to you, and to your ma ... She's all I've got in this world, see....' He broke down crying loudly.

Hard knots had formed in Christy's brain. 'Don't worry, da,' he said, barely noticing that a warder had led his sobbing father away. One thought consumed him: Winchester had found all this out and had told Ahmed. That was why the Arabs had quit the plan which had been going so brilliantly well. His world had come crashing down around him, and it was all down to Winchester. Christy got up and headed for the exit with only one idea in his mind. He was going to London. He was going to kill Simon Winchester.

14.12.79

The queues in Hatton Garden had been getting longer every day. That Friday, they stretched round the corner into High Holborn, all the way as far as Chancery Lane Underground. Commuters and other travellers emerging from one of the busiest stations in London's legal and journalistic district had to jostle their way through hordes of people clutching silver articles, desperate to sell their wares, before they became trinkets of little value again.

Two vehicles headed towards Marylebone House along different motorways that afternoon. One was a blue Bentley, bringing Elizabeth Greville down the A1(M), the other a taxi bearing Christy along the M4 from Heathrow.

Simon Winchester was in his study, doing his utmost to sell silver from the nominee accounts. In the ballroom, James Greville sat in one of the leather sofas, a large tumbler of booze by his side, staring at the two portraits on the wall – his father, kind, assured, in command of his world with his gun; then himself, puny, tentative, clutching at his heart. The Platters sang:

> *' … I could start my life all anew … '*
> *' … If I had you … '*

Susan had a nasty task to perform, but before she did it, she gave into an impulse which had been building for several days. She called Marylebone House and said to the receptionist, 'Is Mr Christy O'Donnell back from the States yet?'

'No, he isn't,' replied the girl. 'Can anybody else help?'

Susan knew it couldn't be long before he was back, with silver crashing down around everyone's ears. There would be nothing for him to do in Chicago. She said, 'I'd like to leave a message for him to call me when he does get in. It's Susan Gardner. Will you see that he gets the message, please?'

'I will.'

Susan then dialled Mr Wilson, no longer dreading having to inform him that he either had to stump up another $5,000 variation margin, or try to sell out at today's limit down price of $12.78 because, by Monday, his position was certain to be in deep deficit.

Elizabeth was the first to arrive at the House, ahead of Christy by about two minutes. She went straight to the ballroom, and was appalled at the state of her husband.

'James?'

He gazed distractedly at her.

'You've been drinking, haven't you?'

He looked away, out through the windows at the Park. What a beautiful place it was.

She said, 'Henry called yesterday. He told me you'd been in to see him and ask him for money....'

He looked back at her. 'You won't help Liz, will you?'

'I have already helped you....'

'When have you ever helped?' he cried, rising. 'You're a whore. You slept with Charles, and then you refused to give me money when I needed it.' He shook his fist at the portrait. 'And you, you smug bastard, you thought you were God, you tried to destroy our family ... And so what if I *did* tell John Early to give you a fall ... I didn't know the Land Rover would kill you ... Even if you deserved it ...'

His mouth stopped. Charles Greville's pale grey eyes were gone. All that remained were empty sockets.

The colour drained from James's face, and his mind burst with the question, had someone tampered with the painting? Someone who'd seen his father after the accident? It was impossible. But that's what must have happened ... And now there were these dreadful spasms wrenching at his heart, and they would wreck everything, he knew. He heard Elizabeth from very far away, crying, 'James, James.' And then he had the solution.

'Winchester!' he cried, clutching at his breast. 'It was Winchester who did it.'

'What is it?' Elizabeth cried, 'what is it?'

He suddenly saw her afresh. 'My darling Elizabeth.' He opened his arms and clasped her to his body. 'You are the best wife any man could ever have had ... You do love me, don't you?'

He registered, as consciousness raced away from him, that she was screaming.

Christy picked up the message from the reception desk in the Great Hall and stuffed it in his pocket. He couldn't think just now about Susan. He was trembling too much with rage.

He strode into the study. The comptroller, on the phone at his desk, swivelled his piggy eyes on to him.

'So, you went to see my father in prison....' The words choked in Christy's throat.

Winchester put the phone down and rose off his seat.

Christy was across and on him in a flash. He grabbed the comptroller by the tie knot and collar and violently twisted the whole lot around. Winchester went red and tried to shove the hand off his neck. But Christy was twice as strong as him. Winchester said, half-strangled, 'It was because of Susan....'

'*What?*' Christy loosened his grip.

Winchester shook his collar back into shape. 'She told me about it, and I went to see for myself.'

'Susan?'

Winchester smiled grimly. 'Yes, Susan Gardner. You know, your bloody girl friend from America.'

What the hell did she have to do with this, Christy wondered. 'And so how come she told you about my father?'

'It's all down to the eternal love triangle, I'm afraid,' Winchester explained in a matter-of-fact tone. 'She's crazy about you, and I'm crazy about her. I was hoping that somehow I'd win her from you by exposing you thoroughly.'

Christy's rage rose again. 'And so you went to Dublin because of something Susan told you, got a signed confession from my da, and then you sent this to Ahmed....'

The comptroller's piggy eyes narrowed. 'No. I sent nothing to Ahmed. The only person I showed your father's confession to was the duke. I hoped he'd have you thrown out of working with us. This way you wouldn't come back to London. This way I could try to get Susan somehow to care for me....' He opened a drawer in his desk and withdrew the papers he'd come back from Ireland with. 'These are the originals of the confession and my notes. There are no copies. You can have it all. I thought of showing the stuff to Susan too, but realized that it would probably only turn her completely against me.'

Christy, his theory shattered, asked in puzzlement, 'But then what happened with Ahmed? Why did he pull out like that?

And why exactly has Turki been selling gold short too?'

'The last question is easy enough to answer: the short sales in gold are designed for the Arabs to make a profit on the downside, and cover some of their losses in silver. But why they pulled out of silver is something I hoped *you*'d be able to tell *me*. You see, Mr O'Donnell, I had a call from a friend in Dubai who knows Karim Jamal. Well, my friend asked Jamal just what the hell was going on, and Jamal told him, "Tell Simon Winchester to talk to John Early if he wants any answers. Tell him that it is more important to Crown Prince Ahmed to be King of the Hejaz than to make two billion dollars." '

Mrs Thorpe opened the study door just then. 'It's the duke,' she said breathlessly. 'He's had a heart attack.'

Elizabeth wanted him taken to the Princess Victoria Mary of Teck private hospital, where the Grevilles were always treated. But the paramedics said no. It would have to be St Thomas's, whose cardio-vascular department was second to none in Britain.

Elizabeth went in the ambulance with her husband. He was in a deep coma. Only half an hour had passed since it had happened, but news of it had already flashed out on all the wire services.

'All bets are off now,' said Simon Winchester. 'It's an awful thing to say, but this heart attack is the best possible thing to happen as far as Greville Holdings is concerned. We now have a faint chance to salvage something.'

'How?' said Christy.

'We've got to get our arses down on our chairs and sell not only the nominees' futures contracts, but also as much of the duke's bullion as we can. The Far and Middle Eastern markets are best for trading in physicals, and we're lucky it's a Friday. We'll be able to sell to the merchants who deal with the souk and bazaar traders over the weekend, without having the price haemorrhaging in Chicago in the background while we do it.'

Before he started, Christy made a phone call to Mincing Lane. 'How are you, my sweet?'

'I hate to admit it,' Susan smiled down the line. 'But I'm one whole lot better for hearing your voice.'

'Me too, my love.'

Winchester grimly ignored the conversation and rang a bullion merchant in Abu Dhabi.

'So, you goddamn leprechaun, when do we get to see each other?'

'Maybe tonight, my love. I'll have to go down to St Thomas's Hospital to see how the duke's doing, then I'll come along to Clarendon Place.'

'I heard about the duke, Christy. Will he be all right?'

'The paramedics said it was pretty serious. A massive heart attack. He's in a coma.'

'Look, Christy,' Susan said. 'Instead of you coming to Clarendon Place later, why don't we do this: I'll be busy here till 7.30 today with all the mess that's going on in silver. Why don't I meet you at the hospital straight after? Like this you can spend as long there as you like?' She didn't give voice to the fact that she couldn't bear the idea of just sitting and waiting for him at the apartment.

'All right, Susie, my sweet. We'll do it like that.'

Elizabeth sat by Greville's bedside in the Hammond intensive care unit. From five drip bags, drugs and blood trickled into his mouth, arms, stomach and thigh. A tracheotomy – an incision in the windpipe – had been performed, and a tube passed into this hole, sending oxygen directly into the duke's lungs. Through other tubes hidden by the covers, blood, urine and excreta passed into containers under the bed. Pulse rate and blood pressure counters hummed, their needles casting zig-zag patterns on moving paper tape. The patterns were feeble. From time to time, Greville's eyes flickered with the effort of opening, then gave up.

'I *was* unfaithful with Charles,' she said. 'But not in the sense you always believed. I've never actually said this to you in so many words, James, but I never slept with him. Unless, of course, you count the night I spent in the vault. No, I never slept with anyone but you. I never specifically denied it when you asked me, because I was so shocked you could actually ask me such a question. Afterwards, I swore I'd never answer you if you asked me it again. You had to trust me and believe in my love if we were ever to find that elusive thing called happiness.'

Nurses came by from time to time to check the monitors, adjust the drips, shift things around. Members of the family's staff and friends came in, two at a time, to sit with Elizabeth, by her husband.

In the early evening, Deborah arrived. She kissed her father's slack face many times, rubbed his brow and asked after his condition from her mother, and from nurses and from the couple of doctors who came to check on him.

'He's a fighter,' the senior registrar told her. 'He needs to be. This is the most critical time. He's got to come through the next twelve hours before we can think about doing anything else. His heart took a fair old knock, you see. There's a lot of tissue damage. We'll have to start thinking in terms of a major operation at some later stage, or even a transplant.'

Mother and daughter sat in silence by Greville for some time. Slowly, Deborah plucked up the courage to say finally to her mother, 'I'm pregnant.'

'Deborah!' said Elizabeth in surprise. 'It's surely not Patrick's, is it?'

'No, mother.' Deborah told her who the father was. 'I'm going to ask him to marry me. I'm determined to get it right this time. I *know* he's not from our station in life, but that isn't everything. After what I went through with Patrick, I've realized at last that position is the least important thing in a relationship.'

Elizabeth nodded sagely. 'Deborah, if this makes you happy, you should do it. But be very very sure about just exactly what you're letting yourself in for.'

Jane and Michael Cooper arrived at around the same time as Simon Winchester. Exceptionally, all three were allowed in at Greville's bedside with Elizabeth, though only on condition that Deborah withdrew. She did.

While this new little party was in with Greville, his pulse rate dropped and a consultant was urgently summoned. The adrenaline feed was boosted, the needle responded on the moving tape, and then anxious calm was re-established around the duke.

Outside the ward, Deborah found herself wandering across to the lifts, getting in one and going down to the ground floor. A corridor led from the lift foyer to the old hall, which had a balustraded staircase and two walls studded with plaster busts of eminent past medics. She wandered on into here, and spotted, a couple of seconds before they noticed her, two special people amongst the flow of staff and visitors. Those few seconds were long enough.

The two people she'd seen were Christy and a woman. And Deborah understood in that brief moment that the woman was someone she could never hope to compete with.

Susan was the first to feel the eyes on her, and swivelled her own gaze on to Deborah. Christy followed the direction of her look, then gulped.

'You know her, Christy?' Susan said.

'Yes, sort of. She's an old friend.'

'Uh huh?' Susan's flesh crawled at Christy's tone. 'Seen her lately?'

'Yeah,' he mumbled. 'A few weeks ago.'

'I see.' She was livid by now.

'Hello, Christy,' Deborah said, coming up with a smile. 'Going up to see daddy?'

'Er, yes, hello there.' He stuck out his hand.

She ignored it and gave him a peck on his cheek. 'So this is the woman you love?' She stuck her hand out now at Susan.

Susan took it limply, trying to force a smile on to her lips and failing.

Christy said proudly, 'Meet the woman I'm going to marry, Deborah. Susan Gardner.'

'I'm *so* pleased for the two of you.' It was Deborah's turn to smile. 'Must fly.' She raised a hand and waggled every finger individually at the pair of them. 'Bye now.'

She turned away and headed off towards the main reception hall. On a wall to the left of the great glass fronted area hung a large painting. It was of a man seated calmly amongst abstract objects, his legs crossed. The picture was entitled: *Portrait Surrounded by Artistic Devices,* and it was an acrylic on canvas by David Hockney.

Deborah bought a coffee at the service counter. She sat in one of the comfortable chairs in the reception area and wondered how she could she tell him now that she was pregnant; wondered how she could ask him now to marry her.

'Please, Susan,' Christy said as they waited for the lift to the second floor. 'Won't you forgive me? It was all such a mistake, I realize now. You were right. I should have got out of the whole bloody scheme when you explained the other side of it to me.'

Susan smiled, the dimple in her cheek rather pronounced. 'Christy, there is no getting away from the fact that I love you. But I am inclined to think you're only sorry now because it all failed. If it had kept on going well, you'd still be in Chicago, not sorry at all, and counting your profits, not thinking quite so hard about me.'

He didn't answer. He feared she was right.

In intensive care, Simon Winchester and Jane took turns trying to talk to the duke. Jane had heard that talking sometimes brought around people in a coma. But Greville didn't respond.

After some time, a nurse came and muttered to the Coopers and Winchester that there were several people waiting by now to come and visit the duke.

The three visitors crossed paths at the ward entrance with Christy and Susan.

'Hi Simon,' said Susan, giving the comptroller a kiss on the cheek.

'Oh hello, Susan.' Winchester cast a look at Christy, then shuffled past.

When they came to Greville's bed, Elizabeth said, 'It's kind of you to come, Mr O'Donnell, but who's your charming companion?'

'I hope you don't mind, ma'am,' said Christy. Susan gave a little curtsy at the duchess. British nobility at last.

Christy went on: 'Only, she's the woman I'm going to marry. She's called Susan, Susan Gardner, ma'am.'

Elizabeth shook hands with her, at the same time arching an eyebrow at Christy. 'Deborah was here a little while ago,' she said.

'I know,' he said quickly. 'I passed her in the hall.'

Susan giggled, 'Oh he keeps telling everyone that he's going to marry me, ma'am. But I haven't said yes yet. I'm going back to Chicago next week. I've got some serious thinking and acting to do back there before I can even contemplate coming to live in Ireland.'

'Quite,' said the duchess, and gazed at her husband again.

The other two sat down silently in adjacent chairs and observed the sorry figure, whose skin had take on a grey tinge.

'One day,' Elizabeth said softly but firmly to Christy, 'you or Simon Winchester will have to tell me exactly what you got up to with him in the silver market. What brought him to this state.'

He said, 'It was all going so well, see, ma'am. But then something happened to make the Arabs drop out. We heard it was because Ahmed felt it was more important to be king than make 2 billion dollars, and that it had something to do with Johnnie Early. You may know, ma'am, that he's your trainer across at Eden Grange. I'm going to get hold of him and find out....'

Elizabeth put her hand on his. 'There's no need to ask John Early anything, Mr O'Donnell. If you want to know why the

Arabs pulled out of the scheme, I have the explanation.' She now drew a piece of paper from her bag and handed it to Christy. 'Read this, Mr O'Donnell. It's a copy of a letter that I sent by hand to King Musaid of the Kingdom of the Hejaz. I brought this copy down to London from Condrieu to show James, but I didn't get the chance.'

Christy reached for it and raced through its contents. His eyes widened. Susan glanced over his shoulder, trying to figure out what it was all about.

'Why don't you read it aloud to my husband, Mr O'Donnell?' Elizabeth suggested. 'My daughter Jane was here just now, and she tried to talk to James, believing it would revive him. Perhaps this will.'

Christy looked nervously at the duke. Only faint flickers continued to cross the half-closed eyes in the leaden face.

He took his breath, then read the whole letter out loud:

> Your Majesty,
>
> In your part of the world, you would consider me, a wife, disloyal for divulging the following to someone outside the family. But, for reasons you would never understand, I have to do it. You see, your brother, the Crown Prince Ahmed, is engaged on a risky venture with my husband. Now, I don't know a great deal about your brother and nor, frankly, have I cared to find out. My concern is my husband. The man who brings you this letter is Mr John Early, the horse trainer at our family's racing stables. He was the one who was driving the vehicle out of which my father-in-law, the previous Duke of Marylebone, fell and died. I want you to do one thing when you have finished reading this: I want you to ask Mr Early if my husband telephoned him on the morning of the accident and instructed him to make such a fall happen deliberately. I want you to watch very carefully Mr Early's reaction to the question, never mind his verbal answer. Then I want you to form your own judgement and act as you will. I beg your forgiveness for putting you through what may seem an unnecessary task, but you see, Your Majesty, I have realized that I have to do this for my husband's benefit, because it is my duty. I fervently hope that you will do for me what I ask, and thank you in advance.
>
> Sincerely,
>
> Elizabeth Greville, Duchess of Marylebone.

Christy glanced up at the duchess's face. She looked serene.

'I asked Mr Early to do me a little errand, as a surprise for my husband, you see, Mr O'Donnell. I asked him to personally deliver that letter to the king. I had made all the arrangements for his reception there. Early was delighted to do any service for me after what happened at the Grange on 5 January.'

Susan hadn't fully absorbed the implications of what either Christy or the duchess had said, but she nevertheless had the strongest feeling that the duke's eyes flickered with understanding.

James Greville, third Duke of Marylebone, died at 4.37 the following morning, without regaining consciousness. Elizabeth was the only person at his side.

March 1980

They drove up in the Jaguar, father and son, on that fine gusty day, through the gates and up to the forecourt before Molly's Castle. When they got out, Stephen just stood there, staring up at the vast Norman structure.

'It's the very same one you showed me when I was four, da,' said Christy. 'I'm sure of it. You said you wanted to build one like it for ma.'

The older man nodded. 'I don't believe it Kit. But it's there, and we're here, and you say it's yours....'

'It's ours da.' Christy put an arm around his father's shoulder and led him in. Vast high rooms. Massive fireplaces. Fabulous views from the windows and the turrets and the battlements, over the lush, rolling lands of County Tipperary, over the gallops and the exercise track Christy had had prepared.

'It must have cost a fortune,' Stephen said.

'Half a million pounds da. The madman who owned it before finally agreed to half what he wanted. But the stables facilities cost three times what I'd budgeted. Bloody builders.'

They went outside later, and around to the stables. Christy had had facilities built for sixty horses, double the capacity of

Twelve Pins, though just now there were only thirty-seven boxes occupied. He led his father now to the one from which Miss Fortune looked out. 'Here you are, da. 'She's all yours to care for and look after.'

Stephen grinned with delight, patted her head lovingly and kissed her. 'She's in fine condition, Kit.'

Christy nodded. 'She'll be the dam of many a great racehorse, I'm sure.'

'But what about the law?' Stephen said. 'She was kidnapped, after all.'

'She belonged officially to Lloyds insurance,' he explained, 'since they were the ones who'd paid out when she was taken. When I told them she'd been found, they had me checked out to see if it had been an inside job. But they couldn't find any proof, and when I mentioned I could keep her for breeding purposes, and asked if 10,000 was a fair price, they sent me the release papers without so much as a blink of an eyelid.'

Stephen looked around the yard. Glorious thoroughbreds stared out from other boxes. 'So who owns all these other horses, then?'

'Five belong to my banker, William Lemon. He's been the best and fairest owner I've ever worked with. Then there are odds and sods belonging to various types, and sixteen belonging to an Arab prince.'

'That'd be the owner of Desert Princess, I suppose?' Stephen said.

Christy shook his head. 'No, da. He couldn't keep his horses with me any more. He rang me on the day I left Twelve Pins to tell me he still thought of me as his friend, but had to part company with me for political reasons. He also said that when he became king he'd maybe send me his horses again. But only maybe. Bloody typical.'

'And will you deal with him again in future?'

'Maybe,' replied Christy. 'Only maybe.'

Stephen laughed.

Molly's coffin arrived in a hearse that afternoon. The old box she'd been buried in had got pretty rotten after seventeen years, but Christy had had it put into a fine shiny new one.

The spot which had been selected had been consecrated by Father John Maher, the local priest, and, to witness the interment, old Farmer and Mrs Regan, Eammon Halliday, Thomas Symes and Santos had all come up from County Galway.

'It's nice to have Molly home with us again, isn't it, Kit?' Stephen said.

He nodded. 'It is.'

'I'll put fresh flowers on it every day, Kit, you can be sure of that.'

They'd made a deal. Christy would pay his da a salary for working at the stables, and his da wouldn't blow more than fifty per cent of it on gambling. Christy hoped it would last for at least some length of time. But Stephen had promised that even if he did ever slip up, the one thing he'd never fail to do was get the flowers. He'd never gamble away what it cost to get the flowers, not even in his darkest moments.

When Molly was down in her new home, they all walked back up the lane towards the castle, where a sumptuous tea awaited them. No-one noticed the small sports car which had waited in the property's driveway, and which slowly followed them, until it got to about fifty yards behind them. Then, at the sound of the engine, one or two glanced back and, as the vehicle approached, Christy was pleasantly surprised to see who the driver was.

In the forecourt before the castle, the car passed them and drew up.

When Deborah got out, Christy noticed she had a bulge in her stomach. They kissed each other on the cheeks, Christy introduced her to his da, and Deborah explained she'd come to stay up at Eden Grange for a few days. She said she thought she'd come to see him while she was in Ireland. Christy said he was pleased she had.

When these pleasantries were done with, Deborah reached into the back of the car and got a briefcase and an envelope out of it. 'Now, Christy,' she said brightly, 'I've got news. I'm getting married, and here's an invitation to the wedding.' She held out the envelope.

'Who's the lucky man?' he said, opening the envelope and reading the name: 'Roger Wellington.'

The others drifted away in the direction of the castle, sensing the two should be left alone.

'You might know him,' Deborah grinned. 'He used to be a good friend of Daddy's.'

Christy looked again at her stomach and a lump grew in his throat. 'I hope you and he are very happy, Deborah.'

She said in a matter-of-fact tone, 'I don't love him, but he and I have been trekking a few times together and I know he'll make a perfect father....' She quickly changed the subject. 'Now, let's talk about you, Christy. I want to know what happened to the girl I saw you with at St Thomas's on the day daddy died.'

He said happily at the thought of Susan, 'She's in Chicago, but she phoned just a couple of days back to say she was coming here in June.'

'Permanently?'

'I don't know, but I do know I'll do everything in my power to make her stay.'

A gust of wind blew from the east, and Deborah nodded. 'She loves you very much, you know, Christy.'

'I love her too, Deb,' he said sincerely.

'I know. Well I really do hope it works out between the two of you.' Another gust in their faces. 'You know mummy asked Simon Winchester to leave? She blamed him for daddy's company being wiped out and endangering the whole family fortune with what he got all those nominees to do.'

'It wasn't his fault, Deb,' Christy said.

She shrugged her shoulders. 'Somebody had to pay.' Now she handed him the briefcase. 'Simon mentioned before he went that daddy had sort of agreed to pay you £700,000 for the work you did with him.'

'Oh?' Christy positioned the briefcase on his knee and snapped off the catches. He had already worked out that a case of this size couldn't contain that amount of money. But he could hope anyway, couldn't he?

Deborah went on, 'Well, I wanted you to have that money, but I just couldn't persuade mummy to agree. She's not going to have all that much left herself, I'm afraid, after covering for daddy. Anyway, I thought you should have this instead. I know daddy would be pleased if he knew.'

Christy lifted the briefcase lid and smiled. Inside, tucked neatly in thick wads of tissue paper, was the little silver horse with the golden globe on its back.